SPACE CITY OUTBREAK

by

Jared Austin

Huntsville, Alabama

SPACE CITY: OUTBREAK

ISBN-13: 978-1-7326412-9-7

Published by Up Past Dawn LLC. Find us at
https://jareddanielaustin.com

Dedication

For my siblings: Jason, Shaun, Karisa, and Briana
Your pursuit of your own journeys inspire me in mine.

Acknowledgements

As I continue along my writing journey, I'm reminded continually that no one can accomplish their goals alone. Friends, family, and others play important roles, or suddenly, unexpectedly, step in to help at a critical juncture.

I'd like to thank Darren Gannuch for providing advice on how to handle the medical issues that crop up during the book, and my brother-in-law, Sean Dafter, for ideas on how to handle many technological aspects.

I'd also like to thank my North Alabama Science Fiction and Cake Appreciation Society (NASFCAS) writing group, who listened to my drafts month after month and provided invaluable critiques to improve the plot. I'd like to thank Kay Glover for all her editing support.

Finally, thank you to everyone who reads my books. I hope I've entertained, inspired, and enriched your lives along the way.

Chapter 1

Neil as Team Captain: Day One

Yellow sand dunes yielded to a wall of giant red sequoias. Neil stood on the line demarcating the desert and forest, heat baking the left side of his face while a cool breeze caressed his thick curly hair around his right ear. The sequoias were tall enough that they should cast shadows over the first row of sand dunes. Instead, the shadows ended at a line parallel to Neil's left foot, so that they looked headless.

"This is as great as your flying Venice sim," Neil said, sidestepping into the desert and bumping Nico Colombo as he did. The wind vanished and the heat from the sun toasted his bare skin; sensors in his silver Space City suit activated a cooling feature that kept him from burning up.

Anand and Devika Singh, twin brother and sister, trudged up a dune in search of the next base—the second of three that Neil requested Nico set up. Anand's bald head glistened with sweat and he looked to have gained more weight over the summer. As team captain, Neil would have to talk with Anand about slimming down a bit. Team grades at the Space City Preparatory Academy were more significant in year two, and he wouldn't keep up if he didn't get in better shape. Devika, by contrast, ran stairs in the Games stadium every day.

Jiro Takeda and Eris Zeigler hunted around the sequoias, in case one of the trees served as a secret entrance to the base. As the best shooter in their year, Eris' assignment to their team was a major coup as far as Neil was concerned. And Jiro, with his short, spindly frame made a great scout.

Rounding out the team, Dirk Fischer and Trini Flores floated around the crowns of the sequoias, dodging the occasional impossibly obese turkey with hummingbird wings; you could get away with defying physics in virtual worlds. But instead of hunting for the second base, the pair debated the merits of the new treaty between Space City and the Ukka on Letos; nevertheless, both were skilled Games players, making them ideal teammates for the increased field exams they'd encounter in year two.

Neil had been a little surprised when he'd learned the pair would be on his team. After all, Dirk was in his final year at the Academy, while Trini was in her third. But for some classes, the Academy mixed the second through fourth year students together a little more. It was going to take Neil a little time to get used to handing out orders to older students. That's why he had asked Nico to create the sim for them. Neil wanted to get a jump on the new year by leading the team through a series of tasks, so he could get used to giving orders, and so they'd get comfortable working together. Nico wasn't on the team, but his virtual settings were so stunning that Neil couldn't pass on one for their excursion.

Studying the map on his wrist-comp again, Neil strode across the dividing line from the desert into the forest. He shivered from the noticeable change in temperature, like exiting a hot tub and jumping straight into a pool. The base should be close by. They were inside the base perimeter, shown as a red circle on his wrist-comp map, but Nico had disguised it well.

Anand and Devika started shouting, drawing Neil's attention. Had they found the base entrance? But the twins raced down a sand dune, waving at them to run. Seconds later, a horde of small brown toads topped the dune behind the siblings, as well as every other dune in the area. A biblical plague descending upon them.

Neil tensed, unsettled by the sheer number of toads headed their way, but unsure how seriously to take the threat. After all, they were *toads*. "Nico, what danger level did you put the sim on?"

"It's not fun without a little danger." Nico scratched at the birthmark on the left side of his neck. "And their spikes are poisonous."

He started to dash into the forest. Neil grabbed a handful of Nico's suit and pulled him up short.

"What're you saying?" Neil asked. "Is the poison lethal? Did you set the sim to match reality?"

That had been a nasty surprise during Nico's Venice sim. The Malsain—an alien race possessing greenish-yellow scales, a forked tongue, and a stench that could make you lose your lunch from the day before, and everything else you'd eaten since then—had developed a high danger setting for the sims to mimic real life. Dangers faced could cause as much physical harm as if they were in the real world. To Neil, that was insane. The Malsain, on the other hand, turned up their collective scaled noses at sims that did anything less than perfectly mimic the real world and the dangers it posed. For some reason, thrill seekers onboard Space City had embraced the high danger setting. Nico was apparently one of those thrill seekers.

That's why Neil had told Nico, repeatedly, not to do that for this excursion.

"It won't kill anyone, but it'll probably hurt pretty badly," Nico mumbled with a guilty expression. "The spikes shouldn't pierce our suits."

"And if they get skin instead of suits?"

"You *may* want to die." Nico tugged free of Neil's grasp and took off.

They must be in the medium danger setting then. On low, there was no real threat in a sim. It was all an elaborate ruse. You could see, touch, smell, even taste, but it was an illusion. The sim tricked your mind into believing things were real. It was primarily used for first-years. For medium danger, the Academy wanted students to take threats more seriously, so they could feel varying levels of pain.

And while Nico had followed his instructions, he hadn't taken it easy on them.

As Neil turned back to check the twin's progress, his mouth went dry as the swarm of toads grew exponentially, new ones cresting the closest sand dunes every second. Why hadn't he clarified the threats with Nico before they entered the sim? As a team captain, he should've known everything before they'd started, same as if he were leading the group on a mission to a real planet. If this had been a class, the instructors would've been docking his leadership scores heavily right about now.

He retreated past the first line of sequoias where Jiro and Eris pointed at the oncoming toads, prepared to lay down cover fire for the twins.

"Poisonous? Really?" Eris demanded, casting a glare at Nico.

He chuckled, eyes darting back and forth between Eris and the toads, as if he were unsure who he should be more afraid of.

"Dirk, Arielle, can you help us out?" Neil called over his tradutor—the language translator and comm device was standard equipment for all exploration.

"Devika, sure. I'm on it," Dirk answered.

"I'll get Devika," Arielle corrected as she flew past Dirk toward the twins. "You get Anand."

"Oookay. I guess I'll get Anand." Dirk followed her.

"Nico, where's shelter?" Neil asked. They couldn't deal with all the toads headed their way. Watching them, he felt a little like a cricket about to get swarmed by multiple ant colonies. His instincts to run were almost overpowering.

"There's a grove to the East." Nico shifted his feet, clearly ready to get moving. "The toads won't enter it."

Arielle guided her scooter down alongside Devika, who refused to leave Anand until Dirk had rescued him. Dirk drew up next to Anand, so he could jump aboard. But when Dirk tried to lift off, the scooter rose no more than two feet off the ground.

"Nico, you should embargo Anand's candy supply for a while," Dirk complained.

Dirk and Anand had a good twenty yards on the toads, but the horde was gaining ground. Neil blinked once, activating his new Academy-issued contacts. The thought-controlled contacts could change their vision in a number of useful and surprising ways. He wanted to zoom in for a better look, and the contacts gave him a close up. Their backs were covered with little needles, much like a porcupine, but there was a greenish sheen to them. The poison Nico had mentioned?

It made his skin crawl. An image came unbidden of those needles piercing his skin over his entire body. He shivered and forced the vision away. He debated asking Nico to identify the toxin, but at this point the knowledge wouldn't do him much good.

Once the scooters were within range, Neil ordered the rest of the team to clear out the nearest toads to give their teammates breathing room. There were so many toads bunched together that they barely had to aim to score a hit. But for every one they shot, countless more remained. At ten yards out, Neil tossed a light grenade over the scooters, sending a mass of toads flying in all directions.

The toads had reached the forest and swarmed around and past the trees the way invaders stormed broken castle gates.

"All right, to the grove." Neil waved for everyone to get moving.

Unlike the toad army pursuing them, Neil and the team were hindered by the massive sequoias. He felt like a slalom skier as he detoured around them; despite the trees, they managed to stay ahead of the toads.

A nip of his ear caused him to duck in surprise. He swatted over his head, half afraid one of the toads had caught him. Instead, a pudgy turkey with a sharp beak dive bombed him, pecking at his ears. Others joined in, attacking the entire team. The turkeys also attacked the toads, swallowing them whole.

Neil pointed the fingers of his right hand at the closest turkey and fired a laser straight into its beak. It squawked and veered away.

"Almost there," Nico called over the tradutor. "A little south of where we started."

Neil modified his course, stumbling as his foot hit a root poking up from the ground. He just maintained his balance.

Up ahead loomed a sequoia with a massive hole in the center, so that it served as a tunnel. Through it, he could make out what had to be the grove. Amber, maroon, and purple leaves adorned aspen trees that huddled together like monks at prayer.

Arielle and Devika reached the grove first. Arielle landed the scooter and they both hopped off. Jiro and Eris weren't far behind. Neil reached the path heading through the sequoia, his lungs burning. He paused to check on Anand and Dirk. At that moment several of the turkeys attacked the pair and their scooter ploughed into the ground, sending both boys toppling over the handlebars. The toads swarmed over their legs and torsos and covered the turkeys.

Neil ran back to help, afraid to shoot lest he hit one of them. To his relief, both boys sprang back to their feet, shedding the toads. But the turkeys were gone. The boys ran, eyes wild. Neil tried to cover them, but it was like fighting off a tidal wave with a water pistol. Nevertheless, it was enough for Anand and Dirk to stay ahead.

It took all Neil's willpower to stand pat and wait for the pair to catch up. He feared being covered by the toads himself, unable to fight free as poison was injected into his body from a thousand glistening needles. His skin itched but he stood his ground until Anand and Dirk reached him, the toads close.

"Are you okay?" Neil asked as he directed them toward the grove and took off.

"Yes," Anand replied as they ran. "Don't think they pierced our suits."

A thump against Neil's back sent a chill through him. He'd been hit; he was sure of it. But there was no follow-on sting. "Faster," he ordered, not liking the panicked tone in his voice.

Up ahead, Nico beamed from the safety of the grove. Neil wondered why he'd thought Nico's sims were a good idea. Between this and the invisible Pandirus in the flying Venice sim, Nico was clearly unbalanced.

Panting, Neil leapt between two trunks into the grove. He kept running until he reached a small pond. Anand and Dirk followed a couple of steps behind him. The others watched the toads, which had ground to a halt beyond the perimeter. None entered the grove. They moved around the sides, as if to surround the place; lay siege to it. That was fine with him.

Neil turned around and shot Nico in the back, lighting up his suit target.

"What?" Nico asked.

Neil glared at him. "Are we safe?"

Nico stabbed a finger at the toads outside the grove. "They're programmed not to enter. The trees might as well be fortress walls."

Anand moved over to the edge of the grove, inspecting the toads, which hopped more urgently at his proximity. "Too bad these aren't real. Can you imagine one in Sergeant Terror's chair before she sat on it?" When Eris and Trini gave him horrified looks, he quickly amended. "I'd have an antidote on hand. A joke only. I don't want to hurt her."

"I can imagine her giving you detention in which you have to walk barefoot across a bed of hot coals because of it," Devika replied sweetly.

Chest heaving in an effort to catch his breath, Neil plopped to the ground beside the small pool. The blue-green water was clear all the way to the sandy bottom. Neil rose to his knees and shuffled closer.

The air smelled damp, as if it would soon rain. He dipped his hands down into the pool and drew up the ice-cold water. When he took a drink, it tasted refreshing, but upon swallowing, he found it disappeared upon reaching his throat. He snorted in annoyance.

Sim. Of course.

It would be the same if he tried to eat anything. He'd get the taste—the sim could deceive his senses—but it wouldn't fill him. Thankfully, he wasn't parched. If he had been, he might've killed Nico over it.

"Neil!" Arielle shouted.

Neil twisted back to see her pointing beyond him, her eyes wide. In the middle of the pond, a round bubble the size of a carving pumpkin had emerged on the surface. It glided toward him. Six others joined it.

He jumped to his feet and retreated a few paces, shoulders tensing. "What are they?"

Nico hurried over to join him. "They're harmless. Touch one."

Neil shook his head. "Not a chance."

"It's okay," Nico said. "I promise, you've nothing to worry about. Check them out."

Everyone crowded around, though no one stepped into the water. The bubbles, now nearly as tall as Neil, paused at the pool's edge.

"Come on guys, someone has to have a spine," Nico huffed.

Since the bubbles had stopped moving, Neil leaned in a little closer to inspect one. It wasn't quite a bubble. Rather a sphere of water. Neil reached cautiously with a finger and tapped it. The bubble burst, dousing him.

As Neil wiped his face, the sounds of several water balloons bursting filled his ears. All of the bubbles had exploded, dousing everyone except Nico, who laughed so hard he cried. Neil shook his hands and arms, trying to remove the excess water… and not strangle Nico.

"You're a skunk sack," Jiro complained.

More water bubbles expanded out of the water. Everyone retreated.

"What are they?" Dirk asked.

"Aqua bombers," Nico replied, chest puffed out.

"Are they real?" Arielle took a couple of steps closer to examine one, but kept her arms tucked at her sides.

"As real as anything in a sim," Nico said.

Arielle rolled her eyes. "I meant, are they based off actual aliens?"

"Oh." Nico shrugged. "Could be. I don't know all the aliens in the universe."

Neil had to hand it to Nico. He was extremely creative in the handling of his sims. Crazy, but creative.

Anand and Devika grabbed Nico's arms, having snuck up behind him.

"What are you doing?" Nico tried to pull away.

"Let's go Space Ace." The twins dragged him to the pool and tossed him, causing the aqua bombers to all burst a second time. Nico lurched up from beneath the water, while the team hooted and hollered.

An alarm went off. Dirk checked the wrist-comp velcroed to his left arm. "We better get going, if we're going to get to the Space City Games Cup."

Neil glanced at his own wrist-comp. Three hours until the start of the championship match. He'd really wanted to complete all three bases, but it had taken them forever to find the first and travel from there to the second. Now he'd need to hurry to make it home. He'd been looking forward to the cup for weeks, ever since Grandpa had informed him they had tickets. He should've worked with Nico on better parameters for their tasks within his setting, rather than giving him cart blanche on everything.

"Nico, it's time to wrap this up," Neil said.

"I can't wait for our Games season to start," Eris said as Nico ended the sim, leaving them all back inside the large round cages in the clean room-like facility that comprised the sim training facility.

Neil couldn't either. After losing the Academy Games championship to Riagan last year, he'd waited all summer for revenge. He'd already circled their first match with the Taurus.

Opening the door to his large metal cage, Neil realized he was dry again. Mere seconds ago he'd been drenched. Amazing what the sim could fool the body into thinking was real.

His wrist-comp beeped at him, indicating a new message from Riagan. Likely an excuse for why he'd missed their first team exercise. There was also a message from Maellyn sent yesterday, promising she'd be home tomorrow. She'd spent all summer on Niveum working to cure the Apidium monkeys from an outbreak. He'd only exchanged a few messages with her since she left. The Apidium seemed to be adjusting well, so she was thrilled. But he was anxious for her return.

Pulling up Riagan's message, Neil read. *Need you ASAP. Guiman has a task for us.*

A task? Right now? Better not take too long. He wasn't missing the Cup. Grandpa had promised they had great seats.

"Guys, I've got to meet Riagan." Neil started for the door.

"You two are thick as thieves," Jiro noted. "What have you been doing all summer?"

"Just some work for my grandpa," Neil lied. He hated lying, but there was no way anyone could know what he and Riagan were up to. It would put them all at risk.

Chapter 2

Riagan on Guard Duty

Riagan's scalp sweated underneath the bald cap. He was dressed in a lightweight replica of the Dahaka's black bone armor. And the insulated armor kept him cool. Why couldn't the bald caps be the same?

Headmaster Dardanos handed Riagan his replica Dahaka helmet, which only made his head hotter. Riagan had argued with Ryan Guiman over the need for the caps, since they always wore helmets, but the old man had insisted on them for their own protection. Dahaka lacked hair, so if Riagan's helmet was ever removed, he'd be instantly exposed. He even had to cover his eyebrows.

"Are we searching for their technology base again?" Riagan asked.

Guiman clutched a staff with wrinkled hands, using it to support his weight. "The Dahaka are meeting in the great hall tonight. You've got guard duty at the doors. I need a report."

Since they'd started spying for Guiman, he had mentioned other spies. However, he'd never mentioned names or introduced them. Only Guiman's connection with Dardanos had been revealed, largely because the academy head personally led their combat training. At first, Riagan had been reluctant to train with Dardanos. The headmaster hadn't left the most positive impression on them during their first year encounters, but the dedication he'd shown to training them over the course of the summer had gradually won him over. Neil, too.

Dardanos trained them in hand-to-hand combat; the guns hidden within their armor were a last resort since it would blow their cover.

He often sparred with them at the same time, and they rarely landed a hit. When they'd started training, Riagan had thought the wheelchair would be a severe handicap for Dardanos. But after only a day of training, Riagan learned it was a shield which Dardanos deftly maneuvered to his own advantage.

A few minutes later Neil arrived, red-faced from exertion. Guiman briefed him on their assignment.

"Why tonight?" Neil complained to no one in particular. "We've got Cup tickets."

Riagan gritted his teeth. How could Neil be concerned with the Games when tonight might get them closer to discovering the traitors who got Rois killed? Nothing mattered more.

"This meeting is critical to our finding out where they'll strike next," Guiman said.

Neil's shoulders slumped, but he moved to don his armor.

Guiman showed them a map of the Dahaka fortress on his wrist-comp, pointing out the great hall. "You won't be allowed inside the council chambers, so it'll be tricky to gather intel."

Neil slipped on his bald cap. It automatically modified its color to match his skin tone. Helmet came last. "Let's go."

"Don't forget to color your contacts," Dardanos said.

Riagan blinked once and thought about his contacts changing to blood red; that was all it took. All Dahaka possessed blood-red eyes instead of whites. Every time Riagan and Neil prepared to travel to Siavash, Dardanos reminded them to change their contacts. Forgetting that simple detail could cost them their lives. Riagan wondered if Dardanos' unfailing reminder was due to a sense of guilt over his failings in regard to Rois last year. Something Riagan could appreciate.

Guiman opened the door to his closet, pressed a few buttons, and a Thorne gateway—everyone called them thorneways—sprang into existence in the doorway. Composed of a black liquid that seemed to suck in all light, the thorneway dimmed the simple home.

The first time Riagan had seen one, it had terrified him. He'd imagined this obsidian gate transporting him to some hell. Only after Guiman had explained how they worked and gone through first, followed by Neil, had Riagan stepped through. Now Riagan held his breath and entered the thorneway without hesitation. Guiman had informed them that holding their breath wasn't necessary, but it remained too instinctual to stop.

An instantaneous shock, like static electricity, covered his entire body before he emerged in an underground tunnel on Siavash. Darkness enveloped them. The tunnel was wet and musty, with the sounds of an underground river nearby. Activating the night-vision in his contacts, Riagan headed away from the river as Neil appeared out of the thorneway. They'd traveled here numerous times over the summer. The tunnel exited into a modest cave filled with a sleeping pallet, an armory chest made of bone wrapped with a scaly hide for holding spare gear, a stove, and a wooden cabinet which held some supplies.

The Dahaka lived a sparse lifestyle, and while this cave belonged to Guiman for his spies, it didn't deviate from that custom. Except the sleeping pallet covered a weapons cache for emergencies.

A wall of bones covered the entrance to the cave. Riagan hurried to a door in the wall and pushed his way out into the Dahaka capital, a vast cave system built into the side of a palisade, with an enormous outdoor plain surrounded by a vast bone wall. In Dahaka tradition, each cave mouth was adorned with a grand entrance built from dinosaur bones that the owning Dahaka warrior—known as an Azios—had killed. The more grandiose the entrance, the greater the Azios' stature.

Only the Azios and their families inhabited the capital. Young Azios left their parents to live in tents on the plain beside the perimeter wall until a cave was vacated. Then the young Azios battled for the right to the vacancy. Typically, an Azios spent no more than a year or two in a tent. They either earned a cave or died trying.

Once the Azios had won his own cave, he first tore down the old bone entrance built by his predecessor, leaving it exposed. He then began constructing a new one from the bones of his own kills. Only once the entire entrance was once again covered could he court a female Dahaka. The entrance evolved as the young Azios proved his prowess, and the more grandiose, the better odds he had in finding a mate. The new mate would dye the bones to create a mural that was intended as a foretelling of their life to come.

The common Dahaka lived in villages outside the capital. Riagan didn't understand the reasoning for this, since it left them exposed to attacks, but from what he could tell, the Azios disdained those in the villages.

Everything appeared so primitive. The kinds of technologies needed for space travel remained hidden. Most of their assignments over the summer had revolved around searching for the Dahaka ships, and Riagan knew Guiman had other spies looking, too, but Mainyu had them well hidden. As far as Riagan knew, no one had gotten close.

"Don't waste time getting to your posts," Guiman ordered over their tradutors.

Since Mainyu's demise, the Azios had been consumed with duels as those with ambition, which was most everyone, tried to assume the mantle of power. And they weren't here to draw attention. Strangely, today only a handful of the young Azios sparred among their tents. The older Azios sat around fires sharpening tusk knives or conversing in hushed tones. The mood was so *out of the norm* that a chill ran up Riagan's spine. Something big was definitely on the horizon. Riagan hoped it was simply that one Azios had gained enough support to assume the mantle of leader. Perhaps they'd start to uncover the other traitors responsible for Rois' death.

With Mainyu gone, contact had ceased between the Dahaka and the traitors on Space City; Guiman assured them there were others besides Jarl, but thus far they'd failed to discover who. It vexed Riagan to no end because rooting out the traitors was his primary motivation. But at the moment, Riagan felt whatever had the Azios in business mode had nothing to do with a new leader. Something else was at stake.

They made their way past Azios sitting around campfires and tents until they reached the great hall near the middle of the capital. The great hall possessed the largest bone entrance, easily three times the size of any individual residence. It was dyed yellow like the sun, the greatest source of power to the Dahaka. Unlike the Azios' homes, this entrance wasn't torn down by each new ruler. It had existed for tens of thousands of years, and depicted the Dahaka ruling the stars.

The great hall held the ruler's quarters, a dining area where many Azios gathered to eat and drink, as well as the council chamber. This would be the first meeting in the chamber since Mainyu's death on Mars.

Reaching the entrance, Riagan raised a hand to open the bone door. It burst open, nearly nailing him in the face. He pulled back, Neil beside him, as an Azios marched out. The boys stood immobile, as the Dahaka stormed past them. Adult Azios paid little attention to the young in training, which is what made Neil and Riagan such valuable spies. Guiman's adult spies kept being challenged to duels, and many of them had died.

With the Dahaka past, the boys hurried inside. A couple of cave tunnels on the left led back to Mainyu's or the future leader's quarters, while others on the right led to the dining hall. At the rear was the council chamber. It possessed its own yellow-dyed bone entrance. Guarding it were two young Azios.

"We're here to relieve you of duty." Riagan held his shoulders back and his head high while glaring at the pair in typical Azios fashion.

"Really?" the one on the left asked. "We have another couple hours?"

Neil took a menacing step toward them. "Those are our orders. Now beat it."

They'd quickly learned that an aggressive approach made them stand out less. Speaking politely marked you as weak, and therefore in need of toughening up.

The second guard slapped the first on the shoulder. "Don't question it. Let's get some food."

"Right," the first said. They rushed toward the dining hall.

Riagan and Neil took their places. The chamber doors stood ajar, no one inside.

"Guess we're stuck here awhile." Riagan took a position to the right of the doors.

"Grandpa had great seats," Neil muttered, moving to the left.

Riagan had wanted to see the Games Cup, too, but they needed to know what was happening tonight.

The next several hours dragged on until Riagan was having trouble staying awake. Periodically he'd check his wrist-comp for the time or new messages. The wait was rather dull. Many of their assignments had involved a lot of standing around. Who knew spying had a lot more moments of boredom than excitement?

He started to wonder if Guiman had been wrong about a meeting when a flood of Azios entered the great hall, streaming back to the council chamber. Several Kali joined them, the black smoke that comprised their forms gliding in. The Kali were long-time allies with the Dahaka, and Riagan had observed many Kali in his time on Siavash. Part of him feared they'd eventually run into General Stribog here, despite Dardanos' assurances that the Kali was committed to realigning his people with Space City. Riagan still had his doubts.

Once the chamber was full, standing room only, the door was closed. No one remained in the hall, so Riagan left his post to press his ear against the door, trying to hear discussion. Everything was muffled, so Riagan paired a wireless mini-amplifier with his tradutor, expanded the range to max, and wedged it as far as he could through the bones that comprised the door.

"—steal it from the Alfar," a Dahaka said.

"Impossible!" another scoffed.

"I've put a plan in place," the first said. "Ragna, I want you and Khaeta to assemble two teams. The Kali, Chenbog and Sverog, will reveal the details when you're within striking distance of Orestes."

Orestes was the Alfar moon orbiting Ourania, but from everything Riagan had learned, attacking the Alfar was foolhardy. The Alfar had unrivaled defensive capabilities. No one challenged them.

Who was the speaker?

Riagan didn't dare open the door. He wished their contacts had a mode that allowed them to see through bone.

"The Alfar will spot our ships well before we're in range to attack," a Dahaka said.

"Do you doubt me, Khaeta?" the first Dahaka asked.

"Of course not," Khaeta replied, voice uneasy.

"The Orestes sensors will be deactivated before you're in range," the first Dahaka continued. "Follow the plan. Pull this off, and no one will stand against us ever again."

"Yes, Mainyu," Khaeta answered.

Riagan turned back to Neil, eyes wide.

"What?" Neil asked.

Mainyu couldn't be alive. They'd killed him. He'd been there. Nothing had remained of the Dahaka leader.

"What are you two doing?" a voice demanded behind them.

Riagan and Neil spun to find two Azios approaching. Riagan tensed. They'd been caught. If there was one thing the adults punished their younger Azios for, it was rule-breaking.

Before Riagan could think how to respond, one Azios grabbed him by the neck and lifted him into the air. Choking, Riagan pounded at the Dahaka's iron grip. Out of the corner of his eye he saw the second had Neil.

"Shouldn't stick your eyes and ears in Azios business." The Dahaka clapped Riagan's temple.

His vision blurred. A second later he was thrown into a wall. His helmet was knocked loose, exposing his jaw.

"Don't let me catch you spying on Azios matters again."

Riagan lay in a heap, mind muddled. The room swayed like a boat on the waves. His body ached. He tried to rise, but the Azios shoved him back down. The Dahaka stood over him a moment longer, before the pair entered the great hall.

Once they were alone again, Riagan righted his helmet and hurried over to Neil, who lay sprawled out on the ground. "We've got to go." He pulled Neil's arm, trying to help him up.

Neil groaned and made no effort to rise.

"Neil, can ya hear me? Neil?"

It took several uneasy minutes before Neil was clear-headed enough to respond. Maybe a concussion? Hopefully not much more, but Riagan couldn't be sure. If they were anywhere else he'd try to carry Neil. But not here. Here, Neil had to move on his own before they could leave the great hall. No Azios could see Riagan helping him. As Riagan tried to get Neil alert and up, his mind raced over the revelation.

Mainyu was alive.

Riagan bit his lower lip until he tasted blood. Mainyu was in the next room, alive, and there was nothing he could do. Not when the Dahaka leader was surrounded by his Azios. All Riagan could do for now was carry the message back to Guiman.

Chapter 3

Maellyn Departs Niveum

Maellyn had never felt a greater sense of accomplishment in her life as when the Apidium monkeys reached their newborn-sized hands up into the clear spheres, past the tiny pink flowers, to grab the gray moths. Seeing the Apidium eat the moths made up for all of the long hours, sporadic rain showers, and jungle humidity, as well as the tremendous effort.

Back in the simulation on Space City, it had taken her much less time to teach Harisha and the other Apidium to use the spheres for food than it took with the real ones here on Niveum. It had taken the entire summer in fact. But now the Apidium turned to the spheres routinely for food instead of hunting the black mosquitoes. For the last week the Apidium had no new cases of the disease, and Maellyn's calculations indicated those numbers should now remain low.

"Your father will be proud," Instructor Fintan said. The four-armed albino monkey, a Macab, offered her a canteen of water, which she gladly accepted. "Your mother would've been, too."

"Thanks." A twinge of discomfort hit Maellyn at the mention of her mother, but she covered it up with a swig of water. "You were the mastermind. All I did was train them."

Fintan waved dismissively. "Anyone can have ideas. Ideas are worthless without someone to turn them into reality. Your hard work, both in simulation last year and here this summer, is what saved the Apidium."

An adolescent Apidium on a nearby branch watched them, eyes trained on Maellyn's hands. Despite its human-toddler-size, the tan monkey possessed a silver ring that circled its face and, combined with the rough, wrinkled look of its skin, made it appear elderly.

The Apidium often gathered around Maellyn and the rest of the science team during mealtime, watching for scraps. Everyone took care to avoid leaving out food. Maellyn held up her hand to the monkey to show she had nothing for it to eat. It sniffed her hand a moment before skittering away into the trees.

"To us both, then." Maellyn raised her canteen as if toasting and took another drink.

Fintan nodded acceptance. "Now that work is done, it's time we returned home."

She smiled, looking forward to getting back to Space City. The school year started in a couple of days, and she had things to take care of first. Plus, she longed to see Neil. Their first and only kiss had been more than two months ago, and they'd done little more than exchange messages since. Her work here had left little time for anything else. Would things still be the same when she returned?

Maellyn collected up her gear before making one final pass through the heart of the Apidium zone where they'd first introduced the spheres. She watched as the Apidium ate flies, picked berries, or groomed each other. She also searched for signs of any sick— unusually lethargic, self-separation from the rest, or missing patches of fur. She hadn't spotted a new case in nearly two weeks, but the habit remained.

Once she'd finished her route and assured herself there was nothing else she needed to do, she headed for the temporary thorneway they'd set up for transport between the jungle here on Niveum and Space City. Roughly the size of a soccer goal, the thorneway was already filled with the black, oil-like substance that indicated it was active. She'd once asked her father why they were black. His reply was that it was best to think of them as black holes. They absorbed light rather than reflected or refracted it.

Standing before the thorneway, a part of her wasn't ready to leave. An irrational part of her feared that if she left now, all their hard work would come undone. But the Apidium were in the Macabs' hands now. She had obligations back home.

And Neil.

A smile broke out on her face at the thought of seeing him again, and she stepped into the thorneway, emerging a second later in the round aluminum cages of the Sims facility.

Dr. Theresa Flores stood waiting outside the cages. It was common procedure for travelers returning to Space City after extended time on an alien planet to undergo a routine checkup at the infirmary, but Maellyn hadn't expected the lead doctor to escort her.

Maellyn opened her mouth to greet Dr. Flores when she noticed her father with a couple of Space City Councilmen: Mr. Daichi Takeda, the chief technologist, and Mr. Carl Fischer, the Space City Ambassador. They ringed Juna. The Azzaro was dressed in gray, eyes flat and full of grief. Four other Azzaro held a black box that resembled a coffin.

Maellyn opened the doors of her cage and exited. She wanted to talk to her father, but the solemn expressions on everyone's faces made her reluctant to intrude. Instead, she sidled over to Dr. Flores. "What happened?"

Dr. Flores leaned close and whispered. "Jarl died. Juna has been granted permission to return his body to Sundara for burial."

Maellyn inhaled sharply, sorry for Juna, though she had no sympathy for Jarl. He'd been responsible for Rois' death after working with the Dahaka to smuggle the CME off Space City to Mars. The Dahaka had attempted to use the device to destroy Space City. It was a horrible perversion of her father's work, which had been designed as an energy generator.

Her anger cooled as she studied Juna's distraught figure. The Azzaro woman had lost everything. First her son. Now her husband.

"How did he die?" Maellyn asked.

"A combination of withdrawal and grief," Dr. Flores answered.

One of the cages had a thorneway opened up inside it. The four Azzaros, with Juna in tow, carried the black coffin through it.

"Withdrawal from what?" Maellyn asked, frowning.

"Chemical hypnosis. While imprisoned, he fell extremely ill. We had him checked out."

Maellyn's heart skipped a beat. "Chemical hypnosis causes addiction?" Neil hadn't shown any withdrawal symptoms, nor expressed any issues after Jarl had injected him.

"Based on our test results, Jarl endured prolonged exposure to chemical hypnosis. Maybe for years." Dr. Flores sighed. "He showed massive signs of withdrawal. Couple that with his learning that Jaya died due to his own actions, he gave up. Died within days."

"What about Neil?" Maellyn asked. "He was chemically hypnotized, too." Neil hadn't mentioned any problems, but that would be just like a boy to hide his own physical ailments. Claim he didn't want her to worry. Maellyn clenched her fists. If Neil was risking himself because he didn't want her to worry, she'd—

Dr. Flores shook her head. "Neil is fine. After Jarl's death, we gave him another thorough exam. He showed no issues. At most he'd had a couple exposures."

Despite the reassurances, Maellyn wanted to talk with Neil herself. And if Jarl was chemically hypnotized as well, who had done it to him? Was there another traitor?

She tiptoed toward the door, thinking it best to catch up with her father later after the sendoff. But he whispered something to Juna, before moving to intercept her. "I'm glad you're here." He hugged her, squeezing. "I know you just got back, but I need you to travel with me."

"Travel where?"

"To Sundara for a few days."

Maellyn was torn. She missed him and loved their opportunities to travel together, but it had been a long summer already. "Do you really need me? I'm a mess and I've no clean clothes. Plus, I was hoping for a few days' rest before classes start."

Her father grimaced guiltily. "I'm sorry. I know it's inconvenient, but it's important. I already had Charlie pack a bag with clean clothes for you."

Better Charlie, their droid butler, than her dad. Charlie had a sense of what clothes fit together thanks to years of careful training on her part.

"Okay." Maellyn sighed. So much for seeing Neil again.

Chapter 4

Neil Attends New Student Orientation

Neil, light-headed from a possible concussion, followed Riagan through the thorneway into Guiman's home. Dried blood caked the inside of Neil's nose. At least his helmet had provided a little shielding or the Azios' punch would have broken his nose.

Dardanos sat at the dinner table eating. His eyes widened when he saw them and he rolled his wheelchair over to the sink. "What happened?"

"Mainyu. He's alive," Riagan said.

Neil stumbled and Riagan caught his arm, steadying him.

"Thanks." Neil's vision swam, forcing him to take a couple deep breaths to clear his head. Riagan led him to a chair at the table.

Dardanos returned with a wet rag, which he tossed to Neil. "Your orders were to listen, not get into a fight."

Neil dabbed at his upper lip with the wet rag, frowning that Dardanos hadn't reacted to the news.

"Did ya hear me?" Riagan asked. "Mainyu's alive."

"What else did you learn?" Dardanos motioned for them to proceed with the report.

Neil lowered the rag. "You already knew?"

Riagan's eyes widened. "You did? How?"

"We did," Dardanos confirmed.

"Why didn't you tell us?" Neil tossed the rag, red with blood, onto the table.

"You aren't privy to everything Guiman and I know," Dardanos replied, crossing his arms. "Now would you please proceed with your report? What is Mainyu planning?"

Riagan turned red-faced, and Neil felt his own face heating. They'd busted their tails all summer long on assignment after assignment. Hiding Mainyu's survival was lousy repayment for all their hard work.

Grinding his teeth, Riagan responded. "Mainyu plans to attack Orestes."

"Why?" Dardanos asked, eyebrows raised.

"Don't know." Riagan shrugged. "A couple of Azios noticed us." He gestured to the bloody rag on the table.

"You got nothing else?" Dardanos brow darkened.

Neil's vision started to swim, so he leaned back in his chair and forced himself to relax and breathe.

"There was something else… eliminating Alfar sensors or something." Riagan pointed at the doorframe behind them. The thorneway had extinguished. "The Dahaka responsible for my sister's death is alive. What are we doing about him?"

"Nothing for now." Dardanos absentmindedly stroked his chin.

Riagan gaped a moment, then gritted his teeth. "Nothing?"

A bout of nausea hit Neil. He leaned forward, staring straight down at the table and swallowed, trying not to get sick.

"The Council rejected any moves against Mainyu," Dardanos said.

"What? Why?" Riagan asked.

Neil clenched his fists and fought the desire to sleep. What would make the Council refuse to act against Mainyu after his attempted attack of Space City last year?

Dardanos leaned forward and laid a hand on Neil's shoulder. "You don't look good."

Neil raised his head and shook it. "I'm fine."

"No, you're not fine." Their headmaster rolled his wheelchair to the side, clearing a path to the door. "You might have a concussion. Riagan, get him to the infirmary to get checked out."

Riagan's lips twisted in a snarl. "Why's the Council protecting Mainyu? Ya can't keep this from us. We deserve to know."

Dardanos' eyes narrowed. "You deserve nothing. You work for us. We tell you what you need to know to accomplish the tasks we assign to you. Now get Neil to the infirmary." He pointed at the door and it was clear they would get no further information from him.

Neil tried to think up an argument that didn't sound childish and whiny. He came up with nothing. Riagan stormed from the house first and Neil rose to follow, a little numb and unsure if that was from his injuries or the revelations.

"By the way," Dardanos said as Neil passed. "If you check out all right, I'd appreciate it if you sat in on the new student orientation tomorrow. Watch the exit, so we don't have any recruits *sneak out early*."

Neil flushed at that reminder. It seemed years ago, instead of one, that he, Riagan, and Rois had snuck out of their own orientation in order to see more of Space City, leading to their first and second unfortunate encounters with aliens.

He couldn't bring himself to answer Dardanos. He just followed Riagan out the door.

*****

Neil entered the auditorium for the new recruit's orientation, feeling better after a night's rest. The doctors had confirmed that he'd suffered a minor concussion. They'd run a few tests and sent him home.

Now as he leaned against the back wall by the doors, he marveled that it had only been a year since he sat in here, eating lunch, having just met Riagan and Rois. At the time, his biggest concern had been getting away from his uncle.

For the first time in a long time, he found himself thinking about his uncle. What had his uncle thought after he left? Had he reported Neil's disappearance? Had he worried about him? And to Neil's surprise, he didn't really care either way. He no longer hated his uncle. All the anger and resentment he'd stored up over years of abuse had dissipated without his even noticing.

He had discovered everything he wanted aboard Space City. Beheld wonders he never imagined when he was living in his uncle's basement. If anything now, Neil pitied his uncle, who was so wrapped up in past losses that he never dared to look forward and dream. That day in the recruiter's office, Neil knew he'd been stupid and scared with his fake ID. But if he'd let fear hold him back, he'd never have set foot in space, nor met Maellyn, Riagan, or the rest of his friends. Never set foot on Mars.

The new recruits trickled in, most whispering in excited packs, eyes and mouths wide as children visiting a zoo for the first time. Others were quiet, hunched in on themselves, awed and a little fearful. Neil wanted to reassure them they had no reason to worry. That this place would prove more amazing than their wildest dreams. He also wondered if he had looked like that last year.

Instructor Shilah Nez stepped up to the microphone wearing his formal uniform, blue buttoned-down shirt with a Space City logo and his nameplate on his left breast, along with insignias on both shoulders marking him as a Senior Master Sergeant within Space City.

"Welcome to the Space City Preparatory Academy," Instructor Nez greeted. "This'll be your home for the next four years. Period."

Instructor Nez proceeded to drone on. Students wouldn't return to Earth for the remainder of their time in the academy. Neil wanted to tell them they wouldn't miss it. He hadn't. There were too many amazing things to do here. But then there hadn't been much for him to leave behind either.

Following that was a discussion of the school's two tenets— scientific achievement and social evolution. As he half listened, a note popped up on his wrist-comp. From Maellyn. She'd sent him a brief message yesterday saying she had to travel with her dad to Sundara and would be back in a few days. She promised to fill him in later. He pulled up her new message.

Hey Neil,
Dad has kept me busy since we arrived on Sundara yesterday. We helped Juna transport Jarl's body back for burial.

The reminder of Jarl's death brought him both sadness and relief. Jarl had chemically hypnotized him to wipe his memory. The knowledge that he'd lost memories both scared and angered him. Yet Jarl had only done so because he'd been under a chemical hypnosis as well. The Azzaro had suffered a lot more loss than a few memories.

Neil read on.

He died from a withdrawal due to a chemical hypnosis addiction. Apparently, he'd been dosed for years. Have you been feeling any side effects yourself?

The question caused his breath to catch in his throat. He hadn't noticed any side effects, and the doctors had re-run tests on him after Jarl's death. But it still unsettled him.

I talked with dad. Turns out Jarl wasn't the traitor. Well, he was, but not willfully. There must have been at least one other traitor to dose him. And likely control him.

Anyway, Dad and I are talking with Azzaro doctors and family members, trying to determine strange behavior that might help us pinpoint when and how the dosing started. Hope to be back soon.

I miss you.

Neil read through the message again while the introduction video played. Jarl might not have been a traitor. Mainyu remained alive. Had they accomplished anything on Mars? He shook his head. Of course they had. They'd prevented Space City from being incinerated, saving a lot of lives in the process. But this news presented one more unraveled piece.

A number of students fidgeted during the orientation video, and a few cast glances at him and the door. He glared back to deter them from trying to sneak out.

When the video ended, Instructor Nez returned to the stage up front. Neil huffed, wondering how long this was going to drag on. The door opened beside him and Cade limped in. He nodded in greeting.

"What are you doing here?" Neil whispered.

"I work for the Academy Monthly now," Cade replied. "My first assignment is a piece for first years on how to acclimate themselves to the Academy and Space City."

Neil snorted. "Does anyone read that thing?"

Cade shrugged. "They pay me to write the articles. Not to get people to read them."

"I'm a little surprised to see you working. Didn't you win a big race this summer? And a million pearls?" Neil didn't know the exact exchange rate in currencies, but it was a lot of money.

Cade dipped his head, scowling. "Technically. But I didn't get to keep the money."

"At this time I'll open the floor to questions," Instructor Nez said. "I'm sure all of you have plenty."

Cade started to type on his wrist-comp, so Neil turned his focus back to watching the new recruits. One boy raised his hand, and when Instructor Nez pointed at him, he rose timidly.

"I heard we're taller in space than on Earth. Is that true?" The boy stood straighter as if to prove it.

Instructor Nez smiled. "That was true during your flights here. The lack of gravity in space allows the ligaments that hold the vertebrae of your spine in place to stretch a little, adding an inch or so to your height. But here on Space City we have our own gravity."

The boy sat down, head bowed as if embarrassed.

Another girl raised her hand and stood when called upon. "Is it true your muscles and bones get weaker in space? And you have to exercise eight hours a day to keep them strong?"

Several of the students groaned and a couple murmured to each other. Neil chuckled at their naivety.

"That also is only true without gravity." Instructor Nez pulled a pen from his pocket, held his arm straight out and dropped the pen. It bounced off the floor. "As you can all see, we've got plenty on Space City. Nothing to worry about."

"I heard some people get sick and vomit in space for no reason," another boy said, grinning evilly at a boy next to him. "Is that because of radiation? Do they die?"

Instructor Nez shook his head. "I assure you that is not the case. Some people experience space sickness, but it is not from radiation. All ships you flew in from Earth protect you from radiation, and you are one hundred percent safe on Space City as well. Nor has there ever been a connection between radiation from the sun and space sickness."

The boy scowled.

A new girl stood. Tall for her age. Taller than Neil himself. "Do people age slower in space?"

Neil snickered. Kids would believe anything.

But Instructor Nez surprised him. "Technically that was true while in Earth's orbit."

Neil gawked. Instructor Nez had to be joking.

"If you lived in Earth's orbit and had a sibling living on Earth," Nez grinned as if preparing a joke, "—after fifteen hundred years you'd have aged one second less than your sibling."

Neil chuckled to himself. The girl glowered in disappointment as she sat down, while a companion next to her grinned smugly.

"All right everyone," Instructor Nez raised his voice so everyone would hear him. "If you'll form four lines in front of Instructors Aldrin and Glenn, and Team Captains Hardin and Gilbright, they will lead you to your dorms and get you settled in." The four moved to Nez's side.

Neil pushed open the door to exit. "Got everything you needed?" he asked Cade.

Cade finished typing on his wrist-comp and put it away. "Got enough." He followed Neil outside.

*****

Neil exited the academy main office planning to find Riagan. He hadn't returned to their dorm the previous night after their mission to Siavash.

In a corner of the quad at the center of campus, a boisterous crowd of students gathered around the flagpoles from which the Space City and academy banners normally hung. Neil hadn't seen this many students crowded in one place since—

Brow furrowing, he marched over and pushed his way through to the center. Caleb Thornton and Adrien Laroque stood on the mini hills next to the flagpoles, running a pair of new silver explorer uniforms up the line toward the mini-booster-like rockets at the top. A couple of young recruits, dressed in jester costumes, helplessly watched the prank, no idea the rockets did nothing more than shoot sparks. Faces red with humiliation, the recruits fidgeted under the jeers from the crowd, and were sweating themselves to death in the jester costumes in this late August heat; sometimes Neil wished Space City didn't do *such* a good job of imitating Earth seasons.

A few paces off to the side from Caleb and Adrien, Patrick Duffy observed the proceedings with a smarmy grin. Up to their old pranks as usual.

Clenching his jaw, Neil stomped over to Adrien until the sallow boy retreated.

"Still think harassing defenseless recruits is cool, huh?" Neil snarled at Caleb. He pulled the clothes down from the flagpole Adrien had abandoned. He hoped his words also shamed the crowd.

Caleb shrugged, smirking. "It's a harmless gag."

"Oh yeah," Neil tossed the uniform to one of the recruits, "—stealing uniforms from flobs who haven't been here a day is *great* fun. Especially if you humiliate them in front of the *entire* student body."

Some in the crowd booed.

Patrick blushed. "You're right. This is juvenile." He pushed Caleb back from the second flagpole and pulled down the other uniform, returning it to the other nervous recruit who mumbled thanks and hurried off, likely to get out of the jester costume as quickly as he could.

For a second Neil stared at Patrick, forgetting what else he'd intended to say. What was Patrick planning?

Caleb looked disgusted at Patrick. "I can't believe you're siding with *him*." Caleb jabbed a finger in Neil's direction. "What happened to you?"

Shaking his head, Patrick said, "It's childish. It's beneath us. Let it go."

Neil blinked. Was this some plan on Patrick's part to throw everyone off before he pulled a bigger prank? But Neil didn't have the time to dwell on it. He had more important matters to attend to, so he pushed on past the dispersing crowd.

"Neil, wait up," Patrick called after him.

But Neil picked up his pace, ignoring him. Patrick grabbed his shoulder.

Neil spun, bracing himself. "What do you want?"

Patrick backed up a step, as if he'd been punched. He dropped his gaze to the ground. "I… never got to thank you for saving my life on Mars."

Neil gaped at him, too stunned to respond.

Brow creased, Patrick looked up. "If…If it weren't for you, I'd be dead."

Studying the courtyard, Neil searched for a trap. But no one was close by. Just Patrick shifting from foot to foot.

After another moment's hesitation, Neil said, "You're welcome."

Patrick relaxed, a tentative smile crossing his features. "I know I pulled a lot of cruel tricks on you guys last year. But I want you to know I'm done with all that."

"Didn't seem that way five minutes ago." Neil jabbed a finger back toward the flagpoles.

Patrick's smile faded and his eyes dropped back to the ground. "I didn't have anything to do with it."

"Right." Neil rolled his eyes. "That wasn't you I saw grinning away while Caleb preyed on the new recruits?"

"Look, I said I was sorry. It was a mistake."

Neil wagged a finger at him. "You might think you're different. But you're the same old Patrick. Willing to hurt others for your enjoyment."

Patrick stood there, shoulders slumped, not arguing.

But Neil wasn't done. "I'm not the one you hurt. You owe your apologies to those new recruits." He spun on his heel, too angry to say more.

Thankfully, Patrick didn't follow.

Chapter 5

Riagan's Lesson

Riagan spotted Guiman working in the gardens outside the spaceport. The old man pulled weeds from around the roses, his staff propped against the bed wall. Those roses were bioengineered to change color in the presence of certain toxins or radiation. It was the reason the garden was built right outside the spaceport. Any incoming visitors would have to pass through the garden, thereby revealing if they tried to sneak any harmful pollutant onboard. Riagan had never considered it before, but as the gardener, Guiman had to be involved in monitoring this.

The garden did serve as a convenient place for Guiman to meet with his spies. They could speak freely without being overheard. In addition to weeding, pruning trees, and picking fruits, Guiman's androids scanned daily for recording devices to ensure the garden was clean.

Today, Riagan hadn't come to talk. He was tired of talking, spying, and training.

Mainyu was alive.

Rois was dead.

Riagan couldn't accept that.

He didn't ask Guiman how they were going to handle the threat. The Council had prohibited action against the Dahaka. Instead, with the old man preoccupied, Riagan made his way across campus to Guiman's home and slipped inside. He had his own plan. A simple one.

He activated the thorneway in the closet doorway. Inky darkness rose into place. This would be his first trip alone, but he didn't hesitate. He darted through to Siavash.

In the darkened tunnel he activated his night vision contacts. After proceeding a few steps, he remembered he had to deactivate the thorneway. It was a task Neil typically handled. Riagan backtracked to the thorneway and slid back the panel covering the controls. The panel was camouflaged to blend in with the tunnel walls, while the thorneway was activated within an old storage room, long since abandoned.

He made his way toward the cave entrance. As he did, he fought to contain the adrenaline rush. Ever since becoming a spy, he'd longed for the opportunity to take down someone involved in Rois' death. He'd thought they'd already gotten the main one responsible, but now he knew they'd failed.

As he made his way, he remembered Guiman's mantra—*emotion has no use to a spy. It clouds the mind. It clouds judgment.* Riagan knew he couldn't afford any missteps with Mainyu, so he took the time to breathe deeply and calm himself.

He marched into the cave and over to the armory chest. He retrieved imitation Dahaka gear. After donning the armor, he moved to the pallet and raised it against the wall, revealing the hidden weapons cache. The light grenades would be the easiest to carry, and he hid four in the disguised slots within the armor. It was time.

A part of Riagan wished Neil was here with him. But since Guiman and Dardanos hadn't sanctioned this plan, Neil wouldn't have come. He'd have protested Riagan coming, insisting they wait for Guiman to develop a plan. Neil wanted to help avenge Rois, felt a responsibility to do so, but not without Guiman's permission. He would follow the rules.

The entire grounds were filled with Azios sparring under a noon sun; everything back to normal. The salty tang of sweat filled Riagan's nostrils, so that he wished their helmets came with scent filters. The Azios were dressed in little more than shorts, their traditional black armor reserved for actual battles or those on duty. Not that the lack of armor made them less threatening. All Azios were heavily-muscled giants. Powdery-white bodies rippled and flexed as they attacked each other with hands, feet, and claws from animals they'd killed. They slashed and cut with knives made from bone. More than a little blood was spilt, and scars covered them all.

Yet it was their crimson eyes that unsettled Riagan. Without those eyes, the Azios might be mistaken for albinos on steroids. With them, the Azios appeared downright demonic. Riagan got chills standing alone among them, his nerves fraying like a rabbit encircled by ravenous polar bears.

The armor he wore indicated he was on duty. No one should bother him. *Emotion has no use to a spy.* He strode forward toward the great hall. He would hide in the dining area until Mainyu's quarters were empty. Then he would sneak in and plant the light grenades around the room, along with a tiny camera. Once he confirmed Mainyu's presence, he'd blow the grenades.

"You, hold," a voice shouted.

Riagan pressed onward, trying to look rushed. The speaker couldn't mean him.

"Why do you flee?" the voice asked.

Riagan halted, grinding his teeth. If he ignored the question, everyone would think he was running away. Brand him a coward. He didn't need this distraction but couldn't proceed without drawing even more undue attention.

Riagan spun on his heels. This Azios also wore full armor. Riagan wondered how he hadn't noticed him before among the rest. The Azios had a good fifty pounds on him.

"I'm on orders from Ragna." Riagan clenched his fists and straightened his back, evenly meeting the Azios' gaze.

"Why aren't your eyes red?"

Riagan swore to himself and blinked to activate the contacts. "I don't know what ye talking about."

The Azios narrowed its eyes, but said nothing. Others were starting to take notice. It was time to get going.

Letting annoyance seep into his voice, Riagan asked, "I'll just let Ragna know ya delay his messengers." He hoped that would be the end of it.

For an answer, the Azios grabbed a six-inch tusk from his waist and tossed it to the ground between them. "I challenge you."

Riagan's mouth went dry. Why was this Azios challenging him when he was clearly on duty? They both were. He hadn't given any provocation.

"Why don't you pick up the knife?" The Azios asked. "Are you afraid?"

He was cornered and knew it. There was no way out of a fight. *Fine*, he thought. At least this gave him a chance to test his fighting skills against someone besides Neil.

Rather than retrieve the knife from the ground, which Guiman had taught them was a trap, Riagan withdrew a 3D printed knife from his armor. It resembled the tusk-knives the Dahaka favored, but was stronger; its hilt was contoured to fit his hand. It seemed ridiculous to fight with a knife when he had better weapons at his disposal, but he couldn't give himself away. Not surrounded by the entire Azios host.

Riagan held up his knife and nodded. To his surprise, the Azios strolled forward and retrieved the knife from the ground, momentarily taking his eyes off Riagan. It was a disdainful move. Riagan was so surprised by the audacity that he failed to take advantage of it. Before he could even think to react, the Azios darted forward. Agile as an angry snake, he swiped at Riagan's belly. Riagan barely managed to leap out of reach. The Azios spun to the side. Planting his legs, he sprang forward. Riagan flinched, bracing for impact, but the Azios dove low past him.

Too late, Riagan pivoted. A sharp burn lit up his calf. A trickle of blood slid down his leg.

Anxious to repay the shallow cut, Riagan slashed at the hand holding the knife, intent on disarming his opponent. The Azios back flipped twice, like a gymnast doing a floor routine, before darting forward to slash again at Riagan's belly. The attack forced him back onto his heels and was followed by a left-handed punch to his jaw. The blow sent him reeling.

Riagan tried to rebound, but a punch to the gut and a jab to the temple knocked him backward. Dazed and arms wheeling, he crashed to the ground. He tensed up, the wind knocked out of him. The Azios dropped onto his chest and blows rained down on his head. Riagan tried to ward the punches off, but they came in rapid succession as if he were facing two or three fighters.

Abruptly the pummeling ceased. Riagan exhaled, heart pounding, ears ringing. He tasted blood. The weight lifted from his chest and he rolled to the side, spitting out blood. Gasping for air, his head swam.

The Azios knelt beside him and Riagan raised an arm to protect himself.

"Return to Space City," the Azios whispered. "Guiman wants a word."

The Azios rose and walked away, leaving him to pick himself up.

Riagan wanted to scream. This had all been a setup. Another spy.

Strange words filled the air, followed by laughing. His tradutor must've been broken during the fight. The laughter all around him drove Riagan to his feet. He couldn't believe how thoroughly he'd been beaten. After training with Dardanos all summer, he'd expected he could at least defend himself. Instead, the other spy had beaten him as easily as a child.

Trying his best to shut out the laughter and jeers from the other Azios, Riagan trudged back toward Guiman's cave. His head ached. But he was determined not to rest or show any further weakness in front of the Azios. Rumors would already start to spread based upon his poor showing in the fight.

When he made it back to the cave, he took a few minutes to compose himself. He grabbed some water from the cabinet beside the wood stove and drank. He wanted answers from Guiman. Why had the spy challenged him instead of simply letting him know he'd been caught? And how had Guiman known what he was up to? Riagan hadn't told anyone his plans.

He finished off the bottle of water and his head cleared; his cheeks and jaw ached, but he'd be all right. Tramping down the tunnel, he hesitated before the thorneway. Once he returned to Space City, he was in for another battle. He needed to collect himself.

Again, he wondered how Guiman had known what he was up to? Even if Guiman had discovered that he'd used the thorneway on his own, how would the old man have alerted a spy in that time?

Unless Guiman always had a spy keeping an eye on him and Neil when they went to Siavash. Perhaps someone kept tabs on Guiman's cave, noting who came and went.

"Why aren't your eyes red?"

He groaned as he remembered the question from his attacker. He'd forgotten to activate his contacts. He'd made it easy on the spy to spot him and realize he'd come on his own. Guiman and Dardanos always reminded them to activate their contacts before traveling through the thorneway on a mission.

He felt like punching himself, but took out his frustration on the button that activated the thorneway instead, then stepped through.

Emerging into Guiman's home, Riagan found the old man reading in a chair. Guiman calmly closed the book and set it on an end table beside him.

Riagan decided to go on the offensive. "Is this how ya treat all your spies?"

Guiman grabbed his cane, clasping it in both hands in front of him, but didn't rise. "It is when the spy is a churlish teenager who needs to be taught a lesson. From the looks of you, I'm guessing your ego is bruised more than your body. I ordered her to give you a warning."

Riagan gaped, his next words dying in his throat. That was impossible. The spy had been bigger than himself.

Guiman's eyes danced. He was enjoying this.

"I went to handle the problem ya can't," Riagan snarled. "The one ya promised me."

"And if you'd succeeded?" Guiman asked. "What would you have done when the Council expelled you from the academy? Might've imprisoned you, too. At the very least sent back to Earth where you'd never travel into space again."

"Ya think I care if I got Mainyu?" Riagan asked, but the threat of imprisonment or being sent back to Earth gave him pause. He hadn't considered such possibilities.

Guiman continued as if Riagan hadn't spoken. "You'd lose the chance to catch anyone else involved in your sister's death. They might go free."

"What others? We've spied for ya all summer and come up with nothing. Mainyu is alive and ya doing nothing to catch him!"

Guiman placed two fingers on the bridge of his nose, as if he had a headache. "I told you spying is a slow process. It requires patience. Now that we know Jarl was chemically hypnotized, we have another avenue to search for clues. This information is vital."

Riagan considered this. If someone else had hypnotized Jarl, what was to stop them from hypnotizing Neil again? Or himself? Or anyone else?

"There are also many different ways to go after Mainyu." Guiman motioned to a wall screen that displayed a Dahaka space cruiser marked with numerous notes highlighting its features and capabilities. "I've sent you and others to locate the ships that allow the Dahaka to travel off planet. Or the technology that makes their armor impervious to our laser weaponry."

But the longer it takes to discover the traitors and stop Mainyu, the greater the danger to everyone. He shook his head to banish that fear. "I don't understand why the Council is blocking us from going after Mainyu."

"It's frustrating." Guiman nodded once. "Often when I devise a plan and the Council shoots it down, a part of me wants to press on anyway. But if you can resist impulsive decisions and go back to planning—use that rejection as motivation to work harder—you'll find your next steps will be even better for it. Figure out the reasons for those rejections and that will often lead to a solution."

"But…" Riagan was at a loss. The argument made sense, but he couldn't come up with any rational reason for the Council to essentially protect Mainyu. "It makes no sense."

"It clearly does to them." Guiman seemed to ponder his next words for a minute. "Politicians are self-serving. They scheme to amass power. It always boils down to that. So we need to find out why is it good for the Council to leave Mainyu alone."

"There can't be a good reason," Riagan said.

Guiman led him toward the door. "I'm not saying you'll like it. I'm saying if you discover that answer, we can prepare accordingly."

And with that Guiman opened the door and shoved Riagan out.

Chapter 6

Maellyn's Volcano Descent

Maellyn entered the white sims facility thrilled to be back in class after the long summer abroad. The first couple of weeks of a new school year were always nice, seeing friends that she missed over the summer and getting acclimated to her new classes.

Trini Flores pulled on a silver Space City suit by the racks, so Maellyn joined her.

"Any idea what Fintan and Nez have planned today?" Maellyn gave Trini a warm smile, then grabbed her own suit from the rack and started to dress. Fran Snelling, Anand and Devika Singh, and a few other classmates entered the facility.

Trini shook her head good-naturedly, pulling on silver gloves. "I figured Fintan would've told you."

"As soon as I got back from Niveum, dad ushered me off to Sundara," Maellyn replied. "Got back late last night."

Trini nodded, giving her a sympathetic smile. "I know how it is. Spent the summer with Aunt Teresa on Letos."

"How was that?" Maellyn slipped her hiking boots back on and began to tie them, noting that they were getting a bit tight. She'd need to get a new pair soon.

"I discovered a new creature." Trini's eyes glowed with excitement. "Satu. Most of the Ukka believed it a myth."

"What kind of creature?" Anand asked as he grabbed a suit.

"Like a plesiosaur," Trini answered. "Satu lives in a lake, near where we stayed."

Anand's jaw dropped, his eyes bulging with excitement. "Have to add that to my thousand worlds."

"Yes," Trini agreed.

Anand looked as if he'd won a lifetime's supply of candy.

Maellyn had to admit this Satu creature sounded intriguing. "So you went to Letos to discover if the creature was real?"

Trini sobered. "There was an outbreak among the Ukka. They were in bad shape. We went to provide medical support."

Anand, Devika, and Fran all took a step away from Trini, unease written on their faces.

Trini held up her hands in appeasement. "I'm not sick. Well, I was. But I helped my aunt study the strain and produce a vaccine. I'm over it, and the Ukka are recovering."

Anand and Devika looked doubtful, but Maellyn knew Dr. Torres would never have let Trini free on the ship if she posed a danger to anyone. She'd have been isolated in the infirmary.

"I'm glad you're better," Maellyn told Trini. "And that you could help. Thinking of going into the medical field?"

Trini nodded with a satisfied smile. "I think so. After my career in the Space City Games, or during the off season. I want to do both. No reason I can't enjoy my passion and help others."

"No reason at all," Maellyn agreed, impressed at what Trini had achieved. Through people such as her, Space City was doing amazing things improving life on a lot of worlds. They were a shining standard of what mankind could do.

"I also gained a little brother in the process," Trini added, smiling.

"Yes, I thought I heard something about that. One of the Ukka, right? What's his name?"

Trini blinked, pausing for a moment before realization dawned on her face. "You heard from your dad?" When Maellyn nodded, Trini added, "His name is Otso."

"I like it. Hope I get to meet him."

"He loves getting butternells at the street fair."

"So do I," Maellyn agreed.

Other classmates began to filter in—Maellyn's cousin Cade who had a little stubble on his chin, Nico Colombo studying something on his wrist-comp, and Christel Manikas and Aileen McKensie chattering away. Caleb Thornton and Adrien Laroque followed on the girls' heels. Pyrrhus, a Traga, resembled a spreading fire as he slid in. Except he didn't grow. Just flowed from one spot to the next. He ignored the suits, which he didn't need, and advanced toward the sim cages. No matter how many times she encountered the Traga, Maellyn's first impulse was one of alarm. She guessed it was every humans' initial reaction to what looked like an uncontrolled fire. But she knew Pyrrhus treated everyone well and was a good student.

"I hope you're all here for Intermediate New Worlds." Instructor Shilah Nez entered carrying a rectangular metal box. With Instructor Nez was Instructor Aodh, Pyrrhus' father.

Maellyn frowned. Instructor Fintan was supposed to teach this class with Instructor Nez. Why was Instructor Aodh here?

Instructor Nez set the metal box on a table and removed the lid. Inside were over a dozen pair of eye contacts. Beneath each pair was written a student's name. "I want each of you to grab a set. If you're inexperienced with them, I can show you how to put them in."

The contacts were one of the newest technological releases of the summer. Neil had already told Maellyn that they were great, but this was her first opportunity to try them out.

For the next ten minutes, most everyone struggled with putting the contacts into their eyes, Maellyn included. The first few times she tried, she would involuntarily blink as soon as her finger neared her eye. Instructor Nez told her to look toward her nose and place the contact on the side of her eye before sliding it over onto her iris. It still took her several minutes to get one in. The second came easier, but felt strange, poking her eyes a little bit.

Her vision didn't automatically change with the contacts in, but she knew they could provide night vision, take x-rays of their surroundings, or zoom in.

"Imagine the view you want, then deliberately blink. It triggers the contacts." Instructor Aodh's words were translated to English by her tradutor. It could translate any language, human or alien.

X-ray might be cool. Maellyn concentrated on x-ray vision and blinked. She expected everything to change to black and white, like a medical printout of a skeleton. Instead, the room transformed to tie dye. Most of the facility was blue. The dozens of large, round metal cages in the room were green. Everyone around her had turned into a hodgepodge of blue, green, yellow, orange, and red in their general shape. It was pretty and cool, but made her feel blind at the same time.

She had to switch the contacts back to a regular view in order to feel comfortable again.

Cade held a hand in front of his face as if warding away a bright light. "Night vision is awful."

"You can't use it with the lights on," Caleb Thornton mocked. "What a flob!"

Cade reddened, but to Maellyn's pleasant surprise, he didn't hang his head in shame at the taunting. Normally, whenever Cade was personally attacked, he would mope for a day or two, but this time he seemed to take it in stride. Was he too absorbed in what the contacts could do?

"Now that you've all had time to get acclimated, we're beginning today's lesson." Instructor Nez moved over to the large metal sim cages.

"We're attending my home planet, Anthea," Instructor Aodh said, his actual voice resembling crackling pops of a campfire. "Specifically, a volcano."

So that's why Instructor Aodh is here instead of Fintan, Maellyn thought. Wait, what?

All the boys exclaimed at this revelation. They were clearly crazy. There were a lot of things Maellyn wanted to see, but the inside of a volcano wasn't on her bucket list.

"I'd rather explore a real volcano," Trini muttered as she climbed into one of the large metal cages.

She was crazy, too, Maellyn decided.

Despite the amazing details of a sim—one couldn't distinguish the difference between one and the real world—some thrill seekers always wanted to visit actual planets. Maellyn preferred knowing they wouldn't be in any real danger inside a volcano.

She climbed into one of the metal cages and found what she at first mistook for a ceiling fan propped against the inside of the cage. Extending from the bottom of it were two horizontal T-bars and a harness. The device was a B-chopper, short for Brainwave helicopter.

The horizontal T-bars rested on her shoulders, with the vertical bars pressing against the sides of her back. The harness strapped her in. She'd seen prototypes a few other times, but this would be her first use.

Once everyone was strapped into their B-choppers, Sergeant Nez activated the sim. The metal cages disappeared, leaving them standing on the summit of a mountain. On one side of the summit, a steep slope led down to a forest. A gray, motionless, cement-like river snaked down a portion of that slope and through the forest. An ocean surrounded the forest on three sides that she could see, so they were likely on an island. She wrinkled her nose, overpowered by a foul stench, part of which reminded her of rotten eggs.

The mountain formed a circle with a deep crater at its center. No, not a mountain. They were standing at the summit of the volcano, staring down its maw. The steep, rugged, treeless slopes covered in dirt and gravel led to a trench.

Maellyn froze up a little, bending her knees with the desire to flatten herself to the ground. It seemed the slightest gust of wind might catch the B-chopper blades and haul her off the summit.

The sky was a dull gray, and the wind was frosty, as was common after a late fall rain.

"This place stinks." Christel Manikas pinched her nose, looking ready to gag. "Do we need to wear gas masks?"

"The smell is part of the simulation, to make it realistic," Instructor Nez answered. "It won't cause any harm."

"I could use a little less realism," Aileen McKensie complained.

Maellyn tended to agree, but chose to keep it to herself. Grumbling never endeared you to the instructors.

Instructor Aodh flowed down a beaten path into the crater. "Who can name the types of volcanoes?"

Maellyn was more interested in what features on this planet caused it to give rise to the Traga. There was a subtle change to Instructor Aodh—a decompression and a slight mellowing to his color—as he descended into the volcano. Maellyn looked for Pyrrhus and found the same changes. They were home. Or at least close enough for comfort.

"Anyone?" Instructor Aodh asked.

No one answered as they hiked down the volcano's interior slope. Maellyn knew she had seen stuff on volcanoes in the past but couldn't remember specifics.

"Volcanoes aren't central to most humans," Instructor Nez told Aodh. "Not like the Traga. But you can rectify the holes in their knowledge."

That seemed to motivate the Traga. He swelled up a little. "There are four main types of volcanoes on every planet we've studied—cinder cones, composites, shields, and lava volcanoes. There are variations to the structure and internal mechanisms on every planet, but they generally break down into one of those four. Does anyone know what type of volcano Virtah is?"

Maellyn and several others held up their wrist-comps to scan the volcano.

"Before you scan it," Aodh added.

Maellyn lowered her wrist-comp as she pressed downward, relieved to be off Virtah's summit. Having something at her back made her feel less vulnerable, more in control.

No one had an answer for this question either, so Aodh said, "Virtah is a shield volcano. Basalt lava flows from it." He appeared to flatten a little when no one showed interest.

Their path forward abruptly ended at a cliff. A twenty-foot drop to the next path. No detours right or left. The only option was to use the B-choppers.

"Time to test your flying ability," Instructor Nez announced. "B-choppers can fly you a short distance." As he spoke, his B-chopper blades began to spin. It lifted him a few feet into the air and he drifted out from the cliff. From there he gradually descended to the path below.

Trini was second in the air; no real surprise. She lifted a foot or so off the ground, followed by Devika.

Maellyn hesitated. How high could the B-chopper carry her? Nez had said they could lift them a little, but what if the wind caught her? She wasn't as heavy as Nez. Could it carry her higher? What if she veered off course and crashed into the crater walls at the wrong point?

Aodh turned to everyone still on the ground. "B-choppers are very responsive to your thoughts. Visualize what you want it to do, and it'll react."

Anand was next off the ground. He pushed the highest, rising a good five feet in the air. Maellyn felt nervous for him, especially when he moved off the cliff. But he flew smoothly after Trini and Devika. Instructor Nez had landed below and was monitoring everyone's progress. Maellyn was the only one left on the ground.

"Maellyn, I would've never guessed you as the type to let fears override reason," Aodh said.

She blushed. She wanted to retreat from the cliff. Logically, she knew this was ridiculous. They were in a sim. Right now her body remained safe inside the metal cage, and everything she saw was fake. Yet the wind whipping around her didn't feel fake. The steep summit slope could cause serious bruises or worse if she fell.

Everyone else had reached the path below now. She was holding things up. Taking a deep breath, she imagined herself rising into the air. Her stomach plummeted as she lifted inches off the ground, even though she could've pointed her toes and still touched down.

"That's good. We'll go together," Aodh encouraged.

How? Maellyn wondered. The Traga couldn't fly as far as she knew.

She wanted to close her eyes, but couldn't guide herself blind. Whole body rigid, she imagined the B-chopper carrying her forward. It inched her toward the ledge.

A gust of wind hit her. Involuntarily, she pictured it carrying her up higher. The B-chopper blades spun faster, lifting her ten feet off the ground. Suddenly, all she could focus on was the steep crater as a whole. The bottom was easily a few thousand feet below. It would be a long fall.

A small squeak escaped her lips.

"Now guide your B-chopper down and join the others," Aodh said, snapping her back to her immediate surroundings.

Biting her lower lip, Maellyn imagined herself sinking. She drifted out past the ledge, taking away all sense of safety. Her skin tried to retreat clear off her body, but she forced herself to press onward.

"I'm here." Aodh slid down the cliff face, keeping pace with her. His being there helped her relax a little.

No more wind gusts tugged at her, and she landed beside the others.

"Why don't we fly the whole way down," Trini suggested. "Would be a lot faster."

Maellyn wanted to slug her for the suggestion.

"We are," Instructor Nez answered. "We've got a long way to go yet before the end of class."

They proceeded to fly down in short jumps. Twenty or thirty feet at a time. They all grew more comfortable and confident. Maellyn wasn't as daring as Trini or Devika, who led the way with Instructor Nez, but each jump was less daunting than the last.

Surprisingly, Aodh and Pyrrhus kept pace with them. Despite following the dips and drops of the crater walls, Aodh herded everyone to keep them close together, moving with a speed Maellyn would never have suspected.

It took ten minutes to reach the crater floor to the fissure, which was wide as a canyon. The jagged walls dipped into darkness. Maellyn's fear of heights kicked in again, but it was partially eased by her growing comfort with the B-chopper.

"Who knows the trio of volcano stages?" Instructor Aodh asked.

"Active," Devika Singh offered.

"Good," Aodh said.

"Extinct," Cade added.

"Another correct answer," Aodh agreed.

No one else offered any answers.

"One more," Aodh encouraged, eyeing each of them in turn with the twin blue fires that let him see the world.

Maellyn tapped her tradutor's earphone, remembering to activate its recording function so she could review later for quizzes or tests. The tradutor transferred the recording to her wrist-comp. She couldn't believe she'd forgotten.

"If it's not active or extinct," Trini frowned, considering "—then it must be, I don't know, hibernating?"

"Dormant," Maellyn said, remembering the term thanks to Trini's thinking out loud.

"Yes!" Aodh confirmed. "Virtah is in a dormant state. Does anyone know how we determine what stage a volcano is in?

Maellyn's ears were now frozen and her lungs stung from the chill. She wished she had a mug of hot tea. It was weird to be standing on a volcano and freezing. But she did remember the answer to Aodh's question. Technology that her father had mentioned.

"We now have the ability to use satellites orbiting a planet to map out a volcano all the way to its source at the tectonic plates and evaluate the state of the volcano," Maellyn said. "There's even an app that allows anyone to access the latest data recorded by the satellites."

"Teacher's pet," Caleb whispered, just loud enough for Maellyn and a few others to hear, but not the instructors.

"Nah, she gets it all from daddy," Adrien said. "I bet she doesn't even study. Just ask daddy for the answers."

Maellyn glowered at them. They both smirked. If they only knew. It was honestly harder for her that her father was the lead scientist. Yes, he and Fintan both kept her informed about the work being accomplished in the science labs, but not only would they never consider giving her the answers to any tests she had to take, they both gave her their own assignments that they expected her to complete. Those were always much harder than anything she received in class. And they insisted she always sign up for advanced classes.

"Are we headed down?" Anand practically danced with excitement.

"After you." Instructor Nez gestured for him to take the lead. Anand leapt, face beaming.

Maellyn jumped third after Trini, proud of herself for not bringing up the rear this time. She guided the B-chopper out into the middle of the fissure, away from the walls, before beginning her descent. Remembering her contacts, she activated night vision. The contacts pulsed and the way below was illuminated in a green glow. The light didn't reveal a bottom to this chasm. Instead, the walls seemed to go on forever.

Cade floated beside her, staring down into the depths. "In Iceland, I think it is, people used to believe that volcanoes were portals to hell." His voice held a little uneasiness.

Observing this seemingly endless pit, Maellyn could almost believe that it went all the way to hell. Add in the fire, smoke, and lava that volcanoes belched forth, raining death and destruction down on anyone unfortunate enough to be too close, and it was easy to understand where the superstition came from.

"If I see any horned demons, I'm ditching you," Maellyn teased.

Cade grinned at the absurdity of such an encounter. "If we see a demon, I don't have to fly faster than it, just faster than you."

It took a few minutes before they spotted a bottom, faster than it should've arrived based upon her view a few moments ago. Maellyn looked back up to gauge the distance that they'd come, only to discover darkness and endless walls above. The sim must have auto-adjusted so they wouldn't have to make the entire descent. They didn't have time for long descents in a two-hour class after all.

The walls spread out as they entered the cavern. Touching down, Maellyn tapped her wrist-comp's flashlight button. Light flared, forcing her to shield her eyes before she remembered to deactivate her contacts' night vision. When she reopened her eyes, the flare and green light had gone; her flashlight, and those of several classmates, lit up the cavern.

The rock walls and ceiling around the fissure were a mixture of colors—amber, blue, turquoise, and maroon. The cavern was cool and damp, not what Maellyn would've expected for the interior of a volcano. Aodh had said Virtah was a dormant volcano, not extinct, which meant it should still have activity down here. Perhaps the instructors had chosen to keep the sim cool for convenience.

Instructor Nez moved over to a man-sized hole in the cavern wall that sloped upward. "This is a branch pipe, an alternate path through which lava travels during an eruption. Blink twice with your contacts to scan the pipe and get information on it."

Maellyn did as beckoned and a block of text appeared in the air in front of her, providing basic details on volcanoes, and highlighting the part concerning branch pipes.

"The information is transferred to your wrist-comp automatically," Instructor Nez added.

Sweet! Now she wouldn't have to use her wrist-comp or drones to scan everything. The contacts would simplify the process.

"You can pull up information on any object or even a person."

People?

Maellyn turned to look at Cade and blinked twice at him. A long list of information including his height, weight, date of birth, parents, brother, and other details appeared next to his body. It was an expansion of the data they'd been able to obtain through their wrist-comps previously, which provided only generic information about their surroundings or those they encountered, such as basic details about the Traga if she were to scan Aodh or Pyrrhus.

"I've heard about this!" Cade smiled broadly, staring back at Maellyn.

She wondered self-consciously what the contacts displayed on her, and immediately turned them off. "Isn't this an invasion of privacy? Not everyone wants people to know this stuff."

"The contact's gather publicly available information found on the internet," Instructor Nez explained. "If you don't want people to know something about you, don't put it out there."

Cade sidled over to her. "It was developed for encounters with aliens you're unfamiliar with. The contacts link back to Space City's databases."

It made sense, but still made Maellyn's skin crawl. What if there were things on record she didn't want others to know? Could she remove it? Or was it permanently out there for all to see?

Cade moved over to a large hole in the floor that led even deeper. "When these were in prototype, involuntary eye blinking led to the contacts displaying information about everything in sight. But now it can tell the difference between intentional and involuntary blinking. Plus, you have to focus directly on the thing you want information on."

The cavern dissolved, leaving them back in the crater above the fissure. Maellyn shielded her eyes as they adjusted to the ample sunlight.

"Apologies for the disorientation," Aodh said. "Class is almost up, but I wanted to give you the chance to see Virtah in its active state."

The base of the crater filled with a roiling lake of lava. There were several shouts of shock and surprise, and Maellyn tensed in fear. Was it about to erupt?

"Nothing to fear," Instructor Nez assured them. "This is all it will do."

Maellyn relaxed, a little. The bright red and orange lava boiled, sending sprays up into the air, resembling the ocean during a storm. It was amazing to behold; not an experience she had ever expected to be a part of. They were no more than ants upon the volcanoes surface. It was a reminder of the amazing power of nature, that created so many forces—both on planets and in outer space—that dwarfed them.

That didn't daunt Maellyn, however. For some, the knowledge of their microscopic place in the universe gave them a sense of futility. In the face of such awesome power, what could they ever truly accomplish? For Maellyn, such displays elucidated how far they still had to grow as a species. No matter what anyone accomplished, bigger challenges always remained.

Challenges accepted.

The sim ended, leaving them back in the sims facility. Everyone started to climb out of the cages and remove the B-choppers.

"Before you go," Instructor Nez said, raising his voice to be heard over all the commotion, "—there is a science competition for all second years. You'll be expected to complete team projects for the competition. More information to come in future classes."

Maellyn sighed. She'd rather jump into the volcano. Her father was one of the judges, so it would be yet another area where he would judge her more harshly than others. She wished she could enter the Apidium project in the competition. After all, it had taken a ton of work, but her father would never accept that. She'd have to come up with something new.

Chapter 7

Neil Has a Falling Out

Neil shuffled into his grandfather's kitchen, setting his suitcase of clothes beside the door. He wished he could sleep another hour or two, but he just had time to grab a quick bite before getting to campus for class. On his way, he needed to review his extra instructions ahead of their Intermediate Battle Tactics class. As team lead, he'd be responsible for directing his group through class activities.

Grandpa stood by the counter, a cup of steaming coffee in his hands, his wrinkled brow stern and focused on his 3D food printer. He didn't look up as Neil entered. It was the first time they'd run into each other since he'd missed the Space City Games Cup. Worse, after everything from the last two days, Neil hadn't even come up with a good excuse. He couldn't reveal the mission to Siavash. Guiman and Dardanos had drilled into them that no one but the Council was privy to the information about the missions. It was the only way to ensure they weren't compromised.

Grandpa typed on his wrist-comp, and the 3D printer went to work preparing his breakfast. Same thing he had pretty much every day. Egg whites, potatoes mixed with onions, mushrooms, and a few spices, and a single piece of toast without butter. The food would print out in a predetermined amount based upon his allotted calories for breakfast.

Neil debated heading to campus and grabbing a quick snack from the mess hall. Before he could make a getaway, grandpa turned around. His calm eyes hid his thoughts. Neil braced for the worst.

"Do you have class today?" Grandpa asked.

Neil picked up his duffle. "In an hour. I should get going."

"I'm glad you're concerned with schedule when it comes to your schoolwork." Grandpa sipped his coffee.

With no good response, Neil slid toward the door.

"Sit down, please."

Neil froze at the edge in grandpa's voice. He had a sudden flashback to living with his uncle. Such a tone from his uncle had always meant a beating was coming. And his uncle was his grandfather's son. How similar were they? His entire body tensing, he sat down at the round glass table with a wooden base that resembled a leafless tree.

"What have you been up to this summer?" Grandpa asked.

"Mostly training with Riagan. I'm a team lead this year, remember?"

"So you missed the Cup because you were training?"

Neil bit his lip. He wouldn't go so far as to disrespect his grandfather with a lie. It was one thing to withhold information concerning his spying for Guiman, but he wanted to avoid an outright lie.

"What're you hiding?" Grandpa pressed.

Neil had no plausible excuse, no magic explanation that would satisfy his grandpa, so he remained silent.

"If you won't tell me, I have to assume you're up to some mischief. As your guardian, it's my responsibility—"

"My guardian?" Bristling, Neil met his grandpa's gaze. "You disappeared more than ten years ago. I thought you were dead. Now you think you can step back in and have a say over how I spend my time?"

Grandpa's eyes widened, not expecting the explosion. Neil hadn't either. He wasn't sure where the outburst had come from, but it was true. Why should he have to tell his grandpa anything?

"If I had known about your mother, I would've—"

"You should've known. How could you accept an assignment that sent you away for so long?"

"I'm sorry." Grandpa appeared to flounder for words.

Neil wasn't finished yet. "And you're not around much now. Any time I'm home, you're busy supporting the Council."

Grandpa frowned, eyes dropping to his coffee. He offered nothing further, and Neil didn't want them. He didn't want explanations or apologies. They fixed nothing.

He rose and grabbed his duffle, but when he reached for his wrist-comp in a side pocket, it was missing. He stalked from the kitchen to his bedroom. It wasn't on his nightstand or dresser.

"Where's my wrist-comp?" He muttered to himself, desperate to get out of there. Whenever his uncle had been taken aback, it been followed by violent outbursts. Neil wasn't anxious to see it repeated.

"Wrist-comp located," an electronic voice said from the bed. He pulled back the covers to find it nestled under his pillow. Must've fallen asleep with it last night and forgotten. But why had it spoken to him? It had never done that before.

The wrist-comp beeped with a new message from Maellyn.

I miss you. Can we get together tonight?

He would reply to it later. As he exited his room, he spotted grandpa still standing in the kitchen by the counter. Neil hurried outside.

Once he was on the way to school, he exhaled. He'd gotten away without incident. Then it hit him that Maellyn would ask the same questions tonight. She would want to know everything he had been up to while they were apart. Not for the first time, it pained him to keep his work a secret from her. He told himself she'd understand, but doubt nagged at him.

He suddenly found himself wishing for another mission from Guiman.

Chapter 8

Riagan Fails to Lead

Riagan reluctantly headed to class. It was the last thing he wanted to do right now, but he was already in deep with Guiman and Dardanos. Skipping would make matters worse. Fortunately, Intermediate Battle Tactics was up first. But it wouldn't take place in the arena today. His wrist-comp provided directions to a new facility over on the University campus behind the science labs. It was labeled the battle chamber. Riagan hadn't heard of it, but the name sounded promising enough.

The facility was long, making him think of a silo lying on its side. Not a single window in the place. The front door was locked, but there was a keypad to the left of the door and his wrist-comp instructions for class had the code. He typed in the code and entered the facility to find Neil and a few others gathered before a door. Riagan hurried over to him.

"The chamber is zero g," Neil said, nodding through a nearby doorway at what resembled a giant beehive. Sticking out from the walls was a complex array of platforms split by shafts of varying lengths, all of it made of mirrors.

Why mirrors? Riagan wondered. Didn't seem like the smartest way to build a battle chamber. And what was the purpose of the platforms along the wall? Since the battle chamber lacked gravity, they could float, rendering the platforms useless.

Jiro Takeda, Eris Zeigler, Dirk Fischer, Arielle Delven, and Pyrrhus were also in attendance, which was a small class if this was it.

Casually, Riagan approached the battle chamber doorway and stretched a leg inside. The normal pressure from gravity vanished around his foot. It wasn't his first encounter with zero g's, but the mix was strange, as if his foot might float away from him.

"Good morning," Instructor Mitch Glenn boomed as he arrived, towering over them. As the primary Battle Tactics instructor, Glenn had been the one to teach them the basics of their explorer suits' laser weaponry. "I see you found the battle chamber without problem."

"Is this all of us?" Jiro asked, casting around for other classmates.

"No, there's another team." Instructor Glenn pointed his meaty hand toward another doorway at the far end of the battle chamber. "They'll come in there. Your goal is to reach their end first."

As Riagan contemplated floating through the chamber, he suddenly pictured it from another angle, remembering a story Rois had made him read a few years back. "I've an idea. Everyone throw yourself feet first into the chamber, so the opposing team is below us. It'll make us more difficult targets."

Neil nodded, grinning. "Smart. Riagan, I want you to lead Dirk, Arielle, and Pyrrhus to what is now the ceiling. From there make your way to the far end. I'll lead Jiro and Eris down. See if we can come at Patrick's team from both sides."

Riagan started to ask Neil how he knew Patrick was on the other team, but he realized Neil must have extra information as their team lead. But Patrick was also a team lead, meaning—

"I don't want Pyrrhus." Riagan glared at the Traga. "He probably schemed with Patrick. He's on our team so he can betray us."

The Traga expanded, the fire that composed its body seeming to bulk up. It was a common Traga attribute when they were angry. "I'm no traitor," Pyrrhus's words translated from his native language by the tradutor. "And Patrick wouldn't ask that."

Undaunted, Riagan walked right up to Pyrrhus. "You're lying."

"He's changed." Pyrrhus' coloring lightened, turning from red to near white, which meant he was angrier, not less. Furious.

Riagan couldn't believe the Traga was defending Patrick. Before he could say as much, Neil stepped between them. "All right, that's enough."

Turning on his heel, Riagan marched back to the battle chamber doorway. "I amn't working with the Traga. Give me Jiro instead."

"That was an order." Neil crossed his arms, glaring. "I *am* the Team Lead."

Riagan could feel the flush rising up his face. He couldn't believe Neil had called him out like this. But Instructor Glenn coughed which, for a man his size, wasn't subtle. So Riagan let it go.

Not wanting to stand there and give in, however, he backed up a few feet from the door and slid back into a stance in preparation to run and launch himself into the chamber. See how far he could get.

As he started forward, Dirk blocked him. "Zero g's," Dirk said. "You hurl yourself into that room and you won't stop until you hit something."

"That's the point, right?" Riagan snapped. "Get to their end first."

"And when you hit the glass barrier in the middle?" Dirk asked, pointing. "At the speed you'll be traveling, launching yourself from a place with gravity into a place without it. Nothing to slow your momentum. Likely break at least one bone when you hit the glass."

The glass platform split the room in half. The platform was riddled with strange indentations and a couple of holes in the floor, the sole means of reaching the opponent's side.

"How does that work anyway?" Eris asked. "We have gravity here, and through a doorway there's suddenly no gravity?"

"There's a shield there," Instructor Glenn said. "Can't see or feel it, but it does the job."

Dirk took the lead, stepping into the chamber. Once inside, he stood motionless, but his body as a whole drifted forward. He rotated around and beckoned for the rest of them to join him.

The others piled into the chamber and Riagan followed them in. The weightlessness was a little disconcerting. Eris did a summersault off a panel toward the wall behind them. Riagan tried to swim toward the wall, but the lack of gravity was startling. His efforts amounted to very little. It made him feel helpless, but his initial momentum carried him into another panel, from which he could push off.

"Don't look her in the eyes," Dirk shouted in warning.

Riagan spun around in alarm. Dirk pointed at Arielle, whose long black hair stood on end, waving about as if with a life of their own.

Arielle tossed her head dramatically backward, then forward, causing her hair to drift around, eventually flowing toward Dirk.

"No!" Dirk mock exclaimed. He froze with his mouth open as if he'd been turned to stone.

"All right let's move to the wall by the door," Neil ordered, swimming over to join Eris.

Riagan followed, along with the rest, and used the wall to orient himself like the others so that the far side was below them. Once they were given a green light, they could shove off the wall, dropping toward the exit below. He intended to shove off as hard as he could, see how far he could get. Now that he wasn't hurtling himself from outside the room into it, he figured he wouldn't pick up that much speed. And Patrick's team wouldn't be able to shoot through the glass divider, so no reason to take their time on this side.

"Teams are in place." Instructor Glenn's familiar booming voice came over their tradutors. "Competition starts in three, two, one, go."

A hiss filled the room and Riagan fell backward, gravity suddenly pulling on them. He wheeled his arms, trying to find something to hold onto. Instead, he fell against a wall below him, hitting hard, followed by several other thuds from his teammates. The breath was knocked from his lungs. For a few seconds, all he could do was gasp. His vision rippled.

"Great plan," Neil muttered, pushing off the wall. It took Riagan a moment to reorient himself. The wall was now the floor.

"Remind me to never take advice from Riagan." Dirk pushed himself to a sitting position, groaning in the process.

The platform that had split the room in half had now become a glass wall. The strange indentations in the wall turned to handholds for climbing. And the gaps in the platform were now near the ceiling a good thirty feet high.

"Why did they start without gravity?" Riagan complained, looking himself over so he wouldn't have to meet anyone else's gaze.

"To disguise the maze."

"Maze?" Riagan looked around, recalling the platforms he'd seen before entering the chamber. There had been shafts among the platforms to the right and left, but he'd been so focused on the path down the middle that he hadn't paid them much attention. A simple modification in how the instructors had presented the battle chamber had prevented him from recognizing the maze.

Neil gestured left. "Riagan, lead your group that way. We'll head right."

Riagan didn't appreciate the trickery. Felt manipulated, like the instructors had given them a simple assignment, then five minutes into class revealed they actually had a pop quiz instead. How was that fair?

"No more bright ideas, okay?" Dirk suggested. "I'd prefer not to take any more lumps."

"How about I shoot ya now? Save them the trouble," Riagan said, but the threat was half-hearted. He led Dirk, Arielle, and Pyrrhus into the maze. He still didn't love having Pyrrhus, but after his own faux-pas, he kept his mouth shut. When they reached a four-way, Riagan asked. "Which way?"

Thanks to the mirror walls, their own reflections surrounded them, shifting as they moved, a constant distraction. It made it difficult to search for their opponents or other surprises.

"Maybe check for heat signatures?" Arielle suggested.

Riagan pointed forward. "How does that help?"

Arielle rolled her eyes. "Living things all give off different heat signatures. That may give us some clues what is down each path."

Riagan didn't have an argument for that, nor any better ideas, so he activated his contacts. The maze transformed to a strange psychedelic array of colors. The walls were awash in blue and green. Dirk and Arielle were predominantly red and yellow with a few patches of green and blue. Pyrrhus, however, was all red and yellow.

"I don't see anything," Dirk said, drawing Riagan's attention back to the reason they'd activated the thermal vision.

Riagan eyed each nearby pathway, finding no other heat signatures. It made sense that they wouldn't have come across Patrick or his team yet. No one could've reached the center wall, even if they'd run and lucked into the shortest route there. But what about other objectives? The instructors hadn't given any. As far as Riagan knew, their sole goal was to get to the other half of the battle chamber and reach the far exit before the other team got here.

"Nothing in x-ray, either," Dirk said.

"Do ya think ya could keep up in x-ray mode?" Riagan asked.

"Sure."

"Arielle, deactivate yours," Riagan said. "I'll stay on thermal. Pyrrhus, can ya even wear contacts?"

Pyrrhus flared a little, expanding slightly. "No." So two of them with normal vision.

"Arielle, ya take point," Riagan instructed. "Pyrrhus, cover our backs." He wasn't about to put Pyrrhus in front and risk him leading them into a trap. He wasn't thrilled at the idea of the Traga behind them either, but he only had so many options.

As Arielle led them forward, Riagan studied the walls, the floor, and overhead. The world had become a strange mixture of color splotches. It also made him feel a little handicapped. A part of him itched to reach out with his hands to feel his way forward, as if they were in the dark. It took determination to ignore the compulsion to deactivate the contacts. See normally. Without this view, they might miss something critical as they explored.

Arielle led them right at the next pathway, followed by an immediate left. They passed straight on through another four-way, generally headed toward the center wall.

A beam of red light shot toward them, zipping past Arielle's head. Riagan gave a strangled shout as he ducked. Dirk dove, pulling Arielle down to safety.

From a crouched position, Riagan searched the path for some sign of where the laser had come from. But there was nothing unusual that could account for it. Again he itched to deactivate his contacts, feeling he was flying blind. "Anyone get anything?"

"Nada," Dirk answered, draped over Arielle on the floor.

"I spot nothing," Pyrrhus added.

"Really?" Riagan asked.

"It looked as if the wall fired at us," Arielle said, voice muffled.

They studied the far wall, waiting. When it appeared another shot wasn't forthcoming, Riagan carefully rose, rotating so that his left shoulder faced forward to minimize the target he presented. He was straightening his legs when a second laser shot struck his shoulder. That part of his suit locked up, making his left arm useless. In his panic, he lost his balance and toppled to the ground. The others shouted in surprise.

"Anyone catch the shooter that time?" Riagan groaned.

"Definitely the wall," Arielle said, sounding spooked.

Riagan couldn't dispute her. He hadn't seen any other heat signatures around the wall right before he'd been shot, but a shooting wall wasn't one of the technologies he was familiar with. "What do we do with it?"

"I think I can help," Pyrrhus said.

The Traga slipped past them. He expanded and flattened into a square. Needing to see this normally, Riagan turned off the contacts. Pyrrhus had mutated into a flat wall of flame. Riagan had to admit he was impressed.

Several shots slammed into the Traga, but he didn't slow. Another round of shots proved equally pointless. At least, Pyrrhus had suffered no obvious damage.

He glided forward to the far wall, shots still striking him without effect, all of it reflected in the glass. There was nothing else Riagan could see there. Once Pyrrhus closed on the wall, he arched back and slammed into it. There was an audible crunch. Pyrrhus transformed back into a humanoid-fire. He inspected his work. Beyond him, a broken robot with holes appeared. Why had they been unable to see it?

Alert for more signs of trouble, Riagan struggled to his feet, the task made more difficult with his left arm locked up. Once he made it to his feet, he followed Dirk and Arielle, who were tense and ready to dive for cover once more if fired upon.

Upon reaching Pyrrhus, Riagan discovered that the holes in the robot were actually an exterior cover which reflected the glass walls around it, making it appear invisible. That cover had been damaged by Pyrrhus' attack, revealing it. But the robot should've still had a heat signature. The thermal vision mode should've revealed it, but it hadn't.

"Thanks for saving us," Arielle said to Pyrrhus. Dirk echoed her gratitude.

Riagan smiled guiltily, but looked away, hoping they didn't notice.

"We should get moving," Pyrrhus suggested.

This time Riagan took the lead, despite not having use of his left arm. He chose not to reactivate the thermal view. It hadn't helped thus far and he didn't want to add a second handicap.

It took them another ten minutes and a dead end before they reached the giant glass wall, which was forty, maybe fifty feet from floor to ceiling. By that time, Patrick and his team had already scaled halfway up the wall on their side. There was no sign of Neil, Jiro, and Eris.

Riagan's sense of urgency kicked in at the sight of Patrick ahead of them. He gave orders to climb the wall. Since he couldn't with his left arm locked up, he would provide cover against Patrick's group. To her credit, Arielle stepped over to the wall first.

"Wait!" Dirk grabbed her arm and pulled her back.

"What?" Riagan snapped. No one in Patrick's group had topped the wall yet but they were close. There was no time for delay.

Dirk stared upward, frowning. "Use your x-ray."

Riagan activated his contacts and flinched. Crawling on the walls not fifteen feet up were a dozen torso-sized, reddish-orange, spider-like creatures. Ones that reflected x-rays only, making them invisible to the naked eye.

"That's creepy," Arielle said, a tinge of anxiety in her voice.

Another three dozen of the creatures were spread out over the wall, all on this side. Patrick's team didn't have to deal with them. How was that fair?

Focusing on one of the creatures, Riagan blinked once to activate the scanning feature in his contacts. A description appeared beside the creature. It was called a T'o'chiwal. It inhabited the tidally-locked planet, Hawking-30c. The latter name felt familiar, but he couldn't place it. According to the description, the spiders were aggressive, especially if their territory was invaded, but weren't poisonous.

Pointing his right hand at one of the closest T'o'chiwal, Riagan shot it. The creature splatted on the ground, accompanied by a gasp from Arielle. When it didn't rise for ten seconds, he toed it. It didn't move, so he deactivated his x-ray vision and the creature disappeared. He reactivated x-ray and it reappeared, still motionless.

"Well, we can kill 'em," Riagan told the team. "Let's clear a path."

But when Riagan looked for another target, he found the T'o'chiwal had all scrambled toward the top of the wall. He aimed and fired at one but missed. The others had similar results.

After a few wasted seconds, Arielle turned to Pyrrhus, a hopeful expression on her face. "Want to climb the wall and whack those things, too?"

Pyrrhus shook. "I can't change shape while climbing. I'd fall if I tried." His head drooped a little.

"It's okay," Arielle assured him. "You saved us before. Now it's our turn."

Riagan grimaced. He could provide some cover fire for Dirk and Arielle part of the way up, but after that they were on their own. He'd be useless once they were three quarters of the way up.

"You made it."

Neil and Eris emerged out of a nearby side path, escorting a limping Jiro.

"What happened to you?" Arielle asked Jiro, frowning and pursing her lips.

"Shot in the leg by an invisible robot," Jiro replied. "Suit's locked up."

"My shoulder, too." Riagan pointed, relieved that he wasn't the only one.

"How did you defeat yours?" Neil asked.

"Pyrrhus turned into a wall and smashed it," Riagan replied, his face heating as he said it.

Neil's eyes widened as he regarded Pyrrhus. "Didn't know you could do that."

Pyrrhus mumbled an affirmation.

"What about you guys?" Dirk asked. "I don't see an invisible robot chasing you."

Arielle slapped his shoulder. "How do you *see* an invisible robot?"

Dirk rolled his eyes. "You know what I mean."

Neil's expression soured. "We split up and came at it from three sides. Took some time, but Eris got close enough for a kill shot."

"Had to also figure out *where* to shoot." Eris lifted her chin and smirked.

"We better get moving," Neil said.

Adrien Laroque was peeking his head over the top of the wall, Patrick and the others close behind.

Riagan scowled. "I can't climb with my shoulder locked. Plus, there's a problem. Try ya x-ray vision on the wall."

Neil glanced upward and whistled. "Guessing those aren't friendly?"

"Friendly isn't a word I'd use." Riagan toed the one at their feet. "I killed one, but the rest are out of range."

"Maybe for you," Eris corrected.

Riagan stepped back and waved a hand for her to take his place. "By all means, show us how it's done."

Instead of aiming with one arm, Eris raised both of hers. She fired. A pair of T'o'chiwal fell. Everyone scrambled out of the way as the creatures hit the ground with a pop, yellowish guts oozing out onto the floor. Eris smirked at Riagan, but her lips turned wry as she glanced back up. The remaining T'o'chiwal had spread toward the sides of the room, too far even for her to shoot.

"We'll have to watch out for the rest while we climb," Neil said. "Jiro and Riagan, will you two watch our backs?"

Neil moved to the wall, but turned back to Riagan as if just remembering. "Oh, and I've got a rope we can use to pull you up once we reach the top."

Riagan snorted like a prodded bull. He didn't relish being carried by the team. "Leave me behind. I can slow down Patrick's team. Give ye more time."

But Neil shook his head. "We have to all make it to win."

As the team started the climb, Riagan studied the T'o'chiwal. They jostled around, agitated, but none ventured closer. Adrien, Patrick, and Aileen McKensie had all reached the top of the wall, but hadn't attempted to come over, appearing to debate how to handle the creatures.

Arielle and Dirk were the fastest climbers and took the lead. Once they were a third of the way up, the T'o'chiwal started to creep inward, their survival instincts warring with their anger at invaders in their territory.

"Ye've got company coming," Riagan warned. But the creatures were still too far for him to shoot.

Arielle climbed faster. Dirk kept pace with her. The farther up the wall the group moved, the more anxious the creatures became. They scurried closer, paused as if testing for gunfire, then hastened in a bit more. Riagan shot the leading edge of creatures, but his shots ricocheted harmlessly off the wall. It did give the T'o'chiwal a slight pause, so he kept it up.

By the time Arielle and Dirk were two thirds of the way up the wall, Pyrrhus a short distance behind, the creatures had gotten dangerously close. Patrick's team had all reached the top of the wall, but were continuing to wait, so that all the creatures were focused on

Dirk, Arielle, and the rest. At Riagan's side, Jiro fired wildly at the T'o'chiwal to their right. He hit a couple; with the way he waved his arms, it was all luck.

Neil and Eris paused halfway, clung to the wall with one arm and shot at the creatures that were closest to Dirk and Arielle. Thanks to the shooting barrage, the pair and Pyrrhus reached the holes in the wall above. From there, Arielle and Dirk straddled the wall and took over shooting so Neil and Eris could resume their climb.

It didn't take long before Neil and Eris made it up to a second hole near the ceiling. Seated atop the wall, Neil removed a long rope from his pack. He tied one end off and dropped the other. It stopped three feet from the floor. It was a slim rope, thinner than Riagan's pinky. But he knew from experience that it was plenty strong to lift him.

Grabbing the rope with his good hand, Riagan offered it to Jiro. "Ladies first."

"I'll get the other one." Jiro pointed to where Pyrrhus was lowering a second rope, which made his skin crawl. It was like a fireman swapping roles with a fire. The rope didn't burn, but Riagan still wasn't sure he could've brought himself to be lifted with that rope forty feet by Pyrrhus. Jiro was a braver man than him.

Riagan tied the rope around his waist the best he could with his good arm. "Pull me up."

The slack in the rope disappeared. It bit into his sides as Neil pulled. Riagan leaned back, putting his feet on the wall so that he could walk up. As he scaled the wall, Jiro kept pace with him. The T'o'chiwal pressed in tighter, infuriated at the continued invasion of their territory. Everyone but Neil and Pyrrhus fired to keep the creatures away. Riagan had to hold on to the rope with his good arm, and therefore was unable to protect himself. He gritted his teeth at his vulnerability. Despite the shots from Eris and the others, the creatures suddenly raced forward. Riagan tried raising his locked arm, but it dangled uselessly at his side.

Beyond them, he noticed Patrick and Adrien climbing over the wall, taking advantage of the T'o'chiwal's focus on him and Jiro to sneak down. Cowards.

One of the creatures leapt at Riagan. He inhaled, bracing for impact, but something struck it and sent it flying backward. Riagan turned right to see Jiro had taken it out and he was firing at others, all on Riagan's side, leaving himself exposed. Riagan didn't look past Jiro, knowing he couldn't return the favor.

Riagan shouted at Neil to pull faster as he climbed. Several of the T'o'chiwal had closed to within a few feet, preparing to leap for him. But Eris, Dirk, and Arielle took them out. As Riagan neared the top of the wall, one T'o'chiwal charged. It dodged shots from the others, but at the last second a firebrand sent it flying away.

Chest heaving in relief, Riagan looked up to see Pyrrhus, who had managed to stretch one arm to double its normal length, half its usual thickness, in order to protect him.

"Thanks," Riagan mumbled, as he reached the top of the wall. Perhaps he'd been wrong about the Traga.

Pyrrhus just nodded and resumed pulling Jiro to the top. Neil offered his hand to Riagan and pulled him onto the ledge between him and Eris.

Take a minute to catch his breath, Riagan checked back for Patrick and his team. They had descended to the floor, having avoided the conflict with the T'o'chiwal.

Lucky. He aimed at Patrick, thinking maybe he could at least slow them down with a couple of good shots, but Neil blocked him.

"Don't bother," Neil said. "We need to get down."

"But—" Riagan protested.

"Our goal is to exit the maze," Neil insisted. "They don't matter."

Riagan nodded, relenting.

Having no time to waste, Neil and Pyrrhus lowered Riagan and Jiro down the far side. Riagan untied the rope from his waist while Neil dropped his end. While the others descended, Riagan gathered up the rope.

When they'd all reached the bottom, Riagan offered the rope to Neil. He deposited it back in his pack before guiding them forward. He directed each of them to guard side paths as they hustled through the maze. Fifteen minutes later they reached the exit. A horn sounded, ending the contest.

"I'd say we got good points today," Neil said, clapping Riagan on the back.

Riagan nodded, impressed at how Neil had managed to lead them through this with minimal injury. He was becoming more comfortable in his role as team lead, and it showed. Meanwhile, during his own brief time leading part of the group through the maze, he'd gotten himself shot.

The instructors had known what they were doing making Neil the team lead.

Chapter 9

Maellyn's Rival

Maellyn waited in the garden outside the spaceport for Neil. The bioluminescent trees shone, giant lanterns in the darkness. Yellow flowers, placed randomly throughout the raised beds, reflected the light from the trees, so that they resembled little stars nestled among the others. As she stood there, Maellyn's mind drifted back to the end of last year when she and Neil had shared their first kiss here. A beginning.

Or so she'd thought.

Then she had left for the summer and Neil had been absorbed in *something* that he'd been reluctant to share. Their beginning had gotten stuck. Or derailed. She hoped tonight's meteor shower would jump start things. Get them back to that feeling, but better.

She tried to ignore the sullen voice that whispered things could never be what they were now that the gang was broken. Was Neil spending so much time with Riagan as an excuse to brush her off?

"This brings back a fond memory." Neil entered the garden. He wore a light brown shirt and jeans, and an infectious grin. She'd always liked the way his unruly red hair curled around his ears. He regularly brushed it back, trying to smooth the hair so it wouldn't stick out, but it always popped right back around the ears.

"I thought we'd have a few more memories by now," Maellyn replied, heart leaping at his arrival.

As he approached, his eyes darted around the garden for a moment, searching, before settling back on her. Looking for signs of danger? The attack from the Dahaka on Mars had changed them all in different ways. For most of the summer, she'd found it difficult to go anywhere alone. She'd worked with Instructor Fintan and as many other researchers as possible at all times. Her tent had been pitched at the center of their encampment so that she was surrounded; nonetheless, she had awoken many nights in a cold sweat from nightmares in which Dahaka pursued her. Did Neil suffer from the same fears?

No. Tonight wasn't about rehashing her fears. That was nothing more than clutter separating them, and she refused to let it get in the way.

He reached for her hand and rubbed the back of it with his thumb. "We have time now."

She blushed, the nerves in her hand tingling from his touch.

"We're going to see a meteor shower?" he asked, his blue eyes reflecting the light from the trees.

She nodded, breath caught in her throat as she stared at his eyes a moment before she hooked an arm around his and led him toward the rear of the spaceport where the shower would be clearest. "This one is special. We're supposed to pass near an asteroid with seven tails. I thought we might be able to enjoy the view alone."

He chuckled. "Last time we came out for a meteor shower, you got mad at me."

"Well don't go shooting them and we'll be fine." That discussion was too close to bad memories, so she guided the conversation. "Sorry for missing our date. Dad didn't give me any warning about traveling to Sundara."

He ran his fingers through the hair over his right ear. "I understand. Learn anything more about who hypnotized Jarl?"

"A lot of dead-ends." Maellyn's insides fluttered. No one on Sundara had had any significant contact with Jarl in a couple years. "He wasn't big on regular checkups, so he hadn't seen any doctors there or here."

They continued on for several paces in silence. She wanted to ask if he'd experienced any side effects from his own chemical hypnotism, but she worried that it wasn't her business. That if he wanted to share with her, he would.

Rounding a corner of the spaceport, which opened up toward the cannons, she spotted the last thing she wanted to see. Eris, clustered together with Nico, Dirk, and Arielle, near the usual crowd of students that had gathered around the cannons to shoot meteors. Maellyn tried to pull Neil toward the empty field at the rear where they could privately watch the shower. But they'd already been spotted. Eris smiled and waved.

"Hey, look who it is." Neil waved back. "There's Nico. I need to find out when he's visiting his father's shop. I need a refill."

To her dismay, the four headed over.

"Heard I missed a good battle tactics class the other day." Nico walked close to Eris, and Maellyn hoped the two of them might be an item.

"Definitely a unique one," Neil agreed.

"Neil saved Riagan's butt," Eris added, smoothing her hair back behind an ear.

Maellyn frowned at the gesture. Nope. Nico held no interest for Eris. Maellyn debated how to politely get rid of them.

"You're the one who did all the shooting," Neil protested. "Dirk and Arielle, too, of course."

Eris looked straight into Neil's eyes as if no one else was there. "We wouldn't have gotten to that point if you hadn't come up with the plan to get us past the invisible robot."

"Yeah, but you took it out," Neil said.

Really? Did he have to give her that many kudos? She had to get this conversation turned to something else. Spotting a stone in Nico's hand, Maellyn pointed at it. "What did you bring?"

Nico's shoulders straightened as he held up a dark gray rock in his open palm, drawing everyone's attention. "It's a meteorite. Or more accurately a chondrite."

The little meteorite had a c-shape with lots of indentations in it, as if it had once been malleable and someone had pressed their fingers all over the surface; similar to the way people press their hands into wet cement to leave their handprints in a sidewalk when it dries. Starlight glinted off the meteorite's surface, and occasional streaks of light from the shower overhead zipped over it.

"A real one? Where'd you get it?" Neil asked, turning all his focus to Nico.

"Mars, after the final exam," Nico said. "It's an enstatite chondrite. It's extremely rare." He offered the meteorite to Eris, who accepted it in both hands but passed it on to Dirk without much interest.

"What makes it so rare?" Dirk examined it.

"It's made from the same original materials as all the planets and moons in our solar system," Nico answered. "It's over four and a half billion years old. Been around longer than all life on Earth."

Maellyn blinked in surprise, intrigued by this bit of knowledge. That unassuming little chunk of rock had flown around in space for all of human history until landing on Mars. It could've been zipping around the solar system when the Earth formed.

Dirk passed the meteorite to Arielle, who examined it for a moment before handing it over to Maellyn. She accepted it reverently. The meteorite was heavier than she expected for its size. It was hard to believe she was holding the most ancient thing she'd ever encountered and actually touched. Perhaps might ever encounter. If she could see a montage from its life in space, what wonders would it reveal?

Recognizing that Neil was also studying the meteorite eagerly, she handed it over to him.

"This is amazing." Neil cupped it in both hands like a precious jewel.

Nico beamed. He pulled a metal bar out of a pocket and pointed it at Neil's hand. As if by magic, the meteorite shot toward the metal bar, sticking to the end of it.

"Meteorites are magnetic," Nico said, to Neil's astonished expression.

"You'll have to show me where you found it," Neil said. "Maybe I can find one, too."

"I'll help," Eris offered. "We make a good team."

Maellyn clenched her fists. It was all she could do to bite her tongue. She longed to snarl at Eris to back off, but Neil stared at the meteorite, oblivious to Eris' flirtation. She didn't want to draw his attention to it.

Nico's grimace revealed that he hadn't missed it.

Poor Nico. And poor her, too. How could she get Neil away from Eris without being rude to the others? Or humiliating Nico?

At that moment the meteor shower soared across the night sky. Everyone turned their attention to the shower. Dozens of shooting stars crossed their night sky. A rapid procession of the white streaks, with a few blues and reds mixed in, as if they were observing the finale of a fireworks display.

Almost immediately, the automatic and student-controlled PADSat cannons began to fire. The auto-cannons took out the largest meteorites well before they posed any real danger to the ship. Students, meanwhile, fired the other cannons, attempting to take out large meteorites before the autos got them, or smaller ones before they burned up in Space City's atmosphere. But despite the fact that lasers traveled at the speed of light, most students couldn't accurately aim to hit the meteorites.

Neil found and squeezed Maellyn's hand, then bent to whisper. "When do we see the seven-tailed comet?"

She leaned into his shoulder. "Did you wear your new contacts?"

"Of course."

"They have two different zoom features. One mimics a magnifying glass, allowing you to study small objects. Even microscopic ones."

Neil held his hand up in front of his face. "That's so cool. My skin looks like dried out, cracked dirt in a desert. It's disgusting!"

"Use some lotion," Maellyn suggested, letting go of Neil's other hand. So much for romance.

"That's got to make lab work easier."

"You have no idea," Maellyn agreed. "The moment these were released, all of the scientists in Dad's facility submitted a purchase request for themselves and their assistants."

"So… this comet?"

"The other thing the contacts do is mirror a telescope, allowing you to study things far away or in space. The comet won't get close enough to be seen unaided. But with the contacts..."

He looked up at the sky. She did, too. She thought of the contacts in telescope mode and all the meteorites in the sky magnified, transforming from shooting stars into walls of light zipping past. She swung her head right toward the East, and the sky whipped by in a blur of motion that made her dizzy; she closed her eyes to steady herself.

Thinking of a reduced magnification, she opened her eyes again. The shooting stars, at the left edge of her vision, were a few times larger than with the naked eye. Now, as she searched the sky for the comet, the stars all blurred, but didn't cause the same dizziness. After a few moments, she spotted it.

"It's over there," she whispered to Neil, pointing at it. Then she realized with chagrin that with his own vision magnified, he wouldn't see her pointing. "To the East of the shower."

After thirty seconds, he said, "I see it!"

She magnified her contact vision further. The comet resembled a ball of light the size of a boulder. Seven long, bluish tails stuck out from the comet, resembling the streaks of light that shoot out from the sun around sunrise.

"The comet isn't passing through the ship's atmosphere," Neil noted. "Why does it have burning tails?"

Maellyn enjoyed the excitement in his voice, and sharing this with him. At the moment, with her vision magnified so that she could only see the sky, and sense and feel him next to her, she could imagine they were alone. "The tails are likely dust ejections from the comet. Speculation is that something changed to weaken its gravity. Dust will continue to spew off it until it breaks up."

The explanation wasn't particularly romantic, but it still looked cool. He put his arm around her shoulder. For a few minutes they stood there, enjoying the view. Then she had a compulsion to see his face, to watch him observing the comet. She turned off the magnification and turned to find him studying her face as if to memorize every feature. Before either of them could say anything, Eris punched him in the opposite arm, breaking them apart.

"Show's over," Eris said.

It was all Maellyn could do not to tell Eris off, but that would make everything worse. Arielle gave Maellyn an apologetic grimace, but said nothing.

Eris pointed back toward campus. "We were planning to hit the mess hall for a late snack. Want to join?"

Neil gave Maellyn a questioning look. Why did he put the decision on her? Surely, he knew she didn't want to go with the others. She wanted to be alone… with him. They could still see the comet a while longer. But she found she couldn't voice her desire.

She nodded reluctantly, and they all started back toward campus. As they walked, Eris was too close on Neil's other side. Maellyn wanted to grab his arm again, but knew she would come off jealous and didn't want to give Eris the satisfaction. Oblivious to the tension, Neil grabbed her hand, squeezing. She relaxed a little.

And enjoyed the wrinkle to Eris' nose.

Chapter 10

Neil Struggles with Secrecy

Neil checked his wrist-comp, as he departed the sims facility. He had an email from Grandpa, their first communication in over a month. The first few days after their argument, Neil had been too angry to even consider talking. When the silence between them continued, he didn't know how to respond. His uncle had never made mention of fights after the fact, as if they'd never happened.

Neil hesitantly opened the email, unsure what to expect.

Neil, there's no apology I can give to make up for not being around for you when your mother died. It's something I regret every day. I can only guess what growing up with your uncle was like; I know my son became an angry man.

Since I cannot make up for the past, let me offer something else instead. I know your mother would be proud of the young man you are becoming, as am I. You're working hard at the academy. You've shown determination in everything that has been asked of you. You've shown true bravery in the face of danger that most men run from. And true humility and loyalty in the way you have stood by your friends.

I would give anything for your mother to see you today!

As of your reading this, I am on my way off ship for a time. Trouble is brewing and I must investigate. I wanted to speak to you personally before going, but I was afraid. Yes, grown men can be afraid. Especially of seeing disappointment or hurt on their grandson's face. I promise I will not be gone long. No more than a month. But once I am back, I will make sure I'm around and available to you. I intend to start making up for my mistakes in any way that I can.

Neil's eyes burned at the references to his mother, but he rapidly blinked to hold back tears. He wouldn't let anyone see him cry. It seemed silly that words should affect him. He couldn't explain it, but hearing his grandfather say that his mother would be proud of him was a salve to his heart. He liked to think that if she'd lived, she would be up here with him. Although he doubted she'd be quite so happy with a few of the things he'd endured since coming aboard. But he couldn't say he regretted any of it. And he hoped she still watched him, thrilled at the future he'd found here.

"Neil." Riagan approached through the crowd of students. "Guiman's got an assignment."

Neil shut the message and noticed a new one from Maellyn. It was short, asking if they were still on for lunch.

"Did ya hear me?" Riagan placed his hand over Neil's wrist-comp to block his view.

Neil yanked his arm free. "Back to Siavash?"

Riagan shrugged, but his expression turned surly. "Not sure, but I think the Council ban is still in effect."

As they pressed through the crowd, Neil mulled this over. "It doesn't make sense. He'll come after us again at some point."

"My guess… he's paying someone. Maybe all of them," Riagan said. "If they're getting rich, why go after him? What else makes sense?"

The possibility turned Neil's stomach. That kind of corruption disturbed him. But he also lacked a better explanation. And if it was true, what could they do about it?

His wrist-comp pinged him, reminding him of Maellyn's email. Before he responded, he needed to know what kind of mission Guiman had for them. What would he give her as an excuse if he couldn't make it? Things would be so much easier if she worked with them.

"I want to ask Guiman to bring Maellyn in," he blurted.

"Ya can't," Riagan replied.

"She'd want to help if she knew."

Riagan crossed his arms, mouth tightening. "With her dad's connection to the Council as lead scientist? How're ya going to convince her to keep this secret from him?"

Neil bit his lip. He hated hiding all this from Maellyn, especially now that she was back. How much worse would it be for her with her father? If she talked to him, all the work they'd done over the summer, maybe all the work Guiman had been doing for a long time, would be put in jeopardy. He resented it, but he couldn't see any way around keeping this from her. At least for now.

As they passed the academy main offices, revealing the spaceport gardens ahead, Riagan grabbed Neil's arm and pulled him sideways. He took off toward the rear of the building. Neil chased after him, confused. Riagan ducked around the facility's rear corner and stopped.

"What are we doing?" Neil asked.

Riagan held a finger to his lips. He peeked back around the corner. Neil looked too, expression puzzled. Ten seconds later, Caleb Thornton emerged from the campus courtyard. He slowed, head darting left and right, searching.

Was he following them? Neil wondered.

Caleb took a few more steps, craning his neck. Finally, his shoulders slumped and he turned back toward the courtyard. Riagan darted forward. Neil followed, half afraid he'd have to stop Riagan from doing something stupid.

"Why are ya following us?" Riagan demanded when they were a few yards away.

Caleb spun toward them, eyes widening. He crossed his arms. "You two are up to something."

"We aren't." Riagan had balled his fists.

Neil wanted to point out to Riagan that engaging Caleb would draw more attention when they wanted less.

Caleb shrugged. "What're you hiding?"

Riagan pointed a finger at Caleb. "None of your concern."

"What if I make it mine?" Caleb grinned as if this were a game.

Riagan took a threatening step toward Caleb, so Neil darted between them, putting a restraining hand on Riagan's chest.

"This won't help," Neil warned, before turning to face Caleb. "Did Patrick put you up to this?"

Caleb's nostrils flared and lips puckered. "Patrick and I don't hang anymore. He got weird."

Neil frowned. He remembered his conversation with Patrick previously. Patrick had insisted he was trying to be different and make up for things he'd done. Was that what Caleb referred to?

"Ever since he got hurt, he hasn't been the same," Caleb lamented. "Insisting we take things easier on newbies. Blowing us off. Refusing to participate in pranks. All around stupid."

"Right." Riagan rolled his eyes. "Ya trying to pull one over on us. Get us to drop our guard."

Caleb glared at Riagan, balling his own fists. "I'm just curious why you two are skulking around."

Neil lowered his head. Dealing with Patrick and Caleb was exhausting. "Good luck. All you'll see is us training in the stadium. That's where we were headed before you interrupted."

"Really? Ursa and Taurus training together? I doubt it." Caleb's chin jutted out. He wasn't going anywhere. They'd have to abort and inform Guiman about their tag-along later.

In the meantime, Neil pretended to check his wrist-comp. "I think I'll grab lunch with Maellyn." As he stepped past Caleb, he glanced back at Riagan. "Text you later to reschedule."

Riagan's angry gaze transferred from Caleb to him. He looked ready to go a few rounds with Caleb, but instead just nodded.

When Neil reached the mess hall doors, he looked back to find Caleb following him, which made him jump a little in surprise. Riagan was lost from sight.

Fine with him. Caleb could watch him eat lunch. A nice, boring afternoon. Boring for Caleb anyway.

Chapter 11

Riagan Spies on the Traitors

Once Caleb was out of sight, Riagan pulled up his wrist-comp and typed a quick message to Neil. *Headed to Guiman's. Will tell him you're detained. Lose Caleb ASAP!!*

To be safe, he took a circuitous route to the stadium, then around the spaceport, past the PADSat cannons where no one could follow him without his knowing. Once he was positive Patrick, Adrien Laroque, or anyone else wasn't following him in Caleb's stead, he proceeded to the garden. By the time Riagan reached Guiman, the gardener was taking stock of the fruit picked by his androids.

Alerted by a droid, Guiman turned as Riagan approached. "Where's Neil?"

"Caleb Thornton tailed us," Riagan answered, frowning. "We split up. Caleb followed Neil."

Guiman studied Riagan for a moment, his face blank. "You aren't being careful enough. If Caleb is onto you, others will be, too. If they aren't already."

Riagan flushed. They'd always made sure they were alone whenever they discussed spying. Never alluded to doing anything special or important when in anyone's company. What more could they do?

"You might start answering my summons separately," Guiman suggested.

"I went to the stadium first. Pretended to head to practice before coming here," Riagan said, anxious to prove he was being careful.

Guiman nodded.

At that moment, Riagan got a new message. He pulled it up. From Neil.

Caleb followed to mess hall. I'm eating with Maellyn rather than try to lose him. Less suspicious. Should catch up in a couple of hours if Guiman still needs me.

Riagan growled and relayed the message.

Guiman picked up a couple purple melons from a basket, examining them. "He's smart to stay away. Caleb will grow bored and lose interest. Trying to lose him will only increase his curiosity and determination."

It made sense, but Riagan fumed anyway. Would Neil's commitment to finding Rois' killers waiver now that Maellyn was back?

Setting aside the purple melons, Guiman retrieved a black box hidden inside the fruit basket. It reminded Riagan of a necklace jewelry box. Guiman handed it over. "Probably best you go alone on this mission anyway."

Riagan removed the lid. Inside was a thin, black, transparent strip, like window tinting. It was the size of his wrist-comp. "What's this?"

"A decryption strip." Guiman scrutinized him as he spoke. "One of my informants notified me that a few scientists are secretly meeting with Vereth Ragna, Mainyu's new second in command, at the Olsin Pedran facility in the city."

"A Dahaka aboard Space City again?" Riagan blinked. "Didn't the Council tighten security after last year?"

"Ragna won't be onboard. He'll speak with the scientists remotely."

Makes sense, Riagan thought. "So what's this strip for? Are we hacking the feed to listen in?"

"I need you to sneak into the facility." Guiman removed a key card from his pocket and handed it over. "We can only listen in from inside. Once you're there, I'll give you further instructions on how to use the decryption strip."

A thrill of excitement coursed through Riagan at the prospect of finally discovering and spying on the traitors, but the prospect also made him uneasy. He'd feel better with Neil to help him.

Guiman placed a hand on Riagan's shoulder. "I need you to be sedulous on this assignment. The scientists cannot discover you. What you learn could be crucial to our exposing these traitors who played a role in your sister's death."

Riagan nodded soberly. He placed the keycard with the decryption strip back in the box and slipped it into his pocket. "I'll get it done."

*****

The Olsin Pedran science facility resembled a glass, hive-like dome that reflected most of the city around it. A steady stream of scientists returning from their lunch hour passed through the main entrance and most of the city streets were filled with passers-by.

A whiff of something foul, like an open sewer pouring onto a fire, caused Riagan to twitch and wrinkle his nose. He glanced around for the source to find a group of Malsain strolling along a walkway. The crowds parted as if they were royalty, but instead of awed expressions and pictures, people were covering their mouths and noses, a few even gulping as if trying not to get sick.

Riagan hoped the Malsain weren't headed to the science facility.

Guiman's instructions directed him to a nondescript door in the side of the facility. Despite the Malsain distraction, he felt as if eyes were on him as he approached the door. He knew it was ridiculous. A silly fear because he was breaking into a facility in broad daylight. But there was no reason for him to stand out. Despite this reasoning, it took all his willpower not to check to see if anyone was watching. Nothing would draw attention faster than him acting suspicious.

Taking a deep breath to calm his nerves, he retrieved the keycard from his pocket and casually swiped it over the card reader beside the door. After a second's pause, the door slid ajar and he entered.

He stood in a room half filled with androids. He froze, waiting for one of them to question him or sound an alarm, but they were all powered down and plugged into solar generators. He guessed they were cleaning droids that tended to the facility at night when they wouldn't interrupt the scientists at work. If it worked like the science labs, other droids aided the scientists with routine tasks during the day and would replace these droids on the charging stations at night. The tinted glass exterior walls doubled as solar panels that powered the facility and these charging stations.

A row of lab coats hung on hooks beside the door leading further into the facility. He donned a jacket before pulling up the facility schematics on his wrist-comp. A red line marked the path Guiman's informant had created for him to follow. It was close to meeting time, so he exited the room to a hall.

The rooms on either side of the hallway held sizable labs where scientists buzzed about their work. He kept his eyes straight ahead and pressed forward at a quick pace. The line on his schematics led to a wide, open stairwell near the center of the facility that curved upward. Most of the scientists returning from lunch strolled toward the elevators, so he chose the stairs.

On his way up, he passed two scientists—one stared intently at her wrist-comp, but the second nodded in greeting. He nodded back, feigning a smile and the scientist's gaze shifted as they passed. As Riagan reached the first-floor landing and rotated for the stairs leading to the second floor, he was joined by a scientist that made him think of a squid walking on its eight arms. Riagan stiffened as they marched up the stairs side by side, half afraid it would try to strike up a conversation. One eye on the creature seemed to regard him as they climbed—it took a lot of effort not to ball his hands—but when they reached the second floor it hurried off, while he kept on up the stairs. He passed a few other scientists who all nodded in greeting but said nothing.

At the fifth-floor landing, he turned right down a new hallway. More labs and a few small conference rooms filled the floor. His instructions led him to an empty computer room with three wall monitors, one long desk, and a few black chairs. Surely the meeting wasn't happening in this room. He had nowhere to hide. An adjoining room perhaps?

He activated the comm frequency on his tradutor. "I'm here."

"You'll need the decryption strip now," Guiman answered.

Riagan removed the black box from his pocket and took out the decryption strip. "What do I do with it?"

"Place it on the bottom left corner of the middle screen."

Riagan did and lines of letters and numbers appeared on the screen behind the strip. "Done."

"Give me a moment," Guiman said.

The letters and numbers rapidly flowed by before a visual popped up on the monitor. Onscreen, four scientists in lab coats: two gray-haired—a man and a woman—as well as a bearded, stooped man. The fourth was an Asian man with glasses.

Riagan touched the screen and zoomed in on the tall, slender gray-haired man. The badge hanging from his left breast pocket read Dr. Johnson. Adjusting to the woman, her badge read Dr. Snelling. Riagan noticed a resemblance to Fran Snelling. Mother? Aunt? He'd have to dig into that later.

The bearded man's rough brown hands momentarily blocked the view of his badge as he adjusted his lab coat nervously. Dr. Crowley. And the last scientist, Dr. Song, focused on his wrist-comp.

Riagan zoomed back out and flinched at the sudden appearance of a Dahaka alongside the scientists. The hologram floated over a black disc on the floor. It wore the familiar black armor, but without a helmet. It's pale, hairless head bore two scars, one running from left ear down his cheek and the second starting above his right eye up over his skull.

"Vereth Ragna," Dr. Snelling greeted. "Do you have a status for us on Siavash's retrogression?"

"According to our latest calculations using your CANVASS, the magnetic field is rapidly decaying," Ragna said. "We've already started losing atmosphere."

The male scientists murmured in surprise. Riagan's own jaw dropped at the revelation. This was the first he'd heard of something wrong on Siavash.

"That can't be right." Dr. Song ran a finger over his wrist-comp screen but he never looked up. "Our models to date don't show such problems for years."

The Dahaka's eyes narrowed. "Are you questioning my results?"

"We need to you review your data is all," Dr. Snelling said to smooth things over. "We need to update our models."

Beside the Dahaka, a second hologram appeared showing a large quantity of numbers. Riagan zoomed in on it. At the top were the words Contamination Analysis Network and Variable Area Satellite Scanning. The numbers were meaningless to him.

Dr. Snelling approached the numbers and studied them for several minutes. When she spoke again, her voice was unsettled. "If these numbers are correct, Siavash will become unlivable within five years or less. Likely less."

Riagan dropped into a chair. Was this the reason the Council refused to go after Mainyu? They believed he would cease to be a threat before long anyway. So why risk a confrontation?

"Brenda, we must forward these results to the Council at once." Dr. Johnson scrutinized the CANVASS numbers as well.

Dr. Snelling typed on her wrist-comp and the hologram of Vereth Ragna froze. "We will, but it won't do any good. Just get us in trouble."

"But we're talking the genocide of an entire alien civilization!" Dr. Johnson exclaimed. "We can't let this happen!"

"The Council doesn't consider it genocide," Dr. Snelling answered. "Not when no one is wiping the Dahaka out. It's an act of God."

Dr. Johnson huffed and turned his back, walking animatedly around the room.

"Genocide or not it's almost too late," Dr. Crowley cut in. "We have to relocate the entire population to a new planet. We haven't even located a viable option yet, and you know none of the populated planets will welcome the Dahaka. If we don't get Council resources soon, there'll be nothing we can do."

"I'm working on it," Dr. Snelling said. "Hopefully, we'll soon have a lot more help from an unexpected corner." She typed on her wrist-comp and the Dahaka's hologram unfroze. "Vereth, we'll add your newest data into our models. With the new projections, I believe we'll have a strong argument."

"We need you to intercede with the Council on our behalf," Vereth Ragna said.

"We're working that, too," Dr. Snelling promised.

To Riagan, it was like watching a wolf ask lambs for assistance. These scientists were mad for even considering aid. A part of him felt guilty at the prospect of letting an entire alien civilization die, but how could they ever trust the Dahaka? Mainyu would exploit or overpower anyone who attempted to aid them.

"We'll continue our search for a suitable planet for relocation," Dr. Crowley promised.

"We are making our own plans as well," Ragna replied.

Riagan snorted. That was code for Mainyu was searching for a suitable planet to attack. A peaceful solution wouldn't suit him. Whatever decision he made, innocents would suffer.

"In the meantime, we have support from a new ally. He has his eye on a Council spot," Dr. Snelling said. "—but he'll need assistance."

"What can we do?" Ragna asked.

Riagan leaned forward in his seat. This couldn't be happening. A traitor was attempting to infiltrate the Council? They'd all be vulnerable to Mainyu if that happened.

"We have some ideas in mind, but they aren't ready," Dr. Snelling answered.

Riagan slammed his fist down on the chair arm. "Give me a name. Who is it?"

"We'll talk again soon when we have news," Dr. Snelling added. A moment later, Vereth Ragna's hologram disappeared. Riagan's screen went blank as well.

"Did ya know any of this?" Riagan asked Guiman over the tradutor.

Silence greeted him, and he started to wonder if they'd lost connection.

"Guiman?"

"I had some knowledge of their problems, yes. I was unaware of the extent."

"What about this new ally?"

"I'll have to look into it."

Riagan lifted himself from the chair and paced the room. On the one hand, Mainyu, the Dahaka, and any traitors working with them were responsible for Rois' and Jaya's deaths. But how much of their present actions were motivated by a desperate need to survive? There was a lot he would be willing to do to survive. Even more he would've done to protect Rois. But Mainyu had tried to wipe out all of Space City. The Dahaka couldn't be trusted.

"Riagan, in that box I gave you are a couple of recording devices. I need you to head to that meeting room and plant them. That way we can gather future intel without another break in."

"Okay." Riagan removed the decryption strip from the monitor and returned it to the black box. A half dozen pebble-sized metallic recording devices lined one side of the box.

The facility schematics on his wrist-comp updated with a new line directing him to the meeting room. He exited the computer room and followed the directions, keeping an eye out for Dr. Snelling or the other three scientists. At present, the last thing he wanted was to run into them. He wasn't sure how he would act.

"Is this why the Council blocked us from going after Mainyu?" Riagan asked, unsettled by the implications of this revelation.

"It plays some role," Guiman acknowledged. "No reason to waste resources on a problem that will solve itself."

Riagan mulled this over for a second. "What's the other reason?"

"There is definitely more to it than that. Some deception going on. I just don't know what."

"And this person seeking a spot on the Council?" Riagan asked. He reached the stairs and headed down toward the third floor.

"That *is* a new piece to the puzzle."

While he walked, Riagan checked his wrist-comp for a message from Neil. It had been hours since they'd split up. More than enough time to lunch with Maellyn, then ditch Caleb. "Have ya heard from Neil?"

"I haven't, but it's just as well," Guiman said. "I think this may be something he shouldn't learn for now."

"Why not?"

"His grandfather has closer ties to the Council than I knew. If he says the wrong thing—"

"Neil would never betray us!" Riagan spoke louder than intended and looked around to see if anyone had noticed. A couple scientists cast him odd looks, but no one stopped him and he hurried on.

"I know he's loyal," Guiman said, "—but his grandfather is family. It's hard to keep secrets from family. And besides, he's a smart man. He might discover something despite your best efforts."

Riagan didn't like the suggestion that Neil might be compromised. He needed Neil's help with all of this. He couldn't do it alone.

"I don't mean to cast doubt on Neil," Guiman said. "He can still play an important role. There just may be some issues that it might be better for all of us if he didn't know."

And what issues might Guiman decide it was best he not know? Riagan wondered. He knew Guiman and Dardanos didn't reveal everything to them, but the reminder wasn't pleasant. Nor was the possibility that he'd have to start keeping stuff from Neil.

Chapter 12

Maellyn Becomes Team Lead

Maellyn chewed the last bite of her hamburger, enjoying the delightful mix of beef, cheese, lettuce, and a ketchup/mayo sauce. She'd missed hamburgers and fries over the summer while on Niveum, and was a little embarrassed to realize she'd eaten more than her share of them since the school year started back up.

"I'm not looking forward to Tereshkova's first exam," Trini said, before nibbling at her pizza.

"I hope there's a curve," Nico mumbled around a mouthful of pizza.

Maellyn nodded agreement. They'd stayed an extra two hours after class discussing the Space City grading scale used to determine whether a new planet or moon would be explored via an orbiter, rover, with human presence, or some combination of the three. Evaluating any new planet's potential resources, while determining how conducive it was to human exploration, was based upon a variety of factors that made it seem prohibitive to explore at all. But Instructor Tereshkova's first exam covered assessing the attributes of a list of planets and prioritizing their level of importance to Space City. So extra study was crucial.

Now, Maellyn finished off her last few fries and pushed her plate away, leaning back in her chair. She needed to burp, but stifled it with a quick drink of water.

"Whose up for dessert?" Nico stood, one eyebrow arching.

Trini shook her head. "None for me, thanks."

Maellyn knew she'd already been bad enough for one day. "I'll pass, too. Saving my desserts for later."

"Even if it won't count against your weekly allotment?" Nico asked, a coy grin on his face.

Maellyn rolled her eyes. "You can't get free desserts from the lunch machines."

The machines were tied into the medical database in order to obtain students' health information, such as height, weight, age, cholesterol levels, and blood pressure, along with a variety of other factors. Students ordered food from the machines. The food was 3D printed on the spot; however, depending on how healthy (or not) the meals they chose at the beginning of a day or new week, subsequent options might be limited in order to ensure they maintained a balanced diet. Each student was allotted five desserts per week. Max. It had been one per day freshman year, but the candy black market had become too successful. The academy leadership had attempted to crack down on it, but when that failed—they never learned Nico's identity—they chose to curb sweets consumption by the lone method under their control.

"Your lack of faith hurts." Nico placed a hand over his heart and feigned a pained expression.

Moving over to the machines, he removed his wrist-comp from its holder on his left forearm and started typing. He held up the wrist-comp in front of one machine and tapped the screen. He waited, eyes greedy.

"What's he fooling with?" Trini asked.

Maellyn shook her head. "Not sure, but we might want to make our exit before someone figures out what he's up to."

The girls gathered up their plates and dropped them off on the dishwasher transport, but as they turned to leave, the lunch machine opened and Nico scooped out a tray with three plates holding large slices of strawberry cheesecake. Nico held them up triumphantly.

He strutted toward their table. "The computer recorded three extra helpings of green beans. What can I say? I'm a health nut."

Despite herself, Maellyn's mouth salivated over the cheesecake. Strawberry syrup drizzled down the sides, and two whip cream flowers crowned the strawberries on top. "How did you do that?"

"Small hack." Nico set the plates on the table and gestured for them to join him.

Trini shook her head, but moved toward the table as if unable to control her feet. "Why do you need to hack for free desserts when you already run the candy black market?"

Nico stared at her as if she'd asked why presents at Christmas was a good thing.

As Maellyn argued with herself over whether to give in since the cheesecake was already there or waste it—food should never be wasted, especially not cheesecake—the food machine Nico had hacked opened up, revealing another tray with three more pieces of cheesecake. Nico's mouth twisted into a grin. He rose, but before he could retrieve this new tray it was shoved out of the machine, spilling the desserts on the floor. In their place emerged a third tray with cheesecake.

"What the—" Nico grabbed his wrist-comp, chewing on his lower lip.

This next tray of cheesecake was shoved out of the machine onto the floor, splattering on top of the previous and a fourth tray appeared from the machine, but this one oozed a white goo. Nico typed furiously on his wrist-comp, but the machine started spitting the goo out, spraying Nico's clothes.

Trini jumped up from the table, the plate with her cheesecake in hand. "Maybe we should get out of here."

"Agreed," Maellyn said.

A ding from Maellyn's wrist-comp alerted her to an incoming message. As she pulled it up, a second chime echoed from Trini's wrist-comp, followed by a third from Nico's. A message from Instructor Fintan.

An urgent matter has arisen that I need to discuss with you. Please report to my office as speedily as probable.

Her stomach clenched. Had the Apidium monkeys had another setback?

Trini frowned, looking puzzled. "Instructor Fintan summoned me. I wonder why?"

He couldn't have already discovered this cheesecake hack, Maellyn thought worriedly.

"Me, too." Nico gave the cheesecake-spewing lunch machine an accusatory grimace, before scooting for the door. "Uh, let's not keep him waiting."

*****

Anand, Devika, and Fran shifted uncomfortably in Fintan's office while the instructor studied something on his wrist-comp when Maellyn, Trini, and Nico arrived. Their presence further confused Maellyn. What could Fintan want with the six of them?

Fintan smiled at Maellyn, gesturing with his two left arms for them to file in. "I'm cheerful you could join me promptly. I have critical information to share. And great opportunity."

So not a setback with the Apidium, Maellyn reasoned. She exhaled. *Nor the cheesecake hack.*

Fintan's gaze turned to Nico, who was wiping cheesecake goo off his uniform with a wet towel he'd grabbed from his dorm on their way.

"I took a spill on our way," Nico said. Fintan accepted the explanation without comment.

He shifted back to the rest of them. "How much do you know about what's happening on Ourania?"

Fran spoke up, face lined with worry. "There's some sort of fungal outbreak."

Maellyn wasn't the least bit surprised that Fran knew a good deal. She obsessively studied all things Alfar. Rumors had it that she even wrote fictional accounts of them now—fan fiction.

"The outbreak is now widespread," Fintan said. "Numerous native plants and trees infected. Even animals and Alfar are catching extremely sick from fungus."

Maellyn frowned. Alfar had a body temperature similar to humans, which was too hot for most fungus. Their immune systems should fight off fungal attacks quite easily.

"The Alfar have tirelessly studied it since its discovery," Fintan said. "They call it Agnostosfaira zymi or Azymi for short."

Another troubling bit of news. As the most advanced race in the known universe, the Alfar had zealously studied their planet and meticulously recorded everything. A fungus they hadn't heard of on their home planet should be impossible.

Trini spoke up. "Are they sure Azymi is a new fungus and not a mutation?"

Fintan waved all four hands dismissively. "It's a mutation. Fungi don't form out of nothing. But it matches nothing on record."

"Someone brought it with them," Anand suggested. "From off planet."

Except visitors weren't allowed on Ourania, accept in rare circumstances, and those permitted were rigorously screened during a three-week quarantine before they were allowed onto the planet.

"They've had no visitors for five years," Fintan said. "They're considering the possibility nonetheless."

Maellyn remembered Fintan mentioning an outbreak a few years back on Niveum that nearly wiped out the Greenbark trees, which held a special place in Macab tradition. The outbreak had been the result of a warming of the planet's average temperature. "Isn't Ourania experiencing higher than normal temperatures the last few years? The Azymi could've survived in a remote corner of the planet until recent warming allowed it to flourish."

Fintan beamed at her, pleased that she had remembered what he'd taught her, but he quickly sobered. "That's the leading theory. They've reached out for support; I'm tasked with putting together a team to assist them."

Maellyn blinked. He couldn't mean them. They were students. Space City had ample scientists much more qualified than themselves.

"If you're willing, the six of you will be my team." Fintan looked at each of them in turn.

No one spoke up. Fran had tears in her eyes. None of them had the experience for this. Well, maybe Trini had some after working with her aunt to treat the Ukka on Letos over the summer.

"Each of you possess useful qualifications," Fintan said. "Maellyn and Trini, you both possess experience treating serious outbreaks in the field. Nico, your computer expertise will be an invaluable resource, as the Alfar won't allow us to travel to Ourania. Devika, we need your ability with mathematical calculations. Anand, I've heard you're quite accomplished with designing and building things with additive manufacturing. And Fran, with your extensive knowledge of the Alfar, I'll be counting on you to smooth interactions with them."

Each of them beamed as Fintan recognized them, including Maellyn. She was thrilled at the opportunity, though it still seemed unbelievable. "Why us? There are others in Space City much more qualified to help."

"We won't be the only ones involved," Fintan allowed. "Dr. Flores is involved, as you would expect."

Trini nodded.

"But Space City cannot afford to assign the entirety of its scientists to this one issue. We will be the primary team and consult with specialists, as needed."

"I expect this will take up a lot of time?" Devika asked. "What about our classes?"

"Your main focus will be this," Fintan answered. "And count as your grades. If it was up to me, you would graduate after this is over. The work you'll be doing and the research you'll need to conduct in the process will be beyond what any students are asked to complete during their four years at the academy."

Maellyn felt buoyed with excitement. It was a tremendous opportunity. And getting to skip their regular classes; now she wouldn't have to prep for Tereshkova's exam. Everyone smiled, Anand and Devika murmuring to each other.

"Are you all in?" Fintan asked.

"Yes!" they all confirmed.

"Great. Maellyn, you'll lead the group and report to me," Fintan said. "You're being promoted to a team lead."

She gaped, embarrassed by the opportunity. She was no more qualified than anyone else. But Fran gave her a thumbs up and Trini nodded encouragingly.

"Each of you will coordinate your activities through her." Fintan moved back to his desk, retrieving his coffee in one hand and wrist-comp in the second. He turned back and sat on the edge of the desk. "Can any of you suggest first steps?"

"When can we look at their work?" Nico asked. "Are they sending us the data?"

"I've already received a fair amount." Fintan held up his wrist-comp. "I will distribute. But once you have it, what will you look for?"

Maellyn mused for a moment, pursing her lips as she considered. "We should compare the Azymi against our database for matches."

"Yes." Fintan agreed.

"We need to determine commonalities among those infected," Trini added, staring at the ceiling in thought. "Previous illnesses. Are patients from the same location? Or recently traveled to the same place? We should compare patients with the rest to determine if any trends emerge."

"A case-control study," Maellyn said, recognizing Trini's line of thinking.

"Exactly," Trini confirmed.

Fran frowned, crossing her arms. "Wouldn't the Alfar have done these already?"

"I expect they have," Fintan said. "But we can offer new perspective. We may spot things they've missed."

"Plus, it's a good way to familiarize ourselves with the data," Maellyn added, itching to begin working.

"Agreed." Fintan turned to Anand. "We've discussed people. What about the plants and trees?"

Anand shifted uncomfortably at becoming the center of attention.

"We need to check if the Azymi is found in the soil or air," Devika said to cover up for him. "Can it survive in water? Determining that could go a long way in helping us discover how it gets transported."

"Good." Fintan set down his wrist-comp and picked up keycards, which he began distributing. "We'll use my lab as primary operation place. Let's get started."

Maellyn's wrist-comp notified her that she had fifteen minutes until her next class.

Well, I guess I don't have class, she thought.

That was a weight off her shoulders. Researching the Azymi outbreak would be a ton of work, more than if she'd stuck with doing her schoolwork, but the thought of it invigorated her. This work meant something. Like her work with the Apidium, she'd have the opportunity to save lives—the Alfar, the animals that co-inhabited Ourania, and even the plant life.

That was something worth doing.

At that moment, Instructor Tereshkova appeared in the door, nostrils flaring as her eyes lit on Nico. They all went silent at sight of her, Maellyn's jubilation sinking.

"Nico, you're in big trouble," Instructor Tereshkova said. "My office. Now!"

He hung his head and marched for the door without a word. Maellyn tensed, waiting for Instructor Tereshkova to demand she and Trini come along as well. Instead, Tereshkova turned to Fintan.

"I'm sorry for interrupting. Nico thought it was a good idea to hack into the food machines for desserts, then fled the scene when things went awry. Left a mess behind."

Fintan clucked his tongue. Maellyn hoped this wouldn't cost Nico his position on the team.

Finally, Tereshkova's gaze swept to Maellyn, mouth drawn in a tight line. "I expect you and Trini to report to mess hall for clean up."

"Yes, ma'am," Maellyn replied, her face burning.

Tereshkova's look of disapproval moved to Trini, who confirmed that she would go as well. Then Tereshkova turned on her heels, marching after Nico. And Maellyn promised herself it was the last time she'd trust one of Nico's hacks.

Chapter 13

Neil Witnesses Patrick's Transformation

Leaning against the academy/university infirmary's waiting room wall, Neil fidgeted with his wrist-comp. Why had Instructor Tereshkova moved class here at the last minute? Did this mean their class presentations on 3D printing were on hold?

He rubbed his eyes. He'd slept poorly last night, dreading giving his presentation on additive manufacturing use in spaceship construction. He'd dreamed that Riagan had skipped class, leaving him to present alone. Instructor Tereshkova had called on him first, of course. He'd risen to march up to the front of the class, only to realize his presentation and all notes had been wiped clean from his wrist-comp courtesy of Patrick Duffy. For the next several minutes he'd stuttered through the presentation, trying to remember the main points. Everyone had started to laugh, which led to the realization he'd forgotten to dress that morning. Ducking for cover behind Instructor Tereshkova's desk, Neil had hit his head, which had woken him from the dream. He'd been hanging half out of bed, head throbbing from clubbing it on the dresser.

Despite knowing it had been a dream, he had checked his wrist-comp for their presentation. Then double-checked this morning while telling Riagan about the dream. Riagan had muttered he wouldn't be surprised if Patrick or Caleb found a way to delete their presentations, before conning someone else into taking the fall for it. That made Neil more nervous, so he'd created a backup copy, which he'd uploaded to Instructor Tereshkova's server ahead of time.

Now as classmates filed into the waiting room, Neil prayed that Instructor Tereshkova postponed their presentations. Maybe then he could guilt Riagan into presenting. After all, Riagan hadn't helped much with preparation, instead spending his time on special tasks for Guiman or Dardanos.

It was strange. Riagan had started handling more tasks on his own, but if Neil questioned him, he'd insist they were simple things. No need for them both.

"Hey Neil, ready for your Games match tomorrow?" Cade tossed his head in greeting as he approached. "Phoenix should be competitive this year."

Neil held up his hand for a fist bump. "You better believe I'm ready to play."

Cade held up his wrist-comp. "Got any quotes for me?"

"Nope. Nothing for Phoenix's bulletin board."

"Fair enough. How 'bout after the game? My editor's pressing me for good quotes in everythin'. It'd really help me out."

"Morning class," Instructor Tereshkova greeted as she and Instructor Aodh entered the waiting room.

Everyone went silent.

"It's special day," Tereshkova said. "Aodh and I listen to you for change." She looked a little too smug at that, dashing Neil's hopes that their presentations would be delayed.

Instructor Aodh gestured to his son Pyrrhus, who stood quietly beside Patrick. "The reason we are in the infirmary today is because Pyrrhus' and Mr. Duffy's presentation has to do with the medical uses of advanced manufacturing."

Neil didn't envy Pyrrhus. Any time Instructor Aodh wanted student participation, he always chose his son first. Rumors had it Instructor Aodh marked off points from Pyrrhus' participation grade each time he missed an answer, though those were few. Having a parent as an instructor couldn't be easy.

Patrick and Pyrrhus led them through a set of double doors. Riagan clapped Neil on the shoulders, to Neil's relief. They walked down a white, bleach-scented hallway past a nurses' desk with a couple of girls in blue nursing scrubs. The class proceeded to a vacant patient room.

Patrick strode over to a black half-orb about waist high on the wall. Pyrrhus retrieved a cart, half covered by a sheet. A couple of three-foot antenna-like poles, with lights and magnifiers, hooked from one end of the cart up and over the center of it. After moving the cart over beside Patrick, Pyrrhus pushed the poles outward off the cart while Patrick activated the orb. It projected a presentation title page into the air.

Riagan leaned over. "How much ya want to bet they paid someone else to do it for them?"

Neil said nothing. Patrick wouldn't surprise him. But not Pyrrhus. He'd never known the Traga to cheat, even with all the pressure his father put on him.

Patrick brushed his hand over the orb, and the projected image changed to that of a human torso, grotesquely ripped open on the right side. Blood smeared much of the torso. Several girls gasped in horror. After a second Neil's eyes popped as he recognized the person in the pic. It was Patrick stretched out on a medical bed in what could've been this room.

"As many know, I was hurt during the attack on Mars last year." Patrick used a laser pointer to circle the wound onscreen. "What you don't know is I had two organ transplants because of it."

Neil's breath stopped short. He'd been there; had seen Patrick's wounds. He'd helped clean them and patched up his suit, but hadn't grasped the extent of the injury. Despite the animosity between them, Neil's skin grew hot. He had never tried to find out if Patrick was okay. It seemed he should've at least known that Patrick had needed organ transplants, and to have felt a moment's sympathy for him.

The projector image changed to a video of Patrick spread out on the infirmary bed, a blanket covering him from the waist down. An IV stand to the left of his head sent an anesthesia drip into his arm. Doctors wielding scalpels and other surgical tools in bloody, gloved hands rooted around in the enormous gash in Patrick's side.

Christel Manikas and Aileen McKensie groaned and averted their eyes from the projection. Neil swallowed back a bit of bile that threatened to come out, but he forced himself to watch.

The projection changed to a different scene where a couple of small, white, tubular devices moved methodically along a railing above Patrick's torso. Using the laser pointer, Patrick circled the white devices. "The doctors did a CT scan of my torso to create a 3D image of it, my liver, and right kidney. Afterward, they harvested cells from the organs and some of the surrounding tissue."

The next video showed Patrick, still in a hospital bed but sitting up, holding two jars with organs inside. One resembled a super-sized pink slug, and the other a lumpy kidney bean as large as his hand.

"Using the digital image from the CT scan, a robotic designer developed print files for a new liver and kidney. Meanwhile the doctors, using my harvested cells, cultured a larger batch. Using the new cells, combined with the design file, they 3D-printed a new liver and kidney for me. The process, formally known as additive manufacturing, took a month during which I remained in the hospital in critical condition, the doctors working hard to keep me alive long enough for the new organs to be grown and transplanted."

Pyrrhus leaned forward conspiratorially. "Word has it the doctors got it completed in a month because they were tired of Patrick's groaning and complaining."

There were knowing chuckles from several of the students.

Patrick smiled good-naturedly. "Can't say I loved staying in the hospital for an extended period of time, but I tried not to wear out my welcome."

Riagan snorted and leaned over to whisper to Neil. "Patrick isn't capable of being considerate. He just knows how to please the instructors." And it seemed to be working. Both instructors looked engrossed.

The next video showed the slug-shaped liver back inside Patrick alongside his other organs, while a white, rectangular machine moved along his torso.

"The liver and kidneys, like all organs, are difficult to print and properly transplant into the body, because they are rich in vasculature."

"Blood vessels," Pyrrhus interjected.

"Thank you," Patrick agreed. "What you see here is another 3D printer spraying tissue cells, blended with a medical gel, so they'll stick in place to help my new organs knit themselves and their blood vessels into place within my body. All told I was stuck in that bed for six weeks."

"When he left, the doctors said if he ruined these, he was on his own," Pyrrhus interjected.

A cynical part of Neil speculated that Patrick and Pyrrhus had created these jokes to butter up the instructors. Yet Patrick's eyes held none of their usual calculation, his mouth devoid of its customary smirk. He seemed to be genuinely having fun.

Pyrrhus pulled the sheet off the cart, revealing a rectangular machine with an open top. "If everyone will gather around, we'll show you a little more of the process."

Curious, Neil shuffled forward with everyone.

"This device is a bioreactor," Pyrrhus informed them.

A piston-like device, half outside the bioreactor, entered through a hole in one side and pushed and pulled a foot-long bar. Between that bar and a second, attached to the opposite end of the rectangular machine, were a half dozen pieces of what resembled pink gum attached to vertical pins in either bar. As the piston pushed and pulled one bar, the pink 'gum' expanded and contracted in between the pins.

Pyrrhus pointed his right limb at the pieces of pink substance. "In addition to the organs, Patrick also needed new muscles—3D printed as well!—to help stitch him back together. But you can't simply throw new muscles into the body. This bioreactor exercises the muscles before they're inserted into the body."

"My new organs were exercised too before transplant," Patrick said. "Though in different machines. The doctors would only let us bring this one to show. And to wrap up our presentation, here's the end result." Patrick lifted his shirt.

Everyone murmured. Neil blinked, unable to believe what he was seeing. Patrick's torso had one long, thin jagged scar, but otherwise, he looked normal. You'd never know he had ever been hurt. If Neil hadn't seen Patrick's face in some of the earlier pictures, and the scar, he might have thought the whole thing was made up.

"My recovery is only one of the many things we now do with 3D printing in the medical field." Patrick lowered his shirt. He stepped back over to his wrist-comp and changed the projected image to a lab filled with older students dissecting organs on tables. "We can print artificial mini-organs that surgeons-in-training can learn on. Or print tissue for use in studying disease. We can even print cancer tumors and other specific medical conditions for study. The possibilities are endless."

He clapped his hands, eyebrows raising as he remembered something. "Oh, I almost forgot. My new organs. The doctors printed sensors into the liver and kidney that monitor their health, making sure they perform as expected and aren't showing signs of deterioration."

"I think those are so the instructors can keep tabs on him," Pyrrhus deadpanned, pointing at Patrick. "You never know what this troublemaker's up to."

Instructor Tereshkova thanked Patrick and Pyrrhus for their presentation. Since no one else had a medical presentation, the class departed the room and headed back toward the infirmary entrance. Neil wished he had thought to arrange for his presentation over at the university science labs.

As they reached the front entrance, EMTs burst inside transporting a hover gurney. Neil and the rest of the class darted out of the way as the EMTs rushed toward the ER portion of the infirmary.

"That's Adrien Laroque," someone shouted.

Sure enough, Adrien Laroque lay on the gurney, eyes swollen shut and blood covering his mouth and chin.

"Is he dead?" Christel Manikas asked.

At Neil's side, Cade snapped a pic with his wrist-comp, before typing.

Patrick shoved his way through classmates and followed after the EMTs, but was stopped by a nurse short of the doors. She was an older woman with dark, wrinkled skin and curly gray hair.

"What happened to him?" Patrick asked.

The nurse shook her head, a regretful expression on her face. "I'm sorry. I don't know. He only just came in."

"Where was he found?" Patrick was frantic. Neil wasn't sure if he'd ever seen Patrick show so much concern for anyone else.

"I couldn't say. I wish I could tell you more."

Patrick stared at the doors as if trying to see through them.

"All right everyone, in light of this, I'm ending class early," Tereshkova said, brow furrowed. She glanced between them and Patrick. "I'll keep you informed as to Adrien's status as I hear."

"What do you think happened?" Neil asked Cade. Had Adrien been in a fight?

"I don't know." Cade finished typing and put away his wrist-comp. "But I'm going to start digging until I find out. I'll have the story by tonight."

Instructor Aodh shooed them from the infirmary. Outside, they found the normal milling of students around the courtyard. No evidence of what had happened to Adrien. Unsure of what to do, but with sudden free time, Neil headed for the dorms. He needed to get some studying done, but doubted he could concentrate much right now.

In the dorms, Instructors Nez, Aldrin, and Glenn, and General Stribog questioned students. Cade stood right behind Instructor Glenn, listening to him question a couple of first years.

One officer guarded the door to Adrien's room, which he shared with Patrick, while others searched inside. Neil watched from a distance, but couldn't tell what they were doing. The room looked tossed, one mattress hanging halfway off the bed and stuff everywhere. But no blood that he could see from his vantage point.

"Ya think he was attacked in his room?" Riagan asked, appearing at his side.

Neil nodded. "Have to think so. Why else would they be in there?"

As they watched, Cade joined them. "Speculation is Patrick did this."

Riagan slapped Neil in the chest. "Why aren't I surprised?"

"Really?" Neil frowned. "Why would he hurt Adrien? They're friends."

"Who knows?" Riagan said, shrugging. "He does a lot of crazy craic."

"And when was he supposed to have done this?" Neil asked. This wasn't adding up. "He's been in class with us."

Cade held up his hands. "That's just what I heard from witnesses."

"Patrick was shaken when Adrien was brought in."

"Acting." Riagan scowled at him. "Throw everyone off. I can't believe ya defending him."

"I'm not," Neil protested. "I'm just shocked."

The Patrick he'd seen in class today, telling them how close to death he'd come. And his apology at the beginning of the year. How could he then put Adrien in the hospital in serious condition?"

"Ya shouldn't," Riagan said, glaring at Neil as if he didn't recognize him. "This is just the latest incident in a long line from Patrick."

Neil didn't argue. If it turned out to be true, he knew he wouldn't be surprised. What surprised him was the realization that he *hoped* it wasn't true.

Chapter 14

Riagan Delivers a Message

Back on Siavash for the first time in a couple months, Riagan struggled to calm his nerves. Knowing that something was going wrong with the planet inspired ridiculous fears that the ground beneath their feet might break apart at any moment. And to compound that fear, the last time he'd been here, one of Guiman's spies, a woman at that, had given him the beating of his life; he still didn't know her identity.

He followed Neil into the arena, built inside an enormous cavern. The Dahaka populace filled rows of benches carved into the cavern's walls; echoes compounded their raucous cries until Riagan wished he had ear plugs.

He shifted in his simple woolen clothes, feeling exposed without the familiar black armor, especially considering the sheer number of Dahaka in the arena. Typically, only Azios populated the capital, but the commoners had been granted access for the start of the Azios Tournament, a gladiatorial-style competition. It was their one time each year inside the capital. They wore woolen clothes, and Guiman had decided that sending Riagan and Neil in the same clothing would provide greater anonymity. They were also wearing bald caps and white body makeup to blend in.

"What is it we're retrieving?" Neil yelled.

When Riagan spotted Neil's hazel-green eyes he started to panic and remind him to activate his red contacts, before remembering they weren't needed today. The Azios possessed red pupils, but none of the commoners did. Guiman hadn't discovered the reason for the difference.

While searching the closest walkways for black smoke, signs of the Kali, Riagan said, "Something that'll verify the data Ragna gave the scientists."

"I can't believe all these Dahaka are in danger." Neil sounded spooked.

Taking in the arena, the commoners didn't look that much different than people from Earth in a more primitive era. Men, women, children; it was strange to see any Dahaka that contrasted so completely with the bloodthirsty Azios. Well, maybe not completely. They were here to witness a gladiatorial tournament after all.

"I can't believe our scientists are aiding them." Riagan almost added or the mysterious person seeking a spot on the Council, but caught himself. It was more difficult to hide things from Neil than others. Neil had proven himself time and again.

"Some of them," Neil corrected. He pushed through the crowd, waving for Riagan to follow. "This way."

They weaved around Dahaka and up a wide ramp. The fetid scent of sweat and grime (even commoners rarely showered) turned Riagan's stomach, making him wish he had nose plugs. He focused on breathing through his mouth instead of his nose.

Three horn blasts reverberated through the arena, alerting everyone to the start of a battle. Down in the center of the arena, a Dahaka dressed in ceremonial green garments from head to toe lowered a horn from his lips. Beside him stood two young Azios, dressed only in loincloths. Not much older than Riagan and Neil, the pair each held an ivory tusk, similar to those attached to the forearms on Azios armor.

The two faced each other, shoulders back, heads high, muscles flexed like serpents poised to strike. The green-clad Dahaka raised the horn to his lips once more. He gave a single, short blast. The arena erupted in renewed cheers, shouts, and waving fists. And the battle began.

One Azios darted forward, slashing with his tusk. The second somersaulted clear of the attack and dropped to a crouch. When the first charged again, the second stabbed at his opponent's knees.

A slap on Riagan's arm startled him from the fight.

"Are you going to help or just watch?" Neil asked.

A sharp object pressed into Riagan's back, around his left kidney, forcing his torso to arch forward. Neil's eyes widened as he looked over Riagan's shoulder.

"Don't turn around," a deep, strained voice warned. "See the tunnel ahead on the left? Move."

The knife at Riagan's back cut into the skin, driving him forward on his tiptoes. He wanted to reach for the tusk hidden in his garments, but it was all he could manage to avoid getting stabbed as they proceeded toward the tunnel.

"Are you Sverog?" Neil asked.

"Hush."

They entered the torch lit tunnel and the point in Riagan's back slipped away. He and Neil turned to find two Kali blocking the tunnel's entrance. The pair had modified their black-smoke bodies into rough semblances of human form. Both held short, narrow gray knives that could barely be distinguished from their hands. That was another mystery Riagan hadn't cracked. How Kali could wield a knife or any other solid object.

"Doesn't Guiman have smarter spies who know how to blend in?" the Kali on the right asked, stepping forward.

Riagan flushed. "None of the Dahaka noticed us."

The Kali sneered. "Commoners aren't bright."

"Are you Sverog?" Neil asked again. "Guiman says you have a package for us."

Sverog looked them up and down. "Are you sure you can deliver without getting caught?"

Riagan ground his teeth.

"This isn't our first mission," Neil said.

"It's not apparent."

Neil bristled and stepped forward. "Do you have the package or not?"

Sverog turned back to his companion. "Chenbog."

Chenbog glided forward bearing a small black box. He handed the box to Neil and retreated.

"Get out of here before the battle's end," Sverog warned. "The only reason you haven't been discovered is everyone is distracted."

The Kali exited the tunnel and disappeared back into the crowd. Riagan scowled after them, still feeling the point in his back where the Kali's blade had been. He wondered if there was a means of reversing the tables on a Kali. After a second, he realized his right hand was shaking from adrenaline.

"Let's go," Neil said, hiding the black box in his garments.

When they got back to the base of the stands, one Azios remained standing on the arena floor, pumping both tusks over his head. The other lay dead on the ground, blood covering his chest. On the far side of the arena floor was a wide pit. The victorious Azios dropped the tusks and picked up the body. He carried it to the pit, held it up to show the crowd, who cheered wildly, then tossed it into the pit.

Riagan's heart clogged his throat as he watched.

With the battle finished, the victor marched from the arena to cheers as a new pair of Azios took his place. One of the new fighters looked in his prime, but the other was older, wiry, with splotchy skin. There was no way it was an even match.

Every Azios fought in the tournament each year. Riagan had asked Guiman how the Azios maintained a sufficient number if they always killed each other off in the tournament. He'd replied that most battles didn't end in one fighter dying. Fatalities occurred when a weak, ashamed Azios forced his opponent's hand. Or in the case of this uneven match, older Azios would seek out young, strong opponents in order to die in battle rather than in bed of old age.

Riagan didn't understand their desire to seek out death, but he also didn't pity them. They survived as a warring society, attempting to kill and steal from anyone. The universe would be a safer place without them.

Chapter 15

Maellyn's Tough Introduction

Maellyn exited first from the thorneway into the Alfar research facility on Orestes, Ourania's moon. It was to be the team's first direct encounter with the Alfar since Fintan had recruited them three weeks prior.

The team emerged from the thorneway behind her, Fintan arriving last. Maellyn always hated traveling through the thorneway. Too much like throwing herself through used engine oil, and the split-second change from one location to another was disorienting.

Her displeasure was replaced by wonder as she took in the massive facility. Its ceiling towered hundreds of feet overhead. Before she could even take one step forward, a dozen metallic drones boxed them in. The drones projected large energy shields that fit together like a Spartan shield wall, blocking the way forward. Maellyn took an involuntary step backward, not having anticipated this kind of reception.

"Good morning," a female Alfar said coldly, as she approached the shield wall. She crossed her arms. "Who are you? Where's Fintan?"

The Alfar was tall and lithe with curly, strawberry-blonde hair that didn't fit her severe demeanor. She wore a pale-yellow blouse and pants.

Maellyn opened her mouth to speak, but Fintan stepped forward in a rush, stopping just short of the drone shields.

"Aili, it's welcome to see you." Fintan gestured behind him. "This is my team. We're here to support."

Aili scowled. "I was expecting your Council to send professional scientists, not children."

Maellyn felt her face redden, mouth tightening as she ground her teeth.

Fintan spluttered. "Aili, each member of my team is highly capable. I personally selected them."

"I don't care if they're the best in your academy." Aili turned her back on them, the drones and shield still preventing them from entering the facility. "We are in a real crisis. I expected better support from Space City."

Maellyn shared uneasy glances with Trini and Fran. Anand and Devika glared at Aili, arms crossed and looking ready to march straight back through the thorneway.

"You have me, and you'll receive support from others," Fintan said. He gestured at the drones. "Will you please let us through so we can talk?"

Aili turned back, eyes flashing. "Fine. But I'm going to have words with Dr. Trevena."

A part of Maellyn wanted to tell Aili that she was spurning his daughter, but she chose to keep her mouth shut. That would sound like sour grapes. Her primary goal in coming today was to first establish a relationship with Aili and convince the scientist that they could contribute. And that wouldn't happen if she let the Alfar's slight get to her.

The drones lowered their shield and departed. Hoping to smooth things over a little, Maellyn stepped toward the Alfar scientist and offered a simple nod of greeting. "Greetings, I'm Maellyn Trevena." She emphasized her last name. But the Alfar didn't give her a second glance. Instead, Aili drew Fintan off to the side to speak alone.

Stomach churning at the brusque treatment, Maellyn turned her focus to the facility. This first area was a large open corridor with doors along the rear wall. To their right, a tall glass dome gave them a view of Ourania. It reminded Maellyn of looking at Earth from space, except the continents were drastically different.

An asteroid drifted into view above the facility. Maellyn's eyes widened in shock at the close proximity. Why hadn't the Alfar diverted it long before it reached this close? Strangely, lights blinked on the asteroid. After a moment's study, she realized it was an enormous ship, larger even than Space City.

She shuffled over to Fran. "What kind of ship is that?"

Fran leaned in close, voice hushed. "It's the *Gunnra Kore*. Brand new. Rumored to be indestructible, even for the Alfar. It possesses more defensive capabilities than the rest of their fleet combined. Rather stunning, right?"

Maellyn nodded. She wouldn't want to go up against that thing in a battle.

A four-car, topless hover train pulled up beside them, driven by a male Alfar with spiky blonde hair and violet eyes. He sat relaxed in the front seat, an arm draped over the back, a wide grin plastered to his face.

"Thank you, Albrin." Aili gestured for them to board the seats on the hover train cars. "I'll take you to my lab."

"What about a tour?" Nico asked.

Aili took a seat next to Albrin, who straightened and moved both arms to the wheel. Her back to them spoke volumes.

"Wow," Trini mouthed to Maellyn.

Maellyn shook her head in disbelief.

Albrin drove the hover train to the doors on the back wall that automatically opened inward, granting them access to a new, but also sizable room. They passed a football field-sized garden packed with exotic plants. A dome, like a pink-hued gas bubble running from the floor up more than one hundred feet high, shielded the garden. It held a plethora of exotic flowers, bushes, vines, and algae-covered tree trunks, but no animals that Maellyn could see. Faint hints of wet soil and pollen wafted across the room, mixing with strange, inorganic smells she couldn't identify.

On their left, they passed a domed glass lab in which droids worked on odd machines, sparks flying, accompanied by a steady humming which made Maellyn think of a refrigerator. The lab was the first in a long line, though most of the others were smaller.

The hover train turned left down a row between labs, which ran on a long distance. The labs made up a giant square, and they'd entered one little corner of it.

"This is the dedicated Ourania health wing," Fintan announced, trying to make up for Aili's cold reception. "Every virus and bacterium on Ourania has its own individual lab here for careful study. Some particularly robust or harmful ones have multiple labs designed to study a virus or bacterium in different environments or phases, for example."

Albrin stopped the hover train at a four-way intersection, and Aili got off. She strode toward a lab on the far-right corner of the intersection without waiting to see that they followed.

Maellyn and the rest disembarked the hover train and followed. Inside the lab, Aili slipped her hand through slits in a machine that reminded Maellyn of a hand dryer. There was a light buzzing and when she removed her hands, they were gloved. Fintan followed suit before motioning to each of them to do so as well. Maellyn slipped her hands in, tense at not knowing exactly how the machine worked. Her entire hands were sprayed at once.

Removing her hands, she examined the gloves closely. They didn't look much different than disposable gloves. She tapped a couple fingers together and could discern no sense of wetness. The gloves didn't tear under the light pressure.

She turned her attention to a digital map on one wall of the lab. A bright red circle covered a majority of it, which she guessed marked the outbreak zone on Ourania.

Aili approached the map and placed a hand on the circle. "The red circle represents the area within which we've recorded cases of Agnostosfaira zymi infection. It's a twenty-square-kilometer patch of swampland. The area is quarantined. Crews are scouring it plus another thirty kilometers for new cases."

The Alfar tapped the screen. The quarantine zone filled with numerous red dots, a heavy collection of which converged around the center. "I've changed the view to show all known outbreaks—plant, animal, or Alfar—based upon where they were discovered. The map can show any of the three individually or in some combination."

"This is amazing." Nico approached the map. "I'd love to see how you put this together."

Lips drawn in a thin line, Aili continued as if he'd said nothing. "Sensors, cameras, and radars throughout the planet are tied to satellite hubs, which connect with in-orbit satellites. We pull the data from the satellites to develop and populate our databases."

Anand frowned. "How does your equipment identify infected plants and animals versus normal, healthy ones?"

Weariness weighed down Aili's face. "That's part of our problem. We can't."

"How does that help us then?" Maellyn asked. What good were endless images and video if it couldn't help them with the problem?

Aili's eyes narrowed. "As I noted, we have scientists on the ground recording new cases. Additional personnel comb through video and images from each case location to pinpoint time of infection, if possible, and determine what other data we can gather. Perhaps part of your time can be spent reviewing the video and images, if that's not asking too much."

Nico scowled. "You didn't bring us here for data collection."

Maellyn huffed, wishing he was close enough to smack. Why do boys always seem to lack tact?

"Nico," Fintan chided.

"Fintan will be in charge of your assignments," Aili said through gritted teeth. "He'll determine how to best utilize your *abilities*. That said, the database of images and video undergirds our work here. It is vital we track the spread and pinpoint its origin."

Devika gestured at the map. "Wouldn't that be somewhere within that circle?"

Aili shook her head. "The fungus isn't native to the area; there's enough Alfar living nearby that it would've been discovered before now if it was local. We expect it was transported from some remote region, but right now we're not even sure how."

Despite her frustration with Aili, Maellyn tried to put herself in the scientist's shoes. The outbreak was not small and caused extensive damage. The Alfar were having major trouble trying to get it under control, or they wouldn't have asked for outside help. As the lead scientist on Orestes, the bulk of the pressure to fix this was coming down on Aili. Maellyn knew that if she were Aili, after asking for and expecting real help from the best scientists her allies had to offer, she'd feel dejected and let down to see inexperienced students show up. And in the present context, Maellyn felt a little overwhelmed, as she had when Fintan first talked with them. Maybe it had been foolish to think they could contribute in any meaningful manner.

Fintan clasped his upper two hands under his chin. "I want you to think for a few minutes about the information I've given you. What are some questions you have for Aili? She has graciously agreed to share her time with us."

Maellyn pulled her wrist-comp from her holder and started sifting back through the highlights she'd compiled. "There's no previous record of the Azymi before now, right?"

"That's correct." Aili sighed as if this were a waste of her time.

Fintan turned to Maellyn. "What does that tell you?"

Maellyn bit her lip. The increased global temperatures on Ourania had likely made more of the planet hospitable to Azymi, but that wasn't enough information to make educated guesses.

"Maybe it's from a different planet," Anand suggested. "That could be why you don't have a record of it."

"How did it get here?" Nico scoffed. "Fungi aren't interplanetary explorers."

"Could've been brought by a visitor." Anand glowered.

"Impossible!" Aili crossed her arms and looked absolutely certain. "Few visitors from other planets are allowed on Ourania. That's why you're here on Orestes. This is as close as you'll ever get."

"I've heard the Alfar make some exceptions," Fran said, voice hesitant as if she feared a denial.

"Rare exceptions," Aili said, unmollified. "And those allowed on Ourania are subjected to careful decontamination procedures. Nevertheless, we've already ruled out such a possibility."

"Told you." Nico slapped Anand's arm.

Anand gritted his teeth and glared at Nico. "*Maybe* someone snuck onto the planet."

"Ourania is impregnable," Aili insisted. "No one even gets as close as Orestes without our approval."

Maellyn finally shared what she'd been mulling over. "The last few years Ourania's average global temperatures have increased. It stands to reason the increases expanded the range in which the fungus can thrive, allowing it to spread beyond its native habitat. That allows us to rule out the poles or other regions in the higher latitudes."

"Yes," Aili acknowledged. "But even accounting for changes in temperatures over a number of years, that still leaves large regions left to search."

"What solutions are you considering?" Devika asked. "Would hybridization work for the plants?" When Anand gave her a confused frown, she elaborated. "Crossing the genes of one plant with another to develop resistances."

"That requires finding plants resistant to the fungus first," Aili replied. "Nothing in the current quarantine zone has proven resistant, and without knowing its natural habitat, we can't search it for resistant plants."

"Rules out gene therapy, too." Devika crossed her arms and slouched.

"You could try vaccines to treat the Alfar and animals," Trini piped up for the first time.

Aili shook her head, eyes lowered. "That's a long process. We've already had our first death, yesterday, and we expect things to get worse."

"Someone died from the fungus?" Maellyn's stomach dropped. Fungi weren't that strong.

Aili clenched her fists, her face strained. "It came as a shock when it happened."

Fintan also looked shaken by the revelation. No wonder Aili's reception had been so cold. The situation was much more dire than they'd realized.

"We've run simulations." Aili turned back to the map. "Despite our quarantine measures, it's out. She pointed to a few cases outside the red circle that Maellyn had missed earlier. "We expect this to spike as we move into summer. Antifungal vaccines will take far too long to make. We're working on some nevertheless. But we need faster solutions or large numbers of Alfar will die."

For a few minutes, no one said anything. Maellyn studied the digital map, trying to process this. She'd thought they were helping fight a problem that threatened the flora on Ourania. And to keep Alfar and wildlife from getting *sick*. They were now in a battle to save lives. Maybe a lot of lives. Where would they even begin?

Fintan stepped over and placed a hand on Aili's arm. "Please convey condolences for us to those affected."

Aili nodded.

Fintan turned back to them with a grim expression. "Now you know the gravity of the situation. I've already given thought to the work each of you could do based upon your skills."

"I know what I should work on," Nico said, his expression was serious and firm.

Fintan's eyebrows rose in question.

"You said you need help making positive identification of outbreak cases," Nico said. "You need a publicly-accessed site where all the photos and videos can be uploaded and viewed by anyone on Ourania and Space City. If we provide instructions on how to identify infected plants and animals and convince everyone to participate, sifting through the data will become more manageable."

Aili pursed her lips. "That many untrained eyes would make lots of errors. We'd have to recheck everything."

Nico nodded. "I can set up a program to tally the number of positive and negative IDs of each photo or video, increasing the probability of correct answers. That should narrow down what the scientists should review for confirmation."

Maellyn smiled. It was a great idea. She wished they'd had something similar last year when treating the Apidium.

"Momma. Momma." A young Alfar boy entered at full speed. He ran with locked, uncoordinated legs over to Aili and threw his arms around her knees.

"Hello, Alvi." Aili placed a hand on the boy's head. "You're early."

"It's lunch time already," Albrin said as he entered the lab.

"Really?" Aili raised her eyebrows.

Albrin nodded.

Aili grabbed her son's arms and started prying him from her legs, but her whole demeanor had changed, warming. "Alvi, I've got some people for you to meet."

Alvi turned, but pressed his back against his mom's legs, a green toy in his hands. He stared at the floor, but said, "Hi." He possessed the same strawberry-blonde hair as his mother, but it was unruly like Neil's.

Maellyn dropped to her knees. "Hello Alvi, I'm Maellyn."

He looked up for a second, cheeks rosy, with a shy grin. "Hi."

"Alvi, can you tell them how old you are?" Aili asked. She bent down at his side, pointing at them. She gave him an encouraging smile.

"Free," he answered.

"Three," Aili corrected.

"Free," he repeated.

Maellyn pointed at the toy in his hands. "What have you got there?"

"Ep." Alvi held up the little green cloth toy, which looked homemade and reminded her of a cross between a T-Rex and a Stegosaurus.

"Elp," Aili said.

Alvi said the creatures name again slowly, sounding it out.

"Elp is cute." Maellyn pointed at the little toy.

He nodded exaggeratedly. Then his stomach growled.

"Alvi, is Elp hungry?" Aili asked.

He nodded again, clutching Elp to his chest.

Aili turned to Albrin. "Will you lead us to lunch?"

Albrin pointed back at the hover train. "Everyone aboard."

Chapter 16

Neil's Thanksgiving Goes Wrong

"I need a favor," Neil and Maellyn said in unison when she emerged from her dorm, coffee in hand.

He opened his mouth, before processing what Maellyn had said, then shut it again. She also hesitated, eyebrows raising in question.

"Go ahead." He gestured for her to start.

"Dad's on travel to Sundara." She shivered and pulled her thick gray coat tighter. "He's missing Thanksgiving, so will you join me instead?"

His shoulders relaxed and he smiled. He'd received an email that morning from grandpa announcing he'd be back soon and requesting they spend Thanksgiving together. Neil knew a serious discussion between them was coming, but he wasn't ready. Having her along would postpone it. "I was about to ask you the same thing."

She hooked an arm through his left. "I figured it'd work since your grandpa's traveling."

They strolled toward the Academy Games stadium. He had practice in thirty minutes and she planned to study in the stands. Afterward, dinner.

"Actually, grandpa'll be back. He'd love to see you. I was hoping you'd join us."

"Wonderful!" Her face beamed. "At your grandpa's place?"

He chuckled. "I don't think grandpa is quite the cook you and your dad are. I'm thinking a restaurant."

"We should invite Riagan," she suggested.

"You're right," he agreed. Why hadn't he thought of that sooner? The holiday would be hard on Riagan, considering he'd spent every previous one with Rois since their parents' deaths. The Irish didn't celebrate Thanksgiving in Ireland, but they two had expanded their tradition to the holidays celebrated aboard Space City. He shouldn't be alone.

"We'll have to make him come."

She was right. Riagan would prefer to stew in the dorms. "I'll handle it," he said.

A chilly breeze hit as they reached the field between campus and the stadium, finding every exposed bit of skin. He shivered and wished he'd worn a jacket, instead of a long sleeve shirt underneath his Ursa uniform.

Picking up the pace a little, he asked, "How is the Alfar outbreak project going?"

She huffed and shook her head. "I'd thought solving the Apidium problem last year was challenging. But we knew plenty about the disease, even if it had mutated and jumped species. We simply had to adapt. With the Azymi fungus, we know little to nothing. It's not a mutation of anything known. In fact, it has little in common with other fungi on Ourania. We're starting from scratch.

"On top of that, the lead Alfar scientist will only communicate with Fintan. She's not happy students are involved."

He frowned, craning his neck to look at her. "Didn't the Alfar ask for your help?"

"Not our help. She wanted Dad and other scientists. She thinks the Council sending students is a slap in the face."

"That'll make it more satisfying when you solve the problem."

She smiled and squeezed his arm.

"Is that thanks for the encouragement, or because it's cold out?" he asked.

She laughed lightly. "Both."

They passed through the arched gateway entrance to the stadium and toward the tunnel leading to the field.

"We'll have to keep dinner short tonight," she said. "I've got too many pictures and videos to search through."

"Would you like help?"

She pulled away right before the tunnel, prepared to head up the stairs to the stands. "You don't want to waste your evening doing that."

"Really," he insisted. "I was looking for a reason to procrastinate studying for a test."

She stepped forward, head tilted up to look at him. "Are you sure?"

"Yeah. I'll always prefer an evening with you, no matter what we're doing." He placed his hands on her shoulders, suddenly wishing practice had been cancelled.

She remained looking up at him, waiting. He leaned forward and kissed her, thrilled at the soft massage from her lips. And her hands lightly pressed against his chest. When she stepped back he kept his hands on her shoulders, wanting to pull her back to him, to kiss her again.

"You have to get to practice," she said, voice a whisper.

"I can be a few minutes late."

But she placed a finger on his chest and nudged. "You better go. And I have to study. I'll see you afterward."

He sighed as she turned and started up the stairs.

*****

Neil and Maellyn pressed through the crowds in the city. Street vendors on all sides shouted out holiday specials. Between two nearby oaks, an upside-down glass fountain hovered over water shooting up into it. A hologram above the fountain advertised Rory's Weird and Unexplainable.

One vendor possessed a giant, transparent balloon, more than twenty feet tall and at least that again wide, which floated above the square. The balloon was filled with hawks, eels, toads, tortoises, and a variety of other creatures all composed from a rainbow of colored gases. The vendor sold the gaseous creatures as exotic pets.

Neil wondered what it would be like to own a pet composed entirely of gas. Couldn't keep it in a pen. What would one eat? Of course, he already had a pet, which Maellyn kept for him. Maybe they could swing by after dinner to see Petey.

An older Murgin bumped into Neil. "Pardon me, sir. How 'bout some smoked anchovies?"

The Murgin had light purple scales—obviously dyed—from head to the bottoms of his four legs. A half dozen gold hoop earrings adorned the gills on both sides of his face.

"None for us." Neil waved away the Murgin, not wanting to get held up.

"I've got a special for Thanksgiving." The Murgin stepped sideways to a cart and opened the lid with a tentacled hand, while scooping out a small tray containing a dozen cooked anchovies. "They are twelve for ten credits."

If the Murgin had been selling butternells, Neil might've been tempted, but not anchovies. "Another time," he said as he spotted grandpa through the crowd.

He and Maellyn hurried forward, dodging a couple young Traga swiftly sliding past. Even after a year and a half onboard Space City, it was a little unsettling to see a Traga bearing down on you. It was like standing in the path of a wildfire, albeit at milder temperatures. They could crank up the heat some, though. Once the Traga had passed, Neil crossed the space to his grandpa.

"Maellyn, you look lovely as ever." Grandpa gave her a quick hug.

"Thank you, Mr. Ericson," she replied. "Glad you're home."

Grandpa smiled before giving Neil a nod. "Should be my last task off Space City for a while. Hoping to see my grandson a little more."

Neil returned the nod. "Finals are in two weeks, then a month of winter break." He decided not to mention that he hoped to spend a good bit of that time either training for the second half of their games season or with Maellyn.

"You mentioned Riagan joining us?" Grandpa looked over their heads, surveying the crowd.

"He said he'd meet us here." Neil turned to look as well, wondering if he should've insisted on coming from campus with Riagan. "Should be here shortly." He hoped Riagan wouldn't blow them off.

"Sure," Grandpa agreed.

Vendors with carts filled much of the square. One advertised powder blue stone necklaces and bracelets from Sundara. Neil spotted the butternell lady. It took all his self-control not to buy some this instant. Hopefully, she'd still be out there in a couple hours when they finished eating. His mouth watered at the thought of the butterscotch-filled pastries, warm and fresh. He'd treat Maellyn.

His wrist-comp chimed that he'd received a message. He checked. It was from Riagan. Pulling it up, he read. *Running late. Meet you in the restaurant.* Neil decided to take that as a good sign. Being late wasn't the end of the world as long as he came.

Sharing the news with grandpa and Maellyn, Neil gestured down the road toward the restaurant. "Shall we head up to Xanders?"

Maellyn marched forward. "Let's go. I'm starving."

All the 3D images along the skyscrapers' balconies for the various vendors on each level were decorated in fall colors and holiday themes. Cartoonish turkeys. Pumpkins. Brown, red, and gold leaves. Cornucopias. Pies. Ears of corn and stalks of wheat. Numerous alien foods and symbols, many of which Neil didn't know the name. The street fair would be filled until the late hours with shoppers and revelers celebrating and spending large amounts of money on the vendors' wares.

They crowded into an already full elevator. On the way up, they stopped at several floors, forcing them to shift around to make room for people to get off and others to jump on. Neil started to sweat in the confined space, so he hoped he wouldn't smell during dinner. It was a relief when they emerged to the cool evening air on a balcony.

"Neil! Maellyn!" Nico squeezed through the crowd toward them, eyes shining. "Are you headed to Xanders?" His portly father, Mr. Colombo, tried to keep up.

"Yes. Having dinner with grandpa and Maellyn," Neil said. "And Riagan is joining us."

"May we join you then?" Mr. Colombo asked, addressing his question to grandpa.

"Of course. More the merrier," Grandpa replied.

Xanders was a glamorous seafood and steak restaurant. Everything on the menu came from foreign planets. Abstract-patterned art pieces decorated the champagne-colored walls, and the silver and copper floor tiles fitted together in random arrangements like puzzle pieces. A couple of large fish tanks held aquatic creatures that reminded Neil of pictures he'd seen of Earth's prehistoric past.

A blonde hostess in a copper top led them back to a table for six. "Can I get all of you something to drink?"

"Purple melon punch, please," Maellyn said as she sat.

"I'll take one, too." Neil chose the seat next to her, noticing as he pulled out the chair that its back design resembled a gothic-style trident; Riagan would appreciate it.

The rest spread out around the table.

"Make it three," Nico added.

The waitress turned to grandpa.

He ran his finger down the menu, scanning a moment. "Space City Stout, please. And a water."

"Merlot for me," Mr. Colombo requested.

Their waiter, an older boy with shoulder length black hair, stopped by to introduce himself, drop off a sliced loaf of pumpernickel, and promised their drinks would arrive momentarily. Mr. Colombo pulled the bread plate over and removed a slice before offering the plate to Neil.

"What held up Riagan?" Nico asked.

Neil accepted the bread plate from Mr. Colombo and took a slice for himself and started to butter it. "He was training this afternoon. Probably lost track of time."

At least that's what Riagan had said. But it worried Neil how single-minded Riagan had become about spying. Riagan was barely attending class anymore, just those he enjoyed. Battle Tactics for example. He'd even missed a couple of Taurus practices, and he loved the Games.

"How's he doing?" Grandpa asked, brow furrowed in concern. "Does he talk about Rois at all?"

Neil bit into the pumpernickel bread, giving himself a minute to consider how to answer. The bread was hot, the melted butter soaked into it. "He's training hard all the time. We both do after last year."

Riagan did discuss Rois quite a bit, but not in the way grandpa meant. It was all focused on Riagan's plans to avenge her death. Neil couldn't blame him. If Maellyn had died in the attack on Mars, too, Neil would've done the same. But he also couldn't say any of this. Couldn't share his work for Guiman, even though it would make everything a lot easier if he could. He understood Guiman's reasons for secrecy, but as he sat at the table surrounded by Maellyn, grandpa, even Nico, his silence felt duplicitous.

Fortunately, the waiter returned with their drinks, saving him from further questioning. "Are you waiting on one more, or do you want to order?"

Everyone looked at Neil. He hesitated, unsure what to say.

"This seat for me?" Riagan appeared, pulling back the empty end chair.

"Riagan!" Maellyn rose to give him a quick hug.

"Sorry I'm late," Riagan said. "Needed a quick shower after training. Figured ye'd prefer not to smell me the whole meal."

"You're not late at all." Grandpa offered Riagan the bread plate.

"I'm glad you're here." Neil felt relief well up inside him. Despite the earlier message, a part of him had feared Riagan would bow out last minute. It was good to see him out in a casual setting, as opposed to on a mission.

Riagan placed a hand on Neil's shoulder and squeezed. "Wouldn't miss it once I learned how much food is involved. Turkey, yams and mashed potatoes, cranberry sauce, stuffing, green bean casserole, and more pies than ya can count. Ya'd have to be mad to miss all this."

Nico pointed at himself. "Choir."

Neil could tell Riagan was feigning his joviality, at least a little, but the fact that he was trying was a good sign.

They gave their orders to the waiter. Everyone chose the Thanksgiving special.

"How are classes going?" Grandpa asked once the waiter had gone.

Riagan grabbed another slice of bread. "Great! Missed a few, but Neil keeps me up-to-date. I pay him back with candy Nico smuggles in."

Mr. Colombo chuckled at that. "You let me know if there's anything Nico doesn't have, and I'll get it to you. Special order."

"I haven't had any chocolate planets in a while," Maellyn said before sipping her purple melon punch.

Mr. Colombo pointed toward Xanders' entrance. "Come to the Caramella after dinner. All of you. Anything you want. It's on me."

"Thanks!" Neil said. Peanut butter fudge would be great.

"Come on, Dad." Nico feigned sorrow. "You're killing my profit margin."

Neil hadn't calculated how much of his earnings—Instructor Tereshkova paid for help with her animal charges—went to Nico, but he was positive he was doing his part to keep the candy black market operating.

Mr. Colombo waved a pointed finger, as if he were lecturing. "Gotta treat your best customers every now and again. They're your best word of mouth. Never forget that."

Nico rolled his eyes, but he was smiling.

The waiter returned with steaming dishes of Cajun smoked turkey, mashed with gravy, corn casserole, mac and cheese, and a number of other sides, spreading them out in the center of the table so everyone seated could dish out helpings onto their plates. Neil was a little disappointed the waiter hadn't brought any pies yet, but those would come after the main course.

"So Riagan, what have you been up to, besides Games training?" Maellyn asked. She took a bite of her turkey.

Neil's stomach lurched.

Riagan shoveled a scoop of mashed potatoes into his mouth and swallowed, before answering. "Mostly training with Headmaster Dardanos. Run errands for him. Deliver messages. Stuff like that."

"What sort of messages?" Grandpa asked, wiping a little gravy off his chin. "I thought everyone sent messages electronically these days?"

Riagan shrugged. "I guess sometimes a written message is easier than making our technology compatible with alien tech. Or convincing them to use ours. But it's all pretty boring. Nothing like the project Nico and Maellyn are working on."

Grandpa opened his mouth to ask more, but Neil quickly assisted Riagan's change of topic. "Nico, Maellyn mentioned you're setting up a site where you can post photos and videos from the Ourania outbreak for people to tag. How's that working out?"

Nico set his fork down and rubbed his hands together. "We're putting together two separate sites, one here in Space City and a second on Orestes. All pics and videos will be duplicated on both sites."

"And we can look at the photos and videos for signs of the fungus?"

Nico nodded. "Each pic you see, you choose *yes* if you spot the Azymi fungus, or *no* if everything looks normal. All the pics are hi-res and you can zoom in on any part. You can also circle what you think is the Azymi in a pic."

"It'll make our lives so much easier," Maellyn said. "Right now I'm having to search them all and record what I find manually."

A crumble of stuffing slipped off Neil's fork onto the napkin in his lap. He brushed it away, hoping no one noticed.

Maellyn leaned in close. "Saw that slob." Her lips were curled into a teasing smile.

Heat rose up his face as he gave her a chagrined smile.

Meanwhile, Nico kept on with the features of his new project. "The program tallies up votes for each picture. It'll allow the scientists to prioritize footage.

"But once we've got both up and running, we still have to combine results with those on Orestes. From there, the hope is we can better set the quarantine zone. And also gauge dense zones. Unfortunately, we can't transmit the data through space. It'd take too long to reach Orestes."

"So transport it through a thorneway." Riagan waved his fork in the air, as if conjuring up a thorneway over the table.

Nico looked pained, like Riagan stole his thunder. "That's true, but we can't keep a dedicated thorneway open all the time."

"Can't our scientists review the results here and provide the findings to the Alfar?" Mr. Colombo asked. "Rather than transmit everything."

"We'll have some of that," Nico agreed.

"You're working this project, too?" Grandpa eyed Maellyn. "What're you doing?"

She swallowed and cleared her throat. "Mostly reviewing reports. So far they're refusing to let us examine any contaminated plants or infected animals firsthand."

Neil paused with a fork halfway to his mouth. "Why?"

"They're treating us like children," Nico piped in.

Grandpa grimaced.

"I'm basically checking for data errors," Maellyn said.

Neil knew that wouldn't satisfy her. She wanted to get her own specimens, study their composition, and help find a cure. And if the Alfar didn't appreciate her abilities, it would be to their detriment.

"Don't underestimate verifying their work." Grandpa took a swig of his beer, then tipped the half full glass toward Maellyn. "Consider the pressure the Alfar scientists are under. They've got a fungus they've never seen before. Spreading unchecked. They're working as hard and as fast as they can for answers. They're bound to make mistakes. By checking their work, you're ensuring they don't go down a wrong path based upon false data."

"I know it matters. I just hoped to do more." Maellyn picked at her food.

"When Nico and I still lived on Torcello Island," Mr. Colombo leaned back in his chair, "—I had this one apprentice, Marcello. Not much older than all of you. He'd worked with his dad as a fisherman. Knew nothing about working in a kitchen. Couldn't tell a meat cleaver from a paring knife.

"And every day he came in wearing pants that were too long, so that he frayed the back legs which would catch under the heels of his shoes, but all he had were old pairs from his pa or other fisherman.

"A month after Marcello arrived, we learned a bishop from Venice was visiting. I was tasked with preparing the meal for his visit. As you can imagine, I didn't get the chance to cook for a lot of important visitors. I spent a week debating which dishes I wanted to serve—Risi e Bisi, Baccala mantecato, and of course my own Tiramisu—and we started to cook.

"Now, I always get fresh cod for my Baccala mantecato. I asked Marcello to strip the skin off the cod, but he grabbed a paring knife and starts butchering it up. He's halfway through my cod before I realize it all looks like mangled haircuts.

"At this point it's an hour before markets close, and the bishop was arriving the next day. A holiday. Markets would be closed. I sent Marcello to buy more. He goes racing out the door, and I swear wasn't six steps down the alley before his pants catch on his shoes and he face plants in a muddy puddle." Mr. Colombo shook his head at the memory of it.

"Marcello springs back to his feet, rubbing his face clean on his sleeve, and rushes off once more. I'm now half afraid what condition the cod will be in when the boy returns, but I've got a kitchen full of food that needs preparing. We're expecting more than one hundred guests in all for the bishop's visit.

"Two hours later, Marcello still hasn't returned from the market. I'm starting to sweat now because the market has closed and there's no second trips if the boy failed. After three hours, I'm cursing up a storm and desperately devising an alternate dish to prepare. Four hours later, Marcello strolls in with lines of fresh caught sea bass over his shoulder.

"I asked him where was my cod? He replies, 'The market was out.' Instead, Marcello had sought out his father's old mates and asked for help. In no time they had caught enough sea bass, an acceptable substitute, to meet our needs.

"I shook my head and got him cleaning the sea bass, but I wasn't about to let him hack it up, too. So I set him on mixing the ingredients for my tiramisu while I prepped the fish.

"The next day, we've got all the food ready for the bishop's visit. All the guests were in the hall, and we started to serve. Everyone was pleased.

"Then came the tiramisu. We set the dessert plates before the guests. Everyone takes a bite, and one by one, along all the tables, the guests start coughing. Everyone's reaching for their waters.

"Groaning to myself, trying to figure out what Marcello could've messed up with the tiramisu, I check with the closest guest. Instead of topping the tiramisu with cocoa powder, Marcello had used chili powder, and with a heavy hand." Mr. Colombo shook his head, chuckling to himself.

"At that point my chest starts killing me. I think I'm about to die, but I try to reach the bishop anyway. I yell at Marcello to get the bishop's dessert plate before he eats any. Wide-eyed, Marcello darts forward, but before he reaches the table his pants catch on his shoes *again*. The boy flops forward, this time face planting in the tiramisu. His hand knocks a martini glass, spraying its contents into the bishop's face, before the boy lands in the bishop's lap.

"The bishop splutters in shock. And as I near them, I hear Marcello say, *Forgive me father for you're wearing gin.*"

The whole table burst out laughing. Tears ran down Neil's cheeks. Riagan doubled over, his food forgotten. It was the first time Neil had seen him laughing in a long while. They got dirty looks from a couple of other tables, but Neil didn't mind.

Maellyn dabbed at her eyes with a napkin. "Just to clarify, am I Marcello in this story? Pointing out my inexperience might hurt instead of help?"

Mr. Colombo sipped his wine. "We all make mistakes. The best and the newest. Aili may not know she needs your help, but she'll thank you for it later. I promise."

Neil dabbed away the tears from his eyes from laughing and noticed his grandpa doing the same.

Riagan leaned over to Neil, his wrist-comp in hand. His face had hardened, his ears reddening. He had a message from Cade.

Checked on status of Adrien Laroque. Editor asked me to find out if there were any changes to report. Found Patrick standing guard, or so he said. He's keeping tabs on Adrien.

"Probably waiting for an opportunity to finish the job," Riagan whispered. "Ya hear the academy cleared him? He's getting away with it."

Neil couldn't think of a good response or even how to feel. They'd seen Patrick weasel his way out of trouble on numerous occasions. But was he that same person or the one who'd apologized earlier in the year? Patrick could simply be there keeping tabs on his friend. Neil wasn't planning to trust him with anything any time soon, but he also refused to get worked up when they didn't know the truth. He had serious misgivings about the belief that Patrick would harm Adrien, one of his few real friends.

As they finished up dinner, Nico pulled out small yellow bags, the ones he and his father wrapped candy in, and handed one to each of them.

"What are these?" Maellyn asked.

"Open them." Nico grinned.

Neil untwisted the tie and opened the bag to find a pair of cookies inside. He pulled one out. It was still warm. "Are these fresh from the oven?"

"New bags I bought for special purposes." Mr. Colombo wore a pleased smile. "They keep things warmed or chilled for a few hours."

"What kind of cookies are they?" Maellyn asked.

"Try them," Nico urged.

Neil hesitated, remembering Nico's prank with the aqua bombers during their trial sim at the beginning of the year. But Nico wouldn't risk his business with pranks.

Neil bit into his cookie and was pleased to find it was chocolate chip; all the chips hidden in the middle. As he chewed, the chocolate melting in his mouth, he looked closer at the center. His name was spelled out inside it.

"How did you do that?" Neil held his cookie with his name toward Nico.

"Oh, mine, too." Maellyn showed hers, with her name written in the middle.

"I 3D printed them. Right before dinner." Nico bubbled in his chair.

Neil shook his head. "No way. You can do that? That's amazing!" Every time he thought he'd gotten used to everything that could be done with 3D printing, something new and incredible popped up. And they tasted fresh baked, reminding him of his mother's cookies.

Maellyn cocked her head a little. "Nico, we weren't supposed to have dinner with you tonight. How did you know you'd run into us?"

"I didn't." Nico removed several more bags from his pack. "I'd made several for friends. Was planning to take them back to campus tonight, but I figured why wait. Sorry, Mr. Ericson. I didn't know I'd see you."

Grandpa waved dismissively, wiping his face with his napkin. "That's quite all right."

Neil removed his second cookie from the bag and offered it. "Take my second."

"I don't need it." Grandpa leaned back in his chair, patting his belly. "I'm already off my diet having this meal tonight. Better not push it."

Neil was glad he didn't have to worry about such things as he finished off the first cookie. He'd eat the second and still get butternells when they left. And never gain a pound. As hard as they trained for the Games and with Dardanos, he often ate extra.

Chapter 17

Riagan Breaks Protocol

"We need a mission. Anywhere." Riagan sat up, kicking his feet off the side of his bed and tossed his wrist-comp onto the desk. "I've got to get out of here."

A week into winter break, and he'd had enough of doing nothing. Guiman hadn't sent them on a mission in more than a month. All he'd say was that they were monitoring the scientists at Olsin Pedran, waiting for actionable intel. Nor had Dardanos had any spare time for training. Even Taurus practices were cancelled until the new year.

Neil lay sprawled out on his own bed, tagging pictures on his wrist-comp for Maellyn. "You can help me if you want."

Riagan's expression soured. "Let's check in with Guiman. There must be something we could do."

"You go ahead." Neil didn't look up from his work.

"Fine." Riagan hopped off the bed, grabbed his jacket from the closet, and departed.

Outside, the ship had already rotated away from the sun, the night shade covering the skyline. A few classmates lounged on the grassy hills in the central courtyard, chatting as they stared up at the stars. Riagan headed north toward Guiman's place. As he reached the edge of the courtyard, he spotted movement off to his left. He turned to see someone duck behind a nearby building. Riagan frowned. Was someone following him?

It was probably his imagination, but he doubled back anyway. A familiar head peeked out from behind the building.

"Caleb?" Riagan went from puzzled to angry in an instant. "Why are ya following me?"

Caleb emerged, eyes narrowed. "What are you doing sneaking around at night?"

"I amn't sneaking. I'm walking."

"Where you headed?"

Riagan marched forward until he stood toe-to-toe with Caleb. "Into the city. We're on break. I'm bored."

"You know I'm going to figure out what you and Neil are up to." Caleb clenched his fists, not backing down.

"Why do ya care?" Riagan fantasized pounding Caleb to get rid of him, but too many people were still hanging out in the courtyard. He didn't need that kind of trouble.

Caleb's expression turned sly. "You two have taken extra care to hide what you're doing. You don't want anyone knowing. Even the instructors. So it can't be anything good, despite your and Neil's holier-than-thou attitudes. Once I figure it out, I can decide what to do with it. Perhaps an anonymous tip to Headmaster Dardanos."

Riagan burst out laughing. It so surprised Caleb that he took an uncertain step backward. Riagan's shoulders relaxed, all the tension draining out of him. Caleb knew nothing despite his efforts. "Ya won't learn anything following me tonight."

With that, Riagan marched back to his room on the second floor. This hiding from Caleb was absurd, and beyond annoying, but he wasn't going to fail Guiman on something so simple. When he reached his room, he glanced back to see Caleb still following him. Caleb entered his own room, but left the door wide open, making it clear he hadn't given up. Riagan opened the door to his room, entered, and slammed it shut.

Neil jumped, casting him a startled look.

Riagan jerked a thumb over his shoulder. "Caleb followed me. Came back to get help ditching him."

"Again?" Neil's eyes flashed.

"Will ya help me? Create a diversion or something."

Neil nodded at their window. "Why make it complicated? Just climb out."

Riagan covered his eyes with his hands at his own stupidity. It was too simple. He should've thought of it. After Caleb's falling out with Patrick, he'd moved across the hall. His window opened up to the courtyard. Riagan marched over to the window and raised it, then slapped Neil on the shoulder. "Take a break. Chances are Guiman will have nothing. We'll hike out and back. Maybe grab a bite in the mess hall. Or head into the city. Gotta be something interesting to do."

Neil stared at his wrist-comp, biting his lip. After a moment's hesitation, he dropped the wrist-comp on his bed. "Yeah, sure. I could use something to eat. Let's go." He stood up and headed over to the door, locking it.

Climbing up onto his desk, Riagan stuck his head out the window and looked for signs of anyone, but the street behind the dorm was empty. He also checked Patrick's window, three rooms down, to make sure he wasn't watching. Despite Caleb's claims that he and Patrick weren't hanging out anymore, he wasn't buying it. But the curtains were drawn.

Shuffling onto the windowsill, Riagan lowered himself out the window, then let go and landed on his feet, dropping to a crouch. A lot smoother exit than when they'd fallen out of Patrick and Caleb's window last year. A second later, Neil landed beside him. Then they slipped away. Too easy. If only all their missions were solved this simply.

It took them fifteen minutes to reach Guiman's house. Riagan knocked. He shivered and rubbed his arms, wishing he'd brought a jacket.

Guiman answered the door, mug in hand, a frown on his face until he realized it was them. "What are you doing here boys? He stood back to let them enter."

Riagan pushed past him. "We hadn't heard from ya in a while. Any new developments?"

The old man chuckled and closed the door behind them. He ambled into his kitchen and refilled his mug with coffee. "I wish I did, but the scientists haven't had any more contact with Ragna, at least via hologram."

"So, no recorded contacts?" Riagan asked. After all that trouble he'd gone through to plant recording devices.

"None so far." Guiman returned to his chair in his makeshift living room, which had only room for one other chair and an end table.

"And the Council?" Neil leaned against a wall. "Why are they stopping us from going after Mainyu?"

Riagan pursed his lips, unhappy they hadn't told Neil, even if he understood the reasoning.

Guiman took a sip from his coffee, then set it on the end table. "I've asked why they've sidelined us on that, but I can't get an answer. If I press, they remind me that I work for them."

Neil threw up his hands in exasperation. "What reason could they possibly have for stopping us from going after Mainyu? He's the number one threat to Space City. To all of us."

Guiman shook his head and sighed. "I can't come up with a rational explanation for this. Even knowing the Dahaka may all be wiped out with their planet deteriorating. Certainly nothing ethical or right."

"Must be something we can do," Riagan said, anxious not to head back to the mess hall, despite the offer to Neil. "Some lead."

Guiman retrieved his cane and hoisted himself back to his feet. "I don't, but you two could head back to Siavash. There's a new Azios tournament."

"Are ya sure?" Riagan's heart jumped. Of course he'd love an opportunity to watch the tournament!

Guiman nodded and gestured toward the thorneway, taking steps toward it. "Of course. Go on. Enjoy yourselves."

"I don't know." Neil rubbed the back of his head. "I've been trying to help Maellyn with checking photos of the outbreak."

"Come on," Riagan said, following Guiman to the thorneway. "Maellyn has a team working with her. She can deal without ya for a few hours. How can ya pass up watching the Azios battle each other?"

Neil remained rooted near the door.

"How about this?" Guiman opened the keypad for the thorneway and typed in the code to activate it. "Make a sweep of the capital while you're there. You should have a little more freedom with everyone focused on the tournament. We still need to find the hidden base where they store their ships."

"Sounds perfect." Riagan held out both hands. "What do ya say, Neil?"

The eagerness was evident in Neil's eyes. "All right, let's go."

"We're going!" Riagan clapped Neil on the back.

With the thorneway activated, Riagan practically skipped over to it. As he entered the thorneway, it prickled every inch of his skin. He opened his mouth to groan, but inside the thorneway there was nothing to transmit the sound from his lungs to his ears. Nor could he see anything. It was as if he'd stepped into a vast nothing—he wasn't even standing on ground. Two heartbeats, amplified like a boxer punching his ribcage from the inside, and he emerged onto the pathway leading up to Guiman's cave on Siavash.

Neil exited a second behind him and deactivated the thorneway. Riagan toggled on the flashlight app on his wrist-comp and rushed up the tunnel toward the cave. They were getting to watch the Azios battles without interruption. No real mission. Just a few hours of fun observing the deadliest warriors in the Universe. What could be more fun?

A quick flash of movement alerted Riagan that something wasn't right as he entered the cave. He tried to halt, heart lurching at the unexpected presence, but something slammed into the back of his head, sending him sprawling to the floor. He lay there, thoughts spiraling. Rough hands jerked him to his feet. He tried to open his mouth to protest. A second blow, this time to the side of his head, sent him plummeting into darkness.

*****

Riagan woke to a tapping sound. His head ached and he had no desire to rise. His dry mouth felt as if someone had dumped powder down his throat. The tapping was rhythmic. "Neil, cut that out." What could Neil be doing to make that noise?

"You okay?" Neil asked, voice strained.

"I feel like crap." His senses started processing the hard ground beneath him, rocks cutting into his back and legs. The air was cool, with a dampness to it. And the smell, like the stadium locker room after practice. None of it fit their room. More like—

The tunnel on Siavash.

Riagan's eyes flew open and he tried to sit up. His stomach pitched. He slumped back, breathing deeply to keep from puking. He and Neil had planned to catch the Azios tournament. Someone had been in the cave. They'd been attacked.

"We were captured," Neil said. "The Dahaka threw us in a cell."

He sat against a stone wall, tapping his grandfather's coin on bars that sealed them in. Minimal light lit their cell, which resembled a side pocket in a cavern. Numerous cells lined the cavern, holding prisoners. In the center of the room were cages which held a variety of animals. It was eerily quiet except for muted cheers that indicated they were near the Azios tournament arena.

"Do ya have any water?" Riagan asked. Even a single gulp would be a blessing.

"Maybe you can lick the stones behind you. They're wet. Not sure where the water comes from."

"Skunk sack," Riagan spat at him. "How did they discover us?"

Neil grunted. "Ambushed us in Guiman's cave. Obviously discovered it was a hideout."

Four Dahaka guards entered the cave. Two opened a nearby cell door and hauled out a prisoner. The second pair inserted long poles with a taut loop on each end through an opening in another cage containing a hairless, yellow and black-striped beast. It pressed against the rear of its cage and snapped at the poles. Its muzzle was streaked with blood from where it had been chewing its cage, trying to escape.

It took the guards thirty seconds or so to ring the loops around the beast's neck. One opened the cage. The beast sprang forward, on the attack, but the poles they clung to kept them out of harm's reach. They muscled the snarling beast through the same door the previous guards had dragged the prisoner.

"What now?" Neil resumed tapping the cage. One of the other prisoners shouted at him to cut it out.

Riagan shrugged. "Why're ya asking me?"

"Oh, I don't know. Maybe cause you're the one that got us into this mess."

Riagan eyed the wet wall behind him, tempted by the grit in his mouth to lick it to get some kind of moisture.

"Any time would be great," Neil prompted

Riagan felt the heat rising around his ears, as if someone was using a blow dryer on them. "I didn't make ya come."

"I wanted to stay in the dorms. I had work to do, but you pushed me."

"Take responsibility for ya actions." Riagan rubbed a hand on the wet wall and sniffed it to see if it was water. He couldn't quite tell.

"Yes, everyone else take responsibility because you sure won't." Neil slammed his arm against the bars. A second prisoner shouted he'd gut both of them if they didn't cut out the noise. For a response, Neil raised his legs and kicked the bars repeatedly, while shouting, "I should've let you come alone."

"Really? Ya wish ya'd let me get captured alone?" After all they'd been through, the admission shocked him.

Several of the other prisoners shouted curses at them.

"No." Neil grabbed the bars in both hands and shook them, before staring at the ground. "No, I don't wish you were in this alone. But I wish we'd just gone to the mess hall. Or into the city."

A hiss and the sudden appearance of a Kali caused Neil to shout with surprise and scramble backward on hands and feet from the cage. Riagan flinched, causing a needle of pain to shoot through his head. He felt nauseous again.

A whistle, like wind through a pipe. The Kali was Sverog. It took Riagan a moment to realize that the whistling was the Kali speaking to them. Riagan felt his ear, but the tradutor was gone. Either the Dahaka had found it or it'd been knocked out during the attack.

"We don't know what you're saying." Neil pointed a finger at his ear and shook his head.

Sverog removed a box, from where Riagan didn't know, and handed it to Neil. Riagan forced himself to his feet, ignoring the complaints from his stomach and head. He walked over to Neil, who was pulling something from the box. A pair of tradutors.

Neil took one and handed the box over. Riagan removed the tradutor and slipped it into his ear.

"I've alerted Guiman to your capture," Sverog said in a hushed tone. "He should have a plan to get you out soon."

Riagan pointed at him. "Can't ya let us out?"

"I couldn't get you out of here safely. I'd only blow my cover."

"We've been captured by the Dahaka and you're worried about a blown cover?" Neil half-shouted.

Sverog hissed again. "Keep it down. There's nothing I can do. I'll let you know when I receive instructions from Guiman." With that he drifted away.

"Wait," Riagan called after the Kali. "Do ya have water?"

Surely Sverog could manage that much. Perhaps a little food. But the Kali exited without a response.

"Jeanie Mac." Riagan slammed his open palms against the bars. Neil had taken a seat once more.

His stomach still upset, Riagan decided there was nothing he could do for the time being. Maybe he could at least sleep a little more. Clear his head. Be ready to move when Guiman came to rescue them.

Chapter 18

Maellyn Endures

Maellyn fought back a yawn and sipped her mocha as she entered Fintan's lab. Nico was ready for his picture-checking site, OutSleuth, to go live and Fintan had requested an eight a.m. update from everyone. She had worked on the gene insertion models with Trini and Fran until three last night. She'd debated staying up at that point, but had to take rest where she could get it these days.

While waiting for the others, she checked her messages. Nothing from Neil. He'd been searching through pics and videos for her, but hadn't turned in any findings. He'd promised them yesterday and hadn't even let her know he'd be late delivering anything. Probably too busy running around with Riagan. Couldn't he see how much she needed his help? Didn't he know the pressure she was under?

Fran and Trini stumbled into the lab, the latter's hair tied back in a ponytail to disguise that she hadn't done anything with it in days. Fran wore a new teal blouse, but those jeans were the same from yesterday, not that Maellyn could judge either of them. The only reason she had anything clean to wear today was because her dad had brought a suitcase full of clothes yesterday that their android butler, Charlie, had washed; she owed Charlie the next Space City Retribution graphic novel—he'd been collecting the series from the beginning. Every time a new novel neared release, Charlie would send her and her father a dozen messages each with a description of the new plotline and the release date. Plus, he'd find particularly difficult or tedious chores—by human standards—that needed doing, complete the tasks and send pictures. Charlie kept the novels on his own shelf in the pantry, which he obsessively dusted. He'd read each new novel once through before it took its place next to its companions on the shelf, then re-read eBook-copies countless times so he wouldn't wear out his prized collection. The latest graphic novel was set to release this weekend.

"I'm beginning to have nightmares of this lab." Trini slumped onto a table, her forehead wrinkled as if nursing a headache. Maellyn certainly had one.

Fran dropped onto the table beside Trini, leaning into her. "I'm here so much awake or asleep I'm having trouble telling the difference."

Fintan and the boys strolled into the lab, the instructor with a big smile on his face. "Good morning ladies. Let me get Aili holo-conferenced in and we can get started."

Maellyn got a whiff of Nico or Anand, she wasn't sure which, as they passed by. She resolved to order that graphic novel for Charlie as soon as the meeting ended. He was a lifesaver.

Nico hurried to the rear of the room, casting his wrist-comp onto the wall screen, while Anand carried an ordinary box that held small devices the size of diamonds. Both boys bubbled with energy. They'd probably gone to bed at a reasonable hour and slept soundly, no concern for the late hours Trini, Fran, and herself kept while helping to stop the outbreak. Boys. Likely believed they were doing the important work of the group, too.

Cade slipped into the room, wrist-comp in one hand and a brown bag in the other. He spotted Maellyn, and shuffled over. "Hey cousin. How's the project coming?"

"Okay at the moment. What're you doing? Don't you have a Game to cover?" Maellyn elbowed him playfully.

He held out his hands expansively. "Fintan asked my editor for a write-up to inform students about your new OutSleuths program. Get them involved. I wanted to expand beyond covering the Games, so I volunteered for the assignment. Was hoping you'd give me the inside scoop."

She chortled. "I doubt you'll find any of this exciting enough to be a scoop."

"Well, I came prepared to bribe if necessary." He handed her the bag.

She took the bag and peeked inside. Two butternells. She pinched off a bite, still warm, and tossed it in her mouth. It was fresh, and she knew that it had come from Ms. Lillith at the Street Fair. No one else made butternells as good as hers.

"Good bribe."

He beamed at her. "I know you."

"Good morning, Aili," Fintan greeted.

A hologram of the Alfar scientist appeared in the center of the room. "Good morning," she said brusquely.

"I wanted to provide an update." Fintan gestured to where Nico waited with details of his site pulled up on the wall screen. "The team has made a lot of progress since we met."

Aili crossed her arms and said nothing.

"We're ready for OutSleuth to go live." Nico beamed. "I fixed the bugs in the picture marking function; changed some of the coding. We're ready to launch as soon as you give the okay. Both here on Space City and on Ourania."

Cade snapped a pic of the program running on the wall screen.

"And we've put together plans for a server farm, to be located at the outbreak site, in a raid configuration to ensure backup," Nico added. "Eventually the goal will be to automate transmission of data from the field to our labs and onto the OutSleuth site."

Fintan rubbed his chin with his upper right hand. "Where are we with competition incentives?"

Maellyn swallowed the bite of butternell and stepped forward, a slight cough to clear her throat. "Ready to go. The person with the highest percentage of positive markers gets a three-month supply of candy from Colombo's Caramella. Two through four each receive a month's supply from Colombo's Caramella, plus a voucher for any shop in the street fair. Fifth through tenth place all receive vouchers as well. Oh, and all ten receive four box tickets to the race or Space City Games match of their choice."

She'd finished that task up two days ago, but hadn't appreciated Nico dropping *that* ball on her the week before. He'd been sitting on it for weeks.

"So glad you're devoting your time to prize collecting," Aili announced drily.

Maellyn bit her tongue as she stepped back to the wall. They wanted public support—public participation—for something they weren't personally invested. That required motivation. A competition was one of the best ways to motivate people.

She also wanted to remind Aili how much time they were spending supporting all of this. Yes, they were getting grades, but taking her classes would've been a lot less time consuming or difficult compared to helping solve an outbreak.

Cade, typing away on his wrist-comp, leaned over to whisper, "Is OutSleuth just for students on campus?"

She shook her head. "No. OutSleuth will be open to all of Space City. We need as much help as we can drum up."

"I'm pleased with the progress." Fintan pointed at Anand's box with his pair of left hands. "Progress on the mechanical flies?"

"Scouts," Nico corrected.

Anand set the open box on the table and typed in a few commands on his wrist-comp. From the box emerged a swarm of tiny gray flies, which Anand had built. The flies formed a funnel in the air.

Cade whistled.

"I've got fifty ready for deployment." Anand watched the flies circling overhead, a smile on his face as if he'd trained a puppy to do tricks. "Maellyn, hold out your hand."

When she did so, he directed a single fly from the group over to land in her palm. The scout had a pair of red eyes no larger than the balls on the end of a pin. Cade snapped another picture of the scout resting in the palm of her hand.

"My scouts can take hi-res pictures or videos," Anand said.

"*My* scouts," Nico corrected.

"Which I had to seriously modify in order for them to work in the real world," Anand said. "You didn't have to worry about physics or geometry in your sim Venice."

Nico opened his mouth to argue, but Fintan held up a hand to forestall him. The pair had been fighting over credit for the scouts ever since Anand was tasked with building them. Maellyn didn't know why it was so important to them or why they couldn't share the credit, but neither had been willing to admit the other had played a significant role.

Anand continued. "The scouts can get close-up shots of infected plants and animals in the quarantine zone. Its mouth contains microscopic tools so it can land on an animal and take blood samples, or a plant and collect some of the infected tissue, which is stored in its black thorax and abdomen."

A sharp pinch in Maellyn's palm caused her to yank it back. "Ouch." She glared at Anand.

He wore a sheepish grin. "Just testing."

Aili examined the flies, eyes narrowed. "We have to weigh the risks of these things spreading the fungus when they take samples."

"They're resilient. I built them to withstand your decontamination process repeatedly." Anand gave her an indignant scowl. "They can enter and exit the quarantine zone as many times as needed without risk of spreading the fungus. And the samples they take will be stored until scientists can remove them within the labs on Orestes."

Aili remained unimpressed.

"They work with a mobile base that can recharge them." Anand gestured to a compact structure that moved on tank treads. "When they plug into the mobile base, they offload their data, which it transmits to the server farm for eventual inclusion into the OutSleuth site. It can also store samples as needed."

"Thanks for the update." Fintan nodded to Anand, then turned to Maellyn and arched an eyebrow. "Anything new on the gene insertion modeling?"

"Before we switch topics," Anand cut in. "I want to mention I'll have five hundred scouts ready in two weeks and fifteen hundred in a month."

"Thank you," Fintan said. "Maellyn?"

Her stomach bubbled as if with indigestion. Really just frustration and stress. "The best way is to show you. Can we head over to the sims facility?"

"Sure," Fintan turned to Aili. "We'll disconnect and call you back when we get there."

Aili nodded and her hologram disappeared.

"How is my Ourania sim working?" Nico's eyes looked greedy for approval. "What do you think of the entwined Elope trees? Pretty much winged it on their scent. I'd heard it was strong and distinctive."

"We've been a little busy studying the quarantine zone. Not much time to notice if it was pretty," Trini said, taking the lead as they departed Fintan's lab.

"You didn't check out my non-infected version?" Nico's mouth gaped and he turned to both Fran and Maellyn to see if they had. Maellyn knew he was meticulous with his sims, trying to get every possible detail right. Between creating it and the OutSleuth website, he'd had his hands full.

"I thought it was beautiful!" Fran bobbed up and down like a toddler given some new toy. "The Athanalux caves were stunning. Where did you even get pictures of it? And I got chills from the song of the Astrial birds." She rubbed her arms and shivered.

Cade walked with Maellyn as they headed over to the sims facility. "Nico created a sim of Ourania?"

"Yes," she confirmed. "Same as those for class, except we run simulations showing the impact of the Azymi fungus on flora and fauna on Ourania over time. It also lets us test out possible solutions. See what works, but in a lot faster manner than in the real world."

"That's cool," Cade said, typing more into his wrist-comp.

She couldn't decide if he genuinely thought it was cool, or was saying that to flatter her.

The fifty cages in the sims facility each resembled a 'cage of death' used for motorcycle stunts at fairs. Maellyn opened the door to a cage and stepped inside, while the others climbed into their own. She loaded the Ourania sim.

Beautiful open country replaced the cages and facility. She breathed deeply, muscles loosening as if the air itself massaged her. Timid, curious golden eyes peeked out from green bushes that seemed to sparkle and ripple under the sun's light. She took a half step toward the hidden creature, but the eyes retreated, reappearing seconds later from inside a fallen log a little further away. It wasn't the first time she'd seen it in the sim, but she'd never gotten a good look at one, whatever it was.

Cade spun around, staring. "I didn't expect... This is amazing. Wow!"

A large bronze bird, similar to an eagle, launched itself from its nest in a tree, its cry a trumpet proclaiming its existence. Its widespread wings, against the backdrop of the deep blue sky, curved slightly inward as if the bird offered a hug.

"An Albawk." Fran pointed at the bird, her entire face smiling. "Nico, you did an incredible job creating one."

He typed on his wrist-comp. "Hold out your arm."

Fran complied and the Albawk swung around, dove, and landed near her shoulder, gripping her bicep. Fran's jaw moved, but was unable to formulate words even to thank him for the gesture.

So like Nico, Maellyn thought. He always seemed to know the sweet thing to do in any moment. Not always the right thing to say, but he instinctively knew what would make someone's day.

The Albawk nibbled at Fran's hair, before it leapt back into the air, circling overhead a couple times, then headed east.

Aili's hologram popped into the sim beside Fintan and he caught Maellyn's eyes and nodded for her to take charge.

Maellyn coughed to draw everyone's attention. "Nico, I hate to cut short your showcase, but will you activate the quarantine zone?"

Nico sighed, but typed in a command. Immediately, a gray fuzz covered all the greenery in the area. She recoiled, her skin crawling. The plants and trees that had seemed to glow before now sagged under the fungus. It wasn't her first view of the effects of the fungus, but the sight still bothered her.

She pulled out a pair of gloves from her back pocket and put them on. Kneeling beside a drooped sapling, she ran a finger over the fungus. "As you know, the Azymi is proliferating unchecked."

Trini stepped forward, projecting a screen into the air from her wrist comp. "The Azymi is finding no barriers among animals and Alfar either." The projection showed a pair of lungs, covered in the gray fungus, resembling those of a smoker. Beside the lungs was a blown up image of the brain, enlarged yeast cells floating through it like ants through a colony. "And it has shown an alarmingly high rate of crossing the barriers into the lungs and brain."

Anand hunched in on himself, as if afraid of the fungus touching him.

Maellyn's knees hurt from crouching, so she rose. "After running comparisons, we've found similarities between the Azymi and a couple strains on Anthea. We're testing genes from the Strawling tree and Fibra for resistance to Azymi. Initial results are encouraging, but we've got a lot of simulations to run."

"That's impossible." Aili crossed her arms, mouth rigid. Her eyes flared. "I told you the fungus couldn't have come from another planet. We have too many safeguards in place."

Fintan held up placating hands. "Similar in the way they attack the flora and fauna only. We're not suggesting the Azymi came from Anthea."

Aili didn't look mollified, but at least she didn't protest further. Maellyn hoped Aili would accept their results. If the Anthea plants did show a resistance to the Azymi, would Aili dismiss their findings because she was so certain the fungus wasn't transported from another planet?

Not that it was a sure thing they would even discover the cure to the Azymi. It was one thing for Nico to develop a website to make it easy for non-scientists to search the data and assist. Or for Anand to develop machines to take pictures or samples. It was another altogether to take those samples and data and create an actual treatment or cure. A small part of Maellyn wanted to walk away and not even try. It whispered to her that she would inevitably fail, so why embarrass herself pretending otherwise. She'd been battling those doubts for weeks and it never got any easier.

"I'm pleased with our progress." Fintan clasped both sets of hands. "These problems are not easy. Yet you are facing the difficulties head-on and persevering."

Trini bit her bottom lip. "It may not be enough. Things are accelerating."

Maellyn closed her eyes, not even wanting to contemplate what they'd learned the previous night. She was surprised Aili hadn't already brought it up.

"The Mortans infection rate is higher than other animals on Ourania," Trini said.

Anand raised an eyebrow. "Mortans?"

"Ourania version of vultures," Trini explained. "They consume carcasses, which helps to limit the spread of diseases. A higher rate of infection and death among Mortans means fewer of them eating carcasses, further unbalancing Ourania. We may soon see a separate outbreak."

"That shouldn't have been reported to you." Aili bared her teeth in an annoyed grin. "That isn't your concern. We can handle normal outbreaks or imbalances in the flora and fauna on Ourania."

Maellyn wanted to argue, to point out that they were already failing with one outbreak. What made the Alfar so sure they could handle a second? She also didn't appreciate Aili hiding things from them. How much had been held back that might hinder them from providing real help. She rubbed her sore eyes, wondering why they were wearing themselves out when their support was so unappreciated.

"Your focus is the Azymi only," Aili said with finality.

This time it was Fintan who bared his teeth, but he held his tongue, choosing for whatever reason not to counter the Alfar. Maellyn wished Aili would accept their help, even if their part was small. They were all working toward the same goal and the consequences of failure were great. So why did Aili scorn their contributions instead of welcoming anyone that might bring them a little closer to a solution?

Chapter 19

Neil Fights

Four guards appeared at the cell's entrance.

Neil tensed, backing away. His fight-or-flight response kicked in, but there was nowhere to run and no weapon within reach. The Azios, on the other hand, possessed arm guards with tusk knives attached to them. Plus, he'd already seen them beat another prisoner who'd resisted until he was bloody and motionless on the ground, before dragging his body from the room.

Riagan rose from the ground and stood at his side.

The guards opened the cell door and entered. Without a word, two grabbed Neil's arms and the other pair seized Riagan. Neil jerked back instinctively, but didn't fight. Whether on his feet or being dragged unconscious or dead, he was going with them and they didn't care how.

Neil barely kept his feet as they marched past snarling beasts in cages. He tried his best to ignore the rising panic. Tears welled up in his eyes, but he bit his bottom lip hard and locked his gaze on the door in an effort to control himself. He would not let them see him cry.

They passed through the same door as all the prisoners before them. It opened on a short hallway. Were they being taken for questioning? The Dahaka must want to know who they were and how they'd gotten here. Would they be tortured for answers?

"Where're ya taking us?" Riagan shouted.

For a moment Neil heard the sound of struggling behind him, then an *ooff* from Riagan, followed by nothing. But he couldn't look back and keep his feet. He hoped Riagan hadn't been hurt badly.

Hauled through a second door, they found themselves in a room filled with benches. Prisoners sat on the benches, heads downcast. Azios paced around the room, dressed in loin cloths, like professional wrestlers with a sunlight intolerance.

From open doorways came shouts and stomping. The arena. They were beneath the stands for the Azios tournament. What were they doing here?

The guards deposited them roughly on a bench and chained their wrists and ankles. Neil raised his arms to waist level before the chains caught. He could only shift his legs a half step in any direction.

"You okay?" he asked Riagan, whose head was bowed.

Riagan spat blood on the ground. "If I was any better, I'd be ya."

Neil rolled his eyes.

The arena crowd roared.

"I guess we're in line to battle in the tournament," Neil said. He shivered and an acidic burp welled up from his stomach. He stared around the room, searching for some means of escape.

"You two are up soon, humans." A Dahaka youth sat on the bench across from them. Muscular in traditional Dahaka fashion, he resembled a professional fighter.

Riagan lunged at the Dahaka; his chains caught and dropped him to his knees.

The Dahaka appraised Riagan for a moment. "Good. You'll need that anger. I'm Rashn."

Neil wasn't sure how to take the Dahaka, but he figured talking to him wouldn't be harmful. "Neil."

Riagan bit his lower lip and refused to speak.

"We're going to be paired in the arena." Rashn clasped his hands in his lap, seemingly at ease.

"The two of us against you?" Neil asked, surprised the Dahaka was giving them a heads up.

"We'll face a few beasts first," Rashn replied. "Get by those and we'll fight each other. It won't be easy."

Riagan rose as far as the chains allowed, straining until Neil thought the manacles would cut his wrists. "Will we be given weapons or do ya get to slaughter us defenseless?"

Rashn scowled. "I'm not an executioner. I fight fair."

"Fair? Last year your people ambushed student teams during their final exam on Mars."

Jaw tightening, Rashn replied, "I wasn't involved. I live by the Azios code."

Neil was taken aback. It was the last response he'd expected from the Dahaka. Haughty boasts, yes. Scorn at their failings. Not apparent disapproval for Mainyu's actions.

"But I know many… most, have turned from the code." Rashn's face flushed.

"I've never heard of the code," Neil said, anxious for something to keep his mind off the battle to come.

Rashn nodded. "It's no longer popular to speak of it. Not since Mainyu became ruler. He disdains the code as antiquated. Argues it holds us back from establishing ourselves as equals with Space City. I'd argue it's our aggression that holds us back."

Neil didn't know how to respond. He'd never heard such rationality from a Dahaka. Was he an anomaly or representative of a past version of the Dahaka as his words implied? "Can you tell me about this code?"

"Never run from an aggressor. Never attack a defenseless opponent." Rashn held both hands together as if creating a bowl. "That one also means never attack a weak opponent. Usually. There is no honor in defeating a helpless foe."

"What about a woman?" Neil asked.

Rashn raised an eyebrow. "Why would our code prohibit fighting a woman? They're not inferior opponents. Are human females weaker than males?"

Neil opened his mouth to speak, but as he processed the question it gave him pause. Maellyn, Eris, and many of the other girls at the academy were anything but weak. They'd demonstrated their abilities countless times. And yet the compulsion to never attack a woman was ingrained into every cell of his body. The very idea of fighting a woman made him sick with revulsion. He didn't know how to answer the question.

"Your code's a joke." Riagan cast the Dahaka a disdainful expression. "We saw a powerful Azios slaughter an old one who was clearly inferior." Riagan nodded toward the arena. "Out there."

Rashn shook his head, eyes burning, lip curled back in a snarl as if Riagan had gravely insulted him. "That battle was a show of respect, a recognition of the old Azios' former strength and skill. He had earned a warrior's death. To refuse him would've been the dishonor."

Neil didn't understand that desire to ever seek death. The Dahaka weren't the first culture to prize a warrior's death over living to old age. Just because you weren't as strong as in your youth didn't mean that all purpose for life had ceased. His grandfather proved that. He never quit working to make Space City safer. He wasn't as strong as he'd once been, but he refused to let that stop him from making a difference.

"Is there more to your code?" Neil asked.

"Defend your brothers and sisters in battle," Rashn answered. "Even at the expense of your own life. Never leave anyone behind."

Another Azios smacked a fist across the back of Rashn's head. "Are you such a fossil, you don't see the insult in consorting with humans?"

Rashn ignored him.

It was the first time Neil could remember a Dahaka not react to someone calling them old. He was impressed. As well as with the way Rashn regarded the code. It was strange coming from a Dahaka. "Do any others share your code?"

"A few." There was regret in the Azios voice. "Once, following the code was a point of pride among the Azios. Now it's viewed as a sign of weakness."

Several guards entered and unchained a pair of prisoners from a nearby bench and led them to the arena. Neil breathed deeply to calm his nerves. How long before their turn?

Where was Sverog? Or Guiman? Anyone to rescue them.

Rashn focused back on his hands, breathing evenly, preparing himself. Neil debated asking him more, but what did it matter? They'd soon be forced to fight in the arena, so the last thing he wanted was to go in thinking Rashn was honorable. He wouldn't feel that way if the Azios killed him. Or Riagan.

"We once sought mighty deeds." Rashn clenched his fists, his whole body rigid. "Now we focus on deceit. We measure the greatness of battle through the spoils, rather than the worthiness of our opponent. Once upon a time we revered fallen enemy warriors for their honorable deaths. Now many kill through treachery. Or torture the weak and defenseless." His face had distorted in disgust.

"Why stay then?" Neil asked. "If you hate Mainyu's rule, why not leave?"

"I belong to my people," Rashn said, shoulders slumping. "I keep the code as best I can, but I cannot abandon my people." He rose and stalked off.

"He's just trying to disarm us." Riagan glared at Rashn's back. "Trying to get in ya head."

It was possible, but Neil didn't think so. Rashn appeared genuine. Unfortunately, that wouldn't matter when they entered the arena. Maybe it was better if he assumed Rashn was lying. It would make the fight easier. Of course, if they won, what would happen then? He couldn't imagine the Dahaka would allow them to go free.

The crowd went wild. The stands over their heads shook. How much weight could the ceiling hold before it collapsed, burying them?

Amidst the shouting and vibrations, four guards returned and hauled Neil and Riagan to their feet, unchaining them. It was their turn.

Bile rose up in Neil's throat. He forced it back down, rather than add the humiliation of sicking up in front of the guards.

The Azios pulled him, stumbling, toward the tunnel up to the arena. Rashn walked solemnly ahead of them.

"Don't we get any armor?" Neil asked. "Or something to defend ourselves with?"

The guards snorted.

Apparently Rashn had lied. He'd been messing with them as Riagan had said.

Where was Sverog? Why hadn't Guiman gotten them out of this?

A new concern hit him as they neared the arena floor. Would Maellyn or his grandpa ever know what happened to them? Would Guiman risk exposure of his efforts and spies in order to tell them what happened? He had to. Yet Neil had his doubts and it made him angry. He might die and they'd be left with the haunting uncertainty of never knowing what happened to him.

When the guards shoved Neil out of the tunnel onto the arena floor, Riagan a second after, Rashn waited alongside three large cages, inspecting the beasts. Was he here merely to set the creatures loose on them?

The one in the middle resembled a car-sized warthog. A rhino hog. Similar to one anyway. Except this one had a sickly yellow skullcap, a hard turtle shell on its back, and a much longer snout like a crocodile.

A dull thud behind Neil alerted him that a gate had been dropped, sealing the exit tunnel behind them. A pair of long bone tusks were tossed through the bars at his feet.

"Really?" he demanded. "That's it?"

The guards jeered.

Unable to believe they were being sent into the ring with nothing more than a small knife, Neil, nonetheless, snatched the blades up and offered one to Riagan. They didn't even have time to discuss a strategy before the rhino hog had been released. Not by Rashn, who had moved away a safe distance from the cages, but by an armored guard.

The rhino hog wasted no time charging the two of them. Neil tensed, right hand clutching the tusk knife like it was a rosary. He tried to fire himself up, knowing he'd need anger to fight the beasts. But he was a cold furnace. Fear soaked him. He barely had time to form the question—what do I do?—before instinct took over and he dove out of the stampeding beast's way.

He hit the ground and rolled over. The creature barreled on past, its brain not having yet processed that it had missed its targets. Riagan lay sprawled on his back several feet away. Between them raced Rashn. Neil flinched, prepared for an attack, but the Azios sprinted past. As the beast turned to find them, Rashn lunged for it. The tusk knife in his hand pierced the creature's throat. It reared up, crying in pain.

The crowd roared with delight as Rashn retreated several paces out of reach, tense and waiting for a counterattack. The beast bucked once then dropped to its knees. It collapsed onto the ground, sides heaving.

An arm pulled Neil to his feet. Riagan pointed back toward the center of the arena. The last two cages had opened, revealing a pair of predators that resembled scaly bears. Long, sharp canines protruded from gaping maws. Their legs were thick and powerful.

Rapsids. The Dahaka's personal symbol. Many of the Dahaka's myths involved rapsids.

Unlike the rhino hog, these beasts stalked forward, sizing them up. Neil felt an overpowering urge to run, a mouse dropped into a viper's tank. He wanted to beg the guards in the tunnels to let him out. The tusk knife suddenly felt like a toothpick, a woefully inadequate weapon for fighting a rapsid.

"You two take the one on the right." Rashn had appeared at Neil's side. He had cleaned some of the blood from his arm and knife. "Split up. Keep its attention divided. It'll stay on the defensive longer."

Without waiting for agreement, Rashn scooted away from them, waving his arms to catch the attention of the other rapsid.

"I don't want to die," Neil said to Riagan, unable to help himself. The words came unbidden. The admission shamed him.

"Agreed," Riagan replied with a bitter smile.

Following Rashn's direction because he didn't know what else to do, Neil roved right, away from Riagan. He didn't wave his arms to get the rapsid's attention, as Rashn had done. It was all he could do not to run for cover, not that there was any to find.

Coward, he berated himself. Despite the admonishment, he longed for any reprieve. *Someone, please help us.*

The rapsid plodded forward, muscles taut as it prepared to attack. It stared between them, as if there were a third person with them. Neil almost looked over to see if someone else had joined them.

In a sudden burst of speed, the rapsid bolted toward him. A scream filled his ears. He stumbled backward. As he fell to the ground, he pointed the tusk knife at the creature. He used his spare arm to catch himself as best he could to keep the weapon steady between him and the beast.

Something flew through the air, piercing the rapsid behind its forearm. The beast bellowed, jumping sideways, head whipping around to snap at a tusk knife poking out of its side. The angle prevented it from knocking the knife loose.

Riagan's knife.

The crowd roared approval, but Neil knew that meant Riagan was defenseless. Neil jumped to his feet and moved toward Riagan to defend him. The beast snapped at Riagan's knife in its side a couple more times.

"Any suggestions?" Neil asked.

"Don't let it sink its teeth on ya," Riagan offered.

"Helpful."

Finally giving up on removing the knife, the rapsid snarled and leapt forward. In a panic, Neil threw his knife. He wanted to call it back the second it left his hand, but the tusk hurled forward, burying itself in the rapsid's foreleg right below the shoulder. The beast hit the ground and its leg gave out. It tumbled, flipping over itself and landing on its belly. The fall buried the tusk knife deep into the rapsids left foreleg, opposite the side Riagan had already struck.

Now weaponless, Neil took a couple steps backward. He bumped into Riagan.

"It was a good throw," Riagan said. "Not good enough to keep us alive, but hey, we probably weren't killing it anyway."

The rapsid climbed back to its feet, eyes maddened with pain. It retreated, right foreleg limping.

Movement from off to the side drew Neil's attention a half second before the rapsid noticed. Rashn crossed the distance between him and the beast as if launched. The Azzaro slashed at the creature's belly, but it dodged him. Rashn kept attacking, trying for the throat, the eyes, any weak point he could strike. The rapsid snapped at the tusk. After avoiding a slash from Rashn, the beast lashed out with a fore leg and gashed the Azzaro's right arm. Rashn dashed out of reach, but the rapsid charged forward, maddened with pain.

I need to help, Neil thought. But what use was he without a weapon?

Searching around the arena, he spotted the empty cages. They were built from large dinosaur bones, tethered together with rope. If he had his tusk knife still, he could sever the ropes and wield the bone like a club.

Now on the defense, Rashn could only leap out of reach of the rapsid's snapping jaws.

Motionless, Riagan watched.

"Riagan, I need a knife," Neil shouted.

Riagan gave him a puzzled look; the shouts and jeers from the crowd dominated the arena. How could the Dahaka cheer this on? Neil mimicked throwing a knife, then pointed at the cages. Riagan gave him a thumbs-up. Neil hoped they were on the same page.

Rashn ducked below a swipe from the rapsid and darted forward. He slammed his knife into its hide and pulled it free. The beast spun his way, slamming its torso into him and sending him sprawling, the knife knocked from his grip.

Neil held out a hand as if he could hold the rapsid in place to give Rashn time to recover. Instead, the rapsid lunged at Rashn, who managed to roll away and to his feet in the same movement.

Riagan took the opportunity to grab Rashn's discarded knife. The rapsid sensed the movement and turned on him, forcing Riagan backward. The beast roared at him. He paled, unprepared to fight it alone.

Neil knew he needed to do something, but couldn't attack the beast barehanded. Hoping Riagan could last a few minutes on his own, Neil raced over to the cages. He had to dismantle one.

The crowd, thinking he was running for cover, booed. But how many of them would fare any better in his place?

As he examined the crates, he found they'd been shoddily assembled. The rope at one corner of the cage had frayed. There was a gap between the bones. He rotated the cage on its side, placed both feet on the bottom bones to hold the cage down, then grabbed the loose bone, which was the size of his forearm, and yanked upward. It loosened a little.

The crowd groaned, but Neil didn't waste time glancing to see why. He focused on jerking at the loose bone, heaving one, two, three times. It gave a little with each pull. On the fifth attempt, the bone popped free and he tumbled backward to the ground.

As he struggled to his feet, he took stock of Riagan and Rashn. They had retreated to the rhino hog and were using it as a barrier.

"Riagan!" Neil screamed as he charged over, the bone held aloft. He hoped Riagan would hear him over the crowd. Rashn noticed him, grabbed the weapon from Riagan and went on the offensive, shielding him.

Neil reached Riagan and thrust the bone into his arms, then without waiting to check on Rashn, rushed back to the cage to pry a second bone free. Now that he'd already broken one free, it was easier to pull a second loose from that corner and once again yank on it until it came loose. Still, by the time he was done he was panting. But he wasted no time in returning to the fight.

Riagan and Rashn stood several feet apart, the rapsid's attention divided between them. At the sign of a third opponent, it retreated a couple paces, head swinging back and forth. It roared a warning.

Rashn, a gash in his side, motioned past the rapsid. "Drive it toward the pit."

Wielding the bone in both hands, Neil swung at the rapsid. Riagan did as well, but instead of joining in the attack, Rashn ran off. Neil wondered if the Azios was going to get a third club. But he didn't dare look. He focused all his attention on keeping his weapon between the beast and himself.

With each swing of the club, Neil took a step closer, in concert with Riagan. The rapsid growled, swiveling left and right, looking for ways around them. Reluctantly, it gave ground, blood leaking down its side and torso from where two knives were still lodged, hindering its mobility. Once it reached the edge, it dropped to a crouch, snarling. Neil knew another step would drive it to attack out of desperation. He hesitated, unsure what to do next. Riagan also held his ground.

Then, with a scream, Rashn barreled past them, a cage in his arms. The rapsid's attention swiveled to him and it tried to dart away. He rammed it with the cage and the force knocked it off the ledge into the pit.

The crowd roared in delight as Rashn tossed the cage after the beast. Neil let the end of the bone drop to the ground, his shoulders drooping. He exhaled and closed his eyes.

They'd won.

They'd survived.

Opening his eyes, he raised a hand to shake with Rashn, to share congratulations and triumph. But Rashn had turned his back to the pit and pulled his tusk knife from where it was tucked into his waist band. There was no triumph on his face. Only a grim resolve. "This brings me no pleasure, but this is a fight to the death. The Azios allow no quarter to prisoners."

Neil wanted to argue. To protest. After what they'd accomplished, it wasn't fair for them to fight more. But he also knew the argument was pointless. He could see in Rashn's eyes that the Azios didn't want to fight them, but he was already moving into a defensive stance. If he refused, the Dahaka would send someone else in to fight, and he would pay the price for his refusal.

Without further warning, Rashn rushed Neil the way a bull stampedes a matador. Neil sucked in air and jerked the bone upward to ward off the attack. At the last second, Rashn ducked low, slashing with the knife at Neil's gut. Neil sucked in his belly. Before he could think how to respond, Riagan tackled Rashn. The boys struggled on the ground, Riagan trying to pin Rashn down. But with the Azios superior size, Riagan wouldn't hold him down long. Neil held his bone ready, reluctant to attack Rashn after everything, nor accidentally club Riagan.

Rashn managed to shove Riagan off and roll away. The effort gave Neil a clear shot at the Azios. He raised the club to strike, but hesitated.

A trumpeting filled the arena. Three short blasts. Immediately, the stands became chaos.

Rashn scrambled to his feet, knife held loosely at his side. "You're both granted a reprieve." His eyes sparkled with excitement.

The crowd stampeded for the exits.

"What's going on?" Riagan asked. He was back on his feet, bone club at the ready.

"Dinos attacking. Let's go." Rashn sped past them after his fellow Dahaka.

This was the break they needed. Neil exchanged a look with Riagan who gave a nod and they took off after the Azios.

The Dahaka paid them no mind as they joined the crowd pressing their way out of the arena. They were pushed and shoved as everyone fought to get outside first. Neil thought their exuberance crazy and he let anyone who wanted to pass him do so. He was content to be the last one out. His only concern was escape.

Out in the open field of the capital, the Azios rushed to their homes to retrieve armor and weapons. Overhead flew raptor-like green birds with claws on the ends of four wings and nasty talons. Alariles.

They kind of made Neil think of flying anacondas. The alariles dove into the crowd, snatching up the young Dahaka boys as they tried to retrieve weapons from their tents. A few of the largest alariles even attacked full grown adult Azios, attempting to haul them away. The Azios, young and old, fought ferociously. Those caught clawed at the alariles with their bare hands, attempting to wrestle them to the ground. Neil wished he had a weapon at his disposal, but hadn't thought to grab anything on his way out of the arena. He hadn't expected the attack to be this great or close.

Rashn raced toward an alarile, which was snapping at a young boy it was trying to fly off with. When Rashn neared it he leapt off a bench, knife held high. He slashed at the bird's torso. The creature screeched and crashed to the ground, along with its victim, who lay stunned on the ground for a moment before rising to a sitting position.

The giant wall surrounding the capital shook, accompanied by reverberations all along its length from some great beasts ramming it. Neil turned away, dodging through the Azios for Guiman's cave, Riagan on his heels. They didn't want to be here if those walls fell.

Riagan cried out. Neil looked back to find one of the alariles clutching his arm in its sharp talons as Riagan beat at it with his other fist. Before Neil could help, a passing Azios rammed a tusk knife in the alarile's back. It flopped to the ground, leaving Riagan with a nasty gash on his arm.

"How bad is it?" Neil asked.

"Fine." Riagan waved for him to hurry on. "Let's get out of here."

A few minutes later they pushed through the door into Guiman's cave and paused in the darkness, gasping for air. Neil activated the night vision on his contacts, thankful the Dahaka hadn't noticed those.

The place was a wreck. The pallet in the corner had been tossed aside, revealing the weapons cache, which had been emptied. Same with the armory chest and cabinet, all useful gear and supplies taken, and the rest strewn across the floor. Nothing left to fix up Riagan's arm. Not that Neil wanted to delay and risk a Dahaka coming after them.

They moved down the tunnel to the thorneway frame. Neil activated it, breathing deeply now that this was over. He stepped through to Space City. And promptly dropped to the floor beside the thorneway.

"What in the...?" Dardanos wheeled over to Neil's side and placed a hand on his shoulder, Guiman a step behind him.

Neil found himself nodding, unable to speak. Then the pair saw Riagan's arm and started asking if he needed medical attention. Riagan insisted it wasn't as bad as it looked. He marched toward the sink and began rinsing it.

"Glad you got out during our diversion," Guiman said as he retrieved some disinfectant and bandages from a cabinet.

"Diversion?" Riagan asked through gritted teeth as he let the water wash over his arm. "We were thrown into battle with several beasts and an Azios. Would've died if not for a dino attack."

Guiman handed Riagan the disinfectant and nodded. "The attack was the diversion. We tried to get a couple men assigned to guard duty to free you sooner, but that fell through."

Neil blinked, looking up at Guiman. "You managed to get dinosaurs to attack the capital to create a diversion?"

"It's one of the standard emergency plans," Guiman said.

Dardanos moved his hand beneath Neil's arm and lifted to get him back to his feet. "We're just glad it wasn't too late."

Neil tried not to think about how close to death they'd come. In fact, he didn't even want to discuss it further. "Guiman, your cave is compromised. We'll need a new way onto Siavash." A big part of him wasn't sure he ever wanted to go back. He'd known that spying there was dangerous, but he hadn't understood the reality.

"Yes," Guiman agreed. "Once we learned of your capture, I had Sverog look into it. We already have a backup, but that's not important right now." Riagan had finished washing and patting dry his arm. Guiman had retrieved a nanoshot and injected it into Riagan's arm near the wound. The nanobots would seal it. Then he wrapped the bandage around it.

While Neil tried to think what he wanted to do first—sleep, eat, talk to Maellyn, his grandfather—Riagan spoke up. "Did ya find out how the Dahaka discovered the hideout?"

Guiman's lips thinned and his brow furrowed. "We think the Council alerted them."

"At least someone tied to the Council," Dardanos added.

Neil fell back against one arm of the deactivated thorneway. This couldn't be. The Council had nearly gotten them killed. "Why would the Council tell them? How?"

"It seems…" Guiman's voice trailed off. His mouth twisted. "I mentioned before we needed to learn why the Council's protecting Mainyu. It now appears that he works for them."

"What?" Neil and Riagan said simultaneously.

If he hadn't already been leaning against the wall, Neil thought he might've fallen down again.

"The Council had their own connection to Mainyu," Dardanos said. "We're not sure how long, or how they managed it, but when they discovered we were still pursuing him privately, they took steps to shut us down. You weren't the only spies captured."

Without another word, Riagan stormed from the house. Neil stood to go after him.

"I'm sorry." Guiman reached out a hand toward Neil. "I wish I had known before I sent you. I thought it'd be an easy mission. One you could have a little fun on."

Neil grimaced and nodded toward the door. "I better catch up with Riagan. Make sure he's all right."

Chapter 20

Riagan Employs Masked Larva

Riagan jogged up the uneven stone hill in the Academy Games stadium, his breath foggy. He ignored the aching in his chest from the cold January air, and pushed on to the top. The bowl below held ten bronze boxes, but none of the usual guardian beasts let loose for Games matches. He was alone in the stadium.

He rubbed at the scar on his left arm from where the alarile had attacked him on Siavash. They hadn't been back over the last month since Guiman's cave had been discovered. Most of his operations there were in chaos since the leak by the Council. They still had no idea who had leaked the hideout to the Dahaka, so Guiman had sidelined them for the time being, except for small routine tasks here.

Riagan started to descend the cliff to the bowl, pushing his workout. His jaw ached, and he realized he'd been grinding his teeth. He was at war with himself. After Rois' death, he had promised himself he'd find and punish all those involved.

Justice.

Revenge.

The terms didn't matter. Those responsible had to pay. But with the Council tied to Mainyu, despite everything the Dahaka leader had done, it tainted all of this. There was nothing left in Space City to enjoy. Even the training right now. A big part of him wanted to walk away.

Reaching the ground, Riagan jogged along one of the paths through the massive stone hill toward the open field at the stadium's center. Instinctively, he studied the walls overhead, watching for opponents he knew weren't there; his training kicking in despite his misgivings.

He pushed his pace to a sprint until emerging onto the grassy midfield. Neil waved at him from the sidelines, but Riagan ignored him. He rotated and stepped onto the knee-high base of the stone hill. He started the climb once more. His pace slowed back to that of a jog.

Halfway up the hill, Neil caught up with him. Instead of launching into whatever he'd come about, Neil matched his pace. Riagan felt both annoyed at Neil for joining him without invitation, but also relieved not to have to talk. Because that meant trying to figure out what to do now, and he couldn't. He wanted to run until his energy, anger, hope, resentment, determination, and fears had drained out of him with his sweat. At least temporarily.

It always came back. All of it.

They reached the cliff top, descended into the bowl, then returned down a different path. Three passes they made, their breaths the only noise between them.

On the fourth pass up, Neil finally spoke. "We need to go to Rory's Weird and Unexplainable tonight."

"Can't." Riagan bit his lip. He had no intention of playing games. It was Neil's latest attempt to cheer him up, and it wouldn't work.

"You have to."

"Why would I?" he asked, scowling. He stumbled, a rock sliding out from under his foot. He kept his feet, but had to come to a stop anyway. He bent over, hands on his knees, breath heaving, body unable to go on for the moment.

"Spoke with Fran Snelling." Neil leaned back on his heels, hands on his hips. "She and her mother are taking her little brother tonight."

Riagan growled, annoyed at the mention of Dr. Snelling. Another traitor. One of a long list. "I don't care."

"I think her wrist-comp might hold the solution to exposing her and whoever on the Council is supporting the Dahaka. Tonight may give us the chance to *borrow* it."

Riagan turned and walked downslope, listening to his breathing. It was a good idea. But everything they'd done of late seemed to make things worse, to show a greater amount of corruption. What if they found more than they could ever hope to stop? Hadn't they already? At what point did he throw his hands in the air, write them all off, and walk away? Not that he had any idea where to go. Returning to Earth offered no appeal.

"Wrist-comps require fingerprint activation," Riagan said.

Neil smiled again. His eyes held a twinkle. "Bet her thumbprint is all over the device. We'll scan it and print a 3D replica. Nico already put the program on my wrist-comp. Five minutes and we'll have access."

"Ya told Nico?" Riagan couldn't believe Neil had told someone else despite Guiman's express orders against it; his training again. What did it matter?

"Relax." Neil shook his head. "I told him we're breaking into Patrick's phone to look for evidence he put Adrien Laroque in the hospital. Make him pay for something for once."

Riagan's interest leapt at that suggestion. Getting back at Patrick for the things he'd done never seemed to get old. "We should do that, too. Two birds, one stone, as they say."

"Maybe see if we can pull this off first before planning a second attempt?"

It would be better to focus on Dr. Snelling. "Was this ya idea?"

Neil kicked a rock, sending it shooting off across the midfield line. "Yeah, things have been slow. And I know this is hard on you. Thought if we could make progress on something…"

Riagan found he preferred the plan since it was Neil's instead of Guiman's, though he couldn't say why.

*****

Neil groaned and turned his back to the entrance of Rory's Weird and Unexplainable.

Riagan looked at the ticket boxes, trying to figure out what bothered him. Then he spotted Eris in line with Jiro, Dirk, and Arielle.

"Quick, walk away," Neil whispered, taking his own advice.

Eris turned and her eyes caught Riagan's before he could. Her eyes shifted to Neil's back. She smiled and started in their direction.

"Too late," Riagan said over his shoulder. He feigned a smile to Eris. Excuses bounced around his head like bumper cars, none good ones. Neil rejoined him.

"You two going to Rory's?" Eris asked.

Riagan opened his mouth to say no, as if there was any other reason they'd be standing out here in front of the museum, but Neil answered *yes* first.

Dirk strolled over, arm-in-arm with Arielle, who pressed against his side, decidedly content. Jiro trailed behind like an awkward third wheel. Dirk offered his free hand to Neil and they shook. "What was Instructor Tereshkova thinking with that pop quiz today?" Dirk asked.

Neil rolled his eyes. "I don't know. Only three days into the new semester."

Riagan couldn't remember the last time he'd attended class. Strangely, Headmaster Dardanos hadn't mentioned it any of the times they'd met for training or special tasks.

"You joining us?" Dirk asked.

Neil hesitated a moment, before nodding. "Sure. Sounds good."

Biting his lip, Riagan brought up the rear as the group shifted back toward the ticket boxes. As if this wasn't going to be hard enough without more eyes on them. Hopefully, he and Neil could find a way to lose them inside.

Hurrying back to the nearest ticket box, Jiro flashed his academy ID in front of the scanner. A red light swept across the ID, which deducted the admittance fee from his account. A golden ticket popped out. Jiro grabbed his ticket and flashed a mischievous grin, all his earlier awkwardness momentarily gone. "See you inside."

Dirk stepped up to the ticket box next, an arm still linked with Arielle. He held up his ID. "Do you want passes to the space walk, too?" he asked her.

Arielle shrugged. "Whatever you want to do."

The way the pair fawned over each other nauseated Riagan. They'd been normal people last year before spending their summer on Sundara. Now the lovebirds were unbearable.

"I'm up for the Spacewalk." Eris purchased her ticket and stepped aside for Neil. "Care to go, Neil?"

Riagan rolled his eyes. She never gave up.

Neil mumbled noncommittally as he swiped his badge, handed the ticket to Riagan, then swiped for a second ticket for himself and they hurried inside.

The first room they entered inside Rory's had a sign outside the door which read Masked Larvae with X-ray. Techno music blared from inside. They entered and found the room was pitch black. Riagan activated his contacts, giving him x-ray vision. The room exploded into shapes of blue, green, yellow, red, and orange. They weren't strobe lights, but their movements seemed to keep pace with the beat of the music. And the shapes seemed to have substance to them, like rubber.

Must be the masked larvae, Riagan thought.

Some of the masked larvae expanded like fireworks, but rather than fade away they reached a limit, contracted back in upon themselves, and expanded into geometric shapes in different colors. A rainbow-shaped larva looped upward toward the ceiling, as if creating a slide. It touched the ceiling, looped backward on itself to the floor, then rose once more, this time taking ninety degree turns every few seconds.

Riagan moved over to the rainbow masked larva and placed his hand over its rising form. It bumped into his hand and expanded to triple its size before retracting. He reached down and grabbed the larva. Slimy as an earthworm, it shivered in his grasp. He didn't squeeze hard, but it still separated, the bottom half falling away from his hand. The top half slid up out of his hand, despite his effort to hold on. It fell to the ground and started rising as it had before, now in parallel to its bottom half.

Rather than some strange gadget or gimmick, the masked larvae were actual organisms from somewhere in the universe. Most things at Rory's Weird and Unexplainable were real organisms or phenomena. The planet the masked larvae inhabited must be a strange one to explore.

Nearby, a blue larva that expanded in a star configuration, contracted, grew into a purple octagon, contracted, became a spiral, all the while hovering in the air. As it expanded again, Riagan reached out and let it bump his palm. This one felt like a marshmallow. He grasped a corner of it, and as it contracted, the piece in his hand separated from the rest. He opened his hand, palm upward. The little larva expanded to the size of a softball covered in…what? Rubber spikes? It tickled his palm. It grew and shrank in rhythm to the music as if energized by it, same as the others, but never got too big to hold in one hand.

A hand grabbed Riagan's arm, jerking him backward. A red and orange tube bounced forward and back a few times, gripping his arm; it was attached to a much larger red and orange form. After a second, he realized he was looking at someone motioning for him to follow. Had he been noticed tearing off a part of the masked larva?

The figure leaned close. "Let's go," Neil said.

Several other figures headed toward the rear of the room, passing through a curtain, but he couldn't distinguish one from the next. He slipped the larva into his pocket and followed Neil.

Each time someone pressed the curtain aside, a burst of light shot into the room, blinding him. He switched off the contacts as he emerged from the room and blinked, eyes adjusting. Neil and the rest of the group surrounded him in a great hall.

Kids and teenagers filled the hall, milling about, snacking on candy and drinks, while playing with a variety of exhibits. Young kids bounced in a chaotic enclosed pen filled with small, plastic, multi-colored balls which caromed through the enclosed pen, rebounding off the walls, floor, ceiling, and the kids. They must not pack much of a punch because the children howled joyfully as they leapt around.

Neil tapped Riagan's shoulder and pointed near the pen. Riagan bit his lip, taking stock. Dr. Snelling and Fran stood, smiling and laughing, watching the children. Seeing them side by side, the same sandy hair—Dr. Snelling's with streaks of gray in hers—and slender frames, it was easy to tell their relation. Fran had a few inches on her mother. She also stood looser, more comfortable. Despite the shared laughter, there was a rigidity to Dr. Snelling.

"Riagan and I are going to say hi to Fran," Neil said to the group. "See how things are going with the Orestes project. We'll catch up."

Well done, Riagan thought. He took a step toward the Snellings, but Eris piped up. "I'll come with. I'd like to hear how things are going, too." She bobbed forward beside Neil.

Riagan ground his teeth. What she really wanted to know was how long the project would keep Maellyn away from Neil. And now they'd have to try to swipe the wrist-comp with another set of eyes watching. Fortunately, Dirk, Arielle, and Jiro split off on their own.

"Hey Fran," Neil greeted as they approached.

Fran and Dr. Snelling turned questioning looks toward them. Fran smiled as she recognized them. "Hey." She turned to her mom. "Mom, this is Neil Ericson, a classmate."

Dr. Snelling beamed and reached out to shake Neil's hand. "Neil, yes. Quite the student. I've heard lots about you."

"A pleasure to meet you, too." Neil shook her hand, his eyes darting for a brief second to the wrist-comp clipped to her left arm.

Riagan wanted to clap Neil on the back of the head for looking. He hoped Dr. Snelling hadn't noticed.

Fran introduced Eris as well and they exchanged pleasantries while Riagan debated how to inconspicuously grab the wrist-comp. Then he realized Fran was introducing her mom to him. He found it was all he could do to keep his voice calm and greet her. The smile on his face felt fake.

Her lips drew into a line. Could she tell he was faking? Did she suspect something? But all she did was offer a greeting to him as well, if a bit curtly compared to Neil.

Thankfully, Neil spoke up and drew away everyone's attention. "How is the work going on Orestes?"

Fran sighed dramatically and shook her head. "I love the Alfar. Everyone knows I do. But our primary go-to on this is a pain."

Riagan side-stepped out of Dr. Snelling's line-of-sight. He studied her wrist-comp. It would be simple to grab and pull it free from the clip holder. His right hand tingled with the desire to reach for it. But that didn't mean he could do it without alerting her.

"Maellyn mentioned the woman's rough on you." Neil's sole focus seemed to be on Fran.

Fran's jaw dropped as she huffed, eyes flashing annoyance. "She thinks we can't come up with any useful ideas. We've started briefing Instructor Fintan before meeting with her. Then he delivers our progress. Still, she dismisses half our results and inputs."

"It's frustrating, I know," Dr. Snelling spoke up. "It can be difficult when you're young to convince older, more senior scientists that you have anything new to contribute. Something they haven't thought of already. That's especially true if you're a young woman trying to convince older men."

It was strange to stand here listening to Dr. Snelling give her daughter advice, as if it wasn't her that Fran should be warned about.

Did she not understand she was putting her children at risk by helping the Dahaka? If Dr. Snelling and the other scientists succeeded, it would be Fran and her brother who paid the price. Did Dr. Snelling not see that?

A thump off Riagan's leg reminded him of the masked larva in his pocket. Visible only via the x-ray band, it would be invisible out here. The perfect distraction. Fishing the larva from his pocket, he tossed it into the air, aiming for the top of Dr. Snelling's head.

He knew the moment the larva hit her head because she ducked, hollering in surprise, and swatted at her hair, then the back of her neck. The back of her shirt pulsed as if a mouse had gotten caught in there and was struggling to break free. "Get it off me! Get it off!"

"Let me help you." Neil darted forward. With one hand he grabbed her arm. The other hand he balled into a fist. He punched at the thing beneath her shirt, trying to knock it down. Dr. Snelling bucked and grabbed at her back with her free hand, shouting in alarm. Fran wrung her hands, seemingly wanting to help, but unsure how.

The bulge in Dr. Snelling's shirt at last dropped clear and she danced away. Everyone searched the floor for the culprit. Despite knowing the larva was invisible, Riagan instinctively looked for a second, too.

"What was that?" Fran asked, still searching the floor, bouncing on her toes as if ready to scramble if it tried for her. "Did we get it?"

Dr. Snelling heaved, hand on her chest. "It felt like a mouse. I hate mice." She shivered.

Riagan clenched his teeth to keep from smiling. He wished he could retrieve the little masked larva. There were a lot of other uses for an invisible, gooey creature. Thinking of his contacts, he activated the x-ray vision, hoping to spot the larva. But with so many people everywhere, and all the light, it was impossible to spot. Might've even darted beneath one of the rides or exhibits filling the place. So he gave up and deactivated the contacts.

A second later, Neil surreptitiously threw something behind his back. It hit Riagan in the gut and he caught it. Looking down, he realized it was a wrist-comp. His eyes widened. Dr. Snelling's wrist-comp. He clutched it to his waist and covered it with both hands.

"Mommy, mommy, did you see me?" a young boy ran up to Dr. Snelling and grabbed her waist.

"Yes, Nate," she answered, placing a hand on his shoulder while continuing to search the floor, as if afraid whatever had gotten her would come back for round two.

"Mom, can I get a butternell?" Nate asked.

"Sure. We can go get one."

"Oh, me, too," Eris piped up. "Neil?"

"Sure. After you." Neil gestured for the others to go first. The moment Dr. Snelling had moved ahead, her son and Fran in tow, Neil slipped his own wrist-comp from its arm strap and held it out.

Riagan snatched it. Nico's program was already active on the wrist-comp. All he had to do was find a private place to tap into Dr. Snelling's device. He chose the opposite direction from the others and snuck through the first doorway he came to. At the last second, he tensed, barely registering the wall of water before he plunged straight into it. He instinctively held his breath. The room was filled from floor to ceiling. And despite two open doorways, the water didn't flood out of the room.

"Riagan! This is amazing, isn't it?" Jiro strode toward him in slow motion, fighting the water's resistance.

How was Jiro talking underwater?

The water buoyed up his hair, stretching it out and waving it around like seaweed. And Riagan felt the familiar pressure of the water pressing in on him. It was warm. He slipped the wrist-comps into his pocket, thankful they were waterproof, as he turned to back out of the room.

"Wait," Jiro called after him. "Check this stuff out. It has oxygen so you can breathe in it." He'd noticed the telltale signs of Riagan holding his breath: cheeks puffed out, mouth clamped shut, a few bubbles escaping.

Riagan hesitated. His lungs started to burn for air. Every instinct told him not to breathe, that he would drown. But Jiro's mouth hung open and his chest expanded and contracted naturally.

"Come on," Jiro encouraged. "You'll be fine. Watch me." And with that Jiro opened his mouth wide and took a deep breath. "See? I'm okay."

So Riagan opened his mouth and took a small, experimental gulp. Oxygen entered his lungs, alleviating the burn. And the water stayed out, instead of pouring down his lungs, choking him. He took a second, larger breath, still not comfortable with it, but forcing himself to stand pat.

"What is this stuff?" he asked.

Jiro shrugged. "Don't know. New exhibit. Watch this."

He kicked his legs out ahead of him. His body tipped back and floated, as it would in a normal pool. Jiro waved his arms, propelling himself across the room. A few others swam up near the ceiling, using the walls to spin cartwheels. It looked fun.

Riagan jumped and immediately the liquid around him buoyed him, as if he really had become immersed in a pool the moment he moved. Once more his instincts told him to hold his breath, but he forced himself to ignore it as he swam upward and touched the ceiling. He rotated and kicked off a sidewall, propelling himself along the ceiling. He could easily see Jiro in the liquid, unlike water, which distorted things and irritated the eyes.

As Riagan passed by Jiro, he reached out and grabbed his ankle. Jiro jumped and spun, eyes wide, before realizing what had happened.

"You little." Jiro lunged at him.

Grinning, Riagan dove backward, swimming down and away, out of reach.

Caleb passed by the entrance on the far side of the room. Remembering what he was supposed to be doing, and not wanting to risk Caleb returning, Riagan swam to the floor and exited the room, leaving Jiro behind.

To his surprise, Riagan found that he was dry the moment he stepped outside. But he had no time to marvel over the liquid. He located an empty nearby hallway that led to the bathrooms, which offered a little temporary privacy. Hopefully Caleb wouldn't stumble across it. Dr. Snelling would notice her missing wrist-comp soon, if she hadn't already. He needed to get back. He fished the wrist-comps out of his pocket, hoping no one would look that closely. He reactivated Neil's wrist-comp using Neil's code. Then he scanned Dr. Snelling's device.

The scan program found thirty-six fingerprints, twelve of which matched, and were fat like a thumbprint. The other twenty-four had smaller numbers of matches and were thinner. Now that he had the thumbprint, he needed a replica. He slipped Dr Snelling's wrist-comp into a pocket for the moment, and removed a 3D printer.

He waited for it to boot up and connect to Neil's wrist-comp. A few moments later, a blinking green light on the black, baton-like 3D printer indicated it was ready. He set a print cloth on the ground and initiated the print job. The 3D printer floated out of his hand, down to hover right above the cloth. It moved back and forth, depositing layer upon layer on the cloth until a rubbery thumbprint rested there. He snatched it up, retrieving Dr. Snelling's wrist-comp from his pocket. He used the print to activate the wrist-comp.

"Welcome, Dr. Snelling," the device greeted as its screen lit up.

"Why do you have Dr. Snelling's wrist-comp?"

Riagan inhaled sharply, expecting to find Caleb. But it was Jiro who had entered the hallway. His hair was plastered to the side of his face. Riagan grimaced, trying to think up an excuse on the fly. How could he have known Dr. Snelling would have a voice greeting for her wrist-comp?

"Did you steal that?" Jiro crossed the distance between them, studying the wrist-comp.

Riagan decided to work fast instead of responding. He grabbed Neil's device, preparing to connect it to Dr. Snelling's wrist-comp at the bridge port so he could make a complete backup of the data hers contained.

"Did you steal that?" Jiro repeated, his voice taking on a demanding note.

Panicked, Riagan settled on a partial answer. "I think Dr. Snelling might have information about Rois' death."

Jiro frowned. "Why would she?"

Think. Think, Riagan, he demanded of himself.

Jiro's eyes widened. "You think she's a traitor?"

Riagan's jaw dropped, though he kept his composure enough to keep the devices pressed together so the backup wasn't interrupted. How had Jiro come up with that shot out of left field?

"You do." Jiro pressed forward, face alight with curiosity. "You think she's a traitor, too."

Riagan wanted to deny it, but knew anything he said now would sound insincere at best. Instead, he glared at Jiro, wishing he would go away. And what did he mean by *too*?

"You think Dr. Snelling's a traitor?" another voice asked.

Riagan and Jiro both jumped in shock and surprise. Dirk and Arielle had entered the hallway. Did everyone have to go to the bathroom at the same time? Riagan groaned inwardly. This was the worst covert operation ever. Might as well make an announcement over the museum's intercom.

"Riagan does," Jiro answered. "Thinks she helped Jarl."

"I didn't say that!" Riagan protested.

"You think she's involved somehow," Jiro insisted.

"Why would you think that?" Arielle asked. "I can't imagine Fran's mother would do anything like that."

The copy program on Neil's wrist-comp completed and Riagan disconnected the device. He slipped Neil's device back into his pocket. "I have to return this before Dr. Snelling suspects anything. Can we talk later?"

"Fine." Dirk crossed his arms. "But we're coming, too. I want to hear this."

Riagan bit the inside of his lip until it stung, furious with himself for not being more careful. He should've gone into the bathroom and hid in a stall.

Exiting back to the main area, he pressed on through the room to find Dr. Snelling. He didn't wait to see if the others would keep up. Before long, he found Dr. Snelling, her kids, Neil, and Eris scouring the ground around where they'd been earlier. A part of Riagan hoped they were back to look for the invisible shape he'd thrown at Dr. Snelling earlier, but he picked up his pace nevertheless.

Dr. Snelling looked up as he arrived. "Have you seen my wrist-comp? I think it fell off when I was trying to get the mouse off." Her lips curled in disgust. "I'm going to have a word with management."

"I've got it." Riagan held it up and pointed a thumb over his shoulder. "A little kid saw it and took off with it. I figured it was one of ours and had to catch up with him."

The screen on the wrist-comp was still on, so Riagan pressed the sleep button and handed it over. His face itched as he fought to keep his expression neutral. He wanted to smile in pride at coming up with a cover story on the spot.

"Thanks, Riagan." Dr. Snelling accepted the wrist-comp and his explanation. "I owe you. Can I buy you dinner?"

Neil stepped forward between them. "We have to get back to campus. I got a message from Instructor Tereshkova. The Trojan spiders' cage got knocked over. She needs help catching them."

A look of revulsion swept over Dr. Snelling's and Fran's faces.

"Another time," Dr. Snelling said.

"Look forward to it." Neil grabbed Riagan's shoulder and propelled him back the other way.

Riagan exhaled, relieved to get away without Dr. Snelling the wiser, but he also hoped Neil's message was a fake. He hated dealing with the Trojan spiders. Although it would've provided a good excuse to shrug off the others for now.

Once they were well away from Dr. Snelling, Dirk grabbed Riagan's arm, pulling him up short. "Why do you think Dr. Snelling is a traitor?"

Neil missed a step and Riagan grimaced.

Eris' eyes widened and she whispered. "You guys think Dr. Snelling is a traitor?"

Now Neil arched an eyebrow.

Riagan shrugged. "It was an accident. Jiro caught me going through her wrist-comp."

Eris leaned in closer. "You stole Dr. Snelling's wrist-comp?"

Neil grabbed her arm and steered her past actual, fire-breathing komodo dragons, or what looked like komodo dragons. Once more Riagan spotted Caleb eyeing them.

Riagan tapped Neil on the shoulder and pointed him out.

Neil nodded. "Keep up," he said to the others.

He took off in a new direction, picking up his pace. They passed kids swimming in imitation lava. The kids kicked and screamed and played as they would in a normal pool. One little girl climbed out of the pool, skin perfect and unblemished by the faux-lava. After hurrying past a few other exhibits, he ducked into an empty hallway, the others in tow. From there they could easily see if Caleb approached.

When they had all gathered round, Neil said, "I'm sure you guys heard Jarl used chemical hypnosis on me?"

They all nodded, except Arielle, who frowned. "I thought Jarl was chemically hypnotized, too?" she asked. "That he wasn't acting on his own?"

Neil shrugged. "Maybe. Regardless, Jarl did a lot of bad things while he was chemically hypnotized. I wanted to know if I did, too. What am I guilty of?"

Eris and Arielle's eyes widened at this revelation.

It surprised Riagan, too. He had never considered why Neil had agreed to all this spying. Just assumed it was to help him discover who all had betrayed them and caused Rois' death.

"No one would give me real answers," Neil explained. "All anyone would say was that I was fine. I had nothing to worry about. Everything else was too dangerous for me to know."

"Typical." Eris scowled and crossed her arms.

"I wanted to know for myself." Neil's expression was sober, if not a little pained. "I wanted to find out what happened to me. What I had done."

"You aren't responsible for anything you did while drugged." Jiro nodded once, firmly, as if enough said on the explanation.

Riagan wanted to echo the sentiment, but the words stuck in his mouth. He'd never considered what Neil might've done when he was chemically hypnotized. He'd assumed Neil had been knocked out. Had Neil had his own role to play in all that had happened? Had he in some way been contributed to what happened on Mars? Riagan stared at the floor, troubled.

Neil shook his head, clearly not accepting Jiro's answer. "I have to know. And since they wouldn't tell me, Riagan and I are searching for the answers."

"And you think Dr. Snelling has them?" Dirk asked.

Neil shrugged, but held up his wrist-comp. "We believe she has at least some of them."

"We'll help you get them, then." Eris sidled over to him.

Before Neil could respond, Caleb appeared at the far end of the hallway. He grinned, satisfied with himself for finding them.

"You're wasting your time, Caleb," Neil said, walking toward him. "We're all heading out."

The others took his cue, Dirk and Arielle headed back the way they'd come, while Eris and Jiro moved past Caleb, both giving him dirty looks.

"Maybe, I'll join you then," Caleb said, turning to follow Neil. Eris and Jiro marched at Neil's side, forcing Caleb to trail after.

Neil grunted. "Your call."

Caleb turned his attention back to Riagan. "You coming?"

Riagan stood there a moment, undecided, then pointed back behind him. "I'll hang here a little longer." He moved out of the hallway, forcing Caleb to choose between him and Neil. Thankfully, he chose Neil. Riagan wasn't sure he could handle Caleb tailing him at the moment.

Images of their first encounter with the Dahaka replayed in his mind. He remembered the sudden fear that had overwhelmed them. Had they both been chemically hypnotized that day? How long had it lasted? One minute? Fifteen? An hour? Couldn't have been much more than that, but what could he have done in that time? What could he have been made to do that in some small way led to Mainyu's success in smuggling the CME off Space City, led to the attack on Mars, led to Rois' death.

He had already accepted blame for his own failure. But did he share a greater portion than he'd realized? Did Neil? He wanted to shrug it off, to blame Mainyu. Jarl. Even Dr. Snelling. But that didn't seem to be Neil's take.

Chapter 21

Maellyn—One Step Forward, Two Steps Back

Maellyn stood under a tarp—their base camp—which shielded her from the rain pouring down on the Ourania sim. Partially, anyway. The wind whipped the rain sideways, pelting her face and arms. Nico had added the rain into the sim because it would seep down through the soil to the aquifers below ground. But why did he have to make the storm quite so strong?

With all efforts to maintain quarantine on Ourania failing, Trini's latest theory posited that rainwater carried the Azymi down to the aquifers and spread from there. They needed the data to prove it, yet if that was the case, what could they do about it? There was no stopping the rain. In the sim, Nico could end it with a simple coding command. On Ourania, despite all the Alfar's technological prowess, they still couldn't control the weather.

"What is wrong with people?" Nico slammed his fists down on the table, disturbing Devika, who huddled over a computer screen. "I've got less than fifty participants from the city and roughly that many at the academy. Don't they care?"

"They care," Anand answered from the edge of the tarp, arms folded as he watched the storm. "They just don't believe tagging photos makes a difference. That's why I focus on machines only. I assign a task. The scouts carry it out."

The scouts Anand built were the lone positive result they had at present. The little flying machines had done a superb job of scanning and snapping pictures of the fungus in Nico's sim.

"You're such a flob," Nico growled. "All they can do is document the problem. They can't help *solve* it like OutSleuth and my sim."

Anand glared at Nico's back a moment, before typing in something on his wrist-comp. A couple of his scouts sprang into the air, departing into the rain. Maellyn wondered what he was up to. There wasn't much the scouts could do in all this rain.

She didn't have to wait long for an answer. A few minutes later, the pair of scouts returned carrying two aqua bombers—creatures Nico had invented in his sims. But why had he put them in the Ourania sim?

The aqua bombers resembled spheres of water the size of birthday balloons. The first scout moved over Nico's head as he tinkered with OutSleuth on his computer. It dropped the aqua bomber, scoring a direct hit. Nico gasped, body tensing, jaw dropping as the aqua bomber soaked his head and upper torso. Before he had time to react, the second aqua bomber hit, leaving him spluttering.

Anand snickered. Maellyn covered her mouth to hide her own smile.

Wiping the water from his eyes, Nico spun toward Anand. "I'll get you this time."

The aqua bombers had reformed at Nico's feet. He snatched them up, tossing one after the other at Anand's head. Anand easily ducked, so Nico scrambled to his feet, chasing after him. Anand leapt behind the stack of hefty metal storage containers. But Nico was determined. He darted around the right side, forcing Anand to rush behind Devika. Anand's foot caught a leg of her chair, twisting it several inches and nearly dumping her on the ground. She grabbed onto the table with both arms to steady herself, eyes wide. She'd been engrossed in her modeling programs, missing the boys' antics until her brother nearly knocked her over. She shouted after him, then Nico as he whizzed past her, still giving chase.

Anand performed an awkward step-leap over Nico's computer, barely clearing it. Which was a good thing. If he'd busted Nico's computer, things really would've escalated. As it was, Maellyn had to jump backward before Anand plowed into her, Nico lunging for the back of his shirt. Unfortunately, her momentum had her on her heels, and Nico hadn't anticipated Anand dancing just out of reach. Neither had time to react as Nico plowed into her, knocking her backward onto some chairs and they both tumbled sideways onto the ground.

She grunted in surprise. Then she sucked air through her teeth as pain momentarily flared up her arm. She'd caught her elbow on the edge of a chair, which sent a shiver straight up the bone.

"Am I going to have to suspend you boys?" A voice asked from out of the rain.

Maellyn struggled to her feet, holding her right arm close to her chest, though the discomfort was subsiding. Nico scrambled to his feet, an apologetic look on his face as he reached to help her up. Even Anand stared at her, frozen, mouth hanging open, knowing they'd messed up.

Fintan entered the tent carrying four rectangular containers. He gave both boys an admonishing frown.

"I'm sorry, Maellyn." Nico reset the chairs as she dusted herself off.

"You both could've destroyed a bunch of our equipment." Maellyn crossed her arms. "This is too important for you two to act so carelessly. Lives depend on our work."

Nico mumbled another apology, as did Anand.

"Keep it up and you'll soon find yourselves off the team," Fintan said.

Both boys looked sullen at this, but said nothing.

Fintan nodded as if the matter was over and raised the containers he carried. "I've got dinner."

Those three words gave Maellyn's mood an instant boost. She reached for one of the containers. "Let me help you with those."

Fintan relinquished one, which took both of her hands to wield. She needed a hot meal, even one from the academy mess hall.

Anand and Nico both crowded around to help Fintan with the rest of the food. Devika had returned her focus to the computer screen, pouring over the models she was building.

They dug into the containers, pulling out roasted potatoes with onions and peppers; asparagus with butter, garlic, sliced almonds; and toasted loaves of bread with pepper jack cheese melted in the middle.

Maellyn pried open her container and discovered why it had been so heavy. Four purple melons and a large knife had been stuffed into the container. She was hungry enough that she thought she could eat one of the soccer ball-sized melons on her own.

Fran and Trini each grabbed slices of bread and bit into them, strings of melted cheese stretching from their mouths to the bread. Anand prepared a plate with potatoes topped with sour cream, tomatoes cooked with jalapenos, and a butternell on the side. There was also a jug of purple melon punch.

The one thing Maellyn might've added to the meal was a little meat, but hadn't expected any from Fintan. The Macab didn't eat meat, though he kept his views on the subject to himself, preferring to let others choose their eating habits without comment or recriminations from him. He had only spoken of his refusal to consume meat one time in her presence, after she had flat out asked him. Even then, he presented his views as statements of fact about Macab dietary practices and never brought it up again. Since that day, she never ate meat in front of him—not sharing his views, but respecting his choices.

She pulled out a purple melon and cutting board. As she started to cut off a slice, Devika squealed. "It's working!"

Everyone stopped eating and turned toward her. Maellyn froze with the knife halfway through the melon. Devika sat back from her chair, a mixture of awe and relief on her face.

"The cell is active!"

Trini dropped her plate on the table and ran to Devika's side, bending down to study the computer. After a second, she half shouted half laughed. She threw her arms around Devika's neck as she screamed, face beaming.

Maellyn hurried over to join the pair, the melon and knife forgotten. Everyone crowded around, jostling for a view of the peanut-shaped Azymi cell on the monitor. Maellyn expected the fungal cell to pulse like a heartbeat, but it remained stationary.

"How can you tell?" Nico asked, frowning.

Devika pointed to several series of numbers along the bottom of the screen. The numbers cycled constantly. "Those numbers represent the cell's internal processes. It's stable."

The rotating numbers were a bit anti-climactic, but it remained a huge success. Devika had successfully modeled a functioning azymi cell. Understanding how it worked allowed them to test out hypotheses for turning it off.

"How do you know it's accurate?" Maellyn asked.

Devika gestured at the numbers again. "I can read them. They fit what we should see. We used common techniques. We created a flux-balance analysis model to simulate consumption of food by the cell. We used a combination of differential equations and a geometric model to handle the cell replication process. We've built models for DNA damage and repair, protein activation, and even division of the cell contents."

"Could you repeat that in terms we understand?" Anand grumbled.

If he'd been in reach at the moment, Maellyn was sure Devika would've hit or kicked her brother for that comment. Instead, with annoyance thick in her voice, she said, "I used normal math calculations to model how the cell works."

"We have different definitions of *normal*," Anand replied.

At that moment, the cell stretched, elongated, and separated into two identical cells. Everyone cheered, Maellyn as loud as anyone, and took turns clapping Devika on the back. It was a great breakthrough. A lot of work would still be needed to understand the processes well enough to figure out how to reverse them. Even more work to develop a means of attacking or deactivating the Azymi fungus. But maybe it was a turning point.

It wouldn't be much longer before they'd possess enough data from the rain seeping down through the soil to the aquifers to know how much it contributed to the spread of the fungus, which, if true, would exponentially expand the quarantine zone, perhaps beyond their ability to control.

Maellyn tried not to consider that possibility, although it was vital information they needed. For now, she returned to the purple melon and resumed cutting slices for everyone, snipping away bites for herself as she went.

Everyone returned to their plates, now chatting. It was the best news they'd had in weeks.

Fintan's wrist-comp beeped. Smiling and laughing, he activated the wrist-comp, which projected a hologram of Aili's face into the air above him. One look at the Alfar's face and all the humor leached out of Maellyn the way blood spilled from open wounds, leaving her cold and stiff.

"Aili, it's good to see you," Fintan began, then paused, his smile evaporating as he noticed her tear-soaked cheeks. "What's wrong?"

Everyone quieted. Maellyn's throat dried, but she dared not take a drink. She couldn't even remove her eyes from the haunted face before her. Despite her grievances with Aili, she didn't wish that look upon anyone—the despair of someone who has lost something of such value that their life may never be mended. Whatever weighed on the Alfar's shoulders, it was clear she was breaking.

Aili coughed once and a hand appeared, rubbing her cheeks clean. "I was hoping to get an update, Fintan."

He nodded solemnly. "We'll have results on the fungus leaking through the soil to the aquifers by morning. If it's occurring, we should have projections on fungus expansion within the next few days."

She accepted this without comment. The first time Maellyn could remember the Alfar doing so.

"We've also had a breakthrough," Fintan said without a hint of their earlier joviality. He explained to her their success in simulating the fungus cell.

"We've done the same," Aili replied. "I'll alert Albrin. Send your models here and we can compare." There was no excitement or hope evident on her face or inflecting her words.

"Have you received approval for use of the scouts on Ourania?" Fintan asked. Anand perked up at this.

"Their use has been rejected," Aili replied.

Anand's jaw dropped.

Consternation caused Fintan to bristle. "I don't understand. I thought we were close. Our test runs here in the sim have been perfect."

"Our government declared that *spy* technology will never be allowed on Ourania."

Fintan looked at a loss. Anand growled and kicked over a chair, knocking it out from the tarp into the rain.

"It's not spy technology," Fintan said. "We're using it to help locate outbreak cases only."

"Nevertheless, how do we know how all scouts are used?" Aili asked. "Some could be diverted for covert purposes."

Anand shook his head, moving over in front of Aili's hologram. "We can share access to the tracking programs. You can see for yourself what every scout is doing."

"And how would we know every scout is accounted for?"

Anand threw his hands up in the air. "We're allies. Why would we spy on you?"

Aili shrugged. "I'm told you can hand over the plans, so we can build our own and run them here."

"That'll set us back months." Anand found his chair out in the rain and sat down, his back to the tarp. He was drenched in seconds.

Maellyn debated going out to talk with him. This was his primary contribution to the group, and it appeared all for naught now. But his rigid posture told her he needed space for a bit.

"Well, the scouts were the primary purpose of our next planned visit." Fintan's shoulders slumped, and his exhaustion was more apparent than Maellyn could ever remember.

"We have to eliminate all visits to Orestes." Aili looked numb as she spoke. "We have cases on Orestes now."

Maellyn exchanged looks with Trini, whose eyes had widened at the revelation.

"How?" Fintan asked. "I know you've had trouble maintaining quarantine, but Orestes?"

Aili nodded, and her next words sent Maellyn reeling. "Alvi is infected. He's quarantined here." At this, Aili's reserve broke. Tears streamed down her face. She made a couple efforts to restrain herself, before she broke the connection.

Warm tears stung Maellyn's eyes. How had this happened? How could the fungus have been transported from the planet to the Alfar moon? How could little Alvi be one of the sick?

The sim ended, leaving them inside the round metal cages of the sims facility. Maellyn blinked, shielding her eyes as they adjusted to the sudden brightness from all the lights.

Fintan climbed out of his cage. "All of you head to medical. Now."

"Why do we need to visit medical?" Nico asked as they emerged from their own cages.

Maellyn made the connection first. "Orestes was exposed. We don't know when."

"You don't think?" Trini asked, but she couldn't finish the words. Her face paled as she took a few hesitant steps.

They had visited many times. And worse still, had traveled all over Space City since starting their work on Orestes. If even one of them had been infected, and had brought it back here…they had possibly spread it throughout the ship. Everyone would need to be checked out. Perhaps even a quarantine started here.

Chapter 22

Neil's Investigation of Dr. Snelling

Neil lounged in a chair in a corner of the mess hall, a glass of purple melon punch on the table beside his wrist-comp. "I've gone through emails. Ran a search program for my name, Riagan, and Jarl. No hits."

"What about chemical hypnosis?" Jiro asked, before biting into an eggroll.

"A few, but they're encrypted."

"Try Fran as a password," Eris suggested, both hands clasped around a steaming mug of coffee.

Neil snorted. "She'd use a better password than that for encrypted files."

"How do you know?"

He grinned. "Cause I already tried Fran's name."

"Her son, Nate?" Riagan suggested.

Neil shook his head. They all fired off password suggestions based upon what they knew about Dr. Snelling, most of which in reality pertained to Fran. None of it worked.

"What else you got on there?" Jiro asked.

"Lots of research papers and notes, personal and work calendars, and data files I can't run."

He'd also discovered quite a few emails exchanged with the Council, as well as Dr. Trevena, but as he started reading through the unencrypted ones, he realized this was typical since she ran the Olsin Pedran facility. Even the encrypted emails had subject lines that related to new tech. They had a full backup of Dr. Snelling's wrist-comp, and thus far had found nothing useful on it.

"Can you distribute the files so we can help search?" Jiro asked. "Would go a lot faster."

Neil shook his head. "Can't risk anyone discovering we copied Dr. Snelling's files." He'd kept their primary search between himself and Riagan.

"I agree," Riagan said.

At that moment, Neil received an email to his own inbox. Sent from Dardanos. The subject line read *URGENT, all students report to medical immediately!*

"Did anyone else get the email to report to the infirmary?" Jiro asked, frowning.

Neil pulled up the email, but the instructions simply elaborated on the subject, stating all students should make orderly haste to the infirmary. It assured them all that they had no cause for alarm, but it was mandatory.

"What's that about?" Eris asked.

"No cause for alarm?" Jiro's voice held a skeptical note. "This late in the day, no way this is routine."

"You two get over there," Neil said, and held up the wrist-comp. "Riagan and I'll hide this first."

They split up, Neil and Riagan heading for the alley behind their dorm. Neil hated using the alley and purposely avoided it as much as possible. Every time he set foot in the alley he remembered the overwhelming fear that had consumed them without reason or explanation during their first encounter with the traitor—Jarl or whoever it had been. And it seemed completely reasonable to avoid the alley, even if the actual attack took place a good distance from their dorm. Logical or not, part of him felt that if something horrible happened there one time, it could again.

But worse than that, Neil thought it was the complete lack of memory of what happened after he'd been chemically hypnotized that bothered him most. He had no idea how much time had passed between them exiting that basement and fleeing for safety in the garden. What might have been done to him that he couldn't remember? What might he have done? And now that Jarl and Ormazd were both dead, those answers might never come.

He had both hoped and dreaded that maybe over time he might remember. Had asked the doctors about such a possibility, but they had assured him he had no memories to recover. The chemical hypnosis didn't cover up or hide memories. Rather, it inhibited the brain's ability to form new memories while under the influence. The doctors had called it anterograde amnesia. He couldn't retrieve memories of what happened because they didn't exist.

Now they headed for the window to their dorm room, retracing those steps, at least partway, toward a black hole. There was something on the other side of that event horizon, but it was beyond recovery. And he didn't want to experience it again. Didn't matter that that particular threat was long gone. Or was it? Jarl hadn't chemically hypnotized himself.

As they neared their room, Neil held his wrist-comp to his mouth. "Window open."

It rose.

"After you." Neil gestured for Riagan to go first.

Riagan retrieved the custom stepladder they'd 3D printed and hidden behind the recycling bin. With it, he grabbed the bottom sill for their dorm window and hoisted himself up into the room. Neil placed his hands on the ladder, hesitated, feeling chased by the memory, or lack thereof, then climbed up into their dorm room, rolling onto the desk between their beds, then pulling the ladder into their room; he'd replace it later.

Riagan had already crossed the room and locked the door to prevent intrusion. They could hear the chaos of boys rushing out in the hallway, shouting questions or passing gossip about the summons, and didn't want to risk someone breaking in to make sure they'd heard.

Neil dropped to the floor. "Where do we hide it?"

Riagan held a finger to his mouth for quiet. He stepped over to his bed and grabbed the footboard, pulling the bed back a good couple feet from the back wall.

"What are you—" Neil began.

Riagan swiped his hands sideways below his jaw, glaring at Neil. Then he shuffled past, clambered up onto their desk, and slid behind his bed. He dropped to his knees. Neil frowned and moved over to the corner of the desk as Riagan removed a square panel, no bigger than a shoebox, from the back wall. Setting it aside, Riagan held out a hand for Neil's wrist-comp.

"How long's that been there?" Neil whispered, handing over his wrist-comp.

"Since we moved in."

"Why didn't you tell me?"

Riagan placed the wrist-comp into the hole and replaced the wall panel. Once it was covered up, Neil couldn't tell the wall wasn't completely smooth.

"I've always kept a secret spot for valuables." Riagan stood and climbed back over the desk. "Only Rois knew." He shoved the bed back against the wall, then gestured toward the door. "Shall we?"

Neil shook his head in disbelief. "What else have you kept secret from me?"

Riagan shrugged noncommittally as he unlocked the door and stepped out into the hallway.

Looking at the headboard one last time, Neil wished they didn't have to leave the wrist-comp behind. They hadn't found what they were searching for yet, but he felt positive they soon would. And he didn't want to wait. But reviewing it in medical with so many watching eyes wasn't a good idea. It would be fine. And they couldn't ignore the summons.

Most of the boys had departed the dorm, but a few stragglers brought up the rear. Holding the entrance door open, Instructor Glenn boomed for all of them to hurry and get their lazy rear ends to medical as ordered. Neil picked up his pace, not wanting to be the last one out.

They arrived to a packed waiting room, students everywhere. Maliek Johnson stood against the wall, observing the confusion, occasionally fingering the comb sticking up from the rear of his head.

Neil sidled over. "Maliek, any idea what's going on?"

The first year gave him a quick glance, then went back to studying the room. "Rumors."

"Anything that makes sense?" Riagan asked.

Maliek shrugged. "Something about Ourania. Fintan's team. Maybe spread a virus or something."

Neil's mouth went dry. *Maellyn.* "Anyone know what?"

"Supposedly they went straight from the sim facility here. Except Fintan. He's gone to the city." Maliek emphasized this last bit as if it was the most significant piece.

Countless additional questions came to mind, but Neil decided it was time to seek real answers. He pushed through the crowd toward the front desk, but found he couldn't get within five feet. Dozens of students surrounded the desk, grilling the nurses for answers.

"Am I sick?"

"What did Fintan's team bring back?"

"Am I infected? Am I going to die?"

"I don't feel so good. I need to see a doctor."

"I heard the Alfar betrayed us. Deliberately infected us with some virus."

Neil scoffed at this last comment. Then he raised his voice, trying to be heard over the questions and demands of the others. "How about Maellyn? Is she here?"

The nurses, for their part, calmly assured everyone they were going to be fine. The academy was taking precautions to keep them all safe, but didn't respond to anyone's questions directly. They asked everyone to relax. A doctor would see each of them in turn and explain everything. Of course, those assurances meant little when a few minutes later they began to hand out medical masks for everyone to cover their faces. This caused a few hysterics.

As Neil slipped his own mask on, his stomach did flips. How bad was this?

Knowing he wouldn't get answers from the nurses, he weaved through his classmates, making his way toward the doors leading back to the examination room. Everyone was so busy blathering on about what so-and-so's mother had said, or uncle, or their friend of a friend on the Council, or pestering the nurses, that it was easy for him to get to the back door. But half a dozen students blocked the door. He'd have to wait for them to go back first.

He reached for his wrist-comp to message Maellyn, grasped his bare left wrist, and remembered he'd hidden it in his room. He scowled. He considered sneaking back to his room. He could always come back later. It would be hours before the doctors had time to see all of the students.

But as he turned back, he noticed the front doors were now guarded by Instructors Aldrin and Tereshkova. Both turned back any students who tried to leave. No choice but to stay here and get in to the doctor as quickly as possible. Hopefully one of them could tell him if Maellyn was all right.

A few paces to the side, Cade was leaning against the wall studying his wrist-comp.

"Hey Cade, will you message Maellyn?" Neil asked.

Cade looked up for a moment before returning to what he was doing. "Already did. As soon as I heard the rumors. No answer yet."

"What're you working on? This your big new story for the school paper?"

Cade shook his head. "Naw, tagging photos on OutSleuth."

Neil scrunched his nose. He'd done a terrible job helping with that of late. He'd even forgotten to give Maellyn an update, which he'd promised her. He had to get back on that as soon as they found out what they could from Dr. Snelling's data.

"Just doing my part," Cade said. "Did you see the article I wrote on the release of OutSleuth?"

"Oh… yeah. I must've missed that one." In truth, the only thing he read in the papers were the recaps of the Games matches. He sometimes found tidbits on how the teams played that helped with later strategy.

"I think the whole academy missed it," Cade deadpanned.

"Why don't you forward it to me?" Neil asked, feeling guilty. "I promise I'll read it."

"Yeah, sure. Will do!" Cade looked up, eyes shining at this and Neil promised himself he would read that article first thing when he retrieved his wrist-comp.

"Hope it's better than your coverage of our last game against the Chameleons. That was awful. You saw the video replay. I made it to base with the last egg before Matt Ripley."

Cade snorted and returned to marking photos on OutSleuth. "Not how the judges saw it."

"The judges were blind."

It took twenty minutes before Neil was ushered through the doors by an older nurse, who wore a white one-piece medical suit that covered her arms down to gloves, legs and boots, and her head except for her face. And that was mostly covered by a mask; one step down from a hazmat suit.

All the doctors and nurses back here wore the same suit, leaving Neil feeling vulnerable. He suddenly regretted pushing to be one of the first back here. He wanted to ask if he could have one of those protective suits, but guessed they wouldn't have a whole lot of spares to hand out to everyone.

Searching the hallways and open doors as the nurse led him back toward an exam room, he asked, "Do you know if Maellyn is here? Is she all right?"

"I can't comment on another patient's status," she replied in a tone that suggested she got this question all the time and wasn't about to start answering it now.

"So she's a patient?" He missed a step, his heart beating faster.

The nurse kept right on walking. "I simply can't answer."

He wanted to grab her shoulders and shake her, demand an answer. He needed to know if Maellyn was here. Or Nico. Or the rest of her team. Had they been infected with whatever plagued the Alfar? How could they? They weren't even allowed onto Ourania's surface. But the academy wasn't checking out all the students as a drill. Something serious was going on.

The nurse showed him into an empty room with a desk, cabinets, chair, and an examination table.

"A doctor will be with you shortly." The nurse closed the door behind him.

Reluctant to sit on the exam table, wondering who had been on it before him, Neil instead took a seat in the chair to wait. His stomach fluttered. It wasn't his first time in the facility—he'd been required to take a physical at the start of each school year—but this was the first time he fretted about getting sick here. He was sure he wasn't sick. He'd know if he was.

He didn't have to wait long before Dr. Torres entered the room. A quad doc followed her in, hovering a few paces back from her left shoulder. The quad docs, little black drones with four mini helicopter blades to fly, assisted the doctors, carrying blood or other samples.

Neil jumped to his feet, moving clear of the chair.

"Hello, Neil. How are you?" Dr. Torres placed her wrist-comp on the desk. Her eyes were red, face drawn from exhaustion, but she maintained a smile. The quad doc hovered against a wall.

"Fine. How's Trini?" Neil asked. "I heard her team was sent here."

Dr. Torres nodded. She maintained her smile, but it tightened slightly. "She's doing well. All of them are fine. Maellyn, too."

He exhaled, his shoulders dropping. Maellyn was okay. Nothing bad had happened to her. "There're rumors all this is tied to what's happening on Ourania."

"I'm afraid I can't comment on the matter." Dr. Torres leaned against the desk and typed on her wrist-comp. "But right now there's no cause for alarm. We're taking precautions." She set aside her wrist-comp and placed her hands in a machine that resembled a hand dryer. The device—a specialized 3D printer—sprayed disposable gloves onto her hands.

"If you'll remove your shirt, I'll do a quick examination," she said.

He pulled his shirt up over his head, leaving his torso exposed to the cool air in the room, which sent a shiver through him. He placed the shirt on the exam table, feeling a little awkward about being half naked in front of her. "What're you checking for?"

Ignoring the question, Dr. Torres pulled her now gloved hands out of the machine and gestured for him to sit on the exam table. "Have you had any problems lately? Chest congestion? Headaches? Trouble breathing?"

There was a stool at the foot of the table, which he stepped onto. Sitting on the edge of it, he rubbed his now chilly arms. Dr. Torres removed a stethoscope from a desk drawer and crossed over to him. She placed the stethoscope on his back.

"No." He took a couple of deep, measured breaths, fearing for a half second that he might abruptly experience congestion in response to her questions. "I've felt great." The words came uncertain, as if he needed her to confirm he was healthy.

"Good." She stepped around in front of him, looked directly at his chest, blinked once and stared for a few seconds, as if trying to see inside him.

He fought the urge to hunker down and cover his chest with his arms. He knew she was using the contacts to do an x-ray scan. She'd receive preliminary results through the contacts.

"You look good." She replaced the stethoscope in the drawer and retrieved a tongue depressor. "Remove the mask and open your mouth."

He did as he was told, setting the mask in his lap and flattening his tongue as best he could. She flattened it further with the tongue depressor. After searching his mouth, she deposited the tool in a recycling bin and retrieved her wrist-comp. She typed a few notes, then approached and grabbed his left arm, placing two fingers on the inside of his wrist to check his pulse. She studied her wrist-comp as she did so.

Not liking the silence, he spoke up. "I heard Fintan left for the city. Are they doing these checks there, too?"

She let go of his wrist, typed a note in her wrist-comp, then grabbed a blood pressure monitor from the wall, which she wrapped around his left arm.

"I can't confirm anything," she said as she pressed a button on the blood pressure monitor, which began to expand, squeezing his arm. "But I'm sure you can guess how Space City would respond to a perceived threat."

He nodded.

After she studied her wrist-comp for another few seconds, she removed the monitor from his arm. A second later, she retrieved a new blood sample vial and needle, taking a small sample while he waited patiently. Didn't even sting.

"No signs of infection. You're cleared to go." She deposited the blood sample into a small container the quad doc carried. "The nurse will take you out." She headed toward the door.

"Is Maellyn still here? Can I see her?" Despite assurance that she was okay, he wanted to hear it from her himself. That and to find out what had happened to start all this. Dr. Torres might not be allowed to tell him, but Maellyn could.

"She's under supervision with the rest," Dr. Torres replied over her shoulder. She exited the room, the quad doc in tow, before he had time to ask any further questions.

If they'd already been cleared, why were they being kept in the hospital? He donned his shirt. Deciding he wouldn't need the disposable mask anymore since he was headed out, he tossed it in the recycling bin and opened the door. He poked his head out in time to see Dr. Torres entering another room.

Before he had time to think what to do, the nurse from earlier popped up in front of him. "Ready to go?"

He looked over her head, searching the corridor for signs of Maellyn, Trini, or someone else from their team. Plenty of other nurses and doctors hustled by, along with a few patients, but no one he thought would give him news regarding Maellyn.

The nurse straightened up, as if prepared for him to cause some trouble. "This way, please." She pointed down the hall. When he hesitated a second longer, she added, "I can have security escort you instead. We have a lot of people to check and no time to waste."

"Okay."

She led him a little way down the hall and opened a door leading outside. After he stepped out, she promptly shut it behind him.

"Not much for manners," he muttered. He tried the door handle—locked as expected. He wasn't seeing Maellyn for the time being, so he hiked around the infirmary to the courtyard, which was deserted. It was a little eerie.

A yawn pried open his jaws. Sleep would be nice, but he had way too much to do. Hurrying across the courtyard, he slipped into the mess hall and ordered a soda before returning to his room and locking the door.

After guzzling a quarter of the soda, he tossed the bottle on Riagan's bed and grabbed the baseboard. He grunted from the effort of hauling the bed back from the wall. Heavier than they looked.

With enough space for him to access the back wall, he catapulted himself over the desk. He dropped to his knees and removed the panel. Reaching into the hole, he felt around, but found an empty base. Frowning, he reached further in until he brushed the right stud, but no wrist-comp. He moved his fingers along the base until he hit the left stud. Where was it?

He pressed his face against the hole. Nothing. A jittery panic pitched in his stomach. He stuck his arm back in and reached upward as far as his arm would go, but he was sure Riagan had dropped his wrist-comp into the hole. He felt along the base once more. The wrist-comp was gone.

Had Riagan returned first? He'd stayed well back in the waiting room. And without a wrist-comp, Neil couldn't talk to him until he returned. In the meantime, Neil began searching the entire room, trying to contain his unease.

Chapter 23

Riagan Receives an Ominous Message

Sunlight created halos around the trees on the opposite side of the empty courtyard when Riagan exited the academy infirmary. He couldn't remember the last time he'd seen the courtyard vacant. But then again, he never saw five-thirty in the morning either.

He sent Neil a message, letting him know he'd been cleared. One of the last. Neil, having been one of the first back, would have gone straight back to their room hours ago. Assuming he had been cleared. If he hadn't, Riagan hoped he hadn't changed his wrist-comp password recently.

"Riagan, wait up." Eris caught up with him halfway across the courtyard. She bobbed beside him, showing no signs of a lack of sleep. "Heard everyone in Space City has been ordered to report for testing, too. They're freaked."

Riagan shrugged. The Alfar and a lot of others were concerned, but it wasn't his problem. He had enough of his own to deal with right now.

"What'll happen if anyone's infected?" Eris asked.

"Do I look like a scientist?"

"Ooookaaaay." They walked on in silence.

His stomach growled, reminding him he hadn't eaten anything since their summons to the infirmary last night. He decided to stop by the mess hall for a bite to eat. He typed a quick message to Neil, asking if he wanted anything, then picked up his pace. To his annoyance, Eris followed him. Thankfully, she said nothing as they entered the cafeteria and ordered.

A few minutes later, Riagan had a nice to-go box with a ham, cheese, bell peppers and onion omelet, with a side of bacon and toast. Neil hadn't answered his message, so Riagan ordered him the same thing. As he headed for the door, Eris met him, coffee and a bagel in hand.

"Ya know, girls aren't allowed in the boys' dorm before eight a.m.," Riagan said as the mess hall doors slid open.

She rolled her eyes. "Everyone knows Instructor Glenn isn't up before seven. After last night, it'll probably be a lot later than that before he's patrolling the halls."

He started to tell her he wanted to get some sleep after he ate, but knew she wouldn't leave until she'd at least spoken with Neil, so he pressed on to his room.

"Where is it?" Neil demanded as they entered.

"Where's what?" Riagan asked, recoiling at the accusation on Neil's face.

"My wrist-comp. What did you do with it?"

Riagan sucked in a breath of air, his eyes traveling to the head of his bed, which had been pulled back from the wall. The blankets were piled at the foot of his bed, while his desk drawer contents had been dumped out in the middle of it. In fact, all the desk drawers had been emptied on the beds and floor.

"What do ya mean? I just got cleared at the infirmary." He raised the two containers of food. "Stopped to get breakfast first. You're welcome."

Neil pointed at the wall behind Riagan's bed. "It's gone. If you didn't, someone found it."

Riagan dumped the breakfast containers on Neil and leapt over the desk to the space behind his bed. He wasn't thrilled about exposing his hiding spot to Eris, too, but he'd have to find a new one anyway.

The fake panel lay on the ground. It made him cringe a little. He inspected the hole, but it was empty as Neil said. Nor was there any sign of the wrist-comp behind the desk or under his bed. "Who could've found it?"

He checked again, unable to believe someone had swiped the wrist-comp. No one had ever found his hiding places, except Rois, and she'd never told anyone.

Neil shook his head. "Only Jiro, Dirk, and Arielle knew we stole from Dr. Snelling. But why would they take it?"

"They didn't." Eris typed away on her wrist-comp. "They got called back right before I did. You'd been out for hours by then."

"Who then?" Neil asked.

Riagan rubbed his tired eyes, unable to believe this. A part of him wanted to blame Neil. He was the only person who knew about the hiding spot. But Riagan also knew Neil wouldn't reveal it. Nor had he had the time to do so. "Did Dr. Snelling discover our hack?"

Neil shrugged. "Doubt it. Have to ask Nico. He set up the program."

"Dirk says they're ordering breakfast. Just got there after being released." Eris read from her wrist-comp.

Riagan smacked his hand against the headboard as a possibility occurred to him. "Caleb! He's been spying on us."

Neil looked doubtful. "Maybe. Possible, but what are the odds he knew we'd just hidden something of interest. And how did he discover the hole. I still think Dr. Snelling is our best guess."

"I don't know." Riagan gritted his teeth as he sent a message to Jiro.

"Why would she do this?" Eris crossed her arms. "Why not report us? Unless there's more to this than you're telling us."

Neil whistled and turned to stare out the window.

Riagan kicked his headboard. He'd known he should've told Eris to come back later. As he debated how to put her off, his wrist-comp beeped. New message. Sender marked private.

He bit his lip and frowned.

"What is it?" Eris asked, eyeing the wrist-comp.

Instead of responding, he opened the message.

Did you think I'd let you *endanger my scientists?*

A chill ran through him. He re-read the question. It had to be from Dr. Snelling then. He showed the message to Neil, who took the wrist-comp in both hands, scrutinizing. Eris looked over his shoulder.

"How do we respond?" Neil asked.

Frustration stabbed Riagan like a hot poker. He grabbed his wrist-comp back and typed away. Neil and Eris moved to his side to watch.

He wanted to move away from her, but at this point she knew too much.

This won't derail our search, Dr. Snelling.

Send.

Riagan gripped both sides of his wrist-comp, squeezing. All three stared at the screen, waiting with bated breaths.

Fishing for my identity won't help. But since you've interfered in my plans, you're going to help fix them.

"What plans?" Eris asked.

Neil shook his head, expression queasy.

Why would we do that? Riagan typed. If this wasn't Dr. Snelling, this person was at least tied to her in some fashion. That in itself was another lead.

You've inserted yourself into matters where you don't know the players or the stakes. You're a pawn, and as such, you'll follow orders or be removed from the game none-the-wiser.

He had a flashback to last year when he and Neil stood in the garden after their encounter with the traitor. Neil had wanted to act then, but he had insisted they remain silent and do nothing, because they didn't know what they were doing or whom to trust. That stance had in part led to Rois' death. But acting on the threat came with its own risks, and once more, they were groping in the dark with only the barest hint as to the danger.

"What now?" Riagan asked.

"Do we have a choice?" Neil asked. "Besides, it's a new lead. Without Dr. Snelling's data, we have nothing."

"Why do you think its Dr. Snelling?" Eris asked again.

Neil held up a hand to silence her. "Get the request first, then we'll decide what to do."

Riagan nodded, but he also didn't want this person to think they were too eager. *Ok. What is it you want?* He imagined obtaining some weapon or other piece of technology, like heroes always pursued in stories. Something the antagonist coveted and there was a race to see who would get it.

Travel to Siavash for the Emperor's Ruby. When you return, I'll have further instructions.

"A jewel?" The request was decidedly anti-climactic.

Neil scowled and turned away. "We can't go back to Siavash."

"Back?" Eris spluttered, wide eyes sweeping back and forth between them.

Neil hunched in on himself as he realized what he'd revealed. Riagan almost threw his wrist-comp at him for the faux pas. Neil dropped to a sitting position on his bed, giving an uneasy smile. "Okay. Yes, but we can't say more."

"No." Eris wagged a finger at Neil. "We're helping you, and you're hiding stuff from us?"

Unable to process two conversations at once, Riagan resumed typing. Let Neil dig himself out of this one.

Our means of getting there is compromised.

"They're not related," Neil said.

"How is traveling to Siavash not related?" Eris exploded.

Neil cast a panicked look at the door.

Eris crossed her arms, but lowered her voice. "You and Riagan have scurried around campus in a hush since last summer. Traveling to Siavash apparently. But it's not related to the answers we're seeking from Dr. Snelling? Or these mysterious messages?" Eris arched an eyebrow, daring Neil to deny it.

Riagan opened his mouth to tell Eris off for butting in, but his wrist-comp buzzed with a new message.

Further instructions will be sent at the appropriate time. Until then, keep this discussion between us.

To his shock, the entire chain of messages dissolved from his wrist-comp, leaving no proof to show anyone. He gaped.

"Okay, it may be related," Neil allowed, "—but we still can't tell you. I'm sorry but you'll have to trust us. We're being as open as we can."

And stay away from my scientists.

This message also evaporated before Riagan could show Neil.

Eris turned to Riagan, but he shook his head, dazed at the ability of whomever had contacted them to wipe things off his wrist-comp. In fact, it reinforced the danger of what they were involved in.

Knuckles rapped on their door.

Eris jumped and gasped. Riagan gripped the headboard, at a loss after the direction the last few minutes had taken. Neil lurched to his feet and walked to the door.

It was Jiro. "What happened to your wrist-comp?"

While Neil recounted what had happened since their summons to medical, Riagan leaned against his desk. He hated not knowing who was ordering them around. A part of him still suspected Dr. Snelling, but they had no way to confirm and they couldn't act upon such an assumption. Based on the messages disappearing off his wrist-comp, he felt safe in ruling out Caleb, as much as it pained him to do so. He didn't think Caleb smart enough to pull that off.

Eris pointed at Riagan's wrist-comp. "You think it's Dr. Snelling, but won't tell us why?"

"I'm sorry we can't reveal more." Neil looked visibly sick. "Walk away if you want. We'll understand. All we ask is you keep this between us for now."

This whole thing was spiraling out of control. This was why Guiman had insisted they keep their spying a secret. Had drilled the need into them all year. Why hadn't he and Neil rejected their offer of help after stealing Dr. Snelling's wrist-comp?

Eris exhaled loudly. "This isn't good. We should report this."

"We have no proof." Riagan held up his wrist-comp to show her the messages were gone.

Eris' eyes widened at this and Neil gaped, before burying his face in his fists.

"You're going to do it?" Jiro asked, his expression showing he thought they'd lost their minds. "No questions or precautions?"

"We'll run it by Dardanos," Neil said.

That seemed to calm Eris. "Dardanos. Okay."

That was the last thing Riagan wanted to do. They couldn't do so without letting Dardanos know they had gone out on their own to steal Dr. Snelling's wrist-comp. That would not go over well. But maybe he could help them discover who the messenger was.

The warning to keep quiet flared across his brain. No. Alerting Dardanos would complicate matters. And perhaps destroy their sole lead right now. He was tired of wasting time with no leads. He needed to pursue this one. Preferably just Neil and himself.

Chapter 24

Maellyn Regrets a Break

Maellyn met Neil outside the elevator in the science labs. It was their first evening alone in months, and she was pleased he dressed up for the occasion, wearing a purple silk shirt and black slacks from which hung the golden pocket watch she'd bought him for Christmas.

"You look stunning," Neil said, staring at her dress. "Reminds me of a mountain stream."

The blue dress flowed to green and back as she moved, different parts of it catching the light.

"Thank you!" She brushed her hair back behind her right ear, her hand grazing the columbine earring—tiny lavender flower growing in a little pot. "I love that shirt on you."

"How are you doing?" Neil asked. "I was relieved when I got your message. You're clear?"

"I'm fine. All clear," she said, but she turned to hit the call button for the elevator so he couldn't see her mouth tighten as she blinked back tears that threatened to overwhelm her. She didn't want to fret over Alvi tonight. She needed one evening where she wasn't worrying. Just for a few hours.

She'd almost cancelled tonight. What right did she have to relax, or for romance, when so many Alfar were suffering from the effects of Azymi? But it was Fintan who had forced her out of the lab for the evening, insisting she rest her brain. *Do something, anything,* he'd said, *that gives you a break from obsessing over the problems we're trying to solve. Recharge so you can come back stronger.*

But it was hard to get away from it fully.

"Travel to Orestes is suspended," she said, "—to prevent spread of the fungus."

"Sounds smart. But can you still work on it?" he asked.

"Oh, yes. Plenty to do. Too much, really." She rubbed her arms, trying not to agonize over the number of tasks waiting on her. Maybe she should've argued harder against taking the night off.

She needed to review Devika's models showing Azymi-infected fauna. The current model predictions weren't matching up with what they were seeing in the field. Add to that the revised document Fran had given her that outlined why the Alfar needed to accept use of the Scouts to study the outbreak area. Fran had gotten inputs from Arielle on certain bits of language that needed to be in the document if they wanted a positive response from the Alfar. That document needed to be sent tomorrow.

The elevator door pinged open.

"Everyone else on your team fine?" Neil asked as they entered the elevator.

"Yes, they're great. Everyone's cleared." She pressed the button for the Astronarium and took a deep breath, trying to clear her head. "It really was all precaution."

He nodded. "That's good." For a moment, they rode the elevator in silence, before he asked, "Where is it you're taking me?"

This made her smile. She'd visited the Astronarium so many times that she sometimes forgot most students didn't have access. It afforded them the perfect opportunity to be alone. "It's a surprise."

The elevator door opened upon an expansive hallway. Floor to ceiling windows on either side revealed direct views of space. Most nights you could find lab students down here toiling away on one project or another, but tonight they had the Astronarium to themselves.

She led him to one of the window panels and tapped on it, activating a preprogrammed zoom; one of her favorites. Immediately, a long spiral galaxy appeared across a dozen window panels. Golden specs of light swathed in clouds of blue and green and red.

His jaw dropped at the sight. "How did you do that?" He reached up and placed fingers against the panel, as if to touch the stars.

Smiling, she squeezed his arm, pulling him close. "The windows are telescopes. What you're seeing is a galaxy light years away."

"I had no idea this was down here." He turned to her, eyes wide. "How did I never know this was down here?"

"We scientists keep it to ourselves. If everyone knew about this place, we'd be overrun. Instead, it's a quiet spot to study and conduct experiments."

"I don't see anyone else tonight."

"Being the lead scientist's daughter does come with a few advantages." She crossed the hall and tapped on another window. The nearest panels displayed a stellar mass black hole, which resembled a crescent ring of light.

She bit her lip. It wasn't her programmed visual. One of the students must've forgotten to change the settings back after wrapping up for the day.

"All the windows magnify?" He gestured down the hall.

"Four miles worth." She steered him along. "Scientists and students apply for and are assigned sections on which to work. Each window has multiple channels, allowing multiple visuals, or a group can share. One channel is always reserved for Dad."

Three chirps from something on Neil caused him to jump, his face turning to an 'O' of apology. He reached back and withdrew his wrist-comp from his back pocket. "I'm sorry. Forgot to silence it."

He clicked on the screen and read the message she couldn't quite see. The wrist-comp caught the faint overhead lights. It looked polished and shiny, as if it were brand new. Then he shut off the device and dropped it into his back pocket. "No more interruptions."

"Did you get a new one?" she asked.

"Yep, just today," he replied.

"Was something wrong with your last one?"

"It's lost."

"No idea where you might've lost it?"

He shrugged, but his face had a strange twist to it, as if he was lying, or at least not being completely honest. She stared at the floor as they resumed walking. Yet another thing he was hiding, and she couldn't understand why. As if something had changed between them after their summer apart. He had this wall he used to shield part of himself. Riagan, too. At first, she'd believed it small, insignificant. She had disliked the secrets, but had her own and it had seemed like a trivial barrier. Now it loomed between them, a great steel dam. What did it hold back?

Did he not trust her? She wanted to ask. Perhaps he thought his silence protected her from something. That had been her go-to explanation whenever he'd avoided questions previously.

An uncomfortable silence had grown between them, as if the black hole on the window panels had sucked all the romance out of the night. She moved forward uncertainly, pulling away from him.

"What is happening?" She crossed her arms with a shiver.

"What do you mean?" But from the expression on his face, she could tell he both understood and dreaded her question.

She wanted to let it go. Forget about it. But this had to be done. She couldn't accept secrets, even well-intentioned ones, if that's what they were.

"I'm working so hard right now," she said. "I rarely get good sleep. Taking time off to eat seems selfish when there are lives on the line." She gestured toward his chest then hers. "This is supposed to be my break. Yet it's become a struggle. You're closed off."

He raised his hands a little as if to defend himself, before dropping them back to his sides. His eyes fell to her feet, his shoulders slumped. "I don't want to keep anything from you. None of this is how I want it."

"But you do nothing to change it. It's a choice *you* make to share or remain silent. To be open and honest. Or to guard your secrets."

He turned his back to her, running his hand through his unruly hair. "Look. I… Riagan… It's just—"

She wanted to remind him that she shared everything she was doing with him. She had wanted to tell him, because by doing so, he could better understand her. That led to a possibility that cut at her. Was he hiding all this because he didn't want her to understand him better?

When he turned back, his eyes held guilt and regret. "Eventually I hope I can explain. Believe me, I want to. I just… can't. Yet."

Her wrist-comp chimed a tune and she groaned inside, closing her eyes. It was the special tune for Fintan's group, a message from one of them. They'd only contact her in case of an emergency.

The wrist-comp was inside a special pocket in the back of her dress, allowing her to disguise it. Slipping her hand into the back pocket, she removed the wrist-comp as she opened her eyes.

He stood closemouthed now, waiting.

The message came from Trini. It was brief.

Soil drainage map complete. Quarantine is useless.

She cursed in her head. As far as emergencies went, this was close to the worst bit of news she could've gotten.

"I'm sorry. I've got to go." Tears filled her eyes. She wanted to drop to the floor and curl up in a ball.

"What's wrong? What happened?" He placed a steadying hand on her arm; she realized she'd been swaying. He gently grabbed both of her arms, stabilizing her. She wished he would pull her into an embrace.

Before he could, she backed away, knowing she couldn't stay and feel sorry for herself or anyone else. Nor could she listen to empty apologies.

She turned and ran down the hall toward the elevator. "Our work. Things got a lot worse."

"What can I do to help?" He came after her.

"I... I don't know if you can. Or if any of us can." Nor was she sure any longer that she wanted his help.

Chapter 25

Neil Tracks an Emperor's Ruby

An air of anxiety enveloped the group as Neil led them into the sims facility. Jiro and Eris had never traveled to Siavash, and it was a mission no one wanted. Neil wasn't thrilled at returning to Siavash, but at least they weren't entering the capital again. The only reason he'd agreed to go was because Dardanos had argued this might be what they needed to discover who on the Council was tied to Mainyu.

Going in their Space City camouflage uniforms instead of the imitation Dahaka armor also bothered Neil, but Guiman had insisted no Azios traveled outside the capital in the armor. For them to wear it would immediately alert any Azios they encountered, which Guiman also insisted was unlikely due to where they were traveling. And the Space City camo would protect them better.

Neil chose one of the sims cages and activated a thorneway. Black liquid filled up the cage, which sent a chill up his spine. He'd traveled many times, but the process never felt comfortable.

"Ready?" Neil asked, looking from Eris to Jiro since it was their first trip to Siavash. It was Dardanos who decided to keep them in the fold, at least as far as their investigation into Dr. Snelling, but not before he chewed out Neil and Riagan thoroughly for their risk-taking.

No one answered, so Neil stepped through.

They emerged from the thorneway into a shallow cave, morning sunlight streaming in through the mouth. Only the cave's sharp hook at the back allowed the thorneway to be hidden from passersby.

The cave exited to a forest of tall, deciduous trees covered in golds and reds. Fall in full bloom on Siavash. They caught glimpses of the Dahaka capital a few miles to the north, which was closer than Neil had hoped they'd be. But it was far enough away, and perhaps early enough in the morning, that the only sounds were that of a swift flowing river somewhere to the south.

Jiro and Eris both walked rigidly, arms raised and ready to shoot if they saw any signs of trouble. Seeing them made Neil conscious that he was doing the same, muscles tense. It was important to be on guard—they were in a hostile environment—but they'd make a mistake if they remained too tense.

"Think of this like our missions for class," he said, pleased that his voice came out steady and commanding. "Stay focused on your surroundings. Keep calm. Follow procedure."

Eris responded first. "Scouts, three-hundred-yard perimeter search."

A pair of gray scouts, no bigger than flies, rose up off her left shoulder and flew off in opposite directions. Neil hadn't even noticed they were there until they took off.

Jiro blinked. "How did you get scouts?"

"Anand asked me to test his prototypes," Eris replied. She shrugged like it was routine.

Neil knew she'd gotten the prototypes because Anand was smitten with her, but he didn't say so in front of Jiro, who was, too. Neil wished she'd choose between them and leave him alone.

"When did Anand add voice commands?" Neil asked as they headed East. "Nico used his wrist-comp to control the scouts in his sim."

"He made a lot of changes from what Nico originally designed," Eris answered. "I love them. Much better than the mini drones."

Damp leaves shifted underfoot. But every so often Riagan managed to find a dry one to step on. Each time Neil cringed, half expecting a dozen Azios to materialize out of the forest, surrounding them.

Each fall, Hardin had drilled the Ursa team in the stadium forest on moving silently, even with dry leaves everywhere, considering it vital to their success in the Games. Neil hadn't expected that training to help them outside of their games, but he, Eris, and Jiro all avoided the noisome trouble spots. It was hard to believe Gilbright hadn't done the same with Taurus. Once they returned home, Neil resolved to put Riagan through Hardin's training regimen.

Eris' wrist-comp flashed a warning and pulse-beeped. It pierced the early morning hush. Neil spun around, eyes wide. The alarm was loud enough to catch the attention of Azios in the capital. Eris blushed and silenced it.

"Sorry. The scouts' alert program defaults to my regular alarm settings."

"What is that? A bullhorn?" Riagan asked. "Ya wake up to that?"

"Heavy sleeper," Eris said, blushing. "If I don't, I'd never make my morning classes."

Neil hissed for them to quiet as he scanned their surroundings for whatever had caught the scouts' attention. Eris pulled up footage from the scouts on her wrist-comp, but saw nothing identified.

Neil started to ask her to bring up the scouts' radar, when a voice barked, "What are you doing here?"

Eris fired at the voice, her shot striking the bark of a tree as a figure darted behind the trunk. Neil took aim at the tree, as did Riagan and Jiro.

The figure stuck out both hands. "I just want to talk." The voice was familiar, but Neil couldn't quite place it.

"Nobody shoot," Neil ordered, though to be honest, he was half afraid that might cost them. "Who are you?"

Rashn eased his head out from behind the tree, taking measure of them. "You should be quieter. Azios hunt here all the time."

Neil didn't lower his aim. "Are you alone?"

"Just me." Rashn flashed a big smile which surprised Neil. It was a first he'd seen on a Dahaka. He wore simple garments similar to what he'd had on during their fight in the arena.

Neil lowered his own hands to his sides. "Everyone relax." His heart didn't listen. It pounded.

Everyone except Riagan followed suit, though Jiro's and Eris' eyes were wide and glued on Rashn. The tension in the air was like the threat of an avalanche.

Rashn stepped out, apparently deciding Riagan wasn't going to shoot. "Have you been out here since the tournament?"

Eris' and Jiro's gazes drifted to Neil—more secrets he and Riagan had withheld. The revelation would undermine their trust in him.

Neil grimaced. "No."

Simple answers would be best. He liked Rashn, but they needed to minimize risk.

"You're looking for something," Rashn ventured. "This close to the capital without disguises. What's got you dino hunting without a knife?"

"I'm afraid I can't share that." Neil was uneasy that Rashn had guessed even that much.

The Azios bobbed his head from side to side, a Dahaka expression similar to rolling ones' eyes. "It can't be that important. Anything of value is inside the capital."

Neil shrugged.

"I could help you find it faster. Reduce your chances of encounter with another Azios."

"Or lead us into a trap," Riagan growled.

"Come now." Rashn's expression darkened. "You've given me no provocation. I have no reason to harm you."

Neil noted the reference to the Azios code that Rashn claimed to follow. Yet there was nothing in the code about giving aid. "Why would you help us?"

Rashn eyed the ground, as if embarrassed. "After our fight in the tournament, I'd rather not see you get captured again. You earned your freedom. But the others wouldn't agree."

While Neil appreciated the sentiment, he felt a responsibility to keep his team safe. Trusting Rashn even a little was an unnecessary risk. "We know where we're headed. Won't be here long. Let us go on our way."

The Azios held up both hands again. "I can help. Don't reject me because I'm Dahaka."

"Seems like a great reason to refuse," Riagan fired back. Eris echoed his sentiments.

Neil stared past Rashn, considering. They already had the Emperor's Ruby marked on their map. They could find it on their own. But if Rashn had wanted to capture them, he could've alerted others by now. And he might get them to their goal faster.

Perhaps a little test, to see what Rashn knew. "We're looking for the Emperor's Ruby."

Rashn frowned, looking perplexed. "You came here *just* for that?"

It was hardly the reaction Neil expected and he wondered if they were miscommunicating. The tradutors were extremely sophisticated, rarely interpreting alien words incorrectly. But it wasn't unheard of, especially for rare terms.

"If that is all, I can get you as many as you need."

Eris shook her head. "And you're going to do this just because you like Neil and Riagan?"

Rashn took a couple steps forward as if this was all decided. "We fought together. We're battle brothers. What more reason do I need?"

Riagan bristled, not that Neil could blame him. Until Rashn, Neil had considered all Dahaka to be the equivalent of a violent gang. Encounters were to be avoided at all costs. They always kept their guard up around Dahaka.

Yet Rashn had deliberately put himself in a position of vulnerability while offering help. And as a good team lead, Neil had to consider anything that might increase his chances of mission success and keeping everyone safe.

He found himself wanting to trust Rashn. The Azios appeared earnest. But a wrong decision held consequences for all four of them, not just himself and Riagan. And what if they weren't discussing the same thing? The private messenger hadn't given them any clue as to what they were looking for, so how would he know.

Under his breath, Neil said, "Please don't make me regret this."

Rashn stared quizzically.

"We accept," Neil said, motioning for Rashn to lead the way.

The Azios bounced forward, heading northeast, expecting them to follow.

As Neil followed, Eris closed in.

"You sure?" she asked.

His first thought was to decline. How could he be sure? He was trusting the enemy based upon one past conversation and a battle together. But his job as team lead was to bear responsibility for the risks they faced. He must keep his reservations to himself. "Yes," he replied forcefully to make sure his hesitation didn't show.

Eris studied him a moment, nodded, and walked at his side. Neil expected Riagan to come voice his complaints as well, but he remained off on his own.

While Neil had alertly examined their surroundings from the moment they set foot on Siavash, he became even more focused now. He was taking a big risk on Rashn. He intended to make every effort to minimize that risk.

"Neil, I've got another alarm from the scouts." Eris stared at her wrist-comp.

"What is it?" He moved to her side to see what she had on-screen.

The footage from the wrist-comps showed a thick, scaly creature on eight legs, like a weight-lifting, steroid-pumping spider dashing through the trees. Closing fast.

Rashn hissed, rotating as the creature emerged from the forest ahead of them. Neil pointed his gloved hands, taking aim at the creature while he shifted sideways at a measured pace toward the Azios. Just like the scouts in Nico's sims, these gave a poor heads up. He'd have to ask Anand to spend more time working on their range.

"Get back." Rashn didn't take his eyes off the creature. "The Nle'fes bulrushes with incredible speed and power."

Neil chose to hold his ground, trying to pick out where to shoot. A dozen tiny eyes clumped together above a jagged maw in the Nle'fes' bulging center mass. Was it better to shoot the eyes to blind it or the legs to cripple it? He decided to aim for the eyes, noting it would be easier to at least hit the center mass. He fired, lasers striking a few of the eyes, as well as its mouth and body.

The Nle'fes roared, more angered than hurt.

"I said back off," Rashn shouted.

The Nle'fes charged Neil. He fired a second time, his instincts screaming to run. His body hummed with the anticipation of impact, but as the Nle'fes crouched to leap, Rashn collided with it, his arms stabbing like engine pistons. His hands pumped so fast, the knives in his hands were a blur. Rashn's momentum carried them to the ground where they tussled for a few seconds before his body flew backwards, kicked away by the Nle'fes.

Yellow pus bubbled out from the creature's body. It climbed to its feet, stumbled, then righted itself. Once more it charged, this time for Rashn, who had clambered back to his feet.

Dozens of laser shots struck the Nle'fes' legs and side, jarring Neil out of his slack-jawed trance. Riagan, Jiro, and Eris had all joined the battle. Neil chided himself for even the momentary lack of focus. He had faced similar creatures in the Games. Though none this fast.

He raised his arms to shoot once more, but the Nle'fes sprang high into the air, covering half the distance between it and the team, shrugging off their shots.

It bowled over Eris. She screamed from beneath it. Memories of Rois' on Mars flashed through Neil's mind. Desperation drove him forward. Not this time. Not while he could do something to stop it.

Two of the Nle'fes' legs kicked out, catching Jiro in the chest as he tried to help. He flew back into a thicket. And then Rashn dove onto the creature again, stabbing. The impact carried them off of Eris, who lay motionless. Neil rushed to her side, searching for injuries.

Her eyes were open wide and she cringed when she saw him. He didn't see any blood.

The creature wrapped its legs around Rashn's torso, squeezing. Riagan, who was behind the pair, shot the creature in the back. Rashn's arms, loosely pinned to his sides, stabbed one-two-one-two-one-two into its belly. The creature rose up, lifting Rashn from his feet, before it collapsed. Rashn crashed on top of it, still piercing it with his tusk knives. It screamed as it died.

Neil knelt down beside Eris and offered his hand. She jerked away, looking around wildly for the Nle'fes.

"It's dead," Neil said in what he hoped was a reassuring tone. "Are you hurt?"

Tears filled her eyes, but she shook her head. She took his hand and let him pull her to her feet as he stood before she brushed the tears away.

Jiro dusted himself off. Everyone appeared okay.

Neil sighed in relief until Rashn rounded on him, waving a knife.

"I told you to stay back." The Azios marched over until mere inches separated them.

"I was trying to help." Neil couldn't believe Rashn's reaction.

"You pissed it off and nearly got us all killed."

Neil's face reddened.

Rashn turned sideways, raising his voice for all of them. "If you want me to take you to the Emperor's Ruby, everyone will follow my orders from now on. Or I leave now."

"Go on then." Riagan waved dismissively at the Azios. Eris and Jiro added their own protests against taking orders from a Dahaka.

Neil held up his hand to forestall them and barked, "No, he's right. We don't know what we're up against. We need his help."

"We've done fine on our own," Riagan insisted.

"You've been lucky." Rashn glowered at them. "If I hadn't been here, you'd all be dead."

Riagan scowled.

Any doubts Neil had harbored evaporated after seeing Rashn risk his life to protect them from this attack. And he didn't want to waste any more time.

"Please Rashn, lead the way," Neil said.

The others started to protest but Neil silenced them. And when Rashn motioned them to follow, Neil didn't hesitate.

Everyone else fell in line behind him, which was fine with him. If he'd made a bad decision, he'd prefer he faced the consequences, not the rest of them, if at all possible. In reality, he knew they were all in the pot together, and hoped he wasn't tipping them over into the fire.

A message lit up Neil's wrist-comp. He checked it, hoping for a reply from Maellyn. He hadn't heard anything from her since their failed date. He'd sent apologies and tried to go visit her, all to no avail. But instead, the message was a reminder from Instructor Tereshkova about their upcoming exam in two days. And he hadn't gotten any studying done.

"You look troubled." Rashn glanced at Neil's wrist-comp. "Bad news?"

"It wasn't great news." Neil turned back to the forest ahead. "But it's more the message I didn't receive."

"Your female?"

"Yeah, she's angry at me for keeping all of this a secret from her." He held up both hands, gesturing at the landscape as a whole. "Because she doesn't understand the dangers."

Rashn walked in silence, offering nothing.

"And I think she's also mad I've been too busy to help with an important project she's working on."

Rashn chuckled. "I don't know about human females, but ours don't consider that a valid excuse."

"Pretty much the same for us," Neil said.

"So what does she need help with?"

Neil hesitated a moment, but decided there wasn't much harm in Rashn knowing. After all, the Dahaka couldn't take advantage of the outbreak. The Alfar defensive technology required little supervision. "There's a fungal outbreak on Ourania. The Alfar have been unable to control it and asked for Space City support. Maellyn's part of a team researching the problem."

"Does she ask a lot of you?"

"No, not really," Neil admitted. Saying that aloud sent a wave of guilt through him. Instead of going after Dr. Snelling, he could've been helping Maellyn. He was the one who had chosen not to prioritize her. And his decisions had led to more secrets between them.

Rashn dropped the matter, perhaps sensing Neil's discomfort. Fifteen minutes later, Eris pulled them up short.

"I've got more alarms from the Scouts." Eris was pulling up her wrist-comp. A few seconds later, her eyes widened, rising to Neil. There's a lot of Dahaka ahead."

Neil's adrenaline was pumping. They needed to retreat. Quickly. Had they been seen? Rashn had led them into a trap.

He spun on his heels. "Everyone get back now." He took aim at Rashn. "Traitor."

The Azios held up both hands. The tusks were gone, his hands empty. "There's nothing to fear." With one hand he pointed ahead. "It's a village. None of them will cause you harm."

"Why did you bring us here?" Neil asked, ignoring the assurances.

"You wanted an Emperor's Ruby," Rashn answered. "I brought you to a village that has some. It's safer than where you were headed."

"We can't trust him." Riagan strode forward, aiming his hands at Rashn's head, prepared to shoot. "Take him out and let's get out of here."

Rashn's eyes darted toward Riagan and he licked his lips. "Please, look. Just over that hill. The villagers pose no danger."

"Riagan, don't shoot, but keep your aim on him." Neil kicked himself for trusting Rashn, but he wanted to believe him, too.

Neil topped the hill, which revealed a Dahaka village at the bottom. The villagers stared back. Women and children hid behind carts or rushed into simple huts. The men were all gaunt and dressed in simple garments. No black armor, as far as Neil could see. No one rushed to retrieve weapons. Instead they huddled together, fear distorting their faces, as if he and the team were aggressors.

And then it hit Neil that none of the villagers had blood-red eyes. A feature Neil had associated with all Dahaka. Yet these villagers had whites, and it was this that reassured him.

Neil turned back to Rashn. "They've got an Emperor's Ruby? Why would they give it to us?"

Rashn shrugged. "Why not? They're in plentiful supply. Women pick them all the time to wear in their hair."

Neil blinked. In their hair? Were the tradutors suffering another translation error? It seemed unlikely. "Really?"

Rashn turned sideways and beckoned for them to follow. "It's a common enough flower."

"We're here for a flower?" Eris' voice disbelieving. But she had relaxed, too.

"That can't be right." Riagan moved to Neil's side. "He's lying."

"I've no reason to lie," Rashn replied. "You'll see." He took a couple steps down the hill and paused to wait for them.

"Or we're talking about two different things by the same name," Jiro said, echoing Neil's fears.

Neil grabbed his wrist-comp and typed a note to their private messenger. *Is the Emperor's Ruby a flower?* He half expected a response ridiculing them.

When nothing came immediately, he decided they might as well continue on and get a look at these flowers. "Where can we get one?"

"Are ya serious, right now?" Riagan demanded. "It's a flower. It can't be what we're looking for. We're wasting time."

"We don't know what we're looking for." Neil glared at Riagan, warning him to stand down. "All we know is its name."

Riagan huffed and pointed at his wrist-comp. "We've got a map. It's Southeast of here."

"That's where the Emperor's Ruby grows." Rashn took a step toward Riagan, eyes trained on the wrist-comp and map.

Riagan took a cautious step back and aimed with his free hand at the Dahaka. Neil grabbed Riagan's wrist to stop him from doing something stupid. Rashn had given them no provocation and the last thing they needed was bloodshed right now. Not here.

"You swear no one in the village will attack?" Neil asked.

"Most don't know how to fight," Rashn assured them. "The Azios are all violent. They love it. But out here in the villages, the Dahaka are different."

Neil checked his wrist-comp, but still no answer. It had to be the wrong thing, right? Why would the messenger go to so much trouble for a flower? Unless the messenger was toying with them for amusement. If they had been sent here for the flowers, it would be better to obtain them here, now.

"Let's see them." Neil took a step down the hill, hoping he wouldn't end up regretting this.

Riagan wrinkled his nose, but fell in beside him.

As promised, none of the Dahaka villagers brandished weapons as Neil and the team entered. Instead, they all shied away. Most of them looked half starved, and far too weak to mount a decent attack.

"It's okay. They've come for the Emperor's Ruby." Rashn raised his voice for all to hear. "There's no need to fear."

Rashn's overt attempt to keep everyone calm made Neil wonder if he had woken up in an alternate universe this morning. It was unexpected and outside all experience he'd had with the Dahaka. Perhaps outside the interactions of any human being with the Dahaka.

Instead of caves with massive bone monuments, the village consisted of stone hovels. Rather than Azios gathered around fires or sparring, the villagers tended gardens or fed tethered animals. Most of the Dahaka Neil looked at lowered their eyes, as if afraid to offend him. A number of them ducked into homes or rounded corners, hurrying out of sight.

"Rashn!" A female Dahaka sprinted over. Roughly the same height as Rashn, she possessed a slender build. Long black hair flew like a flag behind her. "I hoped you'd visit. Who are you with?" She showed none of the unease evident on all the others.

Rashn beamed at her. "Vahu, I couldn't stay away. I come with guests. They seek an Emperor's Ruby."

"You come with strange visitors, with the red eyes of Azios, in search of flowers?" Vahu arched an eyebrow.

Neil stifled a laugh as he remembered the red contacts they all wore to help them blend in with the Azios. He had gotten so used to activating the contacts' color change mode when visiting Siavash, that it was routine now. Had the villagers' reaction been because of the contacts? He debated ordering the team to deactivate theirs, but that might cause greater fear and confusion.

"Not everyone is as bloodthirsty as most Azios." Rashn reached up to brush Vahu's hair off her right shoulder. "Some enjoy simple beauty."

Riagan cleared his throat, drawing everyone's attention. "Can we see this Emperor's Ruby?" His lips had thinned, and he looked like he thought this was a huge waste of time.

At his side, Eris' narrowed eyes darted around the village. Searching for any and all possible threats. But Jiro looked relaxed, giddy even.

"Does your mother still collect them?" Rashn asked Vahu.

The female Dahaka remained oriented toward Rashn, but she studied Neil a moment, her eyes meeting his, before dropping to his feet and returning. "Yes." She headed back the way she'd come, and Rashn followed.

A beep on Neil's wrist-comp gave him pause. Riagan and Eris crowded in on either side of him to see for themselves as he pulled up the message from the private messenger.

Yes.

"Ya got to be kidding," Riagan said, shaking his head.

Neil rubbed his chin. What could their messenger want with a flower? Again he wondered if this was all a pointless exercise. Perhaps the messenger was distracting them.

"This is all a big joke to Dr. Snelling." Riagan scowled and looked ready to shoot something. "Make us jump through hoops as payback for stealing her wrist-comp."

The doctor remained first and second through fifth on Riagan's list for the private messenger's identity. Neil had major doubts, but he also didn't have any better alternative.

Rashn and Vahu, several paces ahead of them, were deep in conversation.

"Let's keep up." Neil pushed past his team after the two Dahaka.

They followed Rashn to the rear of the village to a canopy composed from some large, tan animal skins. Beneath the canopy, another female Dahaka, wrinkles on her face and bald patches on her head, wove an orange flower through a reedy basket. Cut orange flowers littered narrow, wooden tables. Beneath the tables were reed baskets, clay pots, and a variety of other simple wooden objects. Many of them had the orange flowers incorporated into them in some fashion.

The moment the older Dahaka woman laid eyes on Rashn, her hands dropped to her hips. "Rashn, why are you taking so long between trips? I'm beginning to think you're taking my daughter for granted."

"I could never do that." Rashn slipped an arm around Vahu's shoulder, pulling her close. "Not that she'd let me, Yaema."

Vahu slapped Rashn's chest affectionately. "You better remember that."

Yaema's gaze drifted to Neil and the rest and she sobered. "Who have you brought?"

"They're humans. They come searching for the Emperor's Ruby."

"Humans?" Yaema said the word slowly, sounding it out as she took measure of them, much as Vahu had earlier. Neil couldn't remember the last time he'd been appraised so thoroughly, as if both Dahaka women had measured, weighed, and assessed him.

"Where are they from?" Vahu asked.

"A place called Space City," Rashn answered.

"They traveled from another planet for an Emperor's Ruby?" Vahu scoffed. "Do they also wrestle long-snouts while fishing for minnows?"

Rashn shrugged. "They were headed to Jagged Rock for them."

Yaema grunted, eyes measuring them again. "Never make it."

Neil grimaced. She hadn't even heard of humans a few minutes ago, but she was already judging them?

"That's why I brought them to you." Rashn moved over and placed his hands on Yaema's shoulders, rotating her toward a half dozen long-stemmed, ocher flowers near the back of the canopy. "I knew you could help."

"Will they pay, or take what they want like your fellow Azios?"

"I'm sure we can find some way to pay." Neil wasn't sure what they had that would be of value to Yaema or the villagers.

Rashn sighed and his shoulder's drooped. "I do what I can. Most of the Azios have forgotten the code."

“And we all suffer for it.” Yaema pulled free from Rashn and crossed her arms.

“I know. I know. You know I hate how the Azios treat the villages.” Rashn held up his hands and looked as if it was an argument he was all too familiar with and weary of. “But I can’t improve things yet. I need to earn my place. Then I can fight to bring back the code.”

Yaema looked like she wanted to say more; give him a good long scolding. Instead she turned back to Neil and the others. She arched an eyebrow at Neil. His mind scrambled, trying to come up with something prudent to say on the matter. He opened his mouth, but shut it again.

Rashn pointed west. “We killed a Nle’fes earlier. I’ll bring the carcass back as payment.”

Yaema and Vahu’s jaws both dropped. “How long ago was this?”

“Maybe thirty minutes ago,” Neil said.

Yaema gave him a quizzical look.

“Give them what they want and I’ll have the Nle’fes back here before the sun hits the zenith,” Rashn replied.

“We can help,” Neil added. The prospect of hauling the creature back here in exchange for a flower wasn’t appealing, but Neil found himself wanting to make a good impression on the old Dahaka.

“A Nle’fes would provide a feast for the village,” Vahu said to her mother.

Yaema grabbed a handful of Emperor’s Ruby flowers from a table and offered them to Neil. “These aren’t enough, but if you bring back the Nle’fes, I can get more. As many as you need.”

“Thank you!” Neil accepted the flowers from Yaema. Normal flowers, pinkish buds in the middle, and a subtle scent like lavender. Sending them here to retrieve some made no sense. But he would show Yaema gratitude anyway, whether this was a waste of time or not. “I promise we’ll get the Nle’fes back to you.” And he meant it. From what he could tell, they needed it.

Yaema’s large smile of gratitude buoyed Neil’s spirits the rest of the day.

Chapter 26

Riagan Betrayed

Jiro popped into the doorway of Neil and Riagan's room. "Check your wrist-comps. Dardanos is announcing a proposal to end the Dahaka embargo."

Riagan lurched up from where he lay sprawled on his bed. "What? Why?" He grabbed his wrist-comp from the desk as Neil lunged for his.

"Everyone knows he wants to run for the Council." Jiro strolled over and dropped onto the bed beside Riagan.

"Why put out this proposal then?" Riagan asked. "Does he want to torpedo his chances?" He couldn't imagine anyone taking it seriously.

Seconds later they had the news feed up. Dardanos on a podium in front of the entrance to the History of the Universe Museum. At his shoulder stood a woman, shoulder-length blond hair, wearing a purple business outfit. Their headmaster had never mentioned her.

A crowd stood on the steps, some holding up signs advocating fair treatment of the Dahaka. Riagan wanted to rush to the city that moment and tear the signs up. What fools would advocate for the Dahaka? Mainyu couldn't be trusted. None of the Azios could.

"The isolation of the Dahaka has to stop." Dardanos jabbed a finger in the air. "They should not be punished as a people or society for the actions of those in power long ago. They have suffered for more than twenty years. It is time for that to end. Time to move forward. Time for Space City to re-establish ties with the Dahaka and help them advance as a society. They are ready.

"That's why I've put forth a proposal to the Council to lift the embargo against Siavash." Dardanos paused as the crowd cheered.

Riagan bit his lower lip. He couldn't believe Dardanos. Actions of past leaders? He knew very well the attack Mainyu had led last year. And the Azios were as blood thirsty as ever. He was privy to all the knowledge they'd gained from their missions on Siavash for Guiman. Was Guiman aware of this?

"I remember the first time I laid eyes on Space City." Dardanos stared over the heads of the crowd as if lost in memory. "Its light filled my eyes and gave me hope. That's what Space City represents. Hope." He rotated his wheelchair and pointed back at the museum. "That hope shouldn't exist solely for humans. Space City should be a guiding light for the universe. It has served as a guide for many alien races we've encountered in our explorations; a friend and mentor that has helped many societies to thrive. And we have in turn thrived from our relations with them."

Dardanos paused, his face turning grim. "Unfortunately, we've also turned our backs on others such as the Dahaka." He held up his hands against sudden protests from some gathered. "I know the embargo was first levied for good reason. The Dahaka started a war that cost a great many lives, and we were forced to sever ties.

"But those who initiated that war are gone. They were defeated. The remaining Dahaka have served their time. They deserve a second chance. So I urge all of you to contact the Council members and ask them to support my proposal. Give us a chance to re-establish ties with the Dahaka. For we are greater in unity and friendship, than in discord."

The crowd cheered. Riagan switched off his wrist-comp and tossed it on the desk. "He's lost his mind." Riagan stood and paced. "How could he release such a proposal?"

"It's a smart move," Dirk said, appearing in the doorway. "The Dahaka are a strong race. They could become great allies if given the chance."

"How can ya say that?" Riagan clenched his fists. "Ya saw first-hand what the Mainyu-led Dahaka are like."

Dirk nodded. "I also heard from Jiro about the Dahaka villagers you met the other day. The poor struggling under Mainyu's reign deserve better."

Riagan glared at Jiro, who hung his head. "This is supposed to be a secret," Riagan growled.

Jiro held up his hands in placation. "I thought Dirk was exempt. He was in on Dr. Snelling's wrist-comp and asked for an update."

"I felt bad that Arielle and I hadn't checked with you since Rory's. I wanted to see if there was anything we could do to help."

Riagan scowled, wishing he could get rid of both of them. Go back to just Neil and himself. There were too many people involved now. How long before the wrong people found out? Like Caleb. Or Patrick.

"But back to the discussion, with the resources at our disposal, there's a lot we can do for the Dahaka while minimizing the threat Mainyu poses," Dirk said.

Riagan threw his hands up in the air, unable to believe the argument. "They're an aggressive warrior race. They don't want our help. They want to destroy us."

Neil sat on the edge of his bed, frowning as if mulling all this over.

"Some do," Dirk agreed. "You can't blame all for the actions of a few."

"Rashn," Neil said quietly. He leaned forward from the bed. "He's not violent. And those villagers, all they want is to survive. They welcomed our help the other day."

Dirk cocked his head a little at Neil's words, but didn't question him.

Riagan's anger flooded through him. He stabbed a finger at Neil. "They're the exception. Rashn admitted it. Any help we give will be controlled by Mainyu and used against us. We'd be strengthening our enemy."

"You'd ignore the suffering of the innocent because you're afraid of those in charge?" Dirk asked, hands out, palms up.

"We can't risk it. We'd be giving them the means to destroy us."

"The villagers happily helped us with the Emperor's Ruby," Neil said.

Riagan scowled. "Where'd that get us?"

The messenger had ordered them to deliver the flower to a specific recycle container in Space City. Eris and Jiro had gone ahead a couple hours early and found anonymous spots to observe the recycle bin. Guiman had set up a camera to record traffic around the bin for a full day. Riagan and Neil had then delivered the flower as requested and departed. After more than two hours had passed without anyone stopping by the bin to retrieve the flower, they had decided to send Eris to check for it. She'd found the bin empty, its contents emptied out the bottom.

"That's not their fault," Neil shot back.

Riagan placed three fingers on the bridge of his nose. "We can't make ourselves vulnerable just to help them. We do that, Mainyu destroys Space City. What then? Who will be helped then?"

"It doesn't have to be one or the other." Dirk's hands were shaking. "We don't have to sacrifice ourselves or allow innocents to endure oppression. We can find another way. Work together to solve the problem."

"What right have ya to ask anyone to risk their lives." Riagan raised his voice. "How many must die, like Rois and Jaya, for ya to accept we can't trust them?"

Dirk grimaced, his shoulders slumped. "If you want peace, you must first provide it to others." He turned and left the room, closing the door behind him.

Riagan felt a strong desire to hurl something at the door. "Can ya believe that one?"

Neil shrugged. "I get what you're saying. I don't want to risk Maellyn or anyone else." His words were flat. "But those villagers, they don't deserve what we saw either. I don't know that we should stand by and do nothing. And I know Maellyn would risk herself rather than let that continue. She's doing it now with the outbreak."

"How can we improve anything? I don't see it while Mainyu remains in charge." Riagan stormed over to the door, needing to be alone.

He did not wish the villagers harm. Nor Rashn. But if Dardanos' proposal passed, Mainyu would essentially be absolved of his crimes. The traitors, too. So Rois' killers would go free. How was that right? How was that fair?

And who would be Mainyu's next victim? Because there would be a next. And another.

Riagan exited the dorm, walking he didn't know where. Everything he'd been working toward for the last year, everything Dardanos had helped them with, could all be for nothing. How could he make such an extreme switch? Unless he wasn't in control of his own actions.

Could he have been chemically hypnotized? They still didn't know who had hypnotized Jarl in the first place. At least it had never been publicly revealed.

Passing by the academy main office, Riagan noticed Guiman toiling away in the garden. It made Riagan laugh every time he saw Guiman out there, a gardener and spymaster. Riagan redirected his route.

"Good afternoon," Guiman greeted when he looked up at Riagan's approach. He sat on a short stone wall, planting new flowers in one of the beds. "What can I do for you?"

"Ya heard about Dardanos' proposal?" Riagan asked.

Guiman nodded, but said nothing. He dug a small hole, dropped a few seeds inside, and covered them up.

"Could he be chemically hypnotized?" Riagan asked.

Guiman laughed. He shook his head and dug a second hole beside the first. "It was a political move."

"Why?" Riagan asked. He'd heard Dirk's arguments, but couldn't believe there were that many who agreed with him.

"There are many who feel Mastracchio and the Council's strategy for relations with alien civilizations is too focused on those who Space City can benefit from, while cutting off those who offer little obvious value."

Riagan frowned. "But we've already connected the Council to Mainyu. They control him."

"Yes, to the Council's secret benefit, not the Dahaka people or us." Guiman patted the dirt over the seeds. "Dardanos is ambitious. If he passes his proposal, it'll give him a lot of power."

"So, he's willing to risk our lives to be a Councilman?"

All those times Dardanos had trained them. Was his sole goal to make them more effective pawns?

"Leaders must always risk their citizens' lives," Guiman replied. "Every time the Council sends people to visit alien civilizations—foe, ally, or somewhere in between—they are placed in situations with some risk."

Riagan waved his hands, grimacing. "That's not the same at all. We don't know those others pose a threat. We know the Dahaka do."

Guiman crossed his arms. "What kind of leader does that make me? I've sent you and Neil among the Dahaka many times. Your lives have been in danger every time. You were nearly killed on a couple occasions."

Riagan bit his lower lip. "That's not what I mean. It's different."

"Is it?"

"Ya trying to stop the Dahaka and root out traitors. Ya saving lives, not needlessly throwing them away."

Guiman's expression softened. "I'm glad you understand the difference, because others will ask you these questions, too. All leaders must expose those they lead to harm. Good leaders struggle with who to risk and when."

Riagan nodded. He thought he understood. But that still didn't solve the problem. "What will ya do about Dardanos?"

Guiman shrugged as he dug a third hole. "Dardanos has chosen his own path. He's free to do so."

Riagan flushed. "So what, Mainyu goes free? My sister's killer."

Guiman grabbed a water pail and moistened the soil around the seeds he'd planted. "Maybe your focus is on the wrong thing."

Riagan blinked. "What do ya mean?"

"As you astutely pointed out, we've already discovered that the Council controls Mainyu now. Since they have stood in our way, perhaps we should refocus our sights in order to get to the goal."

Riagan felt an internal resistance. The last thing he wanted was to turn his attention away from getting Mainyu.

"If not Mainyu, what then?" he asked.

"We still need to look into the Council's connection to Mainyu. Discover why they exposed my operation on Siavash, and maybe we also find out who Dardanos is connected to. Perhaps he is the one leading Dr. Snelling and her team."

Riagan gaped. Why hadn't he thought of that? After what Dardanos had done, there had to be something else in play.

"So, what's next?" he asked.

Chapter 27

Maellyn's Team Compromised

"We're taking every precaution. Why won't the Council approve?" Maellyn didn't consider herself quick to anger. But after reading the latest email from her father letting her know they still didn't have approval to return to Orestes, she wanted to unleash fury on the Council.

The wall screen in Fintan's lab had the map of Ourania pulled up, showing the swiftly spreading Azymi cases. Since their discovery that the fungal outbreak had broken quarantine, confirmed cases had tripled with new ones cropping up daily.

Red-faced, Nico struggled to control himself, biting off what Maellyn assumed were curses directed at the new Alfar technician he was communicating with over comm. The new technician had screwed up something while setting up the new server farm in the ever-expanding quarantine zone, and Nico was desperately troubleshooting. Until that was fixed, they weren't receiving any new data from the expanded zone for the OutSleuth site.

Fintan studied simulation results at the back of the room.

Maellyn slumped into a chair, exhausted. "I get it. They don't want it spreading to Space City, but we've got proper procedures in place."

"That's what we thought before the Azymi spread from Ourania to Orestes, too," Devika replied while working calculations. She coughed a couple times as she unscrewed the cap on her water bottle and drank.

"You okay?" Maellyn asked.

Devika took a few extra gulps of water before speaking. "I'm fine. A little tired is all. Haven't been eating well."

Maellyn laughed, eyeing the last piece of cold pizza on the table, no desire for it. "I hardly remember what a nice meal is like."

What she wouldn't give for a simple night off back home with her father, a home-cooked meal from Charlie on the table. Her stomach growled at the thought of a baked chicken with mashed potatoes, green beans, and hot rolls, along with some fresh purple melon slices.

Nico rose from his corner and walked over to the table. "Any takers on the last piece?" When they all shook their heads, he snatched it up and chowed down while returning to work.

Cade entered the room bearing two mugs of coffee, one of which he set in front of Maellyn.

She sat up straight, grabbing the mug in both hands, inhaling the strong, dark roast scent. "You're my hero, cousin."

Cade smiled. "What time are we recording the video with Aili?"

Nico growled at the mention of the Alfar scientist's name. While his OutSleuth site on Ourania was heavily supported by the Alfar, Aili wasn't providing any of the results back to him. They'd required full control of the site, and were operating this whole project like a one-way street, with all information flowing to them. It was especially frustrating since he'd been the one coordinating the setup of everything.

On top of that, while his sim had helped them develop pretty good models predicting the spread of the quarantine zone, which had confirmed the Alfar's own models, Aili had phrased the results as *telling them what they already knew*.

Maellyn checked her wrist-comp. "Fifteen minutes."

"Thanks for letting me sit in on the video." Cade grabbed a chair and sat down beside her.

"Are you kidding? You're helping us by writing up a companion piece," she said.

He removed his wrist-comp from its arm strap and placed it on the table, flipping out the stand. "Well this has kept my editor happy. And I've almost paid Aidan back for last summer."

She chuckled and shook her head. "I still can't believe you raced in the Tefnot. You going back this year?"

He snorted. "No. I've no plans to visit Araxia again anytime soon."

Anand wandered in several minutes later. Since the Alfar had refused to let him operate his scouts on Ourania, and not wanting all his hard work to go to waste, he had handed over the drawings from which they could build their own. Since then, he'd been communicating round the clock with Alfar engineers on problems they'd encountered during production. He also planned to produce them for sale on Space City, but had made minimal progress on that front until the outbreak was over.

"Live and ready," Nico muttered.

After a few deep breaths and a momentary internal panic that the video feed hadn't kicked on yet, Maellyn smiled as Alvi and Aili popped up on the wall screen. Alvi's damp hair clung to a pale scalp. His eyes were red, the sockets black, as if someone had punched him. Aili had the same black circles, though not as pronounced. There were none of the usual signs of condescension and disdain. All that remained was exhaustion. Maellyn couldn't imagine being in her shoes.

The way Aili held Alvi gave Maellyn a momentary flashback of her own mother tending to her when she was sick as a child. At age six, she'd had a bad fever for a couple days. Couldn't keep any food down. She knew she'd complained bitterly, yet her mum had patiently sat with her, offering her broth or reading stories or holding her while she slept. She'd never felt more loved.

Alvi coughed a couple times, the sound wet and hoarse, but when Aili leaned toward him, he pushed her away. "I'm fine." Then he noticed them on screen and gave them a big grin, one that lit up his entire face, which even his ill-health couldn't diminish. "Maeyin!"

"How are you, Alvi?" Maellyn asked, her mood boosted and fatigue lessened by his enthusiasm.

He clutched Elp in his arms. "I'm great! I know how to heal A-mi."

She grinned at the way he said 'Azymi.'

"Really?" she asked, leaning forward and matching her enthusiasm to his. "Can you tell us about it?"

Alvi eyed his mother.

"Go ahead," she encouraged.

He set Elp in his lap, the toy dino flopping face first onto his leg. "It hurts…" His eyes rose upward, considering, "many Alfar. Me, too." He looked down at his dinosaur and Aili whispered in his ear.

He nodded. "Yes. It first come forever ago. Last year. I hurt two months." At the number, he held up his thumb and forefinger. "Mom no know why."

Maellyn wanted to scoop him up and squeeze him. He was so cute and precious, and how could he be one of the infected?

"Are Maellyn and I trying to help you?" Aili asked him.

Alvi nodded again, rocking his head back and forth. "Mom and Maeyin." He pointed a finger at her, reaching as if to touch her. "They try heal me."

"Hey," Anand protested his lack of credit, but Devika kicked his chin to silence him. He doubled over, gripping the leg in both hands, groaning.

"Mom, Maeyin work hard. So we no sick no more." He picked back up Elp and squeezed it tight, a big grin on his face.

Aili squeezed him tight.

Maellyn fought back tears. "That's right, Alvi. We're going to beat this. We don't want you or anyone else sick anymore."

"I second that." Fran wiped her cheeks.

"Good job." Aili lowered her head to Alvi's. "Now Maellyn has questions for you."

Alvi raised both eyebrows, focusing on Maellyn, as if his mother had told him they had a big surprise for him.

Maellyn coughed to clear her throat and give her a second longer before she spoke. "Alvi, where is the Azymi hurting you?"

Alvi pointed with one finger toward his head then lowered it to his chest. "My head hurts. I hard to breathe. I tired."

"I bet," Maellyn said. "Are you sleeping?"

Alvi shook his head. "I try. I cough a lot."

Maellyn wrung her hands, but kept them below the table, out of view. She controlled her expression, keeping a smile in place for him. "Are many others hurting?"

His eyes darted up to his mother.

She nodded. "Go ahead."

"Yes." His grin had faded. He looked solemn, as if understanding the weight of the question. "My friends hurt. Their parents."

Maellyn heard the break in her voice as she asked him the last question. "What would you say to others who want to help us stop the Azymi fungus?"

Alvi frowned as if considering, scrunching his lips in the process. Aili whispered in his ear once more. "Oh," his expression brightened again. "Please help mom and Maeyin, so I won't be tired." After another pause, he asked, "Did I do it right?"

"You did great!" This time Maellyn couldn't hold back the tears, but she wiped them away so as not to confuse Alvi. "That's exactly what we needed."

Aili echoed her sentiments.

"When you come here?" he asked, and held up Elp for her to see. "Elp misses you."

"I miss Elp, too," Maellyn assured him. "We're trying our best to come back. Soon. I promise."

"Have to beat A-mi first?" he asked.

"Yes. We have to beat it. When we do I'll come to make you better."

"Okay." Alvi beamed.

"Thank you, Maellyn. All of you." Aili offered them grateful, weary smiles. "We have to go now, Alvi. Can you say goodbye?"

Alvi waved both hands at them. "Bye."

"Goodbye. See you soon." Maellyn waved back, wishing more than anything that they could go to Orestes now. She wanted to give Alvi a hug. And reassure Aili that they would beat this.

"Goodbye," Cade added.

The screen went black. The moment Alvi disappeared, a weight seemed to press down on the room again. Maellyn slumped back in her chair and rubbed her eyes.

Cade reached out and placed a hand upon her shoulder, squeezing. "Don't worry. You'll figure it out."

"Yes." She pressed down on the table to lift herself up. "All right everyone, we've got a video to finish. If that doesn't boost activity on OutSleuth, nothing will."

A part of her felt awful. They were exploiting Alvi, but they needed something to motivate people to help out. Alvi, with his innocent charm, could touch people's hearts in a way that she and her team could not. If that video didn't convince people to leap off their couches to help, she didn't know what would.

A message on her wrist-comp popped up. The latest data printouts from Devika's models. She and Fintan needed to review them. Not the most exciting task; such tedious work left her drained. But after the talk with Alvi, she could do it. She would.

Devika slumped forward, head dropping to the table. She groaned.

"Devika?" Maellyn frowned as she walked over and laid a hand on her back. "You okay?"

She moaned, before falling sideways. Maellyn stooped to catch her, but was a little slow, only catching her arms. Devika's torso thudded against Maellyn's legs and sagged to the floor, chin to chest.

"Devika!" Anand shouted.

Maellyn held Devika awkwardly upright, as everyone rushed over.

Fintan arrived first, dropping to a knee at Devika's side. Gently, he lifted her chin. "She passed out." He looked up at Maellyn. "Lay her down. Someone alert the infirmary."

Cade called for medical help as Maellyn lowered Devika onto her back, taking care to keep from banging her head on the floor. Mouth ajar, Devika's chest slowly rose and fell. Fintan placed two fingers to her neck below the jaw to check her pulse.

Anand dropped down on his sister's other side and shook her. "Devika. Devika. Wake up."

"She's got a weak pulse." Fintan felt her forehead. "Bit of a fever. Did she mention feeling sick to any of you?"

"No." Maellyn shook her head, but Devika's face was flushed. How had she not noticed before? "Just said she was tired, like we all are."

The others agreed.

What could be wrong with her? Maellyn's first fear was the Azymi fungus, but doctors had already cleared her, along with everyone else. The Azymi hadn't been transported to Space City and the Council had eliminated all travel to Orestes since. Could she be suffering from lack of sleep or not eating enough? Had the fungus had a dormancy period that allowed it to go undetected? But it had been over a month. That didn't seem plausible.

"I'm going to get her to the infirmary." Anand slipped one arm under Devika's neck and a second around her waist, and started to lift.

Maellyn grabbed one of his arms. "I don't think you should. We don't know what's wrong. You might make it worse."

"We can't leave her." Anand's face was clouded with worry.

"Help will be here shortly," Maellyn promised.

A couple minutes later a pair of male medical attendants arrived, one of which was tall with a nice tan—good looking. That thought made Maellyn bite her lip until it hurt. What was she doing, checking a boy out when there might be something seriously wrong with Devika?

After doing a preliminary exam of Devika, including shining a light in both of her eyes, the pupils contracting, the attendants slipped a gurney beneath her and strapped her to it. The cute one—why was she doing that?—tapped a button at one end of the gurney. It rose up into the air, a hover gurney to carry Devika to the infirmary.

They all followed. Everything else was forgotten. The hover gurney floated along, carrying Devika at a steady pace that made Maellyn crazy. Couldn't it go any faster?

Trini and her mom, Dr. Torres, met them at the waiting room doors to take Devika. Trini promised details as soon as they had them, then disappeared inside. The rest of them had to hang out in the waiting room. Maellyn found a chair and dropped into it. Fintan appeared at her side, touching her arm with a gentle hand.

"Are you okay?" he asked.

"I'm fine," she heard herself saying, but was that true? "Tired. Stressed. The usual."

"Maybe you should rest."

She shook her head. That was something she couldn't do right now. Her worry for Devika wouldn't allow her to relax. Nor Anand's pacing in front of the waiting room doors. She needed something to do. "I should review the latest data Devika had on the fungus models."

Fintan took the seat beside her and patted her hand. "That can wait. You shouldn't worry over that right now."

"I have to. I can't sit here and do nothing." She activated her wrist-comp and pulled up her messages to open the data file.

Fintan sighed, but nodded and leaned back in his chair.

She sifted through the data, skipping past the portions showing the breakdown of the fungus itself, as well as how it operated. She wanted the test data. Particularly the results showing how the fungus responded to heat, cold, various all purpose and specialized drugs, and other treatment methods.

The Azymi infection spread rapidly as the temperature rose, as expected. It slowed negligibly if chilled. Not much to go on there. And so far, the resistance strains they'd tested from Anthea were negative. The fungus continued to grow, spreading through victims until they suffocated, or reduced brain activity caused other serious problems. So far, no one had recovered. They had no leads to go on.

It took every ounce of Maellyn's self-restraint not to scream. It had to be there somewhere. The answer to solving this. She wouldn't accept—wouldn't allow—Alvi to die from it. He had eternity ahead of him.

A short while later, Trini emerged from the back, eyes dazed, shoulder slumped. Anand paused, staring at her. Everyone rose, and Maellyn's breath caught in her throat, knowing it was bad.

"She's got the Azymi fungus," Trini informed them. "Not sure how. But my aunt's sure of it. Space City is exposed."

Chapter 28

Neil Discovers Significance of Emperor's Ruby

Neil and Jiro transported Aileen McKensie, the latest person to come down with the Azymi fungus, to the academy's infirmary. They crossed the barren courtyard with her—unconscious, pale, and sweating—strapped to a hover gurney. Aileen wasn't the first student they'd helped. Nor was she the fifth. Nor twenty-fifth.

Only a couple days had passed since Devika's diagnosis, yet the number of new cases had overwhelmed the infirmary. The staff was so overloaded that Neil and Jiro had been hired on as extra help. They helped bring the newly infected to the infirmary, many of whom were unconscious.

At first, the thought of handling those infected creeped Neil out. He didn't want to get sick himself. But as the numbers ballooned, there was no choice. And he knew that he had to help. He couldn't hide out in his dorm room and let others deal with the problem. He had to step up and do his part. He had to be part of the solution. Or he didn't deserve to be there onboard Space City.

Nevertheless, he wore a medical mask and full length gown everywhere he went—a requirement for all staff at the infirmary—to limit exposure.

The infirmary doors swung open automatically as they approached. Neil and Jiro marched through the waiting room past concerned parents—those who had arrived before the Council quarantined the campus and now couldn't return to the city. Their faces were all masks of anxiety and exhaustion. Neil couldn't imagine what they must feel with their children fighting something with no known cure and a high mortality rate, based on what was happening on Ourania.

Neil and Jiro passed through another set of doors back into the heart of the infirmary. Nurses and doctors rushed by with syringes, IVs, and water. Lots of water.

"Dr. Torres, where do you want this one?" Jiro asked.

Trini's aunt looked up from her wrist-comp and slowed. Her quad doc hovered over her head. She walked over and held her wrist-comp with both hands over Aileen. Moving it from head to waist, she scanned Aileen so she could study the extent of the infection.

"Where was she found?" Dr. Torres asked.

"Her dorm room," Neil replied.

"Any signs of hemoptysis?"

"No." There had been no signs of blood around her mouth or anywhere visible. He'd taken the time to search her trash can for bloody Kleenex and even opened her mouth to check inside. "But she does have an elevated temperature and tachycardia." This last bit meant an increased heart rate. Neil wasn't sure why the doctors couldn't just say that.

Dr. Torres made notes on her wrist-comp before pointing down the left corridor. "Try 132. I believe we have an open bed there."

Neil gave her a gloved thumbs-up and they continued on their way. How many beds remained before they had to start finding alternate options?

The Azymi fungus appeared to spread faster through humans than Alfar. They'd soon need to improvise. Perhaps bring extra beds over from the dorms.

Things in the city weren't much better. The Council had declared a state of emergency. They'd ordered to everyone stay home, except those with special passes, in an attempt to limit the spread of the fungus. Not that it helped, as far as Neil had heard.

In room 132, they found a nurse wiping down Maliek Johnson's sweaty face with a tissue. Maliek had been one of Neil's and Jiro's first pickups, and it had shaken them both. The younger brother of Jack Johnson, the first year had been having an exceptionally good Games season; might've even earned league MVP. Now they just hoped he hung on until a cure was developed.

"How's he doing?" Neil asked the nurse.

She grimaced and shrugged as she inspected his mouth. "A little respiratory distress. Same as the rest. That one?"

"Got the call fifteen minutes ago," Neil said. "Dr. Torres scanned her, but I don't have results."

"Ready?" Jiro asked as he slipped his hands under Aileen's arms to lift her.

"Yeah." Neil grabbed her legs and they eased her from the hover gurney to the hospital bed. He tried not to think about how many of their classmates they'd brought in here. Kids that a week ago they'd been training with, and were now fighting for their lives.

The nurse strode over, waving for them to get out of her way so she could tend to Aileen. Neil and Jiro retreated, knowing there wasn't much else they could do to help. As they started for the door, Neil gave Maliek one last look. He wanted to say something to Maliek, to encourage him that things would be all right. But Maliek was unconscious and Neil felt silly doing so in front of Jiro and the nurse, so he bit his tongue.

"Any word from your grandpa about where the outbreak started?" Jiro asked back out in the hall.

"No. Council's still scrambling to identify how it's spreading. Checked the city's water supply, but it's clean. Same with air filtration. The scientists say they've never seen anything like it."

Jiro shivered. "How is that possible?"

Neil bit his lip. "I don't know."

That lack of knowledge left him paranoid. He scanned himself every couple hours. The results always came back negative. Every time he was surprised, sure that this would be the time he got sick. He also messaged Maellyn regularly to check on her. She'd respond she was fine, but that was it for communication. She and the rest of her team were isolated with the scientists in their labs to focus on finding a cure. He doubted he'd see her again until the outbreak was over. It made the way they'd left things between them all the more painful, especially since he knew it was his fault.

As they strolled down the hall to find out their next assignment, Patrick burst out of a room, eyes wide. His eyes beamed and Neil was sure that beneath his medical mask he was grinning wide. "Get a nurse. Adrien's awake!"

"He's awake?" Neil couldn't quite believe what he was hearing.

"Yes. Nurse! Nurse!" Patrick sprinted down the hallway.

Adrien had been in a coma for going on six months. There was growing doubt that he'd ever awake. And plenty of rumors that the time Patrick spent visiting him was looking for an opportunity to make sure Adrien never awoke. Quite a percentage of the student population believed Patrick had been responsible for putting Adrien in a coma, even after he'd been cleared. Many reasoned that Patrick had always been good at covering his tracks.

Neil had harbored his own doubts until Dardanos told him in no uncertain terms that Patrick had played no role in what happened to Adrien. They'd thoroughly cleared him. But as long as they remained unable to discover who was responsible, the rumors would persist.

Now, as Patrick joyfully shouted for a nurse, those suspicions disappeared. Patrick was genuinely happy that Adrien had woken up.

And right now provided a rare opportunity to find out from Adrien what he remembered. Neil grabbed Jiro's arm and pulled him back. "Let's check on Adrien."

They retreated to the open door from which Patrick had come running. The first bed in the room held an unconscious young boy. Neil couldn't remember his name, but he was a first year.

In the second bed lay Adrien, a nasal cannula in his nostrils, an IV plugged into an arm. As they approached, his eyes turned to them, but not really focused. His already pasty complexion resembled a corpse. Adrien swallowed and his eyes focused on Neil. He tried and failed to sit up.

"Water," Adrien rasped.

A table in the corner held bottled water. Neil retrieved one and a cup, wondering as he did so if the nurses would have a problem with him giving water to a patient before they'd examined him. It probably wouldn't do any harm, so he carried the cup over and held it to Adrien's lips. He took a small sip, followed by a second and a third before turning away.

"How do you feel?" Jiro stood at the foot of the bed, studying Adrien as if looking for something he could do to help.

"What happened?" Adrien asked.

"You don't remember?" Neil asked.

"Remember… what?"

Neil hesitated. They were alone, so this provided a chance to ask Adrien who had attacked him before anyone interfered. Of course, if he didn't remember, they might never know who had attacked him.

"You've been in a coma." Neil watched Adrien's face for any reaction. "Someone attacked you in your room. No one knows who."

Adrien blinked and stared up at the ceiling. He offered no response of any sort. Before Neil could ask another question, Dr. Torres swarmed into the room, her quad doc, a couple of nurses, and Patrick in tow. Dr. Torres pushed past Neil to examine Adrien.

"Neil, Jiro, please leave the room," Dr. Torres ordered.

Neil retreated to the wall to get out of the way, but was reluctant to leave. "We need to know who attacked him."

"I need to monitor his health," she replied, "—which means protecting him from being interrogated minutes after he's woken up."

"I'm not interrogating—"

"Out! Patrick, Jiro, you as well."

Neil gritted his teeth. He didn't see the harm in asking Adrien a few questions, but he wasn't going to argue with Dr. Torres. Jiro and Patrick were already heading out of the room. As Neil walked toward the door, he placed a hand on Adrien's right leg above the ankle and gave him an encouraging squeeze. While Neil had never gotten along well with Adrien, he was glad to see him wake up. It was good to see someone recovering.

"The gardener," Adrien said.

Neil paused, hand hovering above Adrien's leg. Neil turned back. "What did you say?"

"Judy, get him out of the room," Dr. Torres ordered.

The closest nurse rounded on him, jaw set. She was heavyset and looked more than ready to haul him out if needed. He held up his hands to stop her. "I'm going."

Out in the hallway, Patrick and Jiro waited for him, eyes wide. Patrick balled fists. "Did he say the gardener attacked him?"

"No, just said gardener." Neil felt dazed.

"What else could he be talking about?" Patrick's face had reddened.

Neil shook his head. "Could be his last memory. Or something else altogether." Was it possible Adrien was another of Guiman's spies and he'd never told them?

"We have to tell someone!"

Neil laid a hand on Patrick, trying to calm him. "Not yet."

"What?" Patrick glared at him. "We can't let this go."

"We don't even know if what he said is at all related." Neil hoped it wasn't. He didn't want to consider the alternative and what that meant.

"Neil's right," Jiro said. "Adrien just woke from a six-month coma. He suffered brain trauma during the attack. His memories are mixed up. Incomplete."

"And he didn't actually accuse Guiman of anything," Neil added.

Patrick exhaled. "What do we do then? There's been no evidence connecting anyone to Adrien's attack. His memories are all we have."

Jiro held up both hands. "Let's give him time to rest. Let Dr. Torres ensure he's all right. Maybe after that he'll be able to give us more details."

"Okay," Patrick said. "But I'm keeping watch until then. I'm not waiting for someone to discover he's awake and try to finish the job."

"I'll help," Jiro offered.

"Good idea," Neil agreed. "We'll take shifts watching him around the clock." After all, they were spending a good bit of time here at the infirmary anyway. It wouldn't take much extra effort to check in on him.

His stomach rumbled, reminding him that he hadn't eaten today. He excused himself and ducked out a side exit. Thanks to 3D printed food, he could get a good meal whenever he needed from the cafeteria. And the time alone would allow him to think. So many things were happening and all they could do was react.

*****

"Neil!" A voice called.

He looked up to see Rashn and his girlfriend, Vahu, making their way toward him through the middle of the courtyard. Neil's head involuntarily shook, as if to clear itself. But the pair were still there. He looked around, panicking that someone would see them. The courtyard remained empty. How had they gotten to Space City? How had they found him?

"What are you doing here?" he asked. "Do you realize what danger you're in coming here?"

Vahu removed a crude leather wrap from her shoulders. Through an open end he could see dozens of Emperor's Ruby flowers. "These should help cure those sick from Ondrigal. In case you need more."

Neil shook his head, frowning. "I'm not sure what you mean."

"The Ondrigal fungus." Rashn took the flowers from Vahu and offered them to him. "You called it something different, but the symptoms you described are the same. I didn't remember at the time, but Vahu made the connection."

Neil accepted the flower in gentle hands. "And this will treat the fungus?" It couldn't be so simple. The Azymi was from Ourania. Would it have much in common with a fungus from Siavash?

Vahu nodded, expression earnest. "Ground it up with water to make a paste and consume it. Once should be enough. Do you have one sick or two?"

Neil laughed, a hysterical edge to it. "We've got at least forty cases here on campus. More in the city."

Vahu gasped and Rashn blinked in surprise. "How long has this been going on?"

"Maybe four days," Neil replied.

Vahu shook her head. "That's impossible. The Ondrigal attacks children only. And the weak. Those already very sick. But it's slow to spread."

He wanted to laugh and cry at the same time. "It must be different. We get several cases a day."

Rashn frowned. "But it's been more than a week since you visited. Yet you say the sickness has been among you for a few days?"

"There's an outbreak on Ourania as well, among the Alfar. That's what I said Maellyn is working on. It hadn't hit here yet. Or at least we didn't know."

"Then we must get more. Many more." Vahu's voice held urgency and she turned to go.

"Wait." Neil held out a hand for them to stop. "How did you get here?"

Rashn looked a bit sheepish. "After your visit, I followed you back to your black water door."

It took Neil a minute to realize Rashn referred to the thorneway.

"I needed to know how you traveled to our planet," Rashn said. "You passed through it and disappeared. The door vanished."

Neil nodded. He'd have done the same in Rashn's shoes. He had to take precautions. Even if Rashn had trusted them, he couldn't know who all had access to the thorneway.

"Unfortunately, it took me until hours ago to discover how your black water door worked."

That was going to be problematic. Guiman wouldn't be happy that any Dahaka knew how to locate or use a thorneway, even an ally.

"We go back now." Vahu gestured behind her. "Gather some more Emperor's Rubies for you and bring them back. As many as you need."

He started to tell Vahu she didn't need to, but as he opened his mouth to speak it hit him. The private messenger sending them to Siavash in search of the Emperor's Ruby. They couldn't make sense of the request at the time, but what if the messenger knew the Emperor's Ruby could be used to cure the Azymi outbreak? The more he considered it, the more he decided it was the only explanation that made sense.

Which meant the messenger had to be working on the outbreak on Ourania. Or knew an outbreak on Space City was coming. Perhaps both. But if the latter were true, why hadn't they stepped forward with the cure?

Rashn put a hand on Vahu's shoulders and they turned to walk away.

"Wait, let me help you get back without being seen." Neil couldn't believe no one had yet noticed, but then everyone was dealing with the outbreak. There was little time for anything else.

Rashn brushed him off. "I'll get us back. We won't be seen."

"You don't understand. If you get caught—"

"We won't get caught."

Neil grabbed the wrist-comp from his arm and ran over to them, offering it to Rashn. "Take this. I can contact you on it. If we need more flowers, I'll let you know." He showed Rashn how to activate it and use the messaging system.

Rashn nodded. "I wait for your call."

"Thank you." Neil held up the flower to them and inclined his head. "If this works, you don't know what it'll mean to us."

"Maybe it will be the start of better than animosity between us," Rashn said.

Rashn's last words reminded Neil of his discussion with Dirk. Riagan had railed against any alliances with the Dahaka, even after their encounters with Rashn. And Neil had understood. They'd had far more conflicts with the Dahaka. Everyone in the universe had. Yet despite this, Dirk had argued passionately that they all shouldn't suffer for their leader's actions. Maybe Dardanos was right to put forth his proposal.

Neil squeezed the flowers in his hand. *After* they put a stop to the Azymi outbreak. They needed to get people well first.

He reached for his wrist-comp to message Maellyn before remembering he had given his to Rashn. He was going to have to buy another. He couldn't keep going through wrist-comps like this.

Running over to the science labs, he wished he still had access. The facility had been restricted since the day after the outbreak broke onboard.

At the main entrance, he used the general comm system to message Maellyn that he had important information regarding the outbreak. As he waited, he wondered again at the identity of the private messenger. Whoever it was was connected to the scientists. The messenger said as much. But if that was the case, why wasn't Maellyn and her team aware of it?

Of course, it was possible Dr. Snelling and her team were working the cure in the city and hadn't shared it with the Space City U scientists. She was working with the Dahaka, so she'd be aware of the fungus and the cure. Except why hadn't she procured the Emperor's Ruby at the same time as the fungus? And if it was Dr. Snelling and her team, how had they managed to get it on Ourania? And why would they infect the Alfar? They were helping the Dahaka because of the threat to Siavash. So why turn around and harm the Alfar. Space City's allies. There were too many questions and far too few answers.

Maellyn emerged from the labs. She had bags under her eyes, her hair was disheveled, and she'd lost weight.

"Are you okay?" he asked. She clearly needed rest and he started to express his concern, but something held his tongue, a vague sensation it might not be a good idea.

She rubbed her eyes, and when she spoke, there was an edge to it. "I'm fine. We're just… You said you had something that could help us?"

He held up the flowers to her. "This flower, it's called the Emperor's Ruby. It'll help treat those suffering from the Azymi fungus."

She pursed her lips, looking at the flower with skepticism. "How do you know this? Where did you get it from?"

He grimaced. He hadn't considered the need for an explanation on how he'd come by it. He couldn't very well say a Dahaka had given it to him. He opened his mouth then closed it and offered the flower to her.

Lips tightening, she turned to open the door and head back inside. "I don't have time for more secrets. The flower is pretty, but I've work to do."

"It's from Dardanos," he blurted out. She paused, turning back. "He gave it to me to deliver."

"Where did he get it?"

He shrugged. "No idea. Just told me to bring it. ASAP."

She bit her lip as she regarded the flower.

"Mix it with water to make a paste," he said, remembering Vahu's instructions. "After that, feed it to someone sick with the Azymi. That's all I know." He shoved the flowers into her hands. She didn't resist, but her look of doubt remained.

"Please," he began. "I'm trying to help." He wanted to say more. Wanted to touch her, to draw her close. To reassure her that he was on her side and that he was sorry for all the secrets he'd kept.

"Thank you." Her eyes were trained on the flower. "I'll share with the team. We'll analyze it." She opened the door. "I should go now."

He wanted to ask when he could see her again. Wanted to ask if she needed anything. Wanted to ask a great many things, but instead, he said, "Let me know if I can help."

As she slipped through the door, she looked back. Her eyes were dull, shoulders slumped. The exhaustion weighing down on her was easy to see. Nevertheless, she gave him a hint of a smile before the door closed behind her.

Please let this help, even just a little bit. Buy us some time.

Chapter 29

Riagan Delivers Trouble

Riagan entered Guiman's home, anxious to know what task the gardener had for him. Everything had slowed since the quarantines on both the campus and city. The old man emerged from his room, staff in one hand and a silver case the size of a necklace box in the other. He nodded and shuffled over to his table, lowering himself into a chair with a groan. The staff he propped against the table.

"Got a job for me?"

"I need you to deliver a package to Dardanos." Guiman held out the silver case.

Riagan smiled uncomfortably, but accepted the case. "Why after his proposal?" He had sought out the headmaster a couple of times for an explanation, but Dardanos had remained out of touch. His floor in the main office was restricted to all students unless summoned and escorted. He had stopped training Riagan or Neil and didn't respond to any messages. As far as Riagan knew, Guiman and Dardanos weren't communicating either. But every time Riagan brought up trying to find out if Dardanos was the one leading Dr. Snelling and her group, Guiman shut him down without explanation.

"I have important information he needs to see."

"What is it?" Riagan studied the case, but didn't try to open it.

Guiman ushered him to the door. "Please deliver that promptly."

Riagan flushed. "I don't have access to his office."

"The elevator code is 9528."

"I'll get it done."

As Riagan left Guiman's, the only people out were the Space City officers ensuring no one left the academy quarantine zone; Guiman's

245

home was barely inside it. It was rare to see anyone out around campus anymore. Everyone hid in their rooms, hoping that isolation would protect them from the outbreak. No matter how many people got sick, the rest believed that if they took the right precautions, they'd be fine. Riagan didn't see any reason to panic over what he couldn't control.

The late afternoon sun poked out from the side of the main office as if checking to see that the coast was clear. Riagan shielded his eyes with one hand and hurried into the building. Would Dardanos be in his office? Part of him wanted to confront the headmaster, to demand answers. But an equal part of him didn't want an encounter with Dardanos now. He didn't want to hear Dardanos try to justify his proposal.

He called the elevator and the doors opened. Entering the code, he rode the elevator to the top floor. The doors opened on an empty lobby. Dardanos' assistant had either gone for the day or was hiding like all the rest.

The doors to the headmaster's office was shut. Riagan took a deep breath, trying to prepare himself for an encounter with Dardanos. But as he neared the doors, a familiar voice inside the office made him hesitate.

"We've completed the inoculation," Dr. Snelling said. "It'll help the healthy resist the Azymi fungus. I'll deliver yours personally."

How had she gotten through the quarantine between Space City and the campus? What was she doing here?

"And the cure?" Dardanos growled. "Reports are we've crossed fifty percent infected."

Another familiar male voice spoke up. "It continues to present a challenge, but we're working round the clock."

"I need results, Dr. Crowley," Dardanos replied. "Not excuses."

Riagan crept over to the wall, trying to listen and puzzle out what all this meant at the same time.

"Are you sure the Emperor's Ruby can cure the Azymi fungus?" Dr. Crowley snapped.

"The Azymi fungus comes from Siavash," Dardanos answered. "The Dahaka use the flower to cure the ill there."

Riagan nearly choked. He placed both hands over his mouth in an effort to keep silent. It seemed to confirm that one of them had been the messenger who sent them to Siavash to retrieve the Emperor's Ruby, but that had been before the outbreak on Space City.

"How did it end up here?" Dr. Snelling asked.

"Mainyu," Dardanos answered. "He attacked Ourania with it. Not sure how it was spread here."

"I'd heard he was dead," Dr. Crowley said, a tinge of fear in his voice.

"A false report. The truth isn't widely known."

Riagan scrunched his nose. Dardanos knew the attacks on Ourania and here had come from Mainyu. And yet he'd put forth his proposal anyway. Why?

"If Mainyu is behind the attack, how will you get our proposal approved?" Dr. Snelling asked. "Once word gets out."

"I'm afraid that bit of strategy needs to remain private for now," Dardanos informed them. "But we've got time. I'm confident when it goes before the Council, they'll approve. Now, if you'll excuse me, I have other matters to attend to."

Riagan turned to look for cover. The assistant's desk. He scrambled to move the chair out of the way and ducked down beneath the desk, his back pressed against the rear panel.

"Of course," Dr. Snelling said. The door to Dardanos' office opened. "Good day."

How long had Dardanos known Mainyu was responsible for Ourania? And how had Mainyu pulled that off?

"Oh, and send me your inoculation results," Dardanos said. "I'll need to provide them to the Council. They'll want to review themselves before approving its use. Dr. Trevena as well, I'd guess."

The elevator doors slid open. "I will as soon as I return to my office," Dr. Snelling promised.

Riagan's jaw dropped as the realization hit him. Dr. Snelling had asked how Dardanos knew about the Emperor's Ruby. The flower that the private messenger had sent them to Siavash to retrieve. It was Dardanos behind it all. Did Guiman know? Or had Dardanos gone rogue, as he had with his proposal?

Once he was sure the scientists had departed, Riagan crawled out from under the desk. For a moment he stared between Dardanos' office and the elevator, debating whether to continue on with the delivery or leave and try to find Neil. Or Guiman. He was reeling from the stream of revelations and needed their input. For now, it was best to deliver the package as requested, then figure out what to do.

Marching over to Dardanos' closed office door, Riagan knocked. No answer. He knocked again. Nothing. He opened the door and stuck his head in. Empty. Except for the displays of weapons and armor that furnished the office, along with a couple of bookshelves with military-themed titles. And a wide oak desk in the center.

Riagan marched over and placed the silver case in the middle of the desk, wondering as he did so what Guiman had sent him to deliver. Then he scooted out of the office, not wanting to be there when Dardanos returned. He wasn't sure he could keep his composure if confronted right now.

But Dardanos didn't appear as Riagan summoned the elevator. When the doors opened, he was relieved to find it empty. He ducked inside and pressed the ground floor button. The doors closed and the elevator started its descent, allowing him to breathe easier. He had time to figure things out. And get help.

Back in the main lobby, he power-walked to the exit. There was no sign of Dr. Snelling or Dr. Crowley out in the courtyard. He didn't see any point in going after them anyway. They were headed back to the city and the officers guarding the quarantine perimeter wouldn't let him past.

Neil or Guiman first?

An explosion caused him to duck and shield his head.

Black smoke billowed above the buildings to the north. Realizing he wasn't in any immediate danger, Riagan rose from a crouch. Curiosity drew him toward the smoke. A bonfire on the edge of campus. It wasn't until he got closer that he realized the bonfire was Guiman's home. He ran forward.

Burning chunks of Guiman's home lay scattered like driftwood surrounding the wreckage. The officers guarding the quarantine zone had surrounded the conflagration, but there was no sign of Guiman. Had he still been inside?

Riagan pressed forward until an officer stopped him. "Stay back."

Waves of heat struck him. It would take a while to get the fire under control in order to search for Guiman, but if he was inside, he was dead. No one could've survived such an explosion, nor the fire greedily consuming the home.

Nevertheless, he had to say something. "The gardener, Guiman, was he inside?"

The officer shrugged and directed him to back off.

Sirens wailed throughout campus. Not that they were needed. Everyone on campus had heard that explosion. Likely some in the city as well. Help would be on its way.

Riagan spotted a smooth piece of wood not far from the house. At first, he dismissed it as part of the wreckage, but houses on Space City weren't made of wood. And while the other pieces were jagged and many of them smoking, this one was smooth, polished. He examined it more closely.

Guiman's staff. He couldn't walk five feet without his staff.

Riagan retreated a few steps. He must be mistaken. That couldn't be Guiman's staff. But the longer he stared at it the surer he became. And if the cane was here, Guiman must've been, too. Riagan started to circle the house for any sign of the old man, but he was nowhere to be seen. He must've still been in the house. The cane had been thrown out by the explosion.

Stomach churning, Riagan thought he was going to be sick. Guiman was dead. He couldn't be dead. Had he felt anything in the explosion? Had he noticed anything wrong or died oblivious?

And what had caused the fire?

As Riagan stared at the leaping flames, he realized this couldn't have been an accident. All the buildings on Space City had the ability to diagnose problems and deliver a warning or take precautionary measures, such as turn off the power to the entire structure. These kinds of accidents didn't occur on Space City. They were too dangerous because a single uncontained fire could destroy the ship, risking everyone's lives. Too many resources had been expended ensuring this never happened.

No, someone had started this. Someone who wanted Guiman dead. Someone who knew Guiman was more than a simple gardener. But who? And why now?

Everything Guiman possessed had been in that shack. Every piece of evidence they'd gathered. All gone. Destroyed. Nothing to give him any clues.

Except the box Guiman had given him to deliver to Dardanos. Perhaps it held some clue as to why this happened.

Knowing there was nothing he could do to help stop the fire, but wanting answers, Riagan turned and ran back toward the main office. People were starting to gather and drift toward the fire.

Not wanting to be detained with questions, he ducked down a side road. Each time he spotted someone he'd take the next available turn, making a strange zigzagging path back through campus until he'd made his way around to the back side. He entered the main office from the rear entrance. An empty receptionist desk with wilting red flowers in a vase on one corner greeted him. He jogged down the hallway past the auditorium where new student orientation was held, as well as other occasional academy functions, and found the elevators.

For the second time that day he rode the elevator to the top floor, and this time he was sure he didn't want to see Dardanos or anyone else. But if he did, informing the headmaster about the explosion was a good excuse for his presence.

Guiman had been killed. Guiman was dead. It didn't feel real to Riagan. It was like hearing someone speak to you in a foreign language of which you had no comprehension.

Opening the door, he found the office empty. His shoulders relaxed. The silver case remained in the center of the desk, unopened. Crossing the room to the desk, he retrieved the case and lifted the lid. Inside, he found a thin, rectangular piece of glass. Frowning, he picked it up. The moment he touched the glass, letters and numbers appeared on screen. They changed in a rhythmic pattern. Encryption. Which confirmed to Riagan that it must hold something important. Perhaps something that had cost Guiman his life.

He needed a decryption strip. A little black skin that resembled window tinting that could be placed over a screen and decrypt its contents. The top couple of desk drawers were locked. Nor did they have keyholes. How were they unlocked?

The bottom left drawer wasn't quite closed, the lip of the lid sticking out from the desk. He set the glass on the desk and reached down to pull the handle. The drawer slid open.

Inside was a wrist-comp. He tried turning it on, but nothing happened. He dropped it back into the drawer. There were also various thumb drives and, buried beneath another silver case, a thin black strip.

He lifted the case and removed the decryption strip. He placed it onto the glass, taking care to line up the edges of the two in case misalignment caused any trouble with the decryption process. Mostly, he did it because a perfectionist part of him would cringe at the decryption strip being off center.

The strip in place, the letters and numbers on the glass cycled faster. He waited, breath held, for the strip to do its thing. He listened, hoping Dardanos didn't choose this moment to return to his office. If only he had Neil with him to keep a lookout. Too late now.

After ten nerve-breaking seconds, the glass cast a message into the air. Except it was more than a message. There were pictures of the Council members, along with notes.

Riagan read.

Normal protocol requires all Councilmen be removed from Space City during a state of emergency. Owing to the ship's proximity to Mars, that will be the logical choice until the outbreak is under control.

The Council *had* fled. While everyone aboard Space City suffered and struggled to find a solution to the outbreak, the Council ran away to save themselves. He'd assumed they were working hard in the city to solve the crisis. Instead, they'd tucked tail and run.

The glass had other pictures, edges viewable on the right and left sides of the projection. Riagan reached up to touch the right picture, wondering how he might be able to adjust the projection to view it.

The moment his finger reached the picture, the projection rotated. The new picture moved to the center, along with accompanying text. It showed a diagram of the Mars facility where the Councilmen would wait out the outbreak. Why was Guiman sharing all of this with Dardanos?

The next picture identified possible locations around the facility that might be susceptible to attack. Riagan's mouth went dry. Had Guiman uncovered a plot to assassinate the Council? Was he warning Dardanos? This might explain what happened to Guiman. If the traitors planning the attack learned that he had figured things out, they'd want to kill him to cover their tracks. But why had Guiman delivered this information to Dardanos instead of the Council?

Riagan cycled to the next message.

The evidence has been placed showing the boys retrieved the fungus from Sverog. Riagan is the perfect scapegoat, a boy distraught over the loss of his sister who blames the Council for failing to save her.

He dropped the glass onto the desk. Both hands clutched the desk edge, propping him up. The Azymi fungus. Had he delivered it to Space City? Had he and Neil been set up? By Guiman? He had sent them on the mission to retrieve something from Sverog. This message alleged the fungus. Or had someone else set them all up? Whoever it was had created the outbreak on Space City. But why? It didn't make any sense.

There was one more message to be read. Riagan selected it.

The poison is 100% fatal with no antidote. Ensure whoever releases it can't be traced back to you. You want a seat on the Council. This will make you head of it. I expect you to deliver on our deal.
Mainyu

Riagan dropped into the desk chair. Guiman possessed direct evidence that Mainyu was trying to destroy the Council. And it sounded like Dardanos was assisting him. After all, Dardanos was the one who put forth the plan to aid the Dahaka as a means of getting himself onto the Council. They had attacked Space City. This discovery could explain why Guiman had been killed? In fact, it might've been Dardanos who had done it. And who had instructed Guiman to send them to retrieve the fungus from Siavash. The headmaster had played them all along.

But if Guiman had learned all of this, why alert Dardanos by sending this evidence? Perhaps trying to give Dardanos a chance to come forward on his own?

And the outbreak on Ourania. Dardanos had said Mainyu was responsible. The two attacks, if successful, and paired together, would greatly shift the balance of power.

He checked the next picture on the right, and the first one reappeared on screen. The extent of Mainyu's plans was mindboggling. The outbreak on Ourania had started a year ago. How long had Mainyu been planning the attack on the Council? How long had Dardanos been helping?

Riagan removed the decryption strip from the glass and bent to place it back in the drawer. As he did so he noticed once more the silver case already there. He was pressing his luck on time, but he couldn't help himself as he picked it up. What other communications did it hold? What else had they learned concerning Mainyu's plans? Or of the work Dr. Snelling and her team were involved on?

Removing the lid, Riagan placed it on the desk and withdrew the glass. He added the decryption strip and waited. The thumping of his heart and the chill in his veins made him wish he had a way to speed up the decryption process. But all he could do was stand there, stiff, until the glass projected a new set of messages into the air.

A weakened Alfar state allows us more freedom to operate. The Azymi fungus will accomplish this goal, while we remain hidden.
Mainyu

Riagan flipped to the next message.

Your place on the Council needs to be secure. It's the only way.
Mainyu

The next message read:

The best way to get at the Council is to force them to leave Space City. Anywhere else and the chances of a successful attack improve greatly.
Mainyu

Latest message:

I require control of the release of the fungus. I will not have a decimated Space City once I lead. Also, I require samples of this Emperor's Ruby so I can get a team started on the serum. Once you provide that, we have an agreement.
Dardanos

A cold sweat broke out on Riagan. Here was proof that Dardanos was involved in everything. Playing Guiman, Dr. Snelling, and Riagan and Neil, too. All in his quest to get on the Council. How many might die so that he could become a Councilman?

A thump against the receptionist desk outside spurred Riagan into action. He ripped the decryption strip off the glass, eliminating the projection. He debated taking both glasses with him for evidence, but if Dardanos was expecting the new one from Guiman, he would be looking for it. He wasn't getting caught red-handed.

He threw the second glass back in its case and dumped it back in the drawer. Breath held, he slipped the new glass from Guiman back in its case and replaced the lid. He strode around the desk, heading for the door as it opened and in rolled Dardanos. The Academy Head halted mid-push on his wheelchair.

Dardanos' face darkened. "What are you doing here?"

"Guiman's home. It was blown up," Riagan blurted out. "I think he was killed."

He hoped he wasn't in danger of joining Guiman on that journey.

Dardanos scowled. He rolled forward. "What were you doing behind my desk? Did you think you'd find me hidden back there?"

Riagan's palms were clammy. "I was looking for something that might indicate where ya'd gone. I figured ya'd want to know."

Dardanos rolled his wheelchair forward until he was right in front of Riagan. He met Riagan's eyes and studied him. Riagan wanted to drop his gaze, to shift underneath Dardanos' glare, but ignored those urges. He met Dardanos' stare and nothing else.

"Thank you for the message. I'd already been informed. You're dismissed."

"Yes, sir." Riagan nodded and marched from the room doing double time.

As he climbed onto the elevator, he debated what to do now. He didn't have any proof. What could he do? All he could come up with was to find Neil. Between the two of them, they'd come up with a plan.

The elevator door dinged open at the same time a realization hit Riagan. The decryption strip. He'd left it on the second glass in his rush to put it back in the drawer. When Dardanos searched for his decryption trip to study Guiman's new message and found it on the glass in his drawer, he'd know Riagan had been in it.

He had to hide. Had to get off Space City. Nowhere on campus was safe. Probably not in the city either, if he could even figure out a way past the quarantine. And he'd have to lose his wrist-comp. It could be used to track him. But where could he go?

Mars.

If he could find evidence of the attack at the Mars facility, he could take that to the Council. But how could he get there? Until the outbreak ended, all thorneway travel was restricted. He didn't know the answers, but he knew he better come up with some pretty quick.

Chapter 30

Maellyn Struggles Forward

Maellyn ran the sim again and crossed her fingers. "It's gonna work this time."

"Our hypothesis is plausible," Fintan said.

They stood in his lab watching the 3D projection of the sim before them. Human cells hovered in the air, like silly string covered in purple spots which represented the Azymi fungus. Orange cells from the Emperor's Ruby in a solution were introduced, at which point the sim accelerated like a time-lapse video. The flower cells attacked the fungus, latching on to the purple spots and consuming the fungus until the human cells were clean.

Maellyn held her breath. Fintan frowned in concentration, his upper pair of arms crossed over his chest and his lower pair of hands curled into fists and pressed against his hips.

After a ten second pause where the Emperor's Ruby cells and newly healed human cells co-existed, the flower cells resumed their attack, little pac-men gobbling up white dots. They consumed the host cells until Maellyn ended the sim with a stifled curse. The delay had lasted longer, but still no good as a cure.

She rubbed her temples, tired of running endless sims. "We need to modify the Emperor's Ruby cells to deactivate once they consume the fungus."

Fintan shook his head. "Re-engineering the cells will take too long. We don't have time."

"How can the Dahaka use this?" she asked. "Doesn't it attack their cells? It has everything else we've tested."

Since learning of the Emperor's Ruby, all the science teams had bombarded Dardanos with questions. Dardanos had confirmed what he knew, including that he had intel that the Azymi fungus had come from Siavash; he had a Dahaka contact. Questions and rumors had begun flying after that. When she'd asked Neil about the contact, he confirmed he knew the Dahaka as well, which only made her wonder even more what he had been up to this year. But for now she couldn't worry about it. She had to tune that out. Her sole concern was finding a way to make the cure safe for everyone, especially Devika and Alvi. She had to find the solution in time to save them.

"We need a Dahaka test subject," Maellyn said. "Test the cure on their cells. See what happens. Can Dardanos' proposal help us with this?"

She wasn't thrilled with aspects of the proposal, but right now, saving lives took precedence over any difficulties arising from reestablishing ties with the Dahaka.

"Won't be approved soon enough." Fintan clutched the hairs on his cheeks with his hands, a sign he was racking his brain for answers. "It would require an emergency session. The Council is already displeased with Dardanos for blindsiding them with this proposal. They're unlikely to grant emergency review given everything else.

"And even if they reviewed and approved, they'll want a plan for how to re-establish contact with the Dahaka. Procedures will need to be revised for dealing with them in light of their known hostile positions. It'll take months before the Council agrees to a new first contact."

Maellyn dropped her head into her hands. They were so close to a solution. Just needed the Council to get out of the way.

"What time is it?" She checked her wrist-comp. Her eyes widened and she spun for the door.

It was time to travel to Orestes to hand over samples of the Emperor's Ruby for the Alfar scientists to investigate. The Council still hadn't approved her father's procedures for traveling to and from the Alfar facility with the quarantines in place, which seemed pointless now. After all, the outbreak had already spread to both places. And it wasn't fair that her father bore the blame—from the Council's perspective—for the outbreak, despite the fact all travel between Orestes and Space City had stopped the moment the outbreak on Orestes had been discovered. But people always wanted someone to blame.

So, it had surprised her when the Council approved her delivering the samples to Orestes. Apparently, her father's argument that Alfar support on helping with this cure had been a persuasive one. It seemed the Council could be reasonable on occasion.

Nico and Anand entered the central lab for the Azymi research, which had been set up once the outbreak reached Space City.

"How are the flora tests going?" Fintan asked Anand.

Anand shrugged. "Mixed results at best."

Nico cast Anand a dirty look. "That's because you messed up the Scouts sample gathering system."

Anand rounded on Nico. "There's nothing wrong with the sample gathering system. Your software doesn't take into account the differences in various flora."

Both boys curled their fists and looked ready to come to blows. Heated arguments occurred more frequently between them now, ever since Devika was diagnosed with the fungus. Maellyn couldn't imagine what Anand must be feeling right now with his sister in a coma. Yet Nico wouldn't back off their rivalry. Why did boys let their egos get in the way of what was important?

Knowing Anand was desperate for any means of helping Devika, Maellyn stepped in between the boys. "I've gotten approval to deliver samples of the Emperor's Ruby to Orestes." She grabbed his arm and guided him toward the cases she'd set aside for delivery. "Aili wants to get her hands on them immediately. Will you help?"

"They're lifting the quarantine between us and Orestes?" Anand raised an eyebrow.

"Only for this delivery. And when we return, we'll be placed in isolated quarantine in the infirmary until the outbreak has ended."

"In case we get infected while we're there?"

She nodded.

"Even though we could get infected staying here?"

She shrugged and raised her hands, palms up. "Will you help me?"

Anand hesitated, brow wrinkling. "If I'm locked up in the infirmary, I can't help Devika."

She stepped close, making sure their eyes locked. And she lowered her voice, not wanting the other scientists in the lab to overhear. "At this point, getting the Alfar's support may be the only way we solve this crisis. Some are already reaching the conclusion that the Emperor's Ruby is false hope." She didn't want to admit the possibility of defeat, but she also didn't want anyone to die because of her pride.

Anand sighed and grabbed the handles for the pair of aluminum cases and lifted. "Might as well. If we're confined to the infirmary, at least I'll be with Devika."

"Thank you."

She would've liked to ask Trini to come too, but these days she wasn't involved much, too busy helping her aunt in the infirmary with the cases here. She'd been a wreck at first because her brother Otso was stuck alone at their home in the city. Trini was able to communicate with him via wrist-comp, but Maellyn could tell that wasn't enough, so she'd sent Charlie to look after him. She was racking up a debt with the android.

They exited the lab and headed down the long hallway, past numerous empty labs with ongoing experiments, many forgotten while the scientists focused on the Azymi problem. Maellyn was thrilled at the way everyone pitched in, regardless of their specialties, to contribute in any way they could.

Yet as they walked down the hallway past the abandoned labs, she couldn't help but wonder what vital projects were ruined or significantly delayed because they'd been abandoned mid-stream. The Azymi outbreak was widespread and deadly, demanding maximum resources. But these other experiments were part of the cost of the outbreak. And the full consequences might not be known for years.

With that in mind, she decided. They couldn't let fear, blame, and bureaucracy get in the way of curing the Azymi outbreak. That included reaching out to the Dahaka for answers. Activating her wrist-comp, Maellyn typed up a short message to Neil.

Headed to Orestes to share samples with the Alfar. Hoping they can identify a solution. In meantime, could Dardanos arrange a meeting with his Dahaka contact who provided the Azymi fungus?

She sent the message. She didn't know how Dardanos was working around the Council, but right now they were all desperate for solutions.

They exited the facility into the midday sunshine. It was bright and warm, forcing her to shield her eyes. It was the first time she'd been outside during the daytime in a week? Longer?

The fresh air and sunshine smelled like possibility. She inhaled deeply. Spring always made her feel as if anything were possible. Perhaps it was the sun, which seemed brighter in the spring. Or maybe the return of warmth that made her feel as though she were blooming. Or the new leaves and shoots on trees and plants, the promise of new life succeeding the stark nakedness of nature in the winter.

Whatever the answer, she luxuriated in the beautiful day, confident they would soon discover the cure; the Azymi's fate sealed.

Space City officers guarded the entrance to the sim's facility. Maellyn held out her badge, which one of the officers took to examine.

"I'm Maellyn Trevena. You should have received approval for my transport to Orestes."

The first officer handed Maellyn back her ID badge. He looked Anand over. "Who are you? Our instructions didn't include anyone else."

Anand offered the officer his badge. "Anand Singh. I work with Maellyn on the Azymi outbreak."

"We're delivering samples to Orestes," Maellyn said, trying to sound authoritative. "You can ask Dr. Trevena to confirm."

She hoped he would let this slide, but the officer handed Anand's badge back, his face remaining serious. "Wait here. I'll verify."

He entered the sims facility, leaving behind the second officer who had crossed his burly arms and looked ready to put either of them down if they made one false move. It seemed best not to attempt to engage him in conversation, so they waited in uncomfortable silence.

After a couple minutes, the first officer returned. "You're approved for travel. Are both cases sealed and tagged?"

She showed him the locks on the front of the cases. They were secure, their digital tags certifying they hadn't been tampered with. The officers stepped aside.

Inside the facility, they stepped over to the rack of silver explorer suits and black boots. Maellyn started to search for a suit in her size when movement behind the rack caused her to jump back, gasping.

Cade pushed his way through the suits. "I'm glad I caught you."

She held a hand to her heaving chest. "You scared me half to death. What were you doing back there?"

Anand, who had dropped both cases and braced himself for a fight, had relaxed and was checking on the cases.

"I heard you're headed back to Orestes to deliver samples. Some sort of cure to the outbreak." Cade was already dressed in an explorer suit, looking ready for travel.

She crossed her arms. "How did you find out?"

He shrugged and held out a hand to Anand. "Can I help you with one of those?"

"Absolutely not." She caught his wrist. "You don't have permission to travel."

Cade sighed, arm dropping back to his side. "You know how hard it's been for me? My brother the racing star while my bum leg will never let me compete in most races. But now I've found something I'm good at. I'm a reporter. And if I go with you I can get a first-hand account of everything."

She shook her head. "This is different than the interview with Alvi. We could get in big trouble if I let you come. How did you even get in here?"

He turned his back to her and searched the suits on the rack. He removed one and handed it to her. It was her size.

"You told me the Council is standing in your way, slowing down progress with bureaucracy despite the fact we're facing the greatest threat to Space City in decades, if ever."

She slipped the suit on over her clothes, knowing she didn't have time for this argument.

"I've already started writing an article based on what I know and what you've told me." He stacked a pair of black boots on the bench beside her. "Let me make the argument for you to the public. Let me show them the Council is endangering their lives by making the scientists jump through hoops in order to get anything accomplished. If I can get the public on your side, the Council will have to back off."

"He makes a good point," Anand said as he snapped his boot closures. "And what's the worst the Council will do if they find out? They're already putting us in quarantine when we return."

She pursed her lips, not liking that it was two against one. She wasn't against the argument. It had merit. But she also knew that it would be her father that took the blame if anything went wrong.

Sensing her concern, or perhaps reading it on her face, Cade stepped over and slipped an arm around her shoulders. "We're cousins. I'm not going to do anything stupid. I'll just go to listen, so I can write a more persuasive article. And you'll see it before it's published."

"All right." She still had her reservations, but it would be nice to have him along.

Anand held out a sealed test tube. Where had that come from? "Would it be wrong to open a case and replace the sample with this purple melon tree sample? You know, as a control group."

Maellyn snorted, knowing he was mostly kidding. Mostly. But she was glad to see a spark of his usual self. "Anxious to get expelled?"

Anand mock glowered. "Why should I get expelled for using a standard science practice? I won't ruin the spare sample."

She rolled her eyes. "Maybe you're the one I should leave here."

She entered the coordinates for Orestes into a sim cage control panel. A thorneway flowed into existence inside the cage. The familiar shiver ran up her spine, but she ignored it as she entered the thorneway.

They emerged into the research facility on Orestes to find themselves surrounded by eight large Alfar dressed in hazmat suits with face-fit masks. The Alfar were reinforced by a dozen defender drones with their energy shields activated.

Maellyn opened her mouth to argue they didn't have time to waste on this, but she checked herself. If roles were reversed, her father would take the same precautions with visitors from a quarantined area. The show of force was excessive, especially when greeting an ally, but the Alfar had never been known to take chances.

"You possess the samples?" one asked, eyeing the cases.

Anand stepped forward, holding them out. All eight of the Alfar took a step back.

"Stay where you are," the speaker ordered. "Albrin, please check them."

Albrin stepped forward with a flat gray panel. "This will just take a minute. I'm going to scan you."

"We're checked every couple of hours back home," Maellyn commented.

"We can't be too cautious," the original speaker said, unconvinced that any scans Space City administered were worth much.

She decided to let it go. They needed to work together.

Albrin held the panel before Maellyn. Her breath caught in her throat, a part of her fearing the results would come back positive despite being checked less than an hour ago. But after thirty seconds, the Alfar declared her clean, nodded to her, and shifted over to scan Anand.

She exhaled, doing her best to mask her relief at the confirmation she was healthy. Her father had taken every precaution to ensure the outbreak didn't penetrate the labs, to keep the scientists healthy and focused on finding a cure. And it was gratifying to prove their competence to the Alfar.

"He's also clean. Welcome aboard." Albrin nodded to Anand before moving over to check Cade and announce he was clear, too.

The original speaker stepped forward and accepted the cases from Anand. "Follow me."

The lack of introduction or courtesy irritated Maellyn. They'd brought the very thing needed to cure the outbreak; well, if the Alfar could prevent it from also destroying healthy tissue.

The other Alfar ringed Maellyn, Anand, and Cade as if they were prisoners. They marched past the enormous dome-covered garden. Many of the exotic plants drooped and were covered in a white film. Infected. During their first visit, the garden had been vibrant and stunning. She'd hoped to get an opportunity to tour it. Now she just hoped it wouldn't be too late to save it.

The Alfar led them back to Aili's lab. The screen on the rear wall showed the red mass that marked the boundary of the outbreak zone, now grown to three times what it had been during their original visit. Aili stood before the screen, arms crossed, shoulders slumped. She turned at their arrival, eyes darting to the cases. Hope sparkled in her eyes, though it was obscured by her black, puffy eyelids. Her hair was frazzled.

The Alfar carrying the cases placed one on the table in the center of the lab. "Your sample for study. Do you require a guard for the lab?"

"No, thank you. We'll be fine," Aili answered.

The Alfar departed with the second case, the others with him except for Albrin. Maellyn had a strong urge to yell *You're welcome* after them, but she kept that in check.

"Maellyn, Anand, it's good to see you again." The edges of Aili's mouth rose in an exhausted smile. It was the first time Maellyn could remember Aili showing any cheer in their presence, except when Alvi was around. The Alfar scientist turned her attention to Cade. "I don't believe we've met."

"Cade Martin." He stepped forward and offered his hand to shake, which Aili accepted.

Maellyn strode toward the sample case. "I hope this sample is helpful. It appears to be the break we needed. It attacks the Azymi fungus. Just need it to stop there."

Aili moved over to join her as Maellyn entered the code into the digital seal to unlock the case. She opened it to reveal a stem of the flower, along with three vials holding extracted cells ready for use.

"If this isn't enough, we can get more." Maellyn gestured at the contents.

Aili picked up a vial and studied it, as if to appraise its value. "Hard to believe a fungus from Siavash infected Ourania. We haven't had contact with the Dahaka in decades."

Maellyn nodded in agreement. "It matches up. The Council is still trying to determine the source of the outbreak on Space City."

Anand puffed his chest out. Ever since they'd learned the fungus had come from another planet, he'd reminded everyone repeatedly of his initial suggestion to that effect, which had been dismissed at the time.

"As are our leaders." Aili carried the vial over to a microwave-sized black machine. She slid open a door and inserted the vial into a slot in the machine. It hummed.

Aili crossed her arms and turned to them. "Would any of you like a drink?"

“I’m fine,” Maellyn said.

Anand shook his head. Cade, too.

“Is there anything we can do to help?” Maellyn asked. “While we’re here.” She wasn’t anxious to head back to the infirmary. This might be her last opportunity to help.

“I need time to analyze the samples first. Get familiar with them. After that I’ll have questions for you.”

“Of course. In the meantime, how is Alvi doing?”

A flash of pain crossed Aili’s face, which was just as quickly hidden. “He’s in the final stage. He didn’t wake up yesterday. If we’re lucky, he’s got two days. Maybe three. Possibly less.”

Maellyn felt as if Aili had kicked her in the gut. At their current pace, it would be nigh impossible to develop a cure for safe use on patients in that time. She could see the same conclusion in Aili’s eyes.

She fought back tears. She wouldn’t get emotional in front of Aili. It was the last thing the Alfar needed right now.

“Can I see him?” she asked.

Aili nodded. “Albrin, will you take her to see him?”

Albrin stepped forward, having removed the hazmat gear he’d worn upon their arrival. He now wore the familiar yellow clothes of all Alfar scientists. “My pleasure. It’s always good to visit the boy.” He motioned for her to follow as he marched out a side door.

Maellyn gave Anand and Cade a quick glance. “Coming?”

Anand paused hesitantly, eyeing Aili and the sample tubes. “I think I’ll stay. In case Aili has any questions.”

“I’ll go with you,” Cade said, moving to her side.

Albrin led them past a long series of labs that reminded Maellyn of the science labs. It comforted her. Labs always had. In her life, they had always been the source of solutions to life’s many problems. No matter how great the problem appeared, it was dissected in a lab down to its various basic parts. That always made it a little less daunting. From there, all good scientists analyzed those parts, looking for answers to what each part did and how they fit and worked together. Once you understood how something worked, you hypothesized theories for how to counteract a problem and meticulously tried each, revising based upon discoveries along the way. You kept going until a solution was reached.

This process had never failed her.

But with the Azymi affecting her home, her friends, classmates, for the first time she feared failure. She felt personally threatened. Would they find the answers in time?

Albrin led them to a medical area and from there to an area with a glass window. Through it, Maellyn could see Alvi lying unconscious in a bed. Machines with tubes were attached to his face, arms, and chest. Even from here she could tell how pale he was. Her breath caught in her throat.

Cade placed a reassuring hand on her arm, squeezing gently.

"Do you want to go in?" Albrin asked from her side. "You'll need to wear a hazmat suit."

"Of course. Yes. Let's go in."

Albrin led them to a pair of closed doors. A green light flashed over him. Once it finished, the doors opened, allowing them to enter a small room filled with dozens of hazmat suits hanging on racks along one wall. Maellyn hurried to retrieve one and pulled it on over her suit, Cade and Albrin joining her. Once Maellyn had zipped up, Albrin stepped close and pressed a button on the side of her mask. It shrank to fit around her face. For a second, she panicked, feeling like someone had thrown a bag over her head to suffocate her.

"Breathe," Albrin ordered.

She did. After a few deep breaths, she relaxed. She surveyed her surroundings. The mask didn't hinder her vision in anyway.

Albrin moved over to a second door. This time, an orange light passed over the entire room, followed by a green one. It took fifteen seconds, but once it finished, the door opened, permitting them into the room where Alvi and several other patients lay comatose in beds, all hooked up to their own monitoring systems. A doctor studying a monitor near one patient glanced up at their entrance, then went back to what she was doing.

All of them were kids or teens. Alvi looked to be the youngest.

"Are they all in the final stage?" Her voice caught a little as she asked the question.

"They are," Albrin confirmed.

She opened her mouth to ask other questions, but found her voice was gone. Now was not the time. Stepping over to Alvi's bed, she found herself hoping he'd wake up. Talk to her. That would give her reassurance.

His forehead and hair were damp, his lips a dark purple, as if bruised. He'd always been so excited. Curious about everything. Endless energy. The azymi had robbed him of all of it.

Elp lay snug between one of Alvi's arms and his chest. She placed a hand on his arm and Elp, trying to will a little bit of comfort to the boy. The gloves on her hands frustrated her. They were cold and lifeless, serving as a poor medium for contact.

"Hang on." Maellyn squeezed his arm. "We're so close. Just keep holding on. Do you hear me? A little bit longer and we'll make everything right."

She wouldn't let this little boy die.

He had forever ahead of him.

This wouldn't be his end.

She promised.

Chapter 31

Neil Visits Mars

Neil woke in a nurse's chair, his head leaning against the wall. Drool seeped from his mouth down to his chin; he quickly wiped it away. He yawned and rubbed his eyes. He longed for a few more hours of sleep.

"Want some purple melon punch?" Patrick approached, a small cup in each hand.

"Thank you." Neil accepted the cup and downed half of it.

Patrick gestured down the corridor to Adrien Laroque's room. Two officers guarded it. "Dr. Torres checked on him twenty minutes ago. Nothing new."

After Adrien had mentioned Guiman's name when he awoke from his coma, followed by the old man being killed in the explosion that destroyed his home—evidence confirmed it—the Council had ordered officers to prevent anyone from entering Adrien's room except Dr. Torres and his nurses. Neil had volunteered several times to deliver food or medicines to Adrien in order to speak with him, but Dr. Torres restricted access to a couple of nurses.

"You don't have to stay," Patrick said. "I can handle watch."

"What's the point of going back to the dorm?" Neil took another swig of punch. "We're always on call. If I'm already here, I can respond faster." And there was no shortage of work that needed to be done.

The truth was, he found the dorms creepy at this point. It was deathly quiet all the time, a large number of students here at the infirmary. Those that remained hid behind locked doors, refusing to answer for anyone. And with Riagan suddenly missing, he didn't want to stay alone. He had scoured the campus looking for Riagan, and at first had feared he'd been killed with Guiman. But quarantine officers had seen Riagan outside of Guiman's place shortly after the explosion. He'd been fine. So where had he gone?

With nowhere else to turn, Neil had reached out to Dardanos and been turned away. The headmaster declared he had too much on his plate right now to provide any answers, and would reach out when he could. For the time being, nothing was more important than ending the outbreak and taking care of those who were ill. Neil at least understood this last bit, and so he stayed here in the hospital, ready to do his part when asked.

A green light flashed across his wrist-comp, alerting him that he'd received a new message. He pulled it up. From Maellyn.

"What is it?" Patrick asked.

"A message from Maellyn," Neil answered. *Asking me to reach out to Rashn for help.*

He started to type a reply when Patrick leaned forward, looking at his screen. Neil jerked the wrist-comp away, but not before Patrick's eyes had popped wide.

"You know a Dahaka?"

Neil punched Patrick in the arm then pointed toward the guards. "Shush." He couldn't believe Patrick had read his messages. Why hadn't he taken better care to shield the screen?

Patrick leaned close, his voice a whisper. "Seriously? You know a Dahaka?"

Neil rose and grabbed a handful of Patrick's shirt, hauling him to his feet. "Let's take a walk."

He stalked down the hall, Patrick in tow, to a rear exit. The door slid open automatically. Outside, Neil scanned for listening ears. They were alone.

He turned back to Patrick, speaking in a hushed tone. "The Azymi fungus came from Siavash." At least that's what he'd reasoned. The connections fit. "I received a flower from a Dahaka friend—"

"Friend?" Patrick spluttered.

Neil shoved Patrick. "Keep it down."

Patrick frowned, but when he spoke again his voice was hushed. "You have a Dahaka friend?"

"Yes. The flower has properties that counteract the fungus. The scientists are testing it out, but are having problems."

Patrick whistled, shaking his head. "You have a Dahaka friend."

"Yes, anyway—"

"Will you introduce me?" Patrick's voice held more than a hint of eagerness.

Neil rubbed his hands over his face. His first instinct was to deny it, as he'd done all year long, but did it even matter anymore? "Maellyn asked that I get more information. The scientists are struggling to develop a cure."

Patrick rocked back on his heels and rubbed his palms together. "When do we go?"

"We?" Neil pointed at the infirmary. "I thought you weren't leaving Adrien?"

Patrick gazed at the door, a wistful expression on his face. "He'll be fine. He's under guard after all. And meeting a Dahaka. How do we get there?"

Neil gave him an appraising look. He couldn't believe this discussion was even happening. Last year he'd hated Patrick. Riagan still did; refused to consider that Patrick had changed in anyway. But Neil knew he had changed. The question was how much.

Patrick grew serious, as if reading Neil's thoughts. "Come on. You can trust me. I promise."

Neil nodded. He wasn't sold, but he had no one else at this point. Jiro and Dirk had gone to Mars, along with their dads. And he'd need help getting to Siavash. "With the quarantine in place, our sole means of traveling to Siavash is the thorneway in the sims facility, which is guarded while we're under quarantine."

Patrick slapped Neil's chest with the back of his hand. "Leave that to me." He marched for the courtyard. "Get what you need and meet in my room."

They split up at the dorm, heading for their rooms. Neil retrieved his silver explorer suit and dressed. He also typed a quick message to Rashn, hoping he'd remember how to use the wrist-comp Neil had given him. He added candy to his pockets in case he got hungry, before making his way to Patrick's room.

Patrick was digging through a duffle on his bed. The other bed, Adrien's, was properly made. Neil wondered how Patrick felt living alone, knowing his roommate was in a coma in the hospital. Worse, he had to deal with that while many classmates believed he was the one who'd put Adrien in the hospital. If it bothered Patrick, he hadn't shown it.

From the duffle Patrick pulled a couple pairs of handcuffs without the chain that normally connected them; they could've been confused for arm bracelets. They were instead held together by a magnetic current activated when placed on someone's wrists. Besides keeping the wearers wrists confined closely together, it also delivered a shock if the person wearing the cuffs attempted to remove them. He'd never worn a pair, but had heard they were no joke.

"How did you get those?" Neil asked.

Patrick shrugged. "You guys know the pranks I used to pull. Just because I've stopped doesn't mean I've gotten rid of my tools." He also removed a roll of duct tape—no one had developed anything better yet. Patrick handed one set of cuffs to Neil. The second pair he slipped into a suit pocket. "Ready to go?"

That Patrick had kept all of this made Neil question once more how much he could really trust Patrick, but decided at this point he really had no choice.

They took a circuitous route through campus in order to come at it from behind. Once they reached the facility, Neil scanned the rear of the building, hoping for an alternate entrance but there wasn't one, except a roof access. Neither of them had a means to scale the side of the building to get on the roof.

Patrick pointed toward the right side of the facility. "You go that way," he said to Neil. "I'll come around the other side."

"Ok?" Neil asked.

"Lean around the front of the building and take out one guard with your stun setting. I'll get the other. We'll cuff 'em together and lock 'em in a sim cage."

"You want to take out the guards?" Neil asked incredulously, not liking the plan one bit.

"We've got to get past them. I don't know how to draw them away."

Neil shook his head, trying to think of some other means or excuse that would get them inside. But he knew as well as Patrick that the guards were under orders to let no one in the sims facility without special orders from the Council.

"It's not an easy shot either," Neil muttered. This plan was insane.

Patrick's lip curled in a half smile. "Come on. You've shot me from farther than that in our Games matches."

"That's hitting a target on your chest or back. Their suits block stun attacks. We'll have to take head or neck shots. Miss and we won't get a second shot."

Patrick clapped him on the shoulder. "Better not miss then."

Neil groaned. It was all he could do not to bury his head in his hands. "You know they have security cameras in the facility, right?"

Patrick shrugged. "Won't be able to get there before we use the thorneway to travel to Siavash."

"And when we get back?"

"Guess it depends on how bad you want to get in touch with your friend. Didn't you say this'll help us stop the outbreak? Seems worth whatever punishment they give us."

Neil would prefer a solution that didn't get them in trouble, but he guessed this would be one of those times when the ends truly did justify the means. After all, they wouldn't hurt the guards.

"All right," Neil agreed.

He eased forward along the side of the facility, tiptoeing. As he reached the corner of the building, he leaned against the wall, took a deep breath, and checked on the guards at the entrance.

"What are you doing?" a female voice asked from behind.

He jumped, spinning, and barely stopped himself from shooting Eris out of shock. His heart thudded in his chest. "Why are you here?"

"Saw you and Patrick slinking around. Surprised me. I had to know what you're up to." She arched an eyebrow. "Well?"

"Neil, are you ready?" Patrick asked over the tradutor.

"Hold on," Neil replied. "Eris, please. I don't have time to explain."

"You're on some mission again, aren't you?"

He sighed. He had been a terrible spy this year. Too much exposure to too many people.

"I want to go with," she said and he noticed she wore a silver explorer suit, ready to go.

"What? No. You can't."

She leaned sideways, peeking around the front of the building at the quarantine officers, raising a hand as if to draw their attention. He grabbed her arm and pulled her back.

"Seems to me you're trying to get past the officers into the sims facility. I could warn them." She crossed her arms and gave him a look that dared him to test her.

"Neil?" Patrick asked again, irritation creeping in.

Neil gritted his teeth and shook his fists in front of his face. "Eris, please."

"Tell Patrick you're ready."

"What?" His mind was scrambling, trying to come up with a means to get rid of her while also debating if he should tell Patrick to abort.

"Tell. Patrick. You're. Ready." At that, she took aim and fired at the closest guard.

"Now, Patrick! Now!" he hollered into the tradutor.

Neil jumped out from the corner of the building to find one guard crumpled on the ground. The second had turned toward them, eyes widening, arms raising to shoot, then he stiffened up and fell beside his comrade. Peeking out from the far side of the facility, Patrick charged toward the downed officers.

Neil looked around, searching for a witness, but they were alone. He rounded on Eris. "Are you crazy? You could've ruined everything."

She marched past him. "I'd say I saved you from ruining it yourself. You know I'm a better shot."

He clenched his fists and stormed after her. He was going to have to take control of this before one of their reckless actions cost them.

"Eris, get the door," he barked. He pointed at the officers. "Patrick, you get one and I'll get the other."

Neil reached for the closest officer's carotid artery to check his pulse, despite knowing they'd used stun lasers. The officer was breathing fine, just unconscious. Neil bent down and thrust his hands under the guard's arms and lugged him toward the door. He grunted. *Guy must weigh two-twenty. Maybe two-thirty.* He dragged the officer into the sims facility, Patrick following him with the second.

Eris closed and locked the door behind them, then joined Neil. "Let me help."

He let go the right arm, which she grabbed, and they pulled together. Once they had the officer into a sim cage, Neil took a couple deep breaths, before helping Patrick drag the second in with the first. Then Patrick slapped the pair of handcuffs on one of each officers' wrists. Once they exited the cage, Eris locked it, trapping the officers inside until someone came to their rescue.

"Heavier than they look," Patrick complained.

"Let's get going." Neil kept his gaze down, not staring up at the cameras, though it was doubtful they'd get out of this unidentified. He marched to the thorneway generator, knowing they didn't have much time before reinforcements arrived.

The Siavash coordinates were easy to pull up; he had them memorized. In less than thirty seconds, a thorneway was activated inside a sims cage. Neil opened the cage door and gestured inside.

"After you," he told Patrick.

For a few seconds Patrick stared at the thorneway, perhaps realizing what they were really doing and having doubts. Good. Maybe it would make him careful.

"Go," Neil ordered.

Patrick lowered his brow in a determined frown and darted into the thorneway.

"You're up," Neil told Eris.

She nodded and jumped in, looking more eager than Patrick had. Neil took a deep breath, hoping this would go as smoothly as their last trip. And end up being worth it. Then he stepped into the thorneway.

*****

Inside the cave on Siavash, Neil didn't waste any time. He headed straight for the cave mouth, Eris at his side. Patrick held both arms primed to shoot, eyes wide. He rotated, searching the cave for threats. It reminded Neil of his first visit here. Fortunately, they weren't going to be in the heart of the capital among all the Azios. He hoped those days were over.

"There's no need to hide," Neil told Patrick to reassure him. "We need to find Rashn."

Patrick hurried to join them as they exited the cave. He said nothing. Every few seconds he pivoted like a dog surrounded by a guerilla army of squirrels all taunting him.

"Are we headed to the village?" Eris asked.

"Hope not."

Rashn had responded he was on his way, but whether that was from the capital or the village, Neil didn't know.

"What are we doing when we find this Rashn?" Patrick asked.

"See what else he knows about the fungus and the Emperor's Ruby. Arrange a meeting with our scientists." Which he suddenly realized wasn't all that different from what Dardanos was planning with his proposal. And if some of the Azios were like Rashn, that would be a good thing.

But Mainyu wasn't. There could be no peaceful treaty with the Dahaka as long as Mainyu remained in charge. Dirk was right, however. The villagers here on Siavash deserved every effort Space City could make to find a solution.

They continued on for another fifteen minutes, headed in the direction of the village, when Rashn and Vahu emerged out of the trees, both carrying Emperor's Ruby flowers. Patrick yelped and took aim at them. Neil hacked his arms down to ensure they didn't have an accidental shooting.

Rashn stepped protectively in front of Vahu. He had a knife in his hands that hadn't been there a second before.

"It's okay." Neil turned on Patrick, putting himself in the way. "Chill. This is them."

"Sorry." Patrick was tense, but he opened his hand, palms toward them. "I'm sorry."

Rashn's shoulders relaxed. The knife disappeared. He and Vahu approached, though she regarded Patrick distrustfully. "Your message said you needed more Emperor's Rubies?"

"Not exactly," Neil said. "It's not working. I was hoping you could give us more information."

"Oh." Rashn shrugged. "Not sure I can help, but Vahu might can."

"Well, from what I'm hearing, our scientists tested the cells from the Emperor's Ruby. It attacks the fungus, killing it, but also attack the host cells."

Vahu frowned. "I'm not following you."

Neil considered his words. They weren't overly technical, but perhaps some terms didn't translate well.

"We made a medicine from the Emperor's Ruby, but it harms those we give it to."

"I didn't know. Believe me, that was not our intent." Vahu looked worried, as if he had accused her of betraying them.

"Nobody faults you," he said. "We're just trying to figure out what's wrong. Maybe there's something special you do? A mix with the flower? Something special in the way you prepare it?"

Vahu shook her head. "We use only the Emperor's Ruby. Ground it into a paste and give it right away, as I told you."

He bit the inside of his lip, at a loss. Why didn't it hurt the Dahaka? "Do you give people the Emperor's Ruby as soon as you pick it? Do you wait a while?" Perhaps the Emperor's Ruby had to be fresh. Or maybe it needed to dry out for a period of time before use.

"Doesn't matter," Vahu said. "We give them ones we have on hand that have been stored for several days. If we run out, we cut fresh flowers and give them to the sick right away. Nothing harms them."

Neil wished he had more of a scientific background. He didn't know what other questions to ask. He doubted collecting more samples would help.

Patrick looked past Rashn and Vahu. "How far is this village? Or better yet, the capital?"

"You don't want to see the capital," Neil said. "And we don't have time to explore."

"Oh sure. You say that because you've been here before." Patrick slapped Eris on the arm. "What about Eris and I?"

"I've seen the village, too," Eris responded.

Patrick grumbled. "How many of you have been here? Everyone but me?"

Neil ignored him. "Rashn, would you consider returning with us? Speak with our scientists."

Rashn exchanged uneasy looks with Vahu. "Humans are fearful of Dahaka. I understand you are different, but what about your leaders?"

"Hell no," Patrick shouted.

Neil glared at him.

“What?” Patrick shrugged. “Just being honest. Regardless of Dardanos’ proposal, too many still hate and fear them. They’d be locked up the moment they stepped through the thorneway.”

“I don’t agree.” Neil shook his head. Yes, many hated and feared the Dahaka, and they would act irrationally based upon that fear. He knew he had previously, to his shame. Yet when it came to it, he believed Dr. Trevena would accept Rashn’s help and defend him if necessary. The other scientists, too. They would view Rashn as he was, not as prejudices claimed.

“You’ll be safe if you come with us,” Neil assured Rashn. “Trust me.”

Vahu wore a worried expression, but said nothing. Rashn appraised her for a few seconds, before nodding. “If we stand by and do nothing, how can we ever hope for a brighter future for our people?”

A tear appeared in Vahu’s eye, but she kept her head held high, hands at her sides. Neil hoped her fears were unnecessary, but a part of him knew Patrick might very well be right. Would Dr. Trevena have the power to convince the Council and guards to let the Dahaka on Space City without locking them up?

A green light on Neil’s wrist-comp alerted him to a new message. He activated it, anticipating another message from Maellyn. He wanted to ask her to check with her dad about Rashn. Guarantee his safety. But the message was from an unknown sender. For a second, he feared the private messenger was contacting him again.

He pulled up the message.

Come to Mars. There’s a plan to attack the Council. I need your help to stop it.
Riagan.

When had Riagan traveled to Mars? How did he get past the quarantine? What was the Council doing on Mars? Who would attack them?

“What is it?” Eris asked.

“Riagan. Says someone intends to attack the Council,” Neil said. Where could he have gotten this intel? Had Guiman given it to him before his death?

"What?" Eris reached for Neil's wrist-comp.

He turned his wrist so she could read it. "They're on Mars. He asked for help."

Patrick crowded in to look as well. "What do we do?" he asked.

Neil shook his head. He didn't have any idea.

"Contact Dardanos?" Eris suggested.

Neil typed a response back.

Come as soon as we can. Have you contacted Dardanos for help?

The response he got back made him blink twice, thinking he had misread.

Dardanos is responsible. Tell no one. Come now!

"What does he mean Dardanos is responsible?" Patrick asked.

There must be some mistake. Regardless, Riagan needed his help. He was going to help clear this up. "We'll get answers when we get there."

"How are we getting to Mars?" Eris asked.

"Um, through the thorneway," Neil replied. "Same way we came here."

Eris shook her head. "You know the second we return to the sims facility, there'll be officers waiting for us."

He scrunched his eyes shut. She was right. By now, there would be other guards in the sims facility, waiting on them to return. "I don't have the coordinates to Mars."

"I do." Patrick began to search his wrist-comp.

"Seriously?" Neil was taken aback.

Patrick smirked. "My family is well connected. I've got the coordinates to quite a few places."

While Patrick searched for the coordinates, Neil looked at Rashn, remembering he had to go back to Space City. He couldn't send Rashn alone. He turned back to Patrick and Eris. "You two will have to go alone. I need to get Rashn to the scientists."

"No, I can make it on my own," Rashn said.

Neil wanted to agree. He'd rather go to Mars and find Riagan, figure out what was going on. But he couldn't abandon Rashn. If he sent the Dahaka back alone, Patrick was right. The guards wouldn't treat him kindly. "No. You'll need me there to vouch for you."

"I'll take him back," Eris said, though he could see from her expression that she resented it. "Riagan needs you. Patrick has the coordinates. That leaves me."

This still felt like abandoning a friend who needed him. He'd convinced Rashn to go to Space City. The Dahaka was his responsibility; however, returning to Space City now meant abandoning Riagan. And if there was an attack planned against the Council, Riagan was in danger.

Rashn walked over to Neil and placed a hand on his bicep. "It's okay. Your friend needs you. I'll be fine with Eris."

"And me," Vahu said.

Rashn's brow wrinkled and he shook his head. "You can't come. You'll be safer here."

Vahu placed her hands on her hips, glaring at him. "You know little about the Emperor's Ruby. And I'm not letting you go alone."

Rashn grimaced. He placed his arms around Vahu's neck, but she pulled away.

"Please," Rashn said. "I don't want to put you in danger."

"But it's okay for you?"

"One of us has to go, and I won't risk you."

"You're not risking me cause it's my call." She took the lead toward the cave.

Rashn gave Neil a look like there was no reasoning with women, then he followed after her.

It took them a short hike back to the cave. Neil fretted, afraid he was making a mistake sending the Dahaka back to Space City. And what were they walking into on Mars? It seemed unbelievable that Dardanos was planning to attack the Council. Riagan must be mistaken.

Patrick entered the coordinates for Mars into the thorneway activation controls. "Ready?" he asked as the black thorneway materialized in its frame.

"Are you sure?" Neil asked Rashn. "I can go with you."

"Go save your friend. We'll do what we can to help your people."

"Thank you." Neil held out his hand.

Rashn stared at it, a puzzled expression on his face. He reached out his own hand. Neil grabbed it with both his own and shook it.

"What is this?" Rashn asked.

"It's a sign of gratitude," Neil said, grinning. "You're helping us in a big way."

"You would help me if I was in need," Rashn said simply, squeezing Neil's hand in return.

"I would." Neil pulled his hand back, motioned for Patrick to enter the thorneway, then followed him through.

*****

Neil emerged onto Mars to find a couple of Space City officers confronting Patrick.

"What're you doing here?" one asked, weapon drawn. Both officers were tense, with the second rounding his weapon on Neil.

Neil froze, raising his hands in surrender.

"Anyone else coming through?" the second asked.

"Just us," Patrick said, his voice slightly shrill.

They stood in a glass cube the size of a single-story house. A second thorneway frame stood beside the one they'd come through in the middle of the room. A single table along the right wall which held equipment.

"What're you doing?" the first repeated.

"Trying to stop an attack," Patrick answered, making sure his hands were open and out from his sides. "Someone plans to attack the Council."

Both officers' faces darkened, their backs stiffening even further. "How do you know the Council's here?"

Idiot, Neil scolded himself. Why hadn't he anticipated guards here, too? Of course they wouldn't let anyone wander into the facility. He stepped past Patrick.

"It doesn't matter how we know or got here. You have to warn the Council. They're in danger." He hoped earnestness would convince them.

"You're going to need some actual evidence." The first officer sneered. "We're not disturbing the Council based upon the word of two students breaking protocol."

Neil gritted his teeth. What they had wasn't evidence at all. A message. Showing that would only complicate matters further. He wished he had Dirk or Arielle here. With their diplomatic backgrounds, they'd know what would convince the officers to take them seriously. Of course, if Dirk were here, he could contact—

His eyes widened and he grabbed his wrist-comp to type up a message.

"Stop that!" The second officer stepped forward, reaching for the wrist-comp.

Neil pulled back. "I'm just contacting Dirk Fischer. His father is Councilman Fischer." Why hadn't he thought of that the moment they learned of the attack? Dirk could get the warning to his father. The second officer moved to his side to examine the message.

Dirk, I need your help. Patrick and I are at the Mars travel facility. Someone is planning to attack the Council. Officers won't let us past. Can you help?

Neil sent the message and waited for a reply.

"Well?" the first officer asked, keeping his aim on Patrick.

"Hasn't responded yet." Neil hoped Dirk saw the message soon. While they waited, he gestured toward the glass wall that presented the surface of Mars. "Would you mind if we looked out while we wait?"

The officer regarded him for a moment, then shrugged. "Have at it. I'll give you twenty minutes. After that, I'm hauling you back to the ship. Hand you over to Dardanos for discipline."

Patrick opened his mouth, but Neil grabbed his arm and squeezed hard, guessing what he was about to say. Telling the officers that they suspected Dardanos of planning the attack wouldn't go over well. Might get them hauled back to Space City faster. No, their only play was to wait for Dirk to respond. And speak with his father.

"What now?" Patrick asked as they moved over to the wall and stared out.

Neil's wrist-comp buzzed with a response from Dirk. *On my way.* "We wait," Neil said.

It was late evening, half the sun above the horizon, casting the Mars facility in a reddish hue. The facility resembled large, futuristic glass igloos strung together by domed hallways. The domed hallways were covered in what looked like algae. Scanning with his contacts revealed the algae was fungal mycelium. The fungus had been grown on the facility after it had been built in order to provide radiation protection.

That last bit gave him pause. Why did the facility need radiation protection? And if it did, why did Space City conduct their final exams outside on Mars? Weren't they needlessly exposing the students to radiation? He made a note to ask Instructor Tereshkova about that later.

Outside the facility, rows of solar panels gleamed in the remaining sunlight. Beyond them, round platforms filled with small green shrubs covered by a glass-like dome. Neil zoomed in on the shrubs with his contacts. They had an odd turquoise coloration. He scanned the shrubs. While he waited for details, he sent Riagan a message telling him they had arrived and asking where to find him.

The shrubs were synthetic, designed to absorb sunlight to create clean burning fuels that powered several rovers around the facility, a couple of which were parked nearby.

Neil wished to drive one. Would it feel any different from driving on Earth?

"Time to go back." The first officer had an obvious gloat as he flexed his muscles. He'd believed they were lying from the beginning.

Fortunately, before Neil had to argue for more time, Councilman Fischer entered, Dirk in tow. Both officers stiffened and saluted. Dirk's dad nodded to them before turning to study Neil and Patrick.

"I hear you've got a pair of students who snuck past quarantine."

"Yes, sir," the first officer replied. "Was planning to drag them back to the academy for punishment."

"No need," Councilman Fischer said. "I'll handle them."

"Yes, sir," the officers replied.

Taller, but every bit as thin as Dirk, his father wore a stoic expression as he approached. Dirk, on the other hand, looked troubled.

"Come with me," Councilman Fischer directed, leading them out of the travel facility to an empty hallway. "My son says you have knowledge of a plot to attack the Council."

"Riagan, actually, sir." Neil wondered if he should salute as the officers had. "He sent us a message asking for help."

"Let me see it."

Neil pulled up the messages and handed over his wrist-comp. "It doesn't say much."

"You think Dardanos is involved?" Councilman Fischer's eyes flashed. "Your friend must be mistaken."

Neil shrugged. "I'm not sure, sir. I just know what he sent." He'd been hoping Riagan would respond by now.

Councilman Fischer handed the wrist-comp back and motioned for them to follow. "Send him a message and let's go find him. I'm going to get to the bottom of this."

"Yes, sir."

Neil typed a second message to Riagan letting him know he needed an urgent response. He hoped this wasn't all some mistake; otherwise, they'd be in a lot of trouble. They'd already be in hot water when they returned to Space City. More than a simple detention with Instructor Tereshkova. Maybe a month's worth of detentions with her. Would Dardanos expel them for this if it all turned out to be nothing?

The cottage-sized igloos—or pods—Neil had seen were living quarters by and large. They gave way to a handful of larger structures that supported labs, storage units, or restricted areas he couldn't see inside.

"How did you get past quarantine?" Councilman Fischer asked.

Neil sighed, squeezing his eyes shut for a couple breaths. No sense in hiding the truth. The councilman would find out everything once he returned to Space City, if not before. So Neil filled him in, starting with Maellyn's request to reach out to the Dahaka. He didn't elaborate on how they knew the coordinates to get to Siavash or why they knew a Dahaka. And Councilman Fischer didn't question them, though he did arch an eyebrow at a couple of points.

At the end of his recounting of recent events, they marched on in an uncomfortable silence, waiting for Councilman Fischer to respond.

"That was dangerous, trusting a Dahaka," Councilman Fischer said finally.

"It wasn't our first encounter with him."

"That may be, but it's a serious breach in protocol. It will have to be addressed."

Neil rushed on. "I'm confident Rashn and Vahu can help stop the outbreak, which is what matters most, right?"

"If there's one positive of your reckless attack on the officers at the sims facility, it's that they'll be on high alert when Eris returns with the Dahaka."

Neil hoped the officers gave Eris a chance to explain why they were there. What with everyone's nerves wound so tight aboard Space City. He felt a stab of guilt once more for sending Rashn and Vahu with only Eris as an escort. Perhaps he shouldn't have convinced them to travel to Space City at all, regardless of how dire the circumstances.

"Where's your friend Riagan?" Councilman Fischer asked.

As if on cue, Neil received a message. He pulled it up on his wrist-comp. "That would be him now. He's hiding out with a miner family in the southeast quadrant of the facility."

Councilman Fischer's jaw tightened. "That should've been reported. They've risked spreading the fungus here."

"They're just trying to protect a kid," Dirk said. "Are we the only ones allowed to seek refuge?"

"We took appropriate precautions. Can you say the same for Riagan?" Councilman Fischer's tone held clear disapproval.

"Probably not," Dirk admitted, but he raised his chin defiantly. "But the family would've tested him to ensure he wasn't infected."

Councilman Fischer regarded his son for a moment, before nodding. "Very well. Let's go see why your friend thinks the Council is in danger."

He led them down several hallways and through several pods—dining halls and other common areas—until they reached the private quarters of the family housing Riagan. The husband and wife were off at work, leaving Riagan alone. Neil was relieved to see he was all right. Riagan's eyes flashed at the sight of Patrick with them, but he said nothing.

"You're the one who believes the Council is in danger?" Councilman Fischer clasped his hands behind his back.

"I'm positive Dardanos' plans to attack," Riagan replied. His eyes were red-rimmed. "Just have to figure out how."

"How do you know this?"

Neil hoped Riagan's reasons for suspecting the Academy Head were good ones. He trusted Riagan, but this was a big leap.

"A few days ago, Guiman gave me a package to deliver to Dardanos," Riagan began.

"The gardener?" Councilman Fischer asked.

Neil coughed, and at Councilman Fischer's sideways glance, he said, "He was a little more than a gardener." Although Councilman Fischer should know that.

Ignoring the comment, Councilman Fischer said, "Riagan, will you please continue with your story." His tone sounded like he already regretted this discussion.

Riagan told them about his delivery to Dardanos, overhearing the Academy Head talking with Dr. Snelling regarding an inoculation for the outbreak, followed by witnessing the explosion that killed Guiman. He'd reasoned that Guiman's demise had something to do with the package he'd delivered to Dardanos, so he returned to Dardanos' office to figure out why. He finished it up with the messages from Mainyu discussing plans to attack the Council.

Councilman Fischer looked thunderstruck at this last revelation, but he recovered quickly. He asked a few clarifying questions, but mostly typed away furiously on his wrist-comp.

Neil had to sit down. All the spying they'd done over the last year, thinking they were exposing the traitors responsible for Rois' death. Instead, they'd been serving one. His stomach roiled. He couldn't imagine how much worse the revelation must've been for Riagan. When had Guiman realized that Dardanos was working with Mainyu?

With the discussion over, Councilman Fischer moved toward the door. "You three can stay for the time being. I need to look into this after I check on the plans to send aid to Orestes. Reports on the attack aren't good."

Neil sat up straight, mouth going dry. "What Orestes attack?"

"The Alfar moon base. We've received word it was attacked. We are prepping a mission to go help."

Chapter 32

Riagan Airlifted

An attack on Orestes at the same time Dardanos planned another here. That couldn't be a coincidence. Dardanos might not have the connections to pull off both attacks, but Mainyu did.

"What kind of attack?" Neil asked. "How bad? Anyone hurt?"

Riagan felt awed at the scope of this. The Alfar, already reeling from the Azymi outbreak, would be devastated if their primary science and technology facility, the place handling their research into a cure for the fungus, was destroyed or seriously damaged. Space City would be in similar shape with the outbreak and the Council destroyed. The coordinated attacks could very well neutralize human and Alfar dominance, at least for a time, as they struggled to recover. And Mainyu would have plans in place to exploit the power vacuum.

"All we can confirm at present is there was an explosion," Councilman Fischer answered.

"Maellyn was on Orestes." Neil's face paled. "Do you have any news about her?"

Councilman Fischer's expression softened, eyes betraying a little exhaustion. "I don't. I'm sorry. And I don't have time for further questioning. I must go." With that, he departed.

Neil stared out the door, saying nothing.

"She'll be fine," Dirk said, placing a hand on Neil's shoulder and squeezing.

Riagan stopped himself from snorting, but not out of a sense of compassion. Instead, the moment he had thought to snort, a sudden pain flared through his shins. It reminded him of all the times Rois' had kicked him when she disapproved of something he was doing. He considered it being realistic, not giving Neil any false hope. Her argument would've been that realistic was an excuse for being cruel.

Still keeping me in line from beyond the grave.

Neil flipped on his wrist-comp and began to type out a message. As he did so, he spoke to Dirk. "Can you find out when your father's sending help to Orestes?"

"Yes," Dirk answered.

Neil finished his message, then jumped to his feet, pacing. "I have to go. I have to find Maellyn. Make sure she's all right."

Riagan had expected the words before Neil even said them. He expected it was all Neil could process right now.

"I'll go," Patrick volunteered.

It took everything Riagan had not to punch him in the face right then. Why was Patrick even here? What had happened in the couple days he'd been gone?

Neil turned to Riagan, a desperate plea for help in his eyes. It made Riagan feel like scum for his answer.

"I can't. I have to find out Dardanos' plan and stop it." He couldn't let the headmaster get away with any of this.

Neil's eyes deadened slightly, but he nodded. It made Riagan wish for a thousand kicks to the shin. But he had no choice in the matter. Right now he had to stop the attack here. The one that *hadn't* happened yet. But it burned him that Patrick would be the one to help Neil.

"I'm staying, too. Arielle is here." Dirk looked guilty, as if staying to help because of her was a sell-out.

Neil shook his head. "Of course. Stay and help stop the attack. Patrick and I can handle it. Let me know what you hear from your dad."

"Of course," Dirk replied.

Neil and Patrick departed.

Riagan turned his back on them, hiding the flush creeping up his face. He was doing the right thing by staying. He couldn't let Dardanos install himself as the new Council leader; Mainyu's puppet.

"What have you discovered?" Dirk asked, shifting from foot to foot, ready to take off, but unsure which direction to head in.

Riagan shrugged and turned back, his expression now controlled. "Very little. As far as I know Dardanos is still in Space City. I have little idea who's setting up the attack. Or how."

"Why didn't you notify the Council?" Dirk asked.

"Accuse Dardanos without evidence?" Riagan asked, wanting to smack Dirk in the back of the head for his naiveté. "Ya think they'd take me at my word? Maybe your word as a Councilman's son."

Dirk grimaced and didn't reply.

"I came to learn what I could. Explored the facility to familiarize myself with the layout; search for anything odd or out of place."

Dirk started typing on his wrist-comp. "The travel facility keeps an official log of everyone who passes through the thorneway. If we get our hands on the log, we might be able to identify unusual visitors."

"And ya have access?" Riagan asked.

Dirk flashed a big smile. "I *am* the son of a Councilman."

Envious that Dirk had managed to come up with more in a couple of minutes than he had in days, Riagan moved to Dirk's side to study what he was doing. "How do we figure out who shouldn't be here?"

"There's a personnel list with everyone who lives and works here. While we can't officially rule them out, I don't believe Dardanos recruited any of them. There have to be easier candidates. I can also match the travel log against the current officers assigned here. Most live onsite, but due to the quarantine, there's been some minor shuffling."

As Riagan watched over his shoulder, Dirk pulled up the lists of Mars' residents and officers and compared them against the travel log for the last week.

One name stood out.

Ryan A. Guiman. Arrived yesterday.

Riagan blinked, sure he was reading that wrong. Guiman was alive? Or had someone stolen his credentials? Whoever had blown up his home and killed him.

"Didn't you say he was killed?" Dirk asked.

"Yeah."

"For a dead guy, he gets around. Arrived last night around ten minutes to midnight." Dirk flipped over to a database that stored facility camera footage.

"Ya can't tap into the facilities cameras, too?" They should've recruited him a long time ago.

Dirk smirked as he entered last night's date and time stamp into the database. "I'm not *supposed* to, but you'd be amazed what I can get into and where I can go by reminding people my father is on the Council. There."

On screen, Guiman strolled out of the travel facility, no crutch in hand. Riagan gaped. They watched him saunter through the facility to an exit. He changed into a suit with helmet for going outside. Once he exited, they lost sight of him on camera.

Dirk rewound the footage to a spot where they could see Guiman's face and took a screen capture. "Doesn't look dead to me."

"We need to find him," Riagan said, relieved to know the old man wasn't dead. He could help them figure out who Dardanos was working with. Probably on it all ready.

"No." Dirk moved to block the door. "If we get in Dad's way, we could compromise the search. I'll send this to him."

Riagan crossed his arms. "Ya heard him. He's getting a team together to go to Orestes. How many officers will he have left to investigate a threat with no evidence? Our best chance is to locate Guiman and see what he knows."

Dirk's chin jutted out and his nostrils flared, as if Riagan had questioned his father's ability.

"I'm just saying." Riagan paused, choosing his words. "The attack could be imminent. We don't have time. Better to at least try rather than wait around and hope we don't die. Think of Arielle."

That got Dirk moving. "You're right. I stayed here to help." They rushed back to his quarters so he could put on his own silver explorer suit.

The room was simple. Bed properly made just like in the dorms. A desk and closet. But this had its own private bathroom, albeit small. And it had its own window, but in the darkness, Riagan couldn't tell what kind of view it had. He also had his own private food printer in a corner. Riagan shook his head, wondering what it must be like.

"I should alert Arielle," Dirk said as he yanked off his shirt. "She'll want to help, too."

"Ya getting dressed. Where is she?"

Dirk gestured out the door to the left. "Three rooms over."

Riagan found her sitting on her bed reading.

"How did you get here?" she asked, sitting up and closing the book, a surprised look on her face.

"We've got a situation. Get ya explorer suit."

She dropped her book and hopped up. "What is it?"

While she dressed in her closet, the door cracked a little, he explained as best he could. Dirk arrived a few minutes later and interjected a couple times. When Arielle emerged from her closet, they headed back through the facility to the last place they'd seen Guiman.

But it had been close to a full day since the old man had arrived. What were the odds they'd be able to track him down? He could be anywhere inside or out? Wherever he was, it would be a quiet spot where few visited. He wouldn't want Dardanos or anyone the headmaster was working with to know he was here.

On the wall across from the exit hung oxygen masks. They were clear, covered the head, attached to their suits, and shrunk to form fit. The suits had a built-in system for pulling oxygen from the air outside.

"Do ya have access to the rovers?" Riagan asked as he donned an oxygen mask.

"It would speed up our search," Dirk agreed. He typed a code into the lock beside the door, followed by a click as the door unlocked.

They stepped outside. Riagan realized it was his first steps outdoors on Mars since their final exam. Since Rois' death. Unbidden tears filled his eyes, which he forced down at the thought of her. He didn't have time to think about her. Not with other lives at stake right now. But she remained there at the edges of his thoughts, a reminder of what could happen if they didn't succeed.

Dirk led them to the nearest rover, but instead of climbing into the driver's seat as Riagan expected, he crawled to the backseat, leaving Arielle to drive. When she caught him looking, she explained, "My dad manufactures these. I've driven them for years."

"Ok." Riagan climbed into the passenger seat.

Arielle gunned the engine and backed up so fast he feared they'd crash into the facility door they'd just exited. Instead, she slammed on the breaks a couple feet shy of the door, shifted to drive, and floored it past the solar panels and shrub domes, kicking up dust as she did so. At the first opportunity, she took a hard left beneath a bridge and into the maze of the facility. He'd seen an overhead view the day before, and it reminded him of a labyrinth of green bullet trains all connected together with various-sized pods; one big home for all Mars personnel. A majority of the workers mined the asteroid belt, providing ample supplies of raw materials for Space City.

"What're we looking for?" Arielle asked without taking her eyes off the road.

Riagan shrugged, realizing he hadn't considered where to go once they'd gotten outside. "Are there more cameras outside the facility?"

"Already on it," Dirk replied from the back seat.

While he searched through the footage from the various facility cameras, Riagan wondered what they would do when they found the old man. It would be nice to find Guiman on his own; have at least a few minutes to ask him about the explosion, the information on the glass he'd delivered to Dardanos, and how he thought they could stop the attack.

Arielle drove through the north part of the facility. Other than satellites dotting the facility roofs, there was little of interest. Green zipped past them. More than once, he grabbed the door handle, pressing himself into his seat, terrified they were about to crash into a wall. But each time, at the last second, Arielle would whip the car left or right down a new path.

"Any luck back there?" Riagan asked, hoping Dirk found something before they were crushed in a horrific collision. He had enjoyed racing the ATVs in the arena on Space City many times, dodging battering rams, barriers, and other drivers. But Arielle took it to another level. He wondered why he'd never seen her racing at the track.

"Take your next left," Dirk ordered from the back seat.

He now had a diagram of the facility projected in the air above his wrist-comp. Most of the facility was in gray, but one building in the southeast corner was highlighted in yellow. Was that where Guiman had gone?

Dirk directed Arielle to take her next two rights, then a left. They had reached an area with larger, nondescript buildings. "Third one on our right."

Arielle braked hard, throwing Riagan against his seat belt. He grunted from the belt digging into his chest.

"What's here?" Riagan asked.

"This area handles facility support systems. Air ventilation, water filtration, waste management, recycling, you name it," Dirk replied.

Arielle jumped out of the rover, Dirk scrambling out behind her. Riagan climbed out his own side. The building lacked any outer doors. As far as he could tell, they'd have to enter the facility from one of the green-covered hallways on either side of it.

From out of the rover's trunk, Dirk removed a thin gray balloon, roughly as long as he was tall. It was attached to a harness and tank. He handed it to Arielle, before removing a second and handing it to Riagan.

"What do I do with this?" Riagan asked.

Arielle started slipping on the harness, while Dirk removed a third balloon for himself.

"We're going to fly up to the roof," Dirk responded.

"Is that where Guiman went?" Riagan donned the harness, snapping together a strap over his chest. The balloon hung behind him, extremely lightweight.

"No," Dirk said. "He entered farther up that way," he gestured toward the hallway beyond this building, "-but my wrist-comp picked up an anomaly on the roof. I think we should check it out."

"Should we call for backup?" Arielle asked.

"We're just checking it out," Dirk answered. "If we see anything, we can call for help." He grabbed a thin black line that hung from the balloon; a tube with a button on the end, which he pressed. "This is a graphene balloon. One tap fills it with helium to rise. A double tap vents the gas in order to descend."

As he spoke, his balloon began to expand and rise up over his head. Riagan found his own black tube and pressed the red button. When he looked back up, Dirk's balloon had filled up enough to lift him off the ground, followed a couple seconds later by Arielle. Riagan inhaled sharply as his own balloon pulled on the straps of his harness then hauled him bodily off the ground. The process was slow, and left him feeling like a sitting duck.

"Why aren't there B-choppers here?" Riagan asked.

"The air on Mars is too light for traditional aircraft," Arielle said. "But these graphene balloons and the heated helium we're shooting into them are lighter than the air on Mars. The downside is they don't move fast.

Since there was nothing he could do to hurry the balloons up, Riagan shifted his attention to the roof of the building. There wasn't much to see until they neared the top. A pale orange glow emanated from a compact, square machine—maybe a generator?—which hummed in the middle of the roof. A pipe from the machine had been inserted into a vent running along the back wall of a third level in a haphazard way.

"Double tap when your knees clear the top," Dirk said. He was the first one to set foot on the roof, his balloon venting helium as he landed and walked toward the glowing machine.

It had to be the anomaly that Dirk had picked up. But what was it doing? Riagan guessed the pipe must carry something into the vent. What was the vent for?

A door banged open. As Riagan swung toward it, Dirk collapsed to the balcony. Guiman stood in the doorway, dressed in an explorer suit. He aimed one gloved weapon at Arielle. She gasped, eyes widening. Her whole body tensed. Then she dropped beside Dirk.

Flinching in fear, Riagan started to raise his hand to defend himself, but Guiman already had his other gloved weapon trained on Riagan's chest.

"I wouldn't if I were you," Guiman warned.

Riagan froze. He stared at Dirk and Arielle, both unconscious on the ground, but breathing. "What did you do?" There was a tremor in his voice he wished he could steady.

Guiman closed the door behind him and strolled forward, business-like, no hint of the frailness Riagan had always associated with him. "Stunned them. Their fate depends on you."

For a half second Riagan thought Guiman was saying their lives depended upon how much he'd told them concerning his spy operations. But there was a smirk in Guiman's eyes. Was he messing around?

"I don't understand. Why did ya shoot them? What's going on?"

Guiman clucked his tongue. "You didn't get here without figuring that out."

Riagan stood there, mind scrambling, wondering if Guiman would stun him too if he made the wrong guess. He pointed at the machine. "Is this part of the attack on the Council?"

"It is." Guiman patted the machine, his demeanor calm as if he was out for a stroll.

"How do we stop it?"

Guiman smiled. "Why would I want to?"

Riagan gaped, confused. "Isn't that why ya here? To stop the attack?"

"I guess you haven't figured out much after all." Guiman sighed. "I've given you all the pieces. Is it too much to ask you to put them together?"

Riagan stabbed a finger at the machine. "That won't just harm the Council, but everyone living here." The mining couple that had let him stay with them. They were expecting a child, a baby girl. They'd be collateral damage in this attack—the baby girl without even having a shot at life—if this wasn't stopped.

Guiman nodded once. "The Council must be stopped. This is the only way."

Riagan's gut clenched. "But This. We can't…"

"Still a fool despite everything you've learned this year?" Guiman shook his head in disgust.

Riagan flushed.

"Do you remember when I first approached you, offering revenge for your sister's death if you helped me?"

"I do." Riagan clenched his fists. "Revenge against Mainyu."

Guiman covered his eyes with one hand and shook his head. "How do you think the CME got on Mars?"

"Jarl," Riagan replied.

"By himself?" Guiman guffawed. "You saw the size of the CME. How did he smuggle it off the ship?"

Riagan shook his head. He hadn't considered how the CME had been moved from Space City to Mars. But then Jarl wasn't the lone traitor. "Dardanos could've helped him. Or the scientists."

Guiman groaned, as if dealing with a dense pupil. "Do you know how much security there is on Space City? And what, Jarl and Dardanos simply strolled with a multi-ton machine out of the science labs and off the ship?"

Riagan felt cold all of a sudden. "What're ya saying? The Council put the CME on Mars?"

Guiman slapped the machine and chuckled. "You're finally seeing part of the picture."

"That makes no sense." Riagan felt cold. "Why would the Council risk themselves and Space City by handing the CME over to Mainyu?"

"Who says the CME could've harmed Space City?"

Riagan stared at the old man. "But… If it couldn't… Why?"

"Fear. Show the citizens of Space City a threat—the Dahaka. Present a tangible danger. Then everyone turns to the Council for protection. And the Council becomes more powerful."

Riagan felt as if someone had been using his stomach as a punching bag. "If the Council orchestrated the whole thing, they sent us out for the final exam knowing what would happen. They sent Rois, Jaya, and others out to die."

"And they weren't the only ones. There are many others besides the Dahaka and you who suffer under their influence. That's why I planned this attack, because the Council must be stopped."

A whisper in Riagan's head, *Think of the family's baby girl*. It was too great a sacrifice to make. "We can't do this. Too many innocents."

"I do what I must to protect my people." Guiman took a step toward him. "To liberate them and give us a better future."

"The rest of Space City won't thank you for this. Sacrificing their friends and family."

Guiman laughed. "You're still missing the last piece. I'm not speaking of the citizens of Space City."

Riagan frowned. "Who then?"

Guiman pressed a button and his silver explorer suit darkened and expanded. From somewhere within his suit, he removed two white tusks and attached them to the now black forearms of his armor.

Riagan's mouth went dry. "Mainyu." The real one. He breathed the name more than said it.

"All along you've been looking at this the wrong way. I am not the one you need revenge from. I am the one giving you revenge. Help me."

Mainyu flipped up a panel and hit a few buttons that caused the machine to get louder.

Riagan took a step forward, afraid to fight Mainyu, but also not wanting to let that machine keep running. Rois had died due to the Dahaka leader's orders. How many other innocents would die from this attack? Riagan didn't know if Mainyu spoke the truth, but even if he was, this was too high a cost.

He blinked, using his contacts to snap a picture of Mainyu, even if it was from the back side. It would still be clear that a Dahaka was here. Then dropping to a knee, he fired with his suit weapon at the pipe running between the machine and the vent. It popped. A loud hiss and smoke pooled up from the pipe.

"No!" Mainyu whirled around, firing his gloved weapon.

The shot struck Riagan in the chest, sending him flying backwards. He landed hard, lungs feeling empty as he gasped for breath. Everything ached. His vision clouded over, and he felt himself losing consciousness. He struggled against it. He fought for breath that wouldn't come, and wouldn't come, and then it did. He couldn't raise himself up, but he managed to roll onto his side.

Mainyu bent over the busted pipe, wrapping it with something, but smoke billowed out of the hole, despite the Dahaka's efforts.

"I took a picture of ya and sent it to everyone here," Riagan gasped. "They're coming."

Mainyu spun around, eyes blazing with fury. He charged. Riagan tried to raise his arm to shoot, but Mainyu knocked it away. Without a word, the Dahaka punched him. Firecrackers of light burst in front of his eyes.

A pair of hands lifted him off the ground. He tried to batter at Mainyu's arms, but his own barely responded. He was carried backward a couple steps and thrown.

Chapter 33

Maellyn's Cure

"Space City… incoming…"

At first Maellyn didn't comprehend the announcement over the facility loudspeakers. She cocked her head to listen, but the announcement wasn't repeated.

She turned to Cade as they followed Albrin back toward Aili's lab. "What did it say?"

"We have visitors from Space City," Cade replied.

"Who?"

He shook his head. "Didn't say."

"We need to go find out who that is," Maellyn told Albrin, hoping it was someone with a breakthrough.

The Alfar led them along a side hallway between labs, angling back toward the thorneway through which the visitors would come. It was all Maellyn could do not to run. They had so little time left. She could sense that. And if it was Fintan—and who else could it be?—with a solution, they needed to know immediately.

Don't get your hopes up, she chided.

Drones surrounded the thorneway, shields raised, making it difficult to see who had arrived. An Alfar guard bumped Maellyn as he hurried past, not even hesitating to apologize. A half dozen other guards joined him behind the drones. They were taking no chances.

"Can you see who it is?" Cade craned his neck, trying to see over the guards.

Maellyn shuffled right until she could get a view around the guards and what she saw caused her to do a double-take. A female

297

Dahaka in the company of Fintan and Nico. Their hands up in the air. What was a Dahaka doing here?

"What's the reason for this unscheduled visit?" one guard ordered.

"We're here to help," Fintan half-shouted. "Where is Aili?"

"No admittance without prior authorization. You'll have to leave."

"Please, where is Aili?" Fintan's head swiveled from right to left, searching for the Alfar scientist.

"It's all right, they're here at my invitation," a familiar voice shouted from behind.

Aili was running. Her red-rimmed, tired eyes suddenly held a sparkle. "Lorni, please choose four of your officers to accompany us. The rest may return to their posts."

"This isn't protocol," the primary guard said.

"I submitted the request a few minutes ago," Aili said. "You should receive shortly. In meantime, I vouch for them."

The guard studied the new arrivals before nodding. He issued orders. Maellyn couldn't believe they were letting a Dahaka enter the facility. But then she was just as surprised to see one in the company of Fintan and Nico. Was this Neil's contact?

The drones deactivated their shields and departed. Nico relaxed, but the female Dahaka remained wary. She wore simple leather garments that showed off strong calf muscles. She reminded Maellyn a little of a marathon runner.

"Fintan, tell me you have good news," Aili said. There was a warmth in her voice that had been reserved for her son. For the first time in a while, there was a glimmer of hope on her face.

Fintan moved to Aili and placed four hands on her arms. "I come with expert help." He turned back, waving for the Dahaka to approach. "This is Vahu. She has experience with healing the Azymi fungus among the Dahaka."

So this *was* the Dahaka that Neil knew. He hadn't mentioned the Dahaka was a girl. She chided herself for the twinge of jealousy. It was childish and unimportant. That realization didn't fully soothe her feelings.

Showing no outward sign of doubt or hostility, Aili held out a hand and walked toward Vahu. "I appreciate your willingness to come. Things are bad. Any knowledge you can share would be of great value."

Vahu clasped Aili's outstretched hand in between hers, shaking once. "I will share what I know. Show me to the patients?"

Aili turned to Albrin. "Will you bring a strong patient to my lab?"

Albrin nodded and retreated. The request surprised Maellyn. It was not protocol to test out new medicine on a patient without extensive tests. But then, they were in dire enough circumstances that Aili was obviously ready to bend the rules. Especially if it saved Alvi's life.

"If you'll follow me." Aili gestured for them to follow her.

If the sheer size of the facility surprised Vahu, she didn't show it. Maellyn remembered feeling overwhelmed her first visit. Yet as Vahu followed Aili back toward the labs, she didn't look around. It was as if this were simply another day. She marched like someone on a mission who had no time to take in the sights.

"Impressive," Cade whispered to Maellyn as he stared after Vahu.

"I met her first," Nico said.

Maellyn rolled her eyes and marched after the Alfar and Dahaka.

"Can you tell me how you prepare the Emperor's Ruby for the patient?" Aili asked as they passed the seriously deteriorating garden.

"It's pretty simple," Vahu answered. "Ground the entire flower with a little water until it becomes a paste. Have the patient consume the entire amount."

Aili arched an eyebrow. "You consume orally?"

Vahu gave a curt nod.

Aili stared at the floor the rest of the way to her lab. She appeared to be mulling this bit of information over. Maellyn knew that in oral consumption, the active ingredient from the Emperor's Ruby would be incorporated into the bloodstream and carried to every cell. But oral consumption wouldn't stop it from attacking a patient's cells after it had neutralized the fungus. If the Dahaka were ingesting the flower compound and recovering from the fungus, there must be something in their physiology that protected them. An enzyme maybe?

Albrin had not yet arrived with a patient when they reached Aili's lab. Aili strode to a corner and retrieved a needle and tube, a blood pressure cuff, some tissues, and a small bottle.

"Vahu, may I take a sample of your blood?" she asked.

Vahu blanched, unsettled by the question. "Why would you need to do that?"

Aili placed the needle and other equipment on the center table and pulled out a chair for Vahu to sit in, gesturing for the Dahaka to do so. "We've determined that the Emperor's Ruby is harmful to Alfar and humans."

Vahu's brow knitted, but sat. Her back was straight, perfect posture. "That's what Neil mentioned. I don't understand."

Maellyn felt another jolt of jealousy, which she squashed.

Aili took a second chair and pulled it close to Vahu. "There must be something, maybe microphages, that break the Emperor's Ruby down and prevent it from causing you harm."

Unsure what to do with herself, Maellyn took a seat on the far side of the table. She felt she should say something to contribute to the discussion.

"If you'll permit me," Aili grabbed the tissue and small bottle from the table, "—it will be a small sample. I can test it here right in front of you and show you what I'm doing."

Vahu held her head high and stared at the bottle in Aili's hand in placid contemplation. After a few seconds, she said, "If you tell me everything you're doing, I can permit this."

"Great!" Aili looked re-energized as she grabbed the blood pressure cuff and leaned forward, wrapping it around Vahu's left arm. The Dahaka didn't pull back, simply watched Aili work.

Removing the lid from the small bottle, Aili dabbed some of the disinfectant onto the tissue. "If you'll extend your arm, I'll clean it."

Vahu did as told.

"I'm using a sterilizing solution to remove dirt and bacteria to avoid contamination." After cleaning Vahu's arm, Aili retrieved the needle and tube. "Next, I'll insert this needle into your vein to withdraw a little blood."

"A little?" Vahu asked, eyes trained on the needle as if it were a sword.

Aili placed one hand under Vahu's elbow, and with the other she tested for the vein. "This will sting for a second." She inserted the needle into Vahu's vein. The Dahaka stiffened and grimaced. Blood flowed into the test tube. Aili let it fill up before placing a cotton ball over the needle. She removed it and set it aside while applying pressure to Vahu's arm.

"Maellyn, will you grab me a bandage?" Aili cast her a querying look while with one hand she pointed at a desk in the far corner. "I forgot to get one."

Maellyn jumped to her feet, happy to contribute, even in this small way. They had no time to waste. She sidestepped Anand and Cade and hurried over to the desk. In the top drawer, she found a bandage roll. She pulled free a strip of the bandage and moving to Vahu's side, wrapped the bandage around the Dahaka's arm over the cotton ball Aili held. The Alfar removed her fingers and Maellyn wrapped three times.

Now that they had the blood sample, Aili poured a portion of it into a petri dish. Maellyn removed the now loosened blood pressure cuff from Vahu's arm while Aili pressed three fingers onto the table's surface. It lit up like a computer screen. Immediately, a picture of the bottom side of the test tube appeared on the back wall-screen, greatly enlarged.

Aili retrieved a syringe holding some of the Emperor's Ruby solution they'd developed. She held the syringe over the petri dish. "I'm mixing a sample of the Emperor's Ruby with your blood so we can examine its effects." She squirted a small sample of it on the penny-sized pool of blood in the dish. She pressed her fingers on the table beside the dish and spread them apart. The table operated like a touch screen, and when Aili spread her fingers the image of the blood sample projected onto the back wall grew exponentially until they could see the blood at a cellular level. Instead of a single pool, millions of cells jostled each other—the blood cells red. The antidote was dark gray.

As they watched on-screen, the gray mass attached to the red blood cells and began to envelop them the way a snake inhaled a mouse. The gray mass moved rapidly, as if insatiable.

"This makes no sense!" Aili's arms fell to her sides.

"What is it?" Vahu leaned forward in her chair, staring uncomprehendingly at the wall.

Maellyn felt buried beneath an enormous heavy tarp that was flattening her.

The Alfar scientist turned to Vahu, eyes defeated. "According to these results, the Emperor's Ruby should harm you the same way it does us."

Vahu frowned. "There must be some mistake with your tests. I consumed the Emperor's Ruby as a child when I had the Ondrigal."

Aili marched over to the wall-screen and pointed at the gray cells consuming the red, and turned a furious face back at Vahu. "This isn't a mistake. The Ruby cells are consuming your blood cells."

Vahu's face darkened and she rose from her seat with clenched fists. "I've seen my people give our children the Emperor's Ruby to cure Ondrigal my entire life. It's been used among my people for centuries."

The two were half a room apart, but Maellyn felt compelled to jump between them. "There has to be some explanation. Something we aren't seeing."

"Perhaps she's lying," Anand suggested. "Maybe she knows the Emperor's Ruby is toxic and is trying to convince us to give it to the sick so they'll die faster."

Vahu wheeled on him, face contorted in rage. "I came here freely. Put my safety in your hands to help."

If Maellyn had been standing next to Anand, she would've kicked him. She wished Devika were there to keep her brother in check. As it was, Maellyn glared at him and held up a hand in warning.

Albrin entered with a patient in tow in a hover chair.

Maellyn rotated toward Vahu and spoke calmly. "Will you tell us again how you prepare the flower before its administered?"

Vahu's nostrils flared. She looked ready to battle Anand. Or storm out of the lab.

"Please," Maellyn begged. "We can't do this without your help."

The Dahaka relaxed her fists. "Ground it up with water."

"Nothing else?" Maellyn asked, cocking her head. Water couldn't account for the results they were seeing.

Vahu bristled at the question, so Maellyn rushed on.

"Could you prepare some?" Maellyn retrieved an extra sample from the cases they'd brought. They needed to see everything. And if Vahu was actively helping, she'd be less likely to give up and leave.

Aili retrieved a spare petri dish and a steel pestle from separate drawers along a wall and brought them over to the table. She chewed her lip as she did so, but kept her mouth shut.

Vahu took the flower and picked the orange petals, dropping them one by one into the petri dish, along with the brown bud. Once she'd filled the dish, Vahu retrieved the pestle and started to ground them up. As she worked, she pulled a small bottle from the belt at her hips and removed the lid.

"What are you adding?" Aili asked, lips parted.

"Water." Vahu poured some in the dish and resumed grounding the mixture up.

Aili's nose scrunched and she crossed her arms. Maellyn knew the scientist was frustrated. She was, too. There was nothing Vahu was doing that would make a difference in how the antidote responded to blood and tissue. Yet she forced herself to remain calm anyway. Hopeful.

Once Vahu had a grayish paste, she set aside the pestle and handed the dish to Aili. "Try this."

Mouth twisted, Aili accepted the sample. She retrieved another clean petri dish and placed both in the middle of the table. She added a fresh portion of the sample of Vahu's blood to the clean dish and followed that up with a little bit of the newly formed paste. With a stoic expression, Aili crossed her arms once more to watch on the wall screen.

The cells and antidote mingled, jostling each other, but after a thirty-second count with bated breaths, there was no sign of the flower cells leeching the blood cells.

Aili's jaw dropped when it was clear the paste wouldn't attack the blood sample. "How is this possible?"

Maellyn was also at a loss to explain what they were seeing. It was as if Vahu had cast a magic spell when creating the paste. Magic wasn't the answer. Maellyn knew this. But she couldn't explain what was different.

After several silent minutes, Fintan spoke up. "What's different about the water?"

Aili shook her head. "It's water. H_2O. Same as on every other planet in the Universe. We've studied it."

"How is the water different?" Fintan repeated his question, looking first at Maellyn and then Anand and Nico.

At first, Maellyn couldn't fathom what he meant. Aili was right. There was nothing special in the chemical composition of water. But staring at the small bottle Vahu had brought, it hit Maellyn that the Dahaka didn't filter their water. It couldn't be that simple. Could it?

Water *was* the same everywhere, but what lived in water wasn't. Not on every planet. Not even for every lake, river, or stream on one planet. Different places had their own flora, fauna, and… "There's bacterium in the water. Or other enzymes that got mixed in during preparation."

Eyes widening, Aili reached for Vahu's water bottle, but her hand paused just short of it. Her eyes darted up to Vahu. "May I?"

The Dahaka nodded, lips curling in a vindicated smirk.

Aili retrieved two more clean dishes and poured a bit of the water into one. After that she retrieved a sample of Alfar water from a bottle Maellyn was sure was filtered for the other empty dish.

Maellyn fidgeted. She felt excited at the possibility that they had cracked the nut that held the solution, but she was also uneasy, fearing another dead end. Obstacles had appeared with such regularity up to this point.

Setting both water dishes on the table, Aili typed on the tabletop, as if on a keyboard. A couple of lights rolled past the dishes beneath the tabletop surface. It was scanning the two samples and would analyze them. In a moment, the wall-screen would list everything that was found in the two.

Albrin, off to the side, checked the vital signs of the unconscious patient in the hover chair. Maellyn could see his whole body was tense.

"What do we do once we get the results?" Cade asked. "Try it out on the patient?" He had his wrist-comp in hand and was making notes.

Aili shook her head. "Not yet. We'll need to test it out on samples of Alfar and human cells. Follow that up with tests on diseased samples and see if it still does its job. If all goes well, we make more."

"A lot more," Maellyn said as she considered how many patients they had in this facility, not to mention the ones down on Ourania's surface or those onboard Space City. Plus reserves.

"Would you be willing to provide us with more Emperor's Ruby and water?" Aili asked Vahu.

Vahu grinned. "Of course, my people will provide as much as you need."

The results popped up on the far wall-screen. The two samples were almost identical. But there were trace elements in the Dahaka sample not found in the Alfar one.

Maellyn clapped her hands over her nose, sighing in relief. They had something. Finally!

Alvi. Devika. They could save both of them. She could keep her promise to Alvi. And many more besides.

A loud blast shook the facility. Something struck her head. A sharp pain lanced through her. She collapsed to the ground, which seemed to shake as if from an earthquake. Before she could even begin to process what had happened, she blacked out.

*****

Maellyn woke with a splitting headache. Every part of her ached. Something heavy lay on top of her—a board or table. Her mind scrambled hazily, trying to make sense of where she was. Alarms rang out.

She rotated onto her side to push the board off her, but a sharp pain seared through her palm from shards of glass. She froze, afraid to move and cut herself worse. Her right leg throbbed. So did her chest and back. She needed help.

Opening her eyes, she found herself face to face with Fintan, unconscious on the ground, blood flowing from a cut on his forehead. What had happened?

"Fintan," Maellyn rasped. "Fintan."

He didn't answer. But his chest rose and fell. Slowly.

"Help!" No one answered. "Can anyone hear me? We need help!"

The alarms made her cringe from the vibrations it sent through her skull, accompanied by moans and cries, none close.

She raised her head slightly, bumping it against the board on top of her. The slight movement sent nauseating pain through her. She wanted nothing more than to lie there and wait for help. But from who?

She withdrew her hands into her shirt sleeves to give her a little padding, then pressed her open palms against the ground, forcing herself to push up. Glass poured off her to the ground. Despite the little bit of cushion, more glass shards cut into her palms. She cried out, but pushed up until the board toppled to the side and off her, allowing her to sit up.

Shattered glass covered much of the floor, along with overturned cabinets and drawers. Aili's lab. It was nothing more than a crooked frame, one corner collapsed. All the other labs in the immediate area were in a similar condition.

There had been some kind of explosion, she realized. Perhaps an experiment gone wrong. Massively wrong.

Aili lay on the ground at the base of her fractured wall screen. One arm was bent the wrong way, causing Maellyn to shudder and look away. She felt guilty and forced herself to look back to ensure Aili still breathed, if faintly.

A pair of legs stuck out from the far side of the broken table she'd pushed off herself. Beneath a desk huddled Anand, who shook his head as if trying to clear it. Blood trickled from his nose.

Maellyn grabbed Fintan's upper right shoulder and gave a gentle shake. She inhaled sharply, the cuts on her hands burning. When she withdrew her hands, blood stained his shirt.

"Fintan, wake up." She studied his face, waiting for him to open his eyes. "Fintan, can you hear me?"

She debated shaking him a little more, but was afraid he might have a neck or back injury that she could make worse by moving him. Fortunately, his eyes fluttered open. He groaned, his upper pair of arms reaching up and cupping his head. After a few seconds, his eyes focused on her.

"Maellyn, what happened?"

She shook her head, leaning back in relief that he was conscious. "I'm not sure. An explosion, I think. There's a lot of destruction."

"Aili's lab?" Fintan asked. "We were—"

"Yes." She overrode him. "We're in what's left of it. How do you feel?"

He didn't respond right away, just closed his eyes. A part of her panicked, fearing he'd passed out. Maybe he had some internal injuries she couldn't see. Then he moaned.

"What is it?" She frantically searched his torso for other injuries.

"I'm okay. What about others?"

"Aili is passed out. Anand appears to be waking up." She looked around and spotted other bodies scattered among the rubble all around. She couldn't tell the conditions of most of them. "There are others…" She let her voice trail off, afraid to say out loud what she was thinking in case it became true.

"I'll be fine." He rolled onto his back. "Go help others."

"Are you sure?" She was hesitant to leave him. He didn't seem fine.

"Yes, go." he pushed her hands away.

Reluctantly, she started to rise. Her left leg throbbed and almost dropped her to the ground. She fought to stand, shifting all her weight onto her right foot. Taking a couple test steps, she winced as pain shot through her hips and up her spine. Refusing to let it stop her, she gritted her teeth. She could do this.

A droid flew in, similar to the ones that blocked them at the thorneway when they first arrived. At first she flinched, afraid that it might think she was responsible for all this. Then she feared it might be the cause. Instead, it scanned her.

"Your injuries have been recorded," the drone said in a simple machine-voice. "Stay put. Rest. Emergency personnel are on the way." Then it moved on, scanning others.

The legs sticking out from the table Maellyn had been under belonged to an unfamiliar scientist. When she edged around the table to check on him, the pole piercing his torso let her know he couldn't be helped. Bile rose in her throat, but she forced it back down. Aili and others needed her help.

Turning her attention toward Aili, Maellyn had to bite her lip against the pain in her hips. Her shoulders were starting to ache as well. "Aili. Aili. Are you all right?"

The Alfar didn't respond. Besides the arm bent the wrong way, Aili had a gash in her side, staining her yellow shirt, pants, and starting to pool on the ground. Blood also covered a cheek. Maellyn half fell to the ground beside the Alfar. She needed to stop the bleeding, but there wasn't anything nearby that looked useful. So she removed her shirt and wadded it up, pressing it into Aili's side. The Alfar groaned and shivered, but didn't wake.

A hand on Maellyn's shoulder caused her to gasp and jump.

"How is she?" Fintan asked.

"She needs a doctor."

"Let me take a look at her."

She shuffled a little aside, but kept the shirt pressed into Aili's side. Fintan bent and lifted her eyelids. They were unfocused. Letting the lids drop back shut, he reached for Maellyn's shirt to move it away so he could get a closer look at the wound. He grimaced. "I'll handle this. Check on others."

"Are you sure? I could help."

"I'll manage. There are others who need help as well."

Nodding, she clenched her teeth as she climbed to her feet once more. Her body cried for her to sit, to rest. But there were many others worse off than her. Right now there was no one else to help. At least as far as she could tell. She hoped the drone was correct and rescue crews were coming.

Nico entered the lab, face and arms covered in cuts.

"How do you feel?" she asked him.

"Like a giant armadillo swatted me with his tail," Nico replied. "Twice."

"Need a doctor?"

He waved dismissively. "I'll live. None of the cuts are bad. Just sting like crazy."

Albrin lay sprawled out, face down, legs inside the lab, the rest of him out. Broken glass covered him. Maellyn moved over to check on him, but when she tried to bend down, pain shot up her left hip and back. She cried out.

Nico placed a hand on her arm. "I'll check on him." He dropped to his knees and felt Albrin's neck for a pulse. After several seconds, he looked back up at her with a sober expression. "He's dead."

Maellyn's stomach turned. A sob escaped her mouth, which she covered with a hand. Tears glistened in her eyes. She wiped them away. This was no time for mourning. Not with so many other wounded crying out. She wished someone would silence the alarms.

Turning to search for the next person in need of help, she spotted two people wrapped together beneath a pile of rubble. She hobbled toward them. As she neared she recognized Vahu. And Cade.

"No!" She rushed to them, ignoring the protests from her leg and hips. "Cade! Vahu!"

She dropped to her knees. The pain shooting up her spine made her dizzy. She breathed deeply and grabbed Cade's face with her hands. "Cade. Wake up, Cade." She felt for his pulse. Faint. Same with Vahu.

Nico dropped to his knees beside her and together they pulled away rubble. Chunks of wood, broken glass that she had to take care not to slice her hand open on, and a mixture of broken cabinets and various tools.

They had Vahu's torso uncovered when Maellyn swooned, feeling lightheaded.

Nico placed a hand on her arm. "Maybe you should rest. I can get them free."

She heard the concern in his voice, but shook her head, suddenly too nauseous to speak. After a couple more breaths, her head cleared a little. Her stomach still felt like acid ready to erupt, but she pushed forward with removing a busted drawer from Cade's good leg. She hoped it wasn't ruined.

As she tossed the drawer aside, there was a loud boom and the facility shook. The tremor caught her off balance, and she fell backward, head bouncing off the ground. Her world spun. Pain flared up her back. She tasted blood. She tried to roll onto her side to pick herself up, but her body wouldn't respond. Her whole body pulsed with pain.

"Maellyn!" Nico grabbed her shoulders, lifting to help her up.

More pain lanced through her and she screamed. Mercifully, she blacked out.

Chapter 34

Neil's Crushing Choice

Sirens wailed throughout the Mars facility. Flashing lights cast the halls in an unsettling reddish hue. Neil plugged his ears. It was happening. The attack Riagan had warned them about.

A mechanical, feminine voice replaced the sirens. "The complex has encountered contamination. Please move to the nearest safe zones. The complex has encountered contamination. Please move to the nearest safe zones."

The sirens resumed their howling.

Patrick arched an eyebrow.

"No," Neil mouthed back. He had no intention of going to any safe zone, but wondered what sort of contamination. There had been no explosions. What had happened? Was it a release of the fungus like on Space City?

"There might be people hurt here, too," Patrick said.

"No. Riagan and Dirk are handling it. There are plenty of others here to deal with whatever's happening." He was potentially abandoning people here who needed his help, but he could not stay while not knowing if Maellyn was okay. He had to get to Orestes.

Patrick crossed his arms. "And if Maellyn is fine? What if by going you're leaving someone else in danger just to verify she is unharmed?"

The accusation stung. Neil raised his fists, voice rising. "You spent months guarding Adrien's room at the hospital, even with officers stationed outside his room, to ensure he wasn't hurt."

"I knew he'd been attacked. Could be again." Patrick's voice rose to match Neil's. "We also know something is going on here. We have a duty to help."

"There was an explosion at the facility where she is." Neil was shouting now. "She could be gravely injured. I have to make sure she's safe—" He shook both fists at Patrick and let out a cry of frustration. How could both attacks be happening at practically the same time?

Fortunately, their argument ended as Councilman Fischer arrived with more than three dozen officers in tow. He glared at them as he approached. "Get to the safe zones. Can't you hear the sirens and warnings?"

Instead of arguing, Neil stood tall, trying to sound as professional as possible. "We want to join the rescue party to Orestes. We've got experience helping out in the academy infirmary. We can be of help."

Councilman Fischer opened his mouth, brow darkening. "We're not going to Orestes. We're in a state of emergency here. I'm reinforcing the guards at the thorneway and searching the facility."

"You can't do that!" Neil felt a wave of panic rise up the center of his chest. "We have people on Orestes. We have to help."

"That'll have to wait. Our priority is here." Councilman Fischer marched past them toward the travel facility.

"Please." Neil rushed to keep up. "Maellyn Trevena is there. At least let *us* go." He pointed back toward Patrick, who was following.

Councilman Fischer ignored him, entering the travel facility and checking with the two officers on guard about security around the thorneway, then barking orders for several men to join them.

Neil jumped in front of the Councilman, halting him. "Let Patrick and I go. We'll investigate and send you a report. You don't need us here anyway."

Councilman Fischer's nostrils flared at the interruption, and for a second Neil feared he would order officers to remove him from the way. But though his words still held a commanding tone, he said, "All right, I'll approve your travel to Orestes to determine the status of any Space City residents there. And to provide aid where you can." He turned to the officers. "No one else comes or goes through this thorneway unless you have approval directly from the Council."

And with that he departed the facility, the remaining officers in tow. Neil exhaled in relief.

Neil turned to Patrick, who was stone-faced.

"I can go alone if you want to stay," Neil said, wanting Patrick to come, but wanting to leave it up to him, "but I could use your help. Even if Maellyn is fine, there will be others who need our help."

While the remaining officers initiated the thorneway, Patrick stared back, face impassive. Weighing the options? When Patrick nodded, Neil felt a little weight slide of his shoulders. He was relieved not to go alone.

It took another thirty seconds for the thorneway to come along. Each second seemed to stretch on indefinitely. Every breath Neil took, he was conscious of the fact that Maellyn might at that very moment be taking her last. The agony, the fear of not knowing if she was hurt, needed him, nearly overwhelmed him. He wanted to snap at the officers to activate the thorneway faster.

Once the familiar black liquid materialized, his instinct was to charge through. To his surprise, Patrick darted through first. He followed a step behind. As one foot entered the thorneway, a loud collision behind him was followed by shouts of surprise from the officers. He tried to look back to see what had happened, but had already stepped too far into the thorneway to pull back or stop. The slick blackness enveloped him, throwing him forward.

His next view was of chaos. Cracked walls and sparking, cut electrical lines. A fire raged unchecked within a garden ahead. The smell of smoke was pervasive, and clouds of it rippled along the ceiling far overhead, some shooting out through jagged holes. And there were more sirens, these faster paced and louder than the ones in the Mars facility.

That reminded him of the commotion right as he entered the thorneway, but his concern was momentary. Two dozen turret-gun wielding drones encircled them. Neil and Patrick held their hands up high, afraid to move and provoke the drones.

"Identify yourselves and state your purpose," an electronic voice said.

Neil and Patrick shared a look, unsure how to respond. Mind scrambling, Neil remembered Councilman Fischer's original plan to send a team. "We were sent by Councilman Fischer to provide aid. From Space City."

Yellow lights from the drones enveloped each of them. After a few seconds, the electronic voice spoke once more. "Identities confirmed and admittance approved." The drones retreated.

Neil relaxed. He'd half feared the drones would mistake them for whomever had attacked the facility.

"Where is everyone?" Patrick asked as they moved forward.

There was no one in the immediate area. Before he could respond, something slammed into them from behind, sending them flying. Neil hit the ground hard, the air knocked out of him. He lay there gasping, unable to do much else.

An Azios in black armor sprinted past. It had come through the thorneway after them. The departing drones turned and fired at the fleeing Dahaka. Exploding chunks of floor and wall sprayed in all directions, but the Azios paid them no mind. Neil and Patrick scurried backward toward the thorneway, desperate to get out of the way. The drones pursued the Azios through double doors ahead.

"What in the world is going on?" Neil asked.

Patrick stood, dusting himself off. "Was that a Dahaka? Where did it come from?"

"The Mars facility," Neil replied, worried what that meant. There hadn't been time for a new connection from somewhere else; that had been what he'd seen right before entering the thorneway.

"What?" Patrick's eyes widened. "How did a Dahaka get past all those guards at the thorneway? How did one get to the Mars facility?"

Neil shrugged. It must have something to do with Riagan's warning, but beyond that, he could only speculate.

"What do we do now?" Patrick looked less than thrilled to be here.

Before Patrick could have second thoughts, Neil pointed at the doors ahead. "I guess go after it and search for Maellyn."

"Go *after* the Dahaka," Patrick murmured. He shook his head, but nevertheless followed Neil as he moved forward.

They passed the burning garden, unable to do anything to quell the flames. There was no fire extinguisher in view. The heat was almost enough to drive them backward. Plus there was no one within.

Through the double doors, Neil halted, eyes widening. The Alfar, those healthy or at least only slightly wounded, checked on their brethren amidst the wreckage of hundreds of labs. And from what he could see, there were a lot of Alfar in serious condition. Where would they even start to help?

There were no signs of the Azios or the drones pursuing him. Neil decided the drones and others could handle one Azios. He let his eyes rove for any sign of Maellyn. If he had been scared for her before, the scene before him filled him with despair. What were the chances of them finding her unharmed in all of this?

In the first lab they entered, they found a pair of Alfar sitting against what was left of a wall, one with a bloody scalp and the other covering his ribs. The first Alfar's eyes were a bit glazed over. Likely suffering the effects of a concussion. The second was hunched forward, taking short breaths, face cringing. Neil scanned him with his contacts, confirming the Alfar had broken ribs.

"What's going on?" the Alfar asked. He gestured at all of the destruction. "What happened?"

Neil bent down beside him and grabbed one of his arms, placing it over his shoulder and helping him up.

"Where's your infirmary?" Neil asked.

The Alfar groaned as they stood. He raised his free arm, grimacing as he did so, and pointed further on through the labs. "Follow the corridor outside to the end."

Patrick helped the other Alfar to his feet.

"Let's get you there," Neil said, but the Alfar, who was now taking in the destruction all around them, shook his head.

"I can manage." He gestured to his fellow scientist. "I can get us both there. Others need help more."

"You sure?" Neil asked, feeling maybe he should insist they help.

But the Alfar pulled away. "Go," he insisted.

Patrick handed the concussed Alfar over, though he looked reluctant. The first swayed a little as the pair took a couple steps forward. They didn't make it far before the concussed Alfar vomited on the floor.

"We should help you back to the infirmary." Neil stepped forward, stepping around the puke and trying to get the concussed Alfar's other arm.

"We'll be fine," the second Alfar assured them. "Please, help my brethren." The Alfar limped from the lab, Neil reluctantly watching them leave before moving on.

In the next lab, Neil and Patrick found a body. Fixed, unreactive pupils stared blankly at the ceiling. It wasn't Neil's first dead body, and he found it wasn't any easier this time around, even with this one being a complete stranger. His stomach churned, and he grabbed a cloth from the ground and draped it over the Alfar's body.

"Still think the Mars facility needed more help than this?" Neil asked.

Patrick's lips thinned. He said nothing.

After a second to process what he'd said, Neil looked away, wishing he could take it back. There were no good choices, except to help whomever they could.

As they emerged from the lab, Neil spotted Fintan. The Macab waved for them to join him. Neil was relieved to see the professor. Was Maellyn with him?

Neil spotted Nico kneeling over someone. He jogged toward them, his gut knotting. As they neared, Nico looked back at them, moving out of the way of the body on the ground.

Maellyn lay on the ground, unmoving. Neil's knees weakened, causing him to stumble. The cold dread that been sloshing through him up to now iced over.

He pushed past Nico and fell to his knees at her side. "What happened?" He grabbed her wrist and found a thready pulse, a term he'd only recently learned. He scanned her for injuries with his contacts, which revealed a fractured back, as well as a number of other breaks and internal injuries. They couldn't move her.

"I'm glad you've come," Fintan said. "Are there others with you?"

"Just we two," Patrick answered, expression guilty as if it was his fault no one else had come. "There was an attack at the Mars facility."

"Oh my," Fintan gasped.

On Maellyn's other side, partially covered by rubble, lay Vahu and Cade. Neil couldn't tell if they were alive or dead, but they all needed medical attention now.

"I didn't know she was hurt until she collapsed." Nico's voice was choked, and he placed an uncertain hand on her shoulder.

Tears welled up in Neil's eyes, but he forced them down. "We need a stretcher." Or a substitute. He swiveled on his knees, scanning the area. He spotted Anand half buried beneath an overturned desk inside a nearby lab. The number of their own hurt in the attack sent a shock through him.

"You should find some in the infirmary." Fintan gestured farther on down the aisle of labs. "Straight back."

Neil jumped to his feet and ran. He swerved around or jumped over broken desks, chairs, overturned carts with spilled equipment, and shattered glass. He ignored cries for help, knowing right now Maellyn's life ebbed. She might not have a moment to lose. Some of those cries might be from people in similar shape, but he pushed that thought away, despite the guilt that welled up in its place. He had to help her first. Afterward, he promised himself he'd help anyone else he could.

He identified the entrance to the infirmary by the crowd of wounded Alfar making their way toward it. He was forced to slow down to avoid running into someone, allowing Patrick to catch up. Still, Neil weaved through the crowd, desperate for Maellyn's sake. He shouted for a stretcher as he went.

Slipping between two Alfar who shouted at him for cutting through, Neil entered the infirmary to find many Alfar surrounding the doctors and nurses, pleading for help for themselves or their loved ones in chairs or lying strewn out on the floor. He wanted to shout, to get someone's attention to ask for a stretcher, but that would only add to the din.

"Neil!" Patrick slapped his arm. He pointed out stretchers hanging on a wall off to the right.

It was difficult not to bowl through the crowd as his anxiety demanded. Every pause from someone in the way made him want to explode. But he fought to control his frustration until he got through and grabbed a stretcher off the wall. It was surprisingly light, even for its thin but inflexible frame. These were the same hover gurneys the academy infirmary used; that would make transporting her easier. Thinking of Cade, Vahu, and Anand, Neil grabbed three more down. The four together were a little unwieldy, but Patrick hadn't made it to him yet, and he wasn't waiting. He'd have to carry the gurneys vertically, his head cocked to the side to see the way forward, until they got back out to the labs.

"Clear some room," he shouted to Patrick.

"All right, we need to get through with stretchers." His voice commanding, Patrick waved for people to spread aside and let them through. He reached an older female Alfar with her back to them. He placed a hand on her shoulder. "Ma'am, let us through, please? We need to help some gravely injured."

Quick as lightning, the Alfar grabbed Patrick's hand from her shoulder and spun around, punching him in the gut. He doubled over.

"Don't ever touch me." The gray-haired Alfar pointed a finger at Patrick's nose. "I'm here with my granddaughter. She has the fungus."

From his doubled-over position, Patrick held up a hand. "Sorry about your granddaughter," he wheezed. "We aren't trying to interfere. We have friends who desperately need medical attention." Patrick pointed to the gurneys Neil held.

The Alfar eyed Neil and the stretchers for a moment, as if doubtful they were telling the truth. "It doesn't matter if you do, there's no help," she said.

Neil frowned. "I know there are a lot injured and it'll take a while, but the doctors and nurses will help. They just need time."

"No." The Alfar shook her head, distress overwhelming her features. "They can't. One of the explosions wiped out all the infirmary equipment."

"That can't be. There are lights and power," Neil said.

All the lights were on in the facility, but as he looked closer, into adjoining rooms, he saw dead monitors beside beds. He spotted patients leaned up against a couple of other blank wall screens.

"No backup generators?" Patrick asked.

"Rumors are they were destroyed in the second explosion." A child started coughing in a chair behind the old Alfar woman, drawing her attention away from them.

"Do they have any idea how long things'll be down?" Patrick asked, placing a couple fingers hesitantly upon the Alfar's shoulder.

Ignoring them, she bent down and started whispering to the child. No more than eight or nine, the female child slumped into the chair, damp hair clinging to her scalp.

Worried, but sure he wasn't going to get anymore answers here, Neil held out the stretchers in front of him and shouted for people to make way. The news increased his sense of urgency. He pushed forward. A path cleared, Alfar ducking out of the way of the stretchers. Once outside, he handed two over to Patrick. They activated the four gurneys, so that they would hover along beside them.

Their pace wasn't much faster. They had to climb over debris and rerouted through a busted lab. When they got back to Maellyn and the others, an Alfar scientist had joined them. She kept one arm cradled to her side.

Fintan jumped up when he noticed Neil and Patrick had returned. He pointed at the ground behind Maellyn. "Set a gurney there."

Neil pushed one of the floating stretchers down to the floor beside her. "The infirmary was attacked, too. They can't help anyone."

"What?" The Alfar moved close until she stood over him.

Neil gave her a quick glance, unsettled by her closeness. "That's what we heard. All the equipment is down."

"That can't be. We have three sets of backups for power." Despite her words, she sounded more pleading than commanding.

"We've got them, Aili," Fintan told her. "Go check on things."

She nodded and headed off for the infirmary.

"Neil, get Maellyn's hips," Fintan directed, drawing his attention back. "Nico, her shoulders. I'll support her neck. Ease her onto her side."

Unable to breathe, Neil placed his hands on Maellyn's hips and eyed Nico, who nodded back, his face pale. They waited for Fintan to get in position. Then they rotated her. Neil was terrified she would cry out or stop breathing. But she remained silent, unconscious. As soon as they had her propped up on her side, Fintan scooped up the stretcher and set it against her back, before strapping her in.

On its own, the hover gurney turned so that Maellyn was lying face up. She moaned lightly, then went silent. Neil's heart skipped a beat. The stretcher rose up into the air to his waist level.

They moved Maellyn clear, then Neil, Patrick, and Nico finished digging Cade and Vahu out from the rubble and placing them on stretchers with Fintan's help. Neither stirred, but Fintan confirmed both were still alive, albeit with significant injuries. From what Neil could tell, Cade and Vahu both had cuts all over their hands and arms.

Cade's left leg appeared to be broken. Would it make his limp worse? Blood smeared Vahu's hair, and seeped down onto her forehead and right temple.

Once they were both strapped in, Patrick and Nico led the last gurney to Anand. They lifted the desk off him and loaded him onto the stretcher.

"Everything in the infirmary is wrecked," Aili confirmed as she returned, a comm device in hand. "They have emergency lights and simple tools. Everything else was destroyed. But Alvi is fine for now."

"Back to Space City, then," Neil said.

Fintan nodded agreement and the group started the somber procession back toward the front of the facility. They couldn't travel a straight path. A couple of times they had to cut through a lab in order to proceed. Walking beside Maellyn's gurney, Neil's gaze darted back and forth between her and the way forward, one moment checking that she was still breathing, and the next ensuring the stretcher didn't hit anything. Each diversion increased his anxiety; how long did she and the others have? He tried to shove aside such thoughts.

They gave the fire consuming the garden a wide berth. Neil was pleased to see machines spraying water at the flames, though it greatly increased the smoke. Coughing, they were forced to cover their mouths and noses with their shirts.

When they reached the thorneways, Aili hurried over to the controls. After thirty seconds of nothing happening, she grabbed her hair. "The thorneways won't activate."

Fintan rushed to her side, checking the thorneway control panel.

Neil sweated. Maellyn didn't have time for delays. She needed a doctor now.

Fintan blanched and shook his head. "You're right. We can't get to Space City."

"What now?" A desperation was building in Neil, a need to do something fast though he didn't know what. "She won't survive if we don't get her to a doctor soon."

"Vahu and Cade, either," Nico added, grimacing.

For several seconds they all stared at each other, all at a loss.

It was Aili who spoke up. "They'll have to come to Ourania." She nodded, as if coming to a decision. "It's our one option."

"That's great!" Neil grasped at anything, any bit of hope that someone could help Maellyn before it was too late.

Fintan shook his head. "I can't make that call. Her father… Cade and Anand's families… there must be someone who can fix the thorneway."

Neil couldn't believe Fintan would reject Aili's offer. "We don't have time. They can't wait."

"You don't understand." Fintan looked pained and hesitant. He turned to Aili. "Call someone to get the thorneway working."

Aili shook her head. "The infirmary is down when it shouldn't be. The thorneways are inactive. There's something massively wrong. This won't be fixed within an hour or even a day."

Fintan stared at Maellyn's unconscious body. He looked helpless.

"We have to get help," Neil reiterated. Why was Fintan rejecting Aili's help? Something burned in Neil's gut. He wouldn't allow the Macab to make this call for Maellyn.

But before he could say anything, Aili stepped forward, placing a hand on Fintan's arm. "You saw the scans of their injuries. They don't have much time, especially the girl." She pointed at Maellyn, making Neil's heart thud faster.

Tears welled up in Fintan's eyes.

"You know you can come with them," Aili told Fintan. "You've always been welcome on Ourania."

Neil clenched his fists. "If you don't, I will. I won't let her die."

"You don't understand," Fintan said without looking up from Maellyn. "If we take her to Ourania for healing she can never leave. She'll be there for life. All of them will."

Neil cocked his head, sure he was misunderstanding. "What?"

This time Fintan did look up, eyes mournful. "You don't know the extent of her injuries. How close she is to death. Even if we take her home, it'll be hard for us to save her life. We don't have the technology yet. She'll never be the same."

"What does that have to do—"

Fintan cut him off. "There's a single way to heal Maellyn that is guaranteed to work. It's through the same process that gives Alfar their eternal life. It will save her, but anyone who undergoes the process can never leave Ourania again or they will die. She'll be tied to the planet."

Neil's mouth went dry. He couldn't believe what Fintan was telling him. This was all too much to absorb. The Macab must be wrong. But when Neil looked to Aili, she nodded confirmation.

Now he understood why Fintan wanted to talk to Dr. Trevena. And the families of Cade and Anand. But they couldn't contact anyone on Space City, and Maellyn might not live long enough for them to reach her father by any means. The decision they made here would affect the rest of her life. Her father, Cade's brother, Anand's parents, Rashn for Vahu, they all deserved to make the call for their loved ones, but there was no time to wait.

"We have to save her life," was all he could manage.

"It's our only choice," Nico agreed, face white.

After a seconds pause, Fintan nodded.

"So how do we get her there?" Neil asked. Now that the decision was made, he was anxious to get her to Ourania without delay.

Aili shook her head, pursing her lips for a moment. "I'm sorry, but you cannot come. Only Fintan and your wounded."

"No. I have to be there," Neil said. He wasn't handing her over and waiting here. He intended to personally take her wherever they needed to go to save her. And if it meant she was confined to Ourania for life, he would be there right beside her. It was more important that she live than where.

"Only those who have done the Alfar a great service may join us on Ourania. Something that proves they are one of us." Aili spoke solemnly, showing no regret but also taking no pleasure in the message. "Maellyn has done that, helping us discover the solution to the Azymi outbreak. Tens of thousands of lives will be saved thanks to her. And in the process, she risked her life to do so. The other's, too."

Neil stared at Maellyn's pale form on the gurney. His knees weakened. To save her life, he had to give her up. Maybe forever.

"I helped her discover the solution," he said meekly, not believing his own words, but not wanting to be separated. "I played a part in this."

Aili's placid expression drove him crazy. "Our leaders will not grant you access. She may go. You must stay."

Without his realizing it, several Alfar had arrived. One stepped to his side now to guide the gurney. Neil tensed, knowing he had to let

Maellyn go to be healed. He wanted to argue for another solution, but recognized that might very well cost her her life. He couldn't be responsible for that. After everything else he had done wrong with her this year, he had to do this right.

"I'll go." Fintan stepped over to her gurney, motioning to the other Alfar that he would handle it. "I'll take care of her." The Alfar nodded and retreated. Fintan turned back to Neil. "I'll make sure she's safe."

Stifling a sob that rose up into his throat, Neil stepped back. He couldn't speak, didn't trust himself not to say something that might compromise her life because he didn't want to lose her.

Other Alfar guided the other gurneys forward, replacing Patrick and Nico. Aili led them away, down a new corridor. Once they were out of sight, Neil fell to the ground, hugging himself, his strength sapped.

Patrick took a seat beside him and placed a hand on his shoulder, squeezing. "You'll see her again. I know it may not seem like it now, but you will."

And the absurdity of Patrick being the one here right now comforting him sent Neil into delirious, choking cries of strung-out laughter.

Chapter 35

Riagan Says Goodbye

Riagan fell. He threw out his arms, reaching for anything to stop his freefall. Then the harness he wore jerked him upright. He spun wildly before his back and head slammed into a wall, and he blacked out.

*****

He awoke face down on the ground, every part of him aching. His ears rang. After a few breaths, he realized the blaring was a wailing siren. He covered his head with his hands to ward off the ear-splitting blare. His head felt ready to split in two like a rotted pumpkin.

The harness he wore tugged him marginally upward. All he could manage was to lie there on the ground, taking deep breaths and hoping the pain would subside.

The siren was replaced by a female voice recording. "The complex has encountered contamination. Please move to the nearest safe zones."

The recording repeated two more times before giving way to the siren. Riagan wanted to scream for someone to turn it off. But it was the persistence of the siren which drove him to push himself to his knees. His head sloshed, forcing him to drop back on his lower legs to remain upright.

He was on the ground at the base of a building near tire tracks. Their rover was gone. Had Mainyu thrown him off the roof? There's no way he could've survived such a fall.

Above him, the graphene balloon floated. It had reactivated. A memory surfaced of his graphene balloon harness stopping his fall right before he slammed into a wall. The balloon must have activated on its own somehow.

His head still threatened to split open at the slightest provocation, but the rest of his pain had dulled. Enough that he could think.

Mainyu's machine. Was it still working?

Glancing up at the facility roof across the way, he couldn't see it. Or Mainyu. Or Dirk and Arielle. Mainyu hadn't thrown them off the building. But had he left them unharmed?

He needed answers. As he climbed to his feet, he looked for and found the button to pump helium into his balloon, but when he pressed it nothing happened. The balloon remained filled only enough to float above him. He pressed the button again to no avail. There was no on/off switch Dirk had mentioned. Must be broken.

"Dirk! Arielle!" He cupped his hands to the sides of his facemask. "Dirk! Arielle!"

No response from them. They didn't pop into view. Nor did Mainyu. Riagan hoped that meant the Dahaka had departed. He couldn't believe Guiman was the Dahaka leader. How had he fooled them? How had he fooled his own people? He certainly wasn't the strongest among them. Why did no one challenge his rule?

He brushed the questions aside. They weren't important for now. He needed to get up to Dirk and Arielle, but the massive building lacked a door, as he'd noted earlier. He'd have to enter the facility somewhere else.

Forcing himself to pick a direction, he took a step forward. His balance was a little off and he toppled over. From his knees, he took deep breaths through gritted teeth. His wrist-comp was missing, and scouring the nearby ground failed to reveal it.

Raising his head up, he shouted again. "Dirk! Arielle! Can anyone hear me?"

"The complex has encountered contamination. Please move to the nearest safe zones." The audio recording had returned. At least that meant the sirens had stopped for a few seconds.

After a short trek, he spotted windows in the facility hallways. He jogged over to the nearest, hoping to find someone inside he could alert. There was no one in the first. Or the second. At the third, he spotted an old man inside a room on the opposite side of the hallway.

Banging hard on the glass a few times got the old man's attention. When he turned around, Riagan realized the man was Neil's grandfather. Mr. Ericson's eyes widened in recognition as he emerged from the room, frowning. Riagan held up both hands, palms up, in a sign he didn't know what to do. Mr. Ericson pointed farther down the facility hallway, which Riagan guessed meant that way to a door. Riagan nodded and pressed on until he reached an entrance. As soon as Mr. Ericson spotted him, he clicked some buttons on an entry panel and the door opened, permitting him to step inside. He had to pull the graphene balloon down and inside before the doors could close behind him.

"Riagan, what are you doing here?" Mr. Ericson's expression was one of surprise.

"Looking for help." Riagan removed the harness for the graphene balloon and deactivated his mask. Before he could remove it, Mr. Ericson grabbed his wrist and squeezed.

"Leave that on," Mr. Ericson ordered. "There's poison gas."

Riagan blinked. "What about ya?"

The old man's eyebrows wrinkled. He jabbed a finger in Riagan's face. "Leave the mask on, no matter what."

Taken aback by Mr. Ericson's gruffness, Riagan nodded his understanding. "I will."

"What were you doing out there?" Mr. Ericson asked as he marched back toward the room Riagan had first spotted him in.

"Mainyu's here. Or was here."

Mr. Ericson stopped, head swiveling at him, mouth open. He studied him for a second, maybe trying to figure out if Riagan was joking. Or lying.

"He's the reason for the attack," Riagan explained. "Dirk, Arielle, and I were trying to stop it. I think Mainyu is gone, but they need help. He knocked them out."

Instead of responding, Mr. Ericson resumed his march. He reentered his original room, which held a large machine. The words *oxygen* and *CO$_2$* were clearly marked in a couple places. So something to do with the facility's ventilation systems.

Mr. Ericson grabbed a wrist-comp from a table. "Emergency personnel. Emergency personnel, I'm reporting two people in need of assistance." He turned to Riagan. "Where are they?"

Riagan pointed in the general direction. "The three story building up ahead. On the roof."

Mr. Ericson clicked the comm button on his wrist-comp again. "Emergency personnel, the pair, Dirk Fischer and Arielle Delven, are on the roof of building SE-9. I repeat, Dirk Fischer and Arielle Delven are in need of emergency rescue on the roof of building SE-9."

After receiving confirmation that someone would locate them, Mr. Ericson signed off and tossed his wrist-comp on the table. "Time to get to work."

"Where's ya mask?" Riagan asked. "Do ya need me to get one?"

"It won't do any good." Mr. Ericson fiddled with some knobs and a crank on a large machine that filled the entire back wall of the room, which was larger than any of the living quarters Riagan had seen in the facility.

"I don't understand. If I need one—"

"It's too late." An edge underscored Mr. Ericson's words. "I've already been exposed and there's nothing to be done about it."

Riagan shook his head, ignoring the words. "Let me get you a mask. I'll be right back." He started for the door.

Mr. Ericson spun around, grabbing Riagan's upper arm. "You can't do anything for me now. I've been exposed to too much of the gas. I've got a couple of hours at best."

Riagan stared at the machine, unable to meet the old man's gaze. He shook his head. He tried to pull away, but Mr. Ericson's grip tightened.

"It's too late for me, but not for many others here. Not for you. But I need your help."

Riagan still couldn't look the old man in the face, and he felt his upper lip quivering, but he managed a nod.

"Good." Mr. Ericson let go of his arm and turned back to the machine. "We've got to vent the air system to clear out the poison. After the system is purified, it can start to process clean air for the facility."

Neil's grandfather. Dying. It couldn't be. He had to be wrong.

"Riagan."

"Okay." Riagan's eyes burned. "What is this thing?"

Before Mr. Ericson could start to explain, he began wheezing. He bent over the table, supporting himself with his arms as he gasped for air.

"Let me get help. Please." It was all Riagan could think to say. He didn't know what else to do. Standing here watching the old man die wasn't acceptable. Neil would never forgive him. He wouldn't.

Mr. Ericson lowered himself into a chair and rasped for another ten seconds. He gestured to the machine, the part with *oxygen* marked on it. For a brief moment, Riagan thought maybe the old man wanted oxygen from the machine.

"That's the Contamination Analysis Network from Variable Area Satellite Scanning system, or CANVASS," Mr. Ericson said. "It monitors the facility's oxygen and pollution."

Riagan puckered, feeling sick. Was he betraying Neil by not seeking help?

There are others who need help, too, a voice inside him insisted.

"I need you to vent the oxygen. That's the best way you can help."

"Surely there's someone better qualified than me." Riagan felt daunted. If he messed with the wrong thing, he could cause far more harm.

Mr. Ericson slammed a fist down on the table, causing Riagan to jump. "No time to wait. Every second could mean the difference between life and death for everyone here."

That made Riagan tense up. He wanted to say that knowledge wasn't going to make things any easier. All he could manage was, "How?"

"See the green handle on the left?"

The rubber handle was two steps to Riagan's left. He reached for it. "This one?"

"Raise it up and to the left."

The handle shifted easily, and when it moved as far as it would go it clicked.

"Now turn the valve right to open the tanks to vent the air filtration system," Mr. Ericson ordered.

It took both hands and some muscle to rotate the valve, which Riagan did until it stopped turning. He heard nothing this time, but the needle on the machine gauge drifted toward zero.

"What now?"

No reply. Riagan turned to find the old man's eyes closed.

"Mr. Ericson?"

Mr. Ericson's eyes blinked open. "I'm here."

Riagan exhaled in relief.

"Did you vent the air?"

Riagan nodded. "What now?"

"Once the tanks are empty, close them and initiate a full system sterilization process. After that we can get the system back online to clean and circulate the air."

Riagan started to reverse what he'd done to close the system. "First part done." He looked around, trying to determine which controls might start cleaning out the system.

"This will take a while." Mr. Ericson pointed toward a slender drawer roughly two-thirds of the way down the machine. "Slide that out."

Dropping to a crouch, Riagan pulled the handle revealing more of a tray than a drawer, in which he found a wrist-comp. He tried to pick it up, but the wrist-comp was welded to the tray.

"That's done precisely so it's not removed," the old man said.

Riagan activated the wrist-comp, which asked him for a password to access.

Mr. Ericson coughed several times before speaking. "The code is O – M – F – 1 – \$ – P – C – 4 – 2 – 5 – 8 – 7 – C – R – T."

After Riagan had entered the password, system notifications appeared on-screen. One box flashed red. *Warning. Oxygen levels dropping.*

"Ignore that for now. Type air system sanitization into the search field."

Riagan ran the search and a new program kicked on-screen showing a diagram of the entire facility's air ducts, filtration system, etc. The program asked him to identify which parts of the system needed to be sanitized. He asked.

"Default is the entire system. Hit enter and let it work."

Riagan did so. "How long will this take?"

"Thirty minutes or so. It does all the work. We just monitor progress."

"So we sit here and wait?"

Mr. Ericson grunted. "I think that's all I'm good for at this point."

Guilt flared up, creating a lump in Riagan's throat, making it hard for him to breathe. He'd failed to stop Mainyu's attack before it killed Neil's grandfather. He should've figured all this out faster. He'd had the time. Known Mainyu had an attack planned for days. And now that he'd failed, he couldn't even alert Neil.

"If there's nothing to do, let me go find ya some help," Riagan said. "I'll be back before it's done."

Mr. Ericson shook his head and started a coughing fit. Riagan edged toward the door, but the old man held out a hand to stop him. After ten seconds or so, the coughing subsided. "You need to stay and monitor in case something goes wrong. I can't."

"It can run without me for five minutes. I'll get an oxygen mask and medicine and be right back."

Mr. Ericson gave him a sad smile. "I appreciate the offer, but it truly is too late for me. Nothing you could do will make a difference at this point."

Riagan felt tears rising to his eyes, so he turned his attention to the wrist-comp to check progress. "Maybe ya should contact Neil. Talk to him before…" Riagan couldn't make himself finish the statement.

After a minute, Mr. Ericson asked, "Where is he? Quarantined at the academy right now?"

"He went to Orestes. Maellyn's working on the Azymi outbreak. But there was an attack. He wanted to make sure she's all right." And because of it, he wasn't here with his grandfather. How was that fair?

Mr. Ericson's face brightened. "She's a great girl. I hope she's okay. Neil should focus on her. If he's distracted with me, he might get hurt."

"But he'll want to know."

The old man was the last real family Neil had. The last Neil cared about anyway. Riagan already knew the pain of that loss. He'd give anything for more time with Rois.

"Maybe one day you'll become a father. If you're fortunate, perhaps even a grandfather." Mr. Ericson slumped in the chair, eyes dulling. "Then you'll understand you sometimes have to make decisions for them that they won't like, but are in their best interest. This is one. If never seeing him again is the price I have to pay to ensure his safety, perhaps even Maellyn's, it's one I'll make every time."

Riagan shook his head. He didn't agree. He didn't see how letting Neil know, giving him a chance to say goodbye, would put him in danger. Or Maellyn. And it was a chance Neil deserved.

Eyeing Mr. Ericson's wrist-comp, Riagan debated grabbing it and calling Neil. The old man couldn't stop him.

"Tell him…" Mr. Ericson paused, seeming to consider his words. "Just tell him I'm proud of all he's accomplished."

Riagan raised his hand to reach for the wrist-comp, Mr. Ericson narrowed his eyes. Riagan hesitated. He told himself the old man couldn't stop him, but those eyes held him back anyway. Reluctantly, feeling like a bad friend, he closed his hand and leaned back against the machine to wait.

For the next twenty minutes neither of them said anything, just watched the progress of the sanitization on the comp screen. The only signal when it finished was a beep on the wrist-comp screen.

"Is it ready to refill with fresh air?" Riagan asked.

When there was no answer, he turned back to find Mr. Ericson slumped in the chair, chin on his chest, eyes closed.

"Mr. Ericson?" Riagan stepped over and shook his shoulder. Neil's grandfather didn't stir. "Mr. Ericson?"

Stomach churning, he took a step back. Should he go get help? Or try to figure out how to get the machine running again? But he didn't know where to find help. And everyone needed the clean oxygen.

He moved in front of the comp screen. The oxygen level sensor read zero percent. Beside it were the words, *increase oxygen* over a bar. Riagan touched the bar, which started to rise. The oxygen level percentages rose until it reached one hundred percent.

He exhaled in relief.

It was finished. As Mr. Ericson requested. He had finished the job, so now he was free to go get help. He deactivated his own oxygen mask and removed it before placing it over the old man's head, hoping the process had worked. And that it wasn't too late for Neil's grandpa. Riagan removed the oxygen tank from his back and set it on the table before screwing it back into the mask.

Mr. Ericson didn't seem to be breathing. He needed help.

Boots thudding out in the hall drew Riagan's attention. Before he even made it to the door, officers streamed into the room.

"What are you doing?" one officer asked, pushing past Riagan to check the air systems.

Others crowded around Mr. Ericson, asking what was wrong with him. Riagan was jostled toward the back as the officers checked on the status of the facility. Someone confirmed that Mr. Ericson was dead.

At this, Riagan exploded. "What took ye so long?"

Everyone paused, heads turning toward him.

One man's brow furrowed. "We came as soon as we could. Had our hands full with the wounded at the thorneway."

"At the thorneway?" Riagan blinked, suddenly uneasy. "Wounded?"

"Yes. A Dahaka attacked and fled through the thorneway. While it was open for people going to Orestes."

Neil. He had been waiting to go. Had he been attacked? Was he among the wounded at the thorneway?

As Riagan processed this, everyone turned their focus back to Mr. Ericson and the machine. Dazed, Riagan slipped out the door. Then he started running. He had to get to the thorneway. Had to make sure Neil was okay. And if he wasn't there, then travel to Orestes.

If Neil was there. If Mainyu was there. Then that's where he was going.

Chapter 36

Ceremony for Maellyn

Maellyn awoke to a sense of imperceptible buoyancy. She experienced an extreme lack of sensation—arms, legs, torso—as if nothing touched her, she just floated on air, but couldn't even feel that. Actually, it was worse; she couldn't detect her body. She felt separated from it, like an out-of-body experience, which sent her into disoriented shock.

She tried opening her eyes. They slit marginally, revealing a blue glow. But that small movement gave her a little relief. It was short-lived, however, as further attempts to move yielded nothing. She tensed—at least her mind did—panic rising.

"Relax," a calm voice spoke into her ear.

Maellyn tried to turn toward the voice, to see who spoke to her, but that was as futile as everything else she'd tried to do. Her alarm skyrocketed.

"Calm down." The voice was gentle, intended to be soothing. "You've sustained severe injuries. We're taking care of you. You're in Athanalux."

She tried to open her mouth to ask what had happened, and what Athanalux was. Hoarse mumblings reached her ears. Nevertheless, the voice understood or guessed at her words.

"The explosions in the Orestes labs fractured your back and spine. Caused a number of internal injuries. You're paralyzed."

That was impossible. She didn't feel any pain. If she had a fractured back or spine, she'd feel that, right? But she did seem to be paralyzed. She couldn't control any part of her body. Even further attempts to open her eyes failed.

The blue glow blurred with sudden tears. She didn't understand. She'd been fine. How could this have happened?

"I know this must be overwhelming," the voice whispered, "—but I need you to relax. Everything will go smoothly if you remain calm."

Pressure on her face raised her eyelids, allowing her to see, albeit blurred from her tears. It still brought her immense relief to see her surroundings.

She appeared to be in a cavern. The surrounding walls and ceiling resembled a magma flow that had cooled. Millions of interspersed tiny blue lights dotted the magma flows, lighting up the cavern. A half dozen Alfar, all dressed in monks' robes, walked along beside her. Dozens of other Alfar filled the cavern, observing.

Instead of relieving her anxiety, the whole scene added to her confusion. Were they still within the facility on Orestes? There were no caverns that she was aware of on Orestes. Had the Alfar brought her down to Ourania? If she was paralyzed as the Alfar walking beside her said, why hadn't they taken her to an infirmary for treatment?

The Alfar lowered her to the ground and stepped away to either side. Additional Alfar set down stretchers bearing Anand, Cade, and Vahu—the boys on her left and Vahu on her right. She tried to call out to them, to ask if they were all right, but managed only faint croaks. None of them moved. Were they all paralyzed as well?

In unison, the Alfar spoke, but in a language she didn't comprehend. Her tradutor must've broken in the explosions? She tried to remember if the Alfar that had spoken to her before had spoken in English. She supposed he must have.

Regardless, the words sounded formal, a recitation. Or a ceremony. It echoed off the walls of the cavern, overwhelming her. The Alfar who had spoken to her earlier had tried to reassure her, but she couldn't locate him now.

Four Alfar approached her and removed her clothes, cutting them away. She tried to fight them off, to shout at them to stop, to cover herself, but all she could do was lie there, mortified as they lifted her naked body, this time leaving the stretcher behind. None of them met her gaze. She wished someone would tell her what they were doing.

More Alfar took up Anand, Cade, and Vahu, also naked, and carried them forward several paces. The chants continued as Maellyn was set down on her side in a stream. She had to close one eye, but the water didn't reach up to her mouth or nose. She couldn't say if the water was cold or warm. Her skin didn't goosebump. She couldn't feel it. She tried again to scream, to beg for answers. Nothing came out.

The pair of Alfar in front of her knelt in the water and held her in place on her side. A couple of Alfar knelt behind Vahu—also sideways in the water—and lifted root-like tubes out of the water, which they placed against her back. The tubes latched onto her. Maellyn realized they must be doing the same thing to her and she shuddered.

She wanted someone to tell her what was happening, but no reassurances came. The two Alfar in front of her watched stoically, unaware or unconcerned with her discomfort.

A dozen tubes were now attached to Vahu's back, all congregated along her spine. The Alfar prodded at other things under the water that Maellyn couldn't see or understand. It was all bizarre. And seemed very primitive for a people as technologically advanced as the Alfar. Except for the tubes. Perhaps it was her perception that was off, like her ability to feel or control her body.

After some time, the numbness she'd experienced since awakening gave way to a slight chill. Next, she became aware of the water she lay in, not visually, but the sensation. As if she lounged in a bath long after all the heat had dissipated. Was it a good thing she could feel the water? It had to be better than numbness, right?

Searing pain lanced through her back along her spine. She tried to arch forward, to pull away. She screamed, though it came out as no more than weak moans. Her open eye welled up with tears again. She tried to beg the Alfar to stop, tried to reach out with her hands to draw their attention, but her body responded only to the pain. While they remained motionless. Impassive.

Black shadows crept into the edges of her blurred vision. She felt herself sliding away, as if the flowing water carried her away from her body. Was she dying? Perhaps the damage had been too great for the Alfar to heal.

An image of her mother, Rei Trevena, appeared before her, seated upon the water with legs crossed underneath her, long black hair tied up with a hair stick, wearing an hakama. She smiled at Maellyn as if they were alone, just the two of them. Maellyn wanted to crawl toward her, to climb into her mum's arms as she had as a child when she was scared or in pain. To be held. Cuddled.

Her mum reached out a hand, beckoning Maellyn to come to her.

"Mum," Maellyn croaked. Her left hand twitched. If she could reach her mum, take her hand, all this would be over. The pain would cease. She needed the pain gone, more than she could ever remember needing anything.

The gap between them narrowed. A little closer and their fingers would touch. She longed for that touch.

"No! Go back!" Rois stepped between them. She wore a turquoise dress, her hair wet, feet bare in the water.

"Please," Maellyn begged, wanting Rois to move out of the way so she could reach her mum. It had been so long.

Instead, Rois dropped to her knees and clasped Maellyn's hand. Sympathy was evident in her expression, but there was also determination in her emerald eyes. *"Hold on. I know how bad it is. But I'm here. I'll stay with ya until this passes."*

Maellyn tried to argue. The pain would only end if she took her mother's hand. She tried to pull her hand free. Rois gripped harder.

"I won't let go." Rois' expression hadn't changed, but her body had hardened, becoming an immovable force. *"Ya can do this."*

"I can't." Maellyn was too exhausted and weak to fight.

Rois squeezed her hand. *"Ya can. Ya have much more ahead. Hold on a little longer. Ya future will be worth all of this."*

Rois or her mum? Fight or peace? Every second of life was a fight. A choice to struggle forward. The beauty, wonder, and excitement of life came with a price. Right now, that price was exorbitantly high. Seeing her father again, Fintan, Neil, Charlie—she still owed the android—required paying that price.

Yet thinking about each of them gave her strength. Her Thanksgiving tradition with her father, she wanted more. New projects with Fintan; they were two for two. Who would buy Charlie his favorite graphic novel series? And Neil. Things there were difficult right now, but she wasn't ready to let any of these things go. They gave her the strength to squeeze Rois' hands back. To cling to her.

Fresh tears welled up in her eyes as the pain in her back grew to match a symphony orchestra at the climax. She clung to Rois' hands with every part of her will. Her mother's smiling visage dimmed, flickered, and disappeared.

At last, her back calmed, leaving her in a wrung out, exhausted state. She held on to Rois, worried everything would ramp back up the second she let go. Next time she might not be able to summon the will to fight again.

But the pain didn't rise again. Instead, everything gave way to dreams of what she'd fought to live for.

Chapter 37

Neil Pursues Mainyu

Dying laughter that sounded a little unhinged to his ears, Neil clambered to his feet. Not because he wanted to, but because too many needed his help right now. He couldn't lose it right now.

An Alfar technician arrived and went to work on the thorneways.

"What's wrong with them?" Nico asked the technician.

"Who knows." The technician looked exhausted. "Everything's wrecked."

Nico walked over. "I might be able to help. I'm pretty good with electronics."

"Sure." The technician pointed to a control panel for one of the thorneways, while he set to work on a different one. "I could use all the help I can get. Take off the panel cover."

"Got any tools?" Nico asked.

The technician removed a gray case from a pocket of his pants and tossed it to Nico.

"Great," Nico said, catching the case and opening it up. "We'll have this fixed in no time."

The Alfar snorted. "Sure, if there's no more attacks."

That response made Neil reconsider what he needed to do.

"We're going after the Dahaka," he said to Patrick.

"You want to pursue him ourselves?" Patrick asked, a slight tremor in his voice.

"No, I don't. But if these attacks don't stop, we won't be a help to anyone. We may end up hurt ourselves." Neil set off back toward the labs. He half expected Patrick to suggest that he'd stay and help Nico and the technician with the thorneways, but instead he followed, to Neil's relief. He didn't want to face the Dahaka alone.

They ran past the garden, which was now a smoking, drenched mess. Most of the plants were little more than burnt husks. Through the double doors, he paused, searching for signs of which direction the Azios might have gone in.

Back around the labs, few Alfar remained in the immediate area. Those able to help themselves had trudged back to the infirmary. Most of the moans and cries they'd heard earlier had now ceased. Neil hoped a majority of them were taken care of. But with the infirmary equipment knocked out, he wasn't sure how much help anyone was getting. He didn't know how to fix the power problem. And his medical skills were extremely limited.

So he pressed on past the labs, headed after the Dahaka they'd seen earlier. By now the Azios could've gone in any number of directions, but for the present it was the only lead he had to go on.

The moment they passed through the next set of double doors beyond the labs, the shouts and chaos of battle somewhere ahead caused Neil to raise his guard. Patrick also changed his stance, raising his arms to prepare for a fight. They'd heard nothing a moment before; apparently, the lab area was soundproof.

This new area appeared to be a maze of offices. Downed drones, dead Alfar scientists and officers, shattered glass from office windows, toppled and broken equipment, were scattered everywhere. Neil and Patrick moved quickly but cautiously toward the sounds of gunfire. Neil kept his eyes shifting for obstacles or to check open doors for threats. At each new turn, they paused and leaned around corners to check the way was clear.

They passed a room with a large window showing Ourania. Neil skidded to a halt at what awaited outside the window.

"What?" Patrick asked. "Hear something?" He had his arms up, ready to shoot.

It wasn't the planet that had stopped him, though Ourania was large and beautiful. But there was also a ship. A monstrous craft, like an aircraft carrier in space. Nico had mentioned it after Maellyn's first trip here with her team. The *Gunnra Kore*, the Alfar's newest defensive ship.

Everything clicked into place.

"Come on." Neil waved for Patrick to follow as he darted back into the hall, running.

"Where to?" Patrick asked.

Neil ran along corridors, moving generally toward the docking port for the Alfar ship. Bullet holes riddled the walls they passed. The sounds of gunfire grew, confirming they were close. Rounding a corner, they found themselves behind a wall of drones in a pitched battle with Azios whom had taken refuge in rooms on either side of the corridor.

Patrick grabbed Neil's wrist, yanking him up short. "We can't engage. The drones won't know we're on their side."

He was right, but Neil also sensed they would not find another route to the ship, at least not without long delays. They couldn't afford detours at this point. Before Neil could even begin to formulate a plan, the wall on their left blew outward. He ducked, pivoted, and dove backward, tackling Patrick out of harm's way. Gunfire ceased.

When no further explosions or gunfire erupted, Neil rose to a crouch, wary. A good bit of the corridor wall on the left had been destroyed. The drone wall was shattered. A number of Dahaka were dead as well. Maybe a quarter of what had been there before the explosion. The rest must've escaped.

"Seriously, what are we getting into?" Patrick asked, eyes wide, studying the destruction.

"Mainyu is after the new Alfar ship." Neil remained crouched, waiting to see if any Dahaka would emerge from one of the remaining doorways.

"Mainyu? He's here?" Patrick had a quaver in his voice as he climbed to his feet.

"Yes." Neil rose and took a few steps down the hall, eyeing the Azios bodies to ensure they were dead.

The attack on this base. The Dahaka coming through the thorneway behind them. At the time, he'd figured the Dahaka had been fleeing the Mars facility and took advantage of the open thorneway.

But that ship. That was a prize Mainyu would covet. And it was only accessible from Orestes. It was also heavily guarded.

And that's where the outbreak came in. The Alfar, already weakened by the Azymi outbreak, were in chaos from the attack on the facility. Mainyu had to know they'd find a cure and end the outbreak on both Ourania and Space City. As bad as it had gotten, they'd survive. But while they were all focused on a cure, the ship was Mainyu's prize. With such a ship there were a lot of things Mainyu could accomplish.

"Shouldn't we get backup or something?"

Neil shook his head. "No time, but you're welcome to go back to find help. I'll go on alone."

"I'm with you. Wherever you want to go."

Once Neil felt confident there were no remaining Dahaka in hiding in the immediate area, he picked up the pace. The quiet now that the drones had been taken out unnerved him. They couldn't be all that was left of the defense.

They rounded a corner, reaching a vast hangar filled with aircraft. At the far end, near an exit from the hangar, was an active thorneway. The new Alfar ship loomed in the background.

Before the thorneway stood Guiman, dressed in Dahaka armor. The shock of seeing Guiman alive, and here, caused Neil to pull up. He stared, unable to process what he was seeing.

"Guiman?"

The old man turned back, wearing a disappointed expression. "I thought it would be you who found me first. Not Riagan."

"What're you doing here?"

Guiman spread his arms wide as he rotated back toward the ship. "Isn't it obvious? I'm here for the ship."

"It's a good thing you're here." Neil exhaled. It wouldn't be just him and Patrick. "Mainyu's trying to steal the ship."

Guiman stared at the ground, shaking his head, arms falling to his sides. "You haven't figured it out either. Neither did Riagan. At least not in time."

Neil frowned, confused. Figure what out? What was going on?

"I'm the one stealing the ship."

"You're Mainyu. The real one." Patrick marched forward, raising both arms to shoot.

"And who are you?" Guiman asked, not the least bit alarmed at Patrick's sighting him.

Neil found he couldn't speak. Betrayed. They'd been betrayed. All year long. Chasing Mainyu when he had been leading them the whole time. Dardanos, too, if Riagan was to be believed, which he had no real reason to doubt him.

"Never mind who I am," Patrick said. "We're here to stop you."

Guiman chortled. "I'd love to do this longer, but that's not prudent." He stepped through the thorneway. Patrick fired, but it was too late.

Guiman was getting away. No. Mainyu was getting away.

Neil ran for the thorneway, but instinctively he knew he was too late.

A figure in an explorer suit and wearing B-choppers flew past him. It took Neil a moment to recognize Riagan streaking across the hangar ground and through the thorneway, which closed behind him. Neil shouted in frustration as he reached the thorneway. He tried to call up the last connection on the control panel, but it had been blocked from the other end.

"No!" Neil pounded both fists on the ring.

The *Gunnra Kore* started to pull away.

"We need to warn someone." Patrick stared after the departing ship.

There had to be another way. He couldn't leave Riagan to face Mainyu alone. He glanced around the hangar. There were other ships, but he didn't know the first thing about flying. Probably kill himself trying to take off.

He sprinted back the way they'd come. He had to find the Alfar. Someone must know another way onto that ship. How many times this year had he stood next to Mainyu, taking orders from him? Too many to count. And his inability to connect the old man to the Dahaka leader had allowed Mainyu to attack Orestes.

Maellyn was down on Ourania, possibly dying, because of him.

Cade, Anand, and Vahu, too.

And Riagan, too, if he didn't find a way on board that ship.

But as he ran, he couldn't shake the dread that it was already too late.

Epilogue

Neil sat in a chair, his legs up on the desk in his room, staring out the open window. The impulse to climb out and take off was overwhelming, but he was under surveillance. He was confined to his room for the time being and sneaking out would make things worse. A lot worse.

Nor did he have anywhere to go. Maellyn wasn't hanging out at the science labs, waiting for him to stop by, but at least she was still alive. The day after he'd returned to Space City, he had received a message from Fintan informing him that everyone had survived and were recovering nicely. It would be some time before they were in any shape to communicate.

A knock on his door stirred him. He sprang upright. "Come in."

The door opened and in rolled Headmaster Dardanos, expression concerned. He closed the door behind him. Neil shifted uncomfortably, wanting to ask Dardanos to leave the door open, but couldn't make himself say it.

"How are you feeling?"

Truthfully, he felt uneasy now, but he couldn't say that. "I'm okay." The Council had cleared the headmaster of any involvement in the attack on Mars. But after everything they'd learned this year, Neil wasn't sure he was ready to take the Council's word on that.

"I heard about your grandfather. I'm sorry for your loss. He was a brave man and a hero in saving people at the Mars facility."

Neil stared at the ground, unable to respond. Thinking of his grandfather made breathing difficult, as if an invisible snake squeezed his lungs. It was hard to believe he was gone.

"I also came to clear things up with you personally," the headmaster said. "I know Riagan accused me of being involved in the attack on Mars. And he had good reason for that."

Neil jerked his head up, eyes widening. Was Dardanos confessing? Now he wished he wasn't trapped alone with the headmaster in his room. He could shout for help, but would someone respond fast enough?

"Not because I did it." Dardanos held up a hand, noticing his unease. "I assure you, I'm innocent."

"Then how…?"

"Guiman fabricated evidence against me that he gave to Riagan. Guiman… Mainyu…." Dardanos grimaced. "It's hard to accept they are the same person."

Neil nodded, understanding the sentiment.

"Mainyu conned Riagan. Conned me." Dardanos grimaced at the admission. "It embarrasses me to realize how long I'd been duped by him."

Neil wanted to say they'd all been conned. Everyone on Space City. The Alfar. Probably many others.

"Now I've got to make up for that," Dardanos said. "And I'm hoping you'll help me with that. You've got a level head on you. I could use your support."

"I—I don't know." Neil was taken aback. After his own failures, he'd wondered if he still had a place at the academy. "Grandpa's gone. Maellyn, she's alive, but I may never see her again either. I just…"

Dardanos rolled closer and placed a hand on his shoulder. Neil pulled away, uneasy with the gesture. It was too soon. Everything was confusing.

"I understand." Dardanos let the hand fall into his lap. "You've gone through a lot. I'm sorry about your grandfather. And Maellyn. I hope once you've had time to process everything, you'll see that while I made mistakes, I'm not the villain."

A small nod was all Neil could manage. Fortunately, a buzzing from his wrist-comp on the desk alerted him to an incoming transmission. A video message.

"I'll let you get that." Dardanos wheeled himself toward the door. "If there's anything you need, don't hesitate to come to me."

The call was from an unrecognized sender. Frowning, Neil waited until Dardanos had left the room, pulling the door shut behind him, before answering it.

Riagan popped up on screen. "I made it."

"Riagan," Neil whispered, not wanting Dardanos to hear him. "Are you okay?"

Hair disheveled, Riagan looked tired, but in good spirits. "I haven't been noticed yet. Don't know how long I'll be able to remain hidden. Mainyu has brought a lot of Azios onboard."

Neil wished he were there instead of here alone in his room. If he could've figured things out a little bit sooner. Yet another failure on his part. "What're you doing? Come back."

Riagan craned his neck, searching over the wrist-comp for several seconds. He hunched back down. "This is my chance to take him out. I have to do this… for Rois."

"Not if it costs you your life."

Riagan's expression hardened. "Even if it costs my life."

"Rois wouldn't want—"

"I have to do this." Riagan cut him off. "If I come back, we'll never have the answers."

"That's crazy. Of course we will." Neil's voice started to rise and he eyed the door, half afraid Dardanos might still be listening outside.

But Riagan was shaking his head. "Think what Mainyu accomplished. The planning it must've taken. Marshalling enough resources to cause a deadly outbreak on Ourania and Space City, while stifling any warning. Carrying out dual attacks on Mars and Orestes, sending everyone scurrying in different directions all so he could steal this ship."

Neil saw awe on Riagan's face, and heard it in his voice. It bothered him.

"He didn't do this alone," Riagan continued. "He had help from others on Space City."

"We knew this already," Neil replied, frowning. "Dr. Snelling and her team. You said you think Dardanos was involved as well."

"There had to be more. To pull this off, there has to be many more involved. That's why I have to stay. Learn how he did it. Who helped."

Neil jumped to his feet, pacing. "Let me join you, then." He squeezed the wrist-comp, needing to do something. "Send me coordinates. I'll come alone."

Riagan grinned. "That's why you're my best friend. But I can't get to a thorneway. Too heavily guarded." His head darted up again, searching. "I've got to go. Wish me luck."

"Riagan, no."

The call disconnected. Neil threw the wrist-comp at the wall, enjoying the sound of it shattering. This could not be happening. He was not going to fail Riagan again. Or anyone else.

Marching to the door, he yanked it open. He was going to get answers.

Then, he was going to act.

THE END

About the Author:

Jared Austin is a young adult science fiction author who lives in the Rocket City—Huntsville, Alabama. With Space City and the books in the series to follow, he hopes to show and inspire his daughter and son, as well as all of his readers, that science and technology are not dull subjects, but gateways to a brighter, exciting future.

If you would like to learn more about the series and future novels, visit: https://jareddanielaustin.com

Books in Series:
Space City
Escape
Space City Outbreak
Contact Not Found

Follow me on social media:
Facebook Author Page: www.facebook.com/jareddanielaustin
Instagram: jared_austin1981

Thank you for reading my book! If you enjoyed it, please consider leaving a review. Even just a few words would help others decide if the book is right for them. Best regards and thank you in advance!